JERRY & SHARON AHERN

WRITTEN IN T

Author of the Best-Selling
The Survivalist Series

$7.99 U.S.
$9.99 CAN.

ISBN 978-1-4391-3399-6

9 781439 133996

50799

S ▷ EAN

WRITTEN IN TIME

A NOVEL

BY

JERRY & SHARON AHERN

WRITTEN IN TIME

Copyright © 2010 by Jerry Ahern and Sharon Ahern

A Baen Books Original

Baen Publishing Enterprises
P.O. Box 1403
Riverdale, NY 10471
www.baen.com

ISBN 13: 978-1-4391-3399-6

First printing, November 2010

Distributed by Simon & Schuster
1230 Avenue of the Americas
New York, NY 10020

Printed in the United States of America

10 9 8 7 6 5 4 3 2 1

For our children and
our children's children and our nephew;
in family, there is strength.

A PICTURE WORTH A HUNDRED YEARS

Ellen opened the envelope. There was a copy of a photograph, just a Xerox, but remarkably clear. It was a photograph of Mr. and Mrs. Jack Naile and their two (unnamed) children.

"This has to be an elaborate practical joke, Jack."

"Lemme see, princess."

She handed it to him. Despite the age of the photograph and the fact that it was a Xerox, the resemblance between the Naile family of nine decades ago and the Naile family of today was enough to make her want to throw up.

She'd been looking out the Suburban's open window but now focused on the other items in the envelope. There was a summary of its contents, typed on an old-seeming machine, Arthur Beach's name scrawled at the bottom.

"The Naile family arrived in town in 1896. They were apparently on their way to California for some new business when their wagon suffered an accident and was destroyed. Reduced to only a few personal belongings, the Nailes seemingly had considerable financial resources. There is no material yet available to me mentioning the fate of their descendants, nor concerning how or when Mr. and Mrs. Naile eventually died. The county medical examiner's office burned to the ground in the 1940s, all death certificates archived there destroyed. I'll keep looking.'"

"Holy—"

"Tell him to stop looking, Jack!"

"Startling resemblance, that photograph. I'll say that."

"Jack, it's you and me and David and Elizabeth, and the picture was taken almost a hundred years ago!"

❋ PROLOGUE ❋

John Naile turned the Cadillac off the county highway and onto the black pavement of a pine-flanked single lane road. Not yet that familiar with his latest vehicular acquisition, he took his eyes off the road and glanced at the wood-accented dashboard in order to find the cigar lighter. He found the lighter and pushed it in. There was a half-filled package of Luckies in the cigarette pocket of his single-breasted gray suit. He started to reach for a cigarette.

"You should try being pregnant sometime, John."

"I don't think I'm going to be able to do that, sweetheart," Naile replied, looking over at his wife in the front seat beside him. Audrey was nearing the end of what she called her "first trimester," but hardly looked pregnant at all. The A-line skirt of her maroon suit barely showed a bulge, even when she was sitting.

"No, what I mean is these seats. I don't know what it was about the '63. I mean, John, I really didn't notice it until I got pregnant. But there was no back support!"

"I think it's more your back than it was the seats, babe. The New Yorker was a comfortable car." He'd gone through two Chryslers, one Lincoln, a Mercedes and a Ford Country Squire in search of the perfect car for his wife, all because his father wouldn't buy anything but a Cadillac. When the '64 model year was announced, John Naile surrendered to fate and ordered one.

But John Naile had no intention, however, of abandoning his longtime personal car, the red Thunderbird. He was vice-president of Horizon Industries, the family business. He was married to the girl of his dreams and the arrival of their first child was only six months away. Behind the wheel of the T-Bird, its top off, the sound of its exhaust when he changed gears as throaty as Peggy Lee's singing—sometimes that sporty little roadster was the only way of reminding himself that he wasn't yet thirty.

Adulthood had gotten him used to driving vehicles the size of a sport boat on wheels, but he didn't have to like them.

"You want me to try the radio, John, and see how it picks up out here?"

"Sure, honey."

Audrey apparently found WLS at 89 on the AM band from Chicago, or at least it sounded like she had; it was an Elvis Presley song playing. "Do you think Elvis will last, John? Like Sinatra?"

"I don't know, Audrey. He's got a good set of pipes, though."

"Okay. What was the first movie you ever took me to, John Naile?"

"We saw Elvis in *King Creole* five years ago, one of

the theaters in the Loop, and afterward we went to that deli next to the Chicago Theater and we both had hot pastrami. How's that for being romantic and remembering stuff? Huh?"

"And you ate most of my pickle." Audrey laughed softly, sliding over a little closer to him, resting her head against his shoulder. John Naile still had the "lover's knob" mounted on the wheel of the Thunderbird, but didn't need one to drive the Cadillac one-handed. Maybe cars like this did have their merits. He folded his right arm around his wife. Despite her Jackie Kennedy-esque pillbox hat, he could still kiss his wife's hair. He touched his lips to her forehead. The scent of her hair, her perfume and the new-car smell of the Cadillac's leather seats all mingled very pleasantly. He'd forgotten to light his cigarette and didn't want to at the moment; the smoke would dispel the ambience.

"Glad you married me?" Naile asked.

"Well, I've had to put up with a lot, John, you being rich and all, with Horizon Industries being one of the leading defense contractors and everything, and that White House dinner when we met President Eisenhower and Dick Nixon. Stuff like that. And then there's your mom and dad—they're so nice to me it's almost spooky! The first time I met them, it was as if they expected you to bring me home and they knew we were going to get married."

"Get Mom to show you her crystal ball sometime," Naile laughed. "I never told you about her Gypsy blood, did I? And was that a yes? About being happy you married me?"

Audrey turned her face up toward him and kissed his

cheek. She whispered, "Yes, silly." Her right hand drifted under his jacket, one smooth finger finding an opening between two shirt buttons.

"Quit that!" He wedged his knee against the steering wheel for a split second and feigned a slap at her hand.

"Why'd they make such a big deal about us coming up on a weekday?" Audrey did that sort of thing, picking up a conversation almost randomly. This one dated from when they'd first gotten into the car almost two hours earlier. "I mean, it's always good to see them; I really love your folks. But you said you had a lot of stuff to do at the office with that new rocket-shooter thing and—"

"Beats me, babe," he told Audrey honestly. "All Dad said was that nothing could interfere with us being here this afternoon—not even prototyping the launcher."

Although John Naile handled the day-to-day running of Horizon Industries with a relatively free hand, his father was still president, chairman of the board and chief executive officer. Why Horizon was developing an inexpensively produced, disposable rocket launcher without any indication that the Pentagon was looking for one was something John Naile had never fully understood. With the apparent rush on the research and development so they could move into prototyping, wiping out a full day to come up to the estate was even more enigmatic. "I really don't know," he added lamely, "but Dad'll tell us."

The weather WLS was reporting for Chicago didn't match at all what John Naile saw through the Cadillac's windshield. Usually, central Wisconsin would have worse weather this time of year, but on this day at this moment, it was a classically beautiful November landscape through which they drove. They'd been on the grounds of the estate since twenty feet or so after leaving the county highway. And suddenly, he was reminded of the musical "*Camelot*," the song that Richard Burton sang about the sheer perfection of that mythical kingdom's climate. This was such a place this day, and John Naile wouldn't have been too much surprised to learn that James Naile had decreed it thus.

John Naile glanced at his watch and compared the Rolex to the dashboard clock; surprisingly, they were in perfect agreement that the time was a few minutes after noon. "You know, how Dad's pushing how great Cadlillacs are and everything? I'll say one thing—the clock keeps time."

"I still like the seats, John." Audrey Naile pulled her legs up under her and nuzzled her nose against his neck.

"Is that okay for you to sit like that? All scrunched up and everything?"

"I'm not that pregnant, John. It's still okay for me to do a lot of stuff."

"Hmm," John Naile murmured.

"Hmm, indeed. Maybe after we leave your parents' place, we can—"

"Why don't we spend the night at Lake Lawn Lodge?" John Naile suggested.

"I don't have any clothes with me, John."

"You won't need any for what I've got in mind. Besides, we can buy what we need, or you can borrow something from Mom."

"'Gee, Mary Ann? Could I borrow some stockings and

underwear? Your son and I are going to go misbehave and—'"

"Hush," he scolded his wife good-naturedly. The road was just about to split at the driveway leading to the main house, the fork to the left leading deeper into the property. The turn was a little sharp, and John Naile slowed the Cadillac before making the right. Audrey sat up and smoothed her dress. She slid over fully into the passenger side, turned down the visor and began adjusting her hat and her hair in the vanity mirror. As always, she wore very little makeup; when she woke up beside him each morning, she looked as perfect as if she'd spent hours in front of a mirror.

All of this—the very comfortable living he made, the estate which someday he would inherit, and all the other family investments—was thanks to David Naile, who founded Horizon Industries in 1914 and never made a bad investment in his life. Phenomenal business judgment seemed to be a family trait. James Naile, David's son and John's father, bought large blocks of stock in obscure companies that always grew into dependable profitability. Who would have figured IBM would have gotten so hot? And why would anyone invest in Japanese electronics? John Naile shook his head just thinking about it.

"What's on your mind, besides your fedora, John?"

"I always think about how things got started, every time I drive up here. My grandfather must have been a genius, you know? He piloted Horizon through the Depression as if there wasn't any stock-market crash in '29 at all. Horizon's steel foundries refused to sell scrap metal to Imperial Japan, and our aircraft and munitions plants were already working double shifts before Hitler invaded Poland in '39. And Dad seems to have his father's magic touch. You'd better hope I'm just a late bloomer, babe."

"It's experience, John, and you're getting that."

"Maybe." He nodded soberly. Every once in a while, he'd pick a winner in the stock market, but not that often and never anything that weird. His father and late grandfather possessed skill; with him, it was educated dumb luck.

After his stint in the army at the end of the Korean War, he'd picked up his sidetracked life and gone to college. Because he "knew" his destiny—Horizon Industries— he'd studied business administration, but carried a second major in music. A certain natural proclivity for the piano and the Naile family jawline seemed to be his principal genetic inheritances from his grandfather, the natural business acumen noticeably lacking. He'd begun growing into that, yes, he supposed, since finishing college in '58 and marrying Audrey that same year. But he had a long way to go.

"Haya Goldsmith was raving about your parents' place." Another resurrected conversation appeared magically out of the blue. "Remember when you and your dad had that big dinner for everybody in the international divisions last year? She talked my ear off! Haya loves Tudor; there isn't a Tudor anywhere in Israel as far as she knows! Did you ever date Haya?"

"No, she was only thirteen or so when Dad got her dad to start up the Israeli division for him, and their whole family packed up and left the country." Then John Naile remembered something. "I take that back about dating her, though. The summer before my senior year in high school? Dad took me over to Israel with him on business, and I took Haya to a movie once."

"What movie did you see with Haya?"

John Naile thought about it, but couldn't remember. It was probably just as well that he couldn't, all things considered. Haya was a genuine knockout, the prettiest comptroller anybody could hope for. Finally he said, "Can't remember what movie it was."

"Right. You've got a memory like a steel trap, John."

"No kidding, Audrey. Something old with Humphrey Bogart, I think." Horizon was one of the first companies to pump money into Israel after independence, and— John Naile had learned only in 1960—had secretly smuggled arms to Israel while the fledgling Jewish state fought for its very existence after the British withdrew from Palestine. The man who'd run that clandestine operation for Horizon was the same man David and James Naile had used to coordinate intelligence data for Horizon during World War Two. Horizon had provided Allied Intelligence with a lot of information both the U.S. and Great Britain had cheerfully—and quietly—accepted. The intelligence data concerning the death camps, sadly, the Allied governments had largely—and quietly—chosen to ignore.

Even in late autumn, the landscaping within the immediate vicinity of the main house and its garage retained a pleasant degree of understated, evergreen elegance. The driveway looped toward the eight-thousand-square-foot Tudor's three front steps. John could see the front door opening and his father and mother emerging.

Mary Ann Naile was still a pinup-quality beauty, her son thought. He'd seen plenty of pictures of her from the time when his mom and dad first met and through the years since before he was born. She had a reasonable amount of gray in her shoulder length hair, but didn't dye it. And she still had her figure, too. There was a heavy cardigan sweater draped over her shoulders, beneath it a silk-looking blouse of the identical shade of gray above a black knee-length skirt, sheer stockings and medium black heels. She hadn't fallen into the First Lady look that Audrey only occasionally affected.

James Naile was tall and straight as ever. Facially and structurally, he resembled the great swashbuckler Douglas Fairbanks, Jr., in his role opposite Ronald Coleman in *The Prisioner of Zenda*—or so it had always seemed to John Naile. Only, unlike Fairbanks' character of the dashing swordsman, James Naile hadn't a nefarious bone in his body—and he had more gray hair. He wore a white shirt, blue slacks and black loafers, a pipe—unlit—clenched in the right side of his mouth.

John Naile stopped the car, turned off the engine and climbed out. Before he could cross over to the passenger side, his father was already opening Audrey's door. "How are you, sweetheart?" James Naile swept Audrey into his arms and hugged her. "You look great, kid! Feeling okay?"

"Just fine, Jim. Never better."

"Good! Good!"

John took off his hat, intercepted his mother and touched at her shoulder as he gave her a kiss on the cheek. "Oh, John! It's good to see you."

"What's the matter, Mom? It's like we haven't seen each other for months. But it's less than a week since—"

"It's just that it's today, and today is a funny day, John.

Not funny like funny, but funny like—well, I don't know what."

"Are you guys . . . ?"

"We're fine, the business is fine. Now, go say hello to your father." John put his arm around his mother's shoulders and she rested her head against him for a split second, then announced, "Jim! Aren't you going to say hello to your son?"

"Sure, after I'm through hugging the pretty girl he came in with." James Naile turned around and extended his hand. John took it, and his father leaned forward and kissed him on the cheek. "I like the new car, son."

"Figured you would, Dad. It's a Cadillac, as you've no doubt noticed."

They were all mounting the steps, but before entering the house, Mary Ann said, "Audrey, help me out in the kitchen, will you? We gave everybody the day off, and after Jim and your husband take care of a little business, I thought we could have some lunch."

"Sure, Mary Ann," Audrey responded. "Let me take off my hat and freshen up."

"I'll meet you in the kitchen, then."

John Naile caught an odd look in his wife's eyes as she veered off along the entrance hall. She paused in front of a gateleg table in the hall, set down her purse and looked in the mirror, beginning to remove her hat.

John Naile looked at his father and mother. "What's up, guys?"

James Naile looked at his wristwatch, a Rolex identical to the one John Naile wore. "We don't have a lot of time, John. Mary Ann?"

She paused before answering, her eyes following Audrey as her daughter-in-law walked out of sight. "I know. Linger over making lunch."

"Yeah." James Naile turned to his son. "Come with me, John. Everything you want to know—actually, a lot more than that, in spades—you'll know." James Naile grabbed a vintage brown-leather bomber jacket from the larger of the two hall closets, donning it as he said, "Let's cut through the house, John. It's faster," and started walking.

John, gray fedora in hand, followed his father, looking once at his mother's face to see if he could get a clue as to what was about to transpire. She looked oddly sad.

"Dad? What's going on?" John Naile quickened his pace to come even with his father. They left the main hallway, passed the base of the circular staircase and under it toward his father's office. They passed a small bathroom, a closet, came out from beneath the stairwell and through an open space—sunlight filtered through a floor-to-ceiling bank of windows and washed the checkerboard-pattern black-and-white tiles in a pale yellow light.

James Naile quickened his pace, opened the double doors to his office and passed through. "Close them behind you, John." In some ways, parents never looked at their children as getting past the age of ten or so, John Naile had often thought, and his father's remark had just confirmed it. "And skip the 'Gee, I thought I'd leave 'em open' riposte, alright?"

"Sure."

His father's office was as he always had seen it since his childhood: big, expensive wooden desk; big, expensive leather desk chair; big, expensive leather couch and easy chairs; a coffee table that matched the desk; the side walls of the fifteen-by-fifteen room obscured floor-to-ceiling with built-in bookshelves; the library steps and a ladder on casters (he could never remember the proper name for one of the things, but thought there was one). The far wall was consumed at its center with double French doors leading out onto a small patio; on either side of the doors stood glass-fronted cabinets. The one on the right was a beautifully executed piece showcasing about a dozen long guns, rifles and shotguns evenly mixed, all premier grades from FN/Browning, Beretta, Winchester, Remington and some of the English gun makers. His father never touched them except to clean them; they were investments only.

"Should have offered you a coat, John, or had you get your overcoat from the Cadillac. Long walk to the bomb shelter, and it's a little cold out."

"The bomb shelter? Why are we—?"

"You'll know. Trust me, son."

The cabinet on the left, as they walked through the double doorway and onto the flagstones beyond—"I know! Close the doors."—held a solitary bolt-action Remington, a lever-action Winchester, a lever-action Marlin, a Remington pump shotgun, various knives and an assortment of handguns, some of them cowboy-style single actions, all except the four long guns heavily engraved and, like the guns in the flanking cabinet, investment quality.

"You ever shoot any of those things, Dad?"

"Why? I keep that '97 Winchester pump of your grandfather's in our bedroom, and I've got 1911s stashed all over the house, as you'll recall, I believe."

Once, as a child, John Naile had committed the all-but-unpardonable sin of attempting to show a couple of his buddies one of his dad's .45 automatics. No Roy Rogers matinees for a very long time after that, and a serious feeling of being considered untrustworthy. His father was not a hobby shooter, John Naile had learned, but a dead shot when he needed to be.

That was proven once and forever when they walked into a bank together and the bank was being robbed. John Naile hadn't even known his father ever carried a gun on his person, but suddenly a little pistol just appeared in his father's right hand and the bank robber went down with a single shot in the throat.

That was the first time—John Naile was twelve—that he had realized that there was more to his father than met the eye.

"Why are we going to the bomb shelter?" John Naile plopped his gray fedora on his head, snapped up the collar of his suit and hunched his shoulders as they started into the gardens.

"To watch a soap opera on television."

"What?"

"Remember what they say about asking silly questions, son?"

"I remember, Dad."

"Walk faster. We'll miss the commercial."

"Are we advertising on television? Hey! You can't get television reception underground."

"No shit, Sherlock! Come on."

John Naile reached into his coat and pulled out a Lucky Strike, then lit it with his Zippo. "Television? I haven't liked anything on television since *Have Gun—Will Travel* went off in September."

"Try Richard Boone's new show. An anthology kind of thing. It's pretty darn good." Still trying to keep pace with his father, John Naile heeled out his cigarette.

They passed the tennis courts and the pool and pool house and the garden shed and turned at the end of the line of privet hedge and started toward the small structure that looked like a pump house but was really a disguised entrance to the family bomb shelter.

"Why can't we watch television up at the house? Is this some kind of dirty program Mom and Audrey can't see?"

"Your mother already has the TV on. I bought one of those portable ones and put it in the kitchen. They'll see what we see."

"I don't understand, Dad!"

"Good! You're not supposed to. Yet! You ever wondered why I built the bomb shelter in the first place, John?"

"Oh, gee whiz, I don't know, Dad! Maybe to protect the family and the servants from blast, fallout and radiation in the event of an attack by the Soviet Union?"

His father was opening the pump house door; a flashlight appeared in James Naile's hand just as suddenly as that pistol had seventeen years earlier.

"There won't be a nuclear war, at least not until sometime after the mid-1990s, John." The light switch inside the pump house went on, and James Naile pocketed the flashlight. "And it certainly won't be the Soviet Union we'll be fighting." James Naile actuated the entrance mechanism into the bomb shelter and the fake rear wall of the pump house slipped left; visible beyond it in the lights

James Naile turned on was a wide metal stairwell winding downward.

"I know you were a confidant of President Eisenhower, Dad, and that you get along okay with Jack Kennedy and most of the Kennedy clan, but I didn't realize you knew Khrushchev and those guys, too."

Unbidden, John closed the shelter door, sealing them inside. He could hear the subtle hum of the ventilation system. During normal times, when the structure was occupied, all electrical systems ran off ordinary household current. There were diesel generators standing by that would take over if the shelter was ever to be used for real. As a kid, John had considered the bomb shelter a kind of tree house, only underground. And, like an elaborate tree house, it consisted of several levels.

James Naile took the steps downward, and John Naile followed him. "I built the bomb shelter in order to mask what's on the fourth level, John."

"Fourth level?"

"I do have special knowledge of the future, John. On days like today, I wish to God that I didn't."

They reached the first level of the shelter, some eighteen feet below the surface.

Half of this level was given over to things such as the diesel generators and their backups, with a separate fuel-storage area, sealed off from the rest of the level for safety reasons, on the far end.

James Naile opened another doorway, flipped another set of switches, and John Naile followed him into the next stairwell.

The second level housed, on one side, living and working

quarters for the family and, on the other end, similar but more modest accommodations for the staff, as well as sleeping quarters. At the center were common rooms and storage areas. Within the storage areas were food, water, toilet paper and everything else one might need for a stay of three months, with certain items regularly rotated out of stock and replaced so that everything would be fresh. There was also a vault. James Naile didn't open it, but John Naile glanced at it while his father opened the next doorway. Within the vault were a dozen each M1 Garand rifles, Colt 1911A1 pistols and Remington 870 pump shotguns. Ammunition and all other necessities for the guns were housed within the vault as well.

John Naile closed the door behind them, and they descended to the third level.

The third level was the smallest. There was an office, smaller but otherwise somewhat similar to his father's office in the house, minus windows, of course. On this floor as well there were three bedrooms—the sleeping accommodations for the family. There was a gymnasium, small but efficient, with free weights, a heavy bag and a treadmill.

"Okay, son. Where do you think the entrance to the fourth level is?"

"What?"

"Where do you think I put it?"

"Why would we have a fourth level to begin with, Dad?"

James Naile didn't smile. "You'll know all of that. Where's the entrance, son?"

John stood in the smallish hall, the office in front of him, the gymnasium to his left, the sleeping accommodations to his right and behind him. "Secret stuff there, right?"

"Right. Come on, son. We don't have a lot of time."

"I know—we'll miss the commercial."

"At the very least."

John turned around. "Your office would be too obvious a spot. Yours and mom's bedroom. Right?"

"Right." James smiled, evidently pleased. He led the way into the bedroom. It was a pretty standard room; a chest of drawers, a dresser with a vanity mirror, a large double bed. John started toward the dresser, but stopped, looking intently at the large headboard of the bed. "Bingo, John! That a boy! Help me move this sucker."

Actually, moving the bed was relatively easy, a matter of merely pulling on the footboard, and the bed's headboard pivoting away from the wall. Behind it was a vault door. James spun the dial through its combination and unlocked it. "Your mother and I are the only ones who know the combination. I'll give it to you to memorize." James reached into the darkness beyond and flicked light switches. The staircase beyond was like the ones connecting the other levels.

"This place must have set you back a small fortune, Dad."

"Not too bad, really; it helps owning your own construction companies and concrete plants." At the bottom of the stairwell, John Naile found himself standing beside his father in what looked like a library or study, book-shelves lining paneled walls. There was a television set—a big one—and there were pieces of unfamiliar electronic equipment. "Here we are, son."

"The Russians will never get you here, Dad."

"Russians, maybe; Soviets, no way, unless future history is to be radically altered. That's why only your mother and I knew about the fourth level until today." As James Naile went over to the television set, almost as an aside he said, "And, by the way, the Soviet Union will officially cease to exist twenty-eight years from now, in December of 1991."

"You mean there'll be a war, then?" John Naile was starting to question either his own sanity or that of his parents. "But you just said there wasn't—"

"Not a war; just evolution, son. The leadership of the Soviet Union will finally realize what folks like us have been saying all along: Communism flat out doesn't work. Economics, son, not philosophy will win out. But that's a long story. Just thank God for Ronald Reagan."

"The ACTOR?"

"That's a long story, too. Anyway, when you feel it's appropriate, John, the secrets I'm revealing to you can be shared with your wife. Someday, that baby Audrey's carrying will need to be told, but not until he or she is an adult and you can be absolutely certain the knowledge won't be abused. That child will someday be the head of Horizon Industries. Unlike you or me, though, during the greater part of his or her tenure, the future will be a mystery."

"The future's a mystery for everybody, Dad." John Naile leaned against the wall, blinked his eyes.

"Not for us, John, thanks to your great-grandparents moving west to Nevada. It's from them that I—and now you—have inherited the records of future history. I don't know if they realized what a moral burden it would be, despite all the care that they took. On the other hand, that knowledge of the future has made Horizon Industries what it is today. I've often considered—but subsequently dismissed—the idea of going to have a chat with your great-grandparents, of trying to tell them that bringing data from the future into the past is more dangerous than they suspect, despite the potential for positive change.

"In the records you'll be reading, John, mention is several times made of eight million Jews being killed in the death camps, for example, but six million were killed according to our perception of recent history. So, maybe the effort Horizon made during the war wasn't for naught. Who can say?"

"Are you alright, dad? You're talking like—well, I don't know what you're talking like. Jack and Ellen, and your Dad and your aunt Elizabeth—they moved to Nevada seventy years ago. So how could you go and talk with Jack and Ellen Naile now? It's my fault. I should be taking on more responsibilities in the company so you and Mom could—"

"Actually, it was sixty-seven years ago that Jack and Ellen Naile moved west, or a little over three decades from now, depending on your perspective."

John Naile stared at his father, then glanced about at the strange trappings in the underground room. Without looking at his father, he said, "What?"

"Ever wonder why I had you learn building and carpentry skills even though you're a rich man's son?"

"Well, I guess you thought it was good for me. Right? Okay, why?"

"Someday you might have to fit out a secret room like this, John, so you'll need to know how. There's a box on the bookshelf there beside you. Take it down carefully, open it and tell me what you see there sealed under the glass inside."

John Naile took the box from the shelf, opened it and looked at the object beneath the glass. Two pages from a magazine article, including a photo of a streetscape from turn-of-the-century Nevada. There were several storefronts visible, one of them reading "Jack Naile—General Merchandise." John Naile looked up from the photo and at his father. "Great-Grandpa's store." He looked more closely at the picture, his eyes drifting down to the bottom of the page. There was a date: 1991. "This date must be screwed up, Dad. You ever notice it?"

"That magazine article is what made your great-grand-parents realize that they were moving west, John, going to wind up in Nevada. A friend sent it to them shortly after the article was published, kind of as a gag. Jack took it more seriously than Ellen—at least at first, anyway. And my father, David, refused to even consider that there was something strange going on. You remember what a hard-head my father always was about almost everything except business," James Naile said. John Naile glimpsed a faint smile crossing his father's lips with the memory. "A fine and generous man of great intelligence and foresight, David Naile. He totally refused to believe, up until the very last minute, that some sort of time anomaly was going to take place and that he and his sister and parents would be caught up in it. But, to be on the safe side, he planned for it, even though he didn't believe in it. The business knowledge he entered the past with enabled him to become the richest man in the state of Nevada. Hell of a guy."

"What the hell is going on, Dad?"

"Take down the copy of *Atlas Shrugged*. Right there on the shelf next to Jack and Ellen's family Bible. The bible was printed next year, by the way, if you care to check the date."

"How can you say 'was printed next year?' What's—"

"Look at the Ayn Rand novel there, in the flyleaf." John Naile took the book and opened it. His father went on. "The book is a 1957 first edition of *Atlas Shrugged*. But there is something stamped into the endpapers."

"'From The Library of Jack and Ellen Naile,'" John Naile read aloud. He stared at his father.

"Now, that volume that you're holding in your hands, John, is one of the few actual books—most of their reference materials were on microfiche, which is like microfilm—but that book and their family Bible and only a few other works were in actual book form when Jack and Ellen Naile packed up the family and moved to Nevada."

John Naile pushed himself away from the bookcase against which he'd leaned. "That's impossible, Dad; you know that. Jack and Ellen Naile moved to Nevada before the turn of the century, and Ayn Rand's book here wasn't published until six years ago."

"If I'd brought you down here six years ago or ten years ago or as soon as you were old enough to read numbers, John, you could have read that same publication date from that same book. You'll have to believe something. And I've got all the proof you or anyone could require confirming that belief.

"Your great-grandparents and my father and his sister, Elizabeth, did indeed move to Nevada just before the turn of the century, but the century I'm talking about was this one, this century—not the last one. When they arrived at their destination, they were not only more than half a continent away from their home in Georgia, but almost an even century back in the past."

Before John Naile could think of anything to say, James Naile looked at his wristwatch and announced, "It's nearly time for Walter Cronkite to come on."

"It's only a little after one-thirty, Dad. All that's on television this time of the day is soap operas. Remember?"

"*As the World Turns*, to be precise, John. See?"

For the first time, John Naile looked at the television screen. There was a picture, all right. "How'd you get—"

"A picture down here? I've got sheathed cable running up to the roof of the pump house up above and to an antenna array. I was down here earlier checking reception. It's perfect. It's a color television, but CBS won't go to color broadcasting for a while yet. Pour yourself a drink, John. You're going to need it. Trust me. What you're about to see is no soap opera."

James Naile placed some sort of black plastic cartridge into one of the unfamiliar-looking electronic gadgets, this particular one right beside the television set. "What's that?"

"It's a VHS videocassette, which will be invented by the JVC Corporation sometime in the future. I don't know exactly when. I have a supply of the cassettes, handmade for me at considerable expense by the boys in our research labs. Both the machine and the cassettes themselves

were copied from equipment owned by Jack and Ellen
Naile. Your great-grandparents had planned to bring
several of these machines to Nevada with them, but the
circumstances of their actual trip came up suddenly. So
they only had one, which doubled as a handheld television
camera. The thing was made by the Japanese, or will be,
depending on point of view. Rest easy; we have stock in
several companies which will be big players in this. And
the Nailes had about a dozen cassettes with them when
the time transfer took place. The original cassettes couldn't
be duplicated or even played until recently, because of the
printed circuitry required for the machine. Getting
images off those old cassettes was almost impossible.
Seems the magnetic surface can start flaking off, kind of
like a photograph fading in sunlight."

"Printed circuitry?"

"Takes the place of cathode tubes—for the most
part anyway. As I was saying, the cassettes were pretty
deteriorated with age, but we were able to salvage
some terrific footage of your great-grandparents, your
grandfather David and your great-aunt, Elizabeth.
Fortunately, the climate in Nevada is usually pretty dry,
so that helped preserve the tapes. The technicians who
helped me never got to see the entire setup, and they
were told that it was top-secret government work. My dad
got me started on the project. It was kind of sweet, really,
watching him sit there in front of a television set, seeing
his parents as they were then, seeing himself and his sister
as teenagers."

"So, these things play like one of the new audio
cassettes?"

"Same principle as magnetic tape, but picture as well as sound, John. We separated the camera concept from the recorder/player, though."

"Then you're going to play a tape right now, and that's how come we'll see Walter Cronkite? This is almost incomprehensible! How'd they get this technology in the past when it couldn't have been invented and hasn't been invented yet? This doesn't make any sense, Dad."

"I'm going to record something. You can look at the copies of the old tapes later. We're about to see history unfolding before our eyes, son, and it won't be pretty to watch. We're going to make a record of it. I don't really know why we should, but maybe I've come to appreciate history the same way you will."

A commercial for Niagara Spray Starch was just concluding. The commercial ended, and there on the screen were a man and a woman in a living-room setting. They seemed to be discussing something, but John Naile didn't care what; his mind was sifting through the bizarre things his father had been telling him.

The television drew his attention again as there was a thudding sound and the words "CBS News Bulletin" flashed on the screen. As his father had predicted, it was the voice of Walter Cronkite, and he was saying, "Here is a bulletin from CBS News . . . "

"Mother of God," John Naile rasped as Walter Cronkite announced that President Kennedy had been shot. The bulletin ended. John Naile took the drink his father offered him. A single malt scotch with no ice. John Naile swallowed half the contents of the glass.

A commercial was on again, a pendulum swinging

back and forth. Nescafé coffee was the product. It was interrupted. Cronkite's voice came on again. "Further details . . ."

John Naile took another swallow of scotch.

In what seemed forever, but could have been the space of a single heartbeat, Walter Cronkite was on camera, in shirtsleeves, looking very tired, less than perfectly prepared. A functioning newsroom was behind him. His desk was littered with telephones and papers.

John Naile listened, closed his eyes as the man whom America would one day trust more than any public official announced the shooting in Dallas, Texas, of President John F. Kennedy.

John Naile opened his eyes. It was an affiliate feed. A negro man wearing a white waiter's jacket caught John Naile's eye: the man was weeping, a crowd of people around him. Kennedy was to have addressed a luncheon, which was the reason for the camera being there.

John Naile heard his father's voice. "President Kennedy is already dead, John. He died a short while ago at Parkland Hospital, never regaining consciousness. History will say that a lone man named Lee Harvey Oswald did the killing but at least well into the 1990s, no one will know for sure. More controversy will surround this assassination than has been associated with any event in American history, including the death of President Lincoln.

"Governor Connally," James Naile went on, "was sitting in the front passenger seat just in front of Jack Kennedy. He was shot, but he's going to be fine. He'll go on to become Secretary of the Treasury." From one of the bookshelves, James Naile took what looked like a photo album.

He opened it to a page showing a dollar bill. "Look at the signature."

John Naile did as he was told. It was Connally's signature.

"LBJ will serve out the remainder of Jack Kennedy's term," James Naile said as if reciting from well-learned rote. "The conflict in Southeast Asia is going to escalate into a full-fledged war that'll last into the 1970s, with thousands of GIs killed. Six months ago, you asked me why I had Horizon Industries gearing up for increased production. What was my motivation for working on that rocket launcher? The answer is that I knew what would happen today, John. I knew Johnson was going to succeed Jack Kennedy in the White House and that he'd knuckle under to the people at Lakewood Industries and other companies like them who've been pushing for a war."

John Naile looked into his father's eyes. "And Lakewood Industries wants a war because it means big bucks. The shits!"

"Exactly, son. And if we let Lakewood Industries profit from the war that's coming at our expense, God knows what Lakewood will push this country into in the next century. Our only choice is to compete for those same defense dollars, and at least give the American taxpayer his money's worth and our GIs equipment that won't let them down. LBJ will effectively rescind an order President Kennedy recently made which would have drastically cut American involvement in Southeast Asia. LBJ's already being sworn in aboard Air Force One. By the time LBJ runs against Goldwater in '64—"

"Senator Goldwater? Barry Goldwater?"

James Naile nodded, took a sip of his drink. "Barry'll be

the Republican standard-bearer. Johnson will withhold information from the electorate about the actual status of the war and Barry Goldwater won't call LBJ on it because Senator Goldwater's knowledge will be privileged information he'll have due to his position with the Senate Intelligence Committee. Barry will lose. LBJ will keep using ground troops, racking up incredible casualty figures. Civil unrest in the United States will come dangerously close to true anarchy. LBJ's vice-president will be Hubert Humphrey, who will run against Dick Nixon in '68 after LBJ declines to run for a second full term. Dick'll win, then run again in '72 and win again, even though he'll be under investigation concerning a burglary at the Democratic national headquarters. Dick'll eventually resign the presidency."

John almost laughed. "The President of the United States resign? Come on, Dad!"

"There are interesting times ahead, John. Oswald—the man I just mentioned as implicated in the killing of President Kennedy? He'll be brought in, but he'll never get to trial. A nightclub owner named Jack Ruby—with apparent ties to organized crime—will shoot Oswald dead in front of the television cameras, live. We'll tape-record that, too."

"This is sick, Dad!"

James Naile nodded agreement. "Sick times, son. There'll be a string of deaths, including Ruby's own from cancer, and Dorothy Kilgallen's. She will be the last news-woman or reporter of any kind to talk to Ruby. She'll die from cancer, too. In years to come, Bobby Kennedy will be killed, and so will Martin Luther King. Throughout this decade and into the next, there'll be rioting in the cities and warfare in Asia."

James Naile pointed to the television screen as he continued. "Walter Cronkite there? He'll retire from anchoring *CBS News* and be replaced by that young kid Dan Rather. We've got records of everything that will take place up until the mid-1990s. You can read through it all for yourself, John, and have your child read it someday."

John asked, "Is it okay to smoke down here?"

"Give me one of those cigarettes, and I'll join you."

John took out the package of Luckies, shook one out for his father and one for himself. James lit both cigarettes from his pipe lighter. "How could we have records of stuff that hasn't happened, Dad?"

"I read it for myself on microfiche when I was about your age, John. Your grandfather chose the day in 1929 when the stock market was going to crash, which of course he'd known about. Of course, Horizon Enterprises was fully prepared in advance, so we actually gained ground rather than lost it during the Great Depression."

"That's crazy, Dad. With this Kennedy thing—why . . . why didn't you just tell J. Edgar Hoover or somebody if you knew that the President was going to be killed? Why didn't you tell Jack Kennedy himself, for God's sake?"

"The same reason why neither your grandfather nor I told your mother about our knowledge of the future before the Japanese bombed Pearl Harbor. We can't risk changing history, and I didn't want your Mom to share in the guilt for that. And, anyway, first thing anyone would say is what you're saying—that it's crazy. After I convinced them with hard evidence, they'd invariably use knowledge of the future in ways which might change the future. We can't risk the future of all mankind in an attempt to save the life of one man or hundreds or even thousands of men.

"And what if Kennedy was still murdered, John?" James stubbed out the cigarette. "How can you smoke these things? What if, even if the government had alerted the Pacific Fleet, the Japs had still gotten through, somehow? What if time heals itself? Say that I'd really been able to prevent what happened just now in Dallas, but somehow in doing so I rewrote the future in such a way that we had that nuclear war we were able to avoid before history was changed? What if I caused the deaths of millions of people, maybe the destruction of all life on Earth, just by tampering with history this one time to save one man?"

James Naile began pacing the room, shook his head, turned off the television set. "It'll still record. No, son, rewriting time is more responsibility than I want on my shoulders, or yours. Just because I have solid connections in Washington doesn't mean I can go in and tell them something like this with any assurance at all that they'll behave correctly, use the knowledge wisely."

John lit another cigarette with the butt of the first one. "This is all true, isn't it?"

"Jack and Ellen Naile are teenagers now, attending the same high school in Chicago. They haven't married yet, of course, but they know one another, and a year from now they'll start dating, and they'll be engaged before they graduate. They'll marry in a few years—in 1968—and they'll have two children. One of those will be David, my father, your grandfather, who'll be the founder of Horizon Enterprises in 1914. Even though your grandfather has yet to be born, John, you're almost old enough to have fathered your great-grandparents—they're only seventeen and fifteen, respectively. And their daughter, Elizabeth, will become one of the most influential women of the early twentieth century."

John found a chair and sat down.

After a long silence, James said, "Let's get out of here in a couple of minutes—our wives will be needing us, and lunch will be ready, anyway. You can tell Audrey if you think it's advisable. I don't know, son; I'd probably wait a while, but do what you think is best. Might want to wait until the night we land men on the Moon. Neil Armstrong will be the first man to set foot on the Moon. That might be a more upbeat way of letting Audrey in on things—just tell her what he's going to say before he says it. That's about six years from now. Think about it."

John Naile could think about nothing else but the future.

CHAPTER
❊ ONE ❊

The building next to City Hall had once been a very small movie theater and had a stage in the back. City Hall itself was even smaller. "I wonder if the city will get the post office once the new post office gets built?"

"If you'd read the newspaper, you'd have a better idea what's going on in town, Jack."

"I've got you to read the newspaper and tell me." Jack Naile drifted the Suburban into the left lane, still paralleling the railroad tracks as they passed the brand-new public-safety complex. He took a U-turn over the tracks at the next crossover, getting over into the right-hand lane. "God help us if that guy wins the presidency, Ellen." He turned right into the diagonal. They were passing the Methodist church when he added, "I mean, I try and give people the benefit of the doubt, and he's a convincing speaker. Sometimes I've gotta remind myself not to believe a single word he says. And I don't buy this moderate

Democrat crap. Thinking of him with the same title as Ronald Reagan and Teddy Roosevelt—ugh!"

"There's nothing you can do but vote for George Bush and hope the rest of the country has the good sense to do the same and reelect him, Jack, so wait until the election before losing your temper. Don't forget to turn at the post office."

Jack Naile made a left and turned onto the one-block long one-way street, the red-brick and gray stone post office at its corner. He parked the Suburban diagonally while Ellen took her keys from the cup holder at the front of the center console. "Bring back a check, kid."

"We'll see if it's there."

"Want me to get your door?"

"I've got it." Ellen slipped out of the front passenger seat and closed the door behind her. Jack Naile hit the power button for the radio, hoping to catch one of his tunes. The station played what he mentally labeled as Afro-American elevator music, but he liked it. Ellen did not. Jack Naile watched Ellen as she walked up the steps. She was just as pretty as—really, prettier than—when he'd married her almost twenty-four years earlier.

It was the dreaded season—summer. Officially, it was still spring, but that mattered little in northeast Georgia. Summer temperatures had arrived in April, by May the humidity joining them. David and Elizabeth were out of school for three months, and that was great, but summer meant editors and everybody else he needed to do business with would be off somewhere frolicking in the sunshine while the usual nasty game of selling new projects and chasing the money owed for old ones became that much more difficult.

Autumn and winter were the best times. Their anniversary was in October. November meant Thanksgiving; Ellen was the best cook in the world, and he'd fight his way past a barbarian horde in order to eat a turkey she'd made—and considering some of the gatherings of relatives they'd had over the years, sword-wielding guys with a permanent case of male PMS would have been a snap to deal with. Just before Christmas, it was their nephew Clarence's birthday. Clarence was like a son to them, raising him since his teens as they had. Right after Christmas came the kids' birthdays, both of them born in January, two years apart. Between their birthdays, the SHOT Show, always an excuse to travel to some city or another. It would be in Houston in 1993, easy driving distance.

And just before Thanksgiving, of course, there was Halloween, which wouldn't be anywhere near as spooky as the first Tuesday after the first Monday in November might be. With all the negative talk about the economy, it seemed to Jack Naile that the press was building a bad situation that really didn't exist, merely in the hopes of unseating the incumbent and electing—Jack Naile shuddered at the thought.

Ellen came down the post-office steps, her long auburn hair bouncing a little as she walked. The instant she opened the passenger-side door, he started to ask, but she answered before the words were out of his mouth. "A lot of junk mail, no weird bills—ohh! And we got the advance check."

"Yes! Pizza for everybody!"

"Do you have to always equate celebrating with pizza?"

"Fine. Make a turkey dinner. I like that better anyway."

Ellen waved the check in front of his face, got out the checkbook and started writing out a deposit slip.

"You never see the character on *Murder, She Wrote* chasing after publishers for a check, do you?" Jack Naile asked rhetorically.

"She makes more royalties than we do, so she probably doesn't have to play chase the check."

"Well, yeah. But we're cool for a while, and all we've got to do is write the little sucker."

"It should be a fun book."

Jack Naile agreed with his wife. Of the dozens of novels they'd done over the years, they'd rarely been able to get some of their pet ideas in print—and this book was one of them. Ellen loved the research end of things and their current magnum opus was far more her idea than his. "Just think about it, kid. Pretty soon, we'll be immersed in El Cid, the Cave of St. John the Divine in the Greek islands and the Great Pyramid at Giza."

"I wish we could go to the Greek islands—nice sandy beaches. I wish we could go anyplace. Egypt would be nice."

"Not in the summer—wrong season. Anyway, we've got some science fiction cons to go to over the summer."

"No sandy beaches, just crowded elevators."

Jack Naile started the car. "Bank?"

"Bank."

"Can you do those photos for me today?"

"This is another one of those roundup articles, isn't it? Guns, holsters, knives?"

"Yeah, well, but the only way I can write it is having the pictures to work from. Only way to organize it."

"I hate roundup articles."

"Well, people like to read—"

"Hey, look at this!" Ellen was sifting through what she had labeled as junk mail. "You've gotta see this."

Jack Naile put the car back in park, and he and Ellen leaned close together over the center console, their heads touching. In her hands she held a page from a magazine. Attached to it was a small piece of paper with a few typewritten sentences. "I see your articles in the gun magazines a lot. Thought you'd get a kick out of this. Looks like somebody in your family was gainfully employed at one time." The note was signed with a name Jack Naile didn't recognize.

"Look at the picture! Look, Jack!"

He didn't have his glasses, but a little squinting helped a lot. A caption beneath a black-and-white photograph described a street scene from northern Nevada in 1903. The street was broad, unpaved, dusty, obviously the main drag. Horses and wagons were in the street, as were various pedestrians. On the far side of the street from the camera was a board sidewalk, several wooden storefronts adjacent to it, the buildings packed together like row housing. One of them, the far left edge of its sign almost obscured by a hanging advertising shingle, read "Jack Naile—General Merchandise."

Jack Naile lit a Camel from a half-empty pack and took the Suburban out of park. He made a right, caught the traffic light and paralleled the railroad tracks, made a U-turn across them and then a quick right into the lot for the bank's drive-thru. "How's about a cup of coffee when we get home?" Jack asked.

"Sounds good."

They were able to pull up at the actual window, Ellen ready with the deposit slip. He signed the check and passed it to the pretty, smiling woman on the other side of the bullet-proof glass.

Jack Naile turned up into their steep driveway and, after stopping briefly to let Ellen out, put the Suburban under the portico; the passenger door couldn't be opened once the Suburban was parked. Parking under the portico always reminded Jack of sticking a size-thirteen foot into a size-twelve shoe. Ellen was already unlocking the house. Jack crossed the broad front porch, and they let themselves in, Jack making a quick right off the shotgun hall and into the office. He wanted to be working on the book, but he had to finish the roundup article. The magazine piece was running too long, but that couldn't be helped. Pretty soon he'd be stuck until Ellen got the rest of the photos taken and they got them back. That, of course, meant better than twenty miles each way to the only place around that developed black-and-whites. He heard the piss-poor excuse for a car that had at one time been a Saab pulling into the driveway. Without looking away from the computer screen, he called out, "David's home, Ellen, Elizabeth. Ellen? You hear me?"

"I'm not deaf!"

The front hallway door was just outside the open door to the office. When Jack Naile heard the door opening, he called out, "Hi, David. Your mom's got something to show you and your sister. Came in the mail. How was summer school?"

"Okay. I'm gonna be late for work, so I've only got a minute."

Jack saved what he'd just written and got up from the creaky old swivel chair his father had given him when he was two years younger than David. The chair was used and looked it. Lookswise, it hadn't changed much since he'd gotten it. But its creaking was getting ominous.

"Elizabeth? You dressed yet?" Jack Naile shouted up the stairs to his daughter. "Come on. See this thing we got in the mail!"

"Coming, Daddy! Just two minutes."

"I don't have two minutes, Dad," David called back over his shoulder as he headed into the bathroom.

"You want a sandwich or something?" Ellen asked as David started to close the door.

David stuck his head out and said, "Yeah. But I've gotta hurry."

"I'm making tuna salad. Want one?"

"Sure."

Jack Naile lit a cigarette. He could hear Elizabeth starting down the stairs. For a fifteen-year-old girl, she had the loudest feet. Maybe it was the shoes.

"When you finish your cigarette, you want a sandwich, Jack?" Ellen asked as he entered the kitchen.

"Sure, princess," Naile said, leaning across the leg of the L-shaped kitchen counter and giving Ellen a kiss on the tip of her nose. "Smells good."

"How can you smell anything with that cigarette? You should quit. David wants you to quit. Elizabeth wants you to quit."

"You want me to quit?"

"Well, if you die because you keep smoking, I can

always marry a rich doctor or something. Go ahead. Expose all of us to secondhand smoke. You don't care."

"Yeah, right." Ellen had achieved the effect she'd sought. Jack stubbed out his cigarette.

"Okay, what's this thing in the mail?" Elizabeth asked.

Jack turned around and glanced at his daughter. She was beautiful, just like her mother, even though she took after his side of the family more. Both kids did, really. Ellen had the gray-green eyes, just like her father and mother. David and Elizabeth had brown eyes, like his. All four of them had the same hair coloring, dark reddish brown, but David's always looked black. David had curly hair like Tom Selleck, but used mousse and all sorts of other stuff to make his hair appear straight, whereas Elizabeth, of course, had straight hair and tried to make it hold a curl.

"Well, what came in the mail?" Elizabeth repeated.

As Jack Naile was about to answer, he heard the toilet flush. "Give your brother another minute. We want to see what both you guys think."

Elizabeth shrugged resignedly and sat down on the deacon's bench at the kitchen table. Jack Naile started to light another cigarette, but Ellen said "Here" and put a dessert plate in his hand with a tuna-salad sandwich and half a kiwi on it.

After what was about two minutes—Elizabeth already had her sandwich and Jack Naile's was half-consumed—David entered the kitchen. "Here," Ellen Naile said, putting a plate in her son's hand. "You want another one, the bread's right there." She took a bite of her own sandwich.

"Where's the thing that came in the mail?" Jack Naile asked his wife.

"Right where you put it." She took it off the kitchen table and handed it to him.

Jack set down his sandwich and sat down at the table. As he opened the envelope and extracted the page cut from the magazine, he declared, "This is really bizarre."

"It's a picture of an old town," David announced, looking over his father's shoulder. Elizabeth had come around to stand beside him. "What's so amazing—"

"Your father wants you guys to look at the name on the store on the far side of the street."

"'Jack Naile—General Merchandise,'" Elizabeth read aloud.

"Ohh. Yeah, that is weird," David announced as he sat down and started eating.

"How's the math class?" Elizabeth asked her brother.

"I'm getting it. I think I'm going to get an A, whereas, if I'd taken it in the fall, well . . ."

"Have you got a store meeting tonight, David?" Ellen asked.

"As assistant manager, I've gotta be there."

"No, I just wanted to double check. You going to have dinner with us?"

"Yeah, sure."

Jack Naile swallowed the bite of sandwich that was in his mouth. "Doesn't anybody have anything to say about the photograph? You guys realize how odd the spelling is for our last name? And then it's even the same first name! I mean, this is really strange. And what an idea for a book!"

"A book?" Elizabeth repeated.

"Why did you ask that?" David asked his sister. "Now Dad'll take the next twenty minutes—"

"Hey, think about it!" Jack insisted. "What would happen to a family just like ours if—somehow—we got thrust back in time to turn-of-the-century Nevada?"

"I'd be late for work," David supplied.

"No, I mean we could have one hell of a book if we used ourselves as the basis for the characters and then worked out all the planning that would be involved and—"

David's smile was indulgent as he told Jack, "It could never happen, Dad. What? Are they going to invent a time machine or something? Are they going to bump into some crazy professor with a DeLorean like Michael J. Fox did in the movies? Nobody's ever going to believe it, Dad, because it couldn't happen in real life. I've gotta go."

David was up. Elizabeth said, "You don't know that it couldn't happen, David. And that is our name on that store almost a hundred years ago. I think Mom and Dad have a good idea."

David didn't say it, but Jack could read his son's thoughts on the young man's face: either "Suck-up" or "You shouldn't humor Mom and Dad on stuff like this; they need to write something serious."

David shot everybody a smile and started down the hall.

Jack was up, Ellen had never sat down for more than a second and Elizabeth was already following her brother down the hall. "We'll wave at you, David."

"Fine. See you guys."

The practice of waving was a family tradition, so much so that anytime David or Elizabeth went out with their friends, all of their friends would wave as well. It went according to a well-established pattern; depending on the clemency of the weather it was conducted either wholly from within the house by the storm door (which also involved flashing the porch light) or from the front porch.

It was a warm—too warm to Jack's way of thinking—and dry day, so the exterior wave option was automatically selected. As David was starting down the front steps, his sister was already saying "Give me a kiss, David." David, of course, did not, but smiled.

David was getting into the Bondo-gray splotched Saab as Jack Naile closed the storm door.

David, an excellent hand with a manual transmission, was already coasting out of the driveway in reverse as Jack went for the customary cigarette.

Jack barely got the cigarette lit in the flame of his Zippo before it was time for the first volley of waves. Jack frequently waved with two hands. Elizabeth sometimes did the two-handed, and that was her selection. Today Ellen, sanest of them all, made her usual one-handed wave. This all transpired as David passed the house. David acknowledged with a gesture halfway between a wave and a salute, accomanied by a slight nod of the head.

Jack Naile took another drag on his cigarette as David made a full stop at the corner. David made the left. About thirty feet after completing the turn, it was time for the second volley. Jack again used the two-handed option, as did Elizabeth. Ellen one-handed it. David, in turn, acknowledging the second volley, honked the Saab's horn.

Jack took another drag from his cigarette, walked down the front steps and dropped the filterless cigarette to the concrete, crushing it under his foot.

The wave was officially over.

"So, you want to help your mother and me with the book, Elizabeth?"

Elizabeth, already starting to go inside, responded, "Let me think about it."

"That's fair, Jack," Ellen interjected.

"It'd beat watching *Oprah* and *Donahue*, kid."

"If I were sixteen instead of fifteen, I wouldn't watch that much TV."

In fairness, she hung out with her friends a lot, read a lot of Danielle Steele and was waiting on word about a part-time job. Sometimes she even helped out in the office. Jack shrugged his shoulders and lit another cigarette. He could sympathize with Lizzie; not being old enough to drive had to suck . . .

The scrunchy in her ponytail was giving Ellen a little headache, so she took it off, stopping in the downstairs bathroom to run a brush through her hair. That done, she continued on her way to the office. As she entered the room, Jack wasn't writing. He was picking up the telephone. "What are you doing? I thought you were working on the book or the article or something. You're trying to find out more about the photo, right?"

Jack looked up from the telephone's keypad and their eyes met. "I'm checking with that little town's chamber of commerce. For the heck of it. Wanted to, ahh . . ."

Jack had pretty eyes—so dark—even when peering out

from within a sheepish smile. "Fine." Ellen sat down at
her desk. Their two desks dominated the center of the
office, the fronts of the two desks facing, touching. Jack
believed in UFOs, thought Bigfoot was the missing link
and, every once in a while, got into serious discussions
about the JFK assassination, about which he was actually
quite well-informed. After over twenty-three years of
marriage, dating four years before that and knowing each
other as friends for three years before that, she was used
to Jack's penchant for going off on tangents.

Ellen picked up *The Skeptical Inquirer* and began
looking through it. She could hear her husband talking,
but wasn't really paying attention until she heard him put
down the receiver and say "Shit."

"What?"

"The historian's out of town for a while and can't be
reached."

"He'll be back." As she said that, her eyes drifted across
the photos on the wall nearest the hallway. There was a
big painting of John Wayne as he looked in *Hondo* and,
next to it, a color photograph of Richard Boone as he
looked in *Have Gun—Will Travel*, one of Jack's favorite
old television programs. Jack even had a hat like Richard
Boone had worn, low-crowned and black; one of Jack's
holster-making friends had made an almost perfect
duplicate of the hatband.

On other walls in the room there were pictures of Clint
Walker, Clayton Moore and Jay Silverheels—mingled with
photos of David and Elizabeth. There was even a picture
of Theodore Roosevelt, one of Jack's big heroes, in his
cowboy mufti, standing beside a large black horse.

Ellen wondered just what it was that her husband was hoping to find out about the photograph they'd been mailed? Did he really wonder if, somehow, they were— "No," she said aloud.

"What, princess?"

"Nothing. Why don't you get back to work, Jack? I'll get out of your hair." As she left the office and entered the hallway, her eyes flickered toward the hall tree. The black Stetson was there, lurking . . .

Unlike departures, there was no arrival ritual, no waving at all. Ellen's thirty-four-year-old nephew, Clarence, merely let himself in through the front door of their house with his own key and sang out his characteristic "Hi. It's me." "Hi" was Northernese for "Hey, y'all!" All of them were Illinois-born damned Yankees who came to Georgia in the late 1970s. Non-damned yankees, of course, were the kind who were merely passing through. Only Liz, who was less than two when they migrated southward, had what Jack Naile' still thought of as a Southern accent. However, Elizabeth could turn it on and off like a faucet, as required.

Jack got up from the kitchen table, stepped into the hallway and responded, "Hiya, Clarence! Ellen's got dinner nearly ready. Good to see you, son!"

For the time that Clarence was in Air Force Electronic Intelligence, in Greece for the last three-and-one-half years of his hitch, they had seen him precious little. Since then, after a year doing pretty much the same thing, but as a civilian, he had moved to Atlanta and taken a job managing a multiplex, which Jack had always thought was a waste of talent. However, it did allow more frequent socializing, for which he, Ellen and the kids were grateful.

Clarence was Ellen's late sister's son, after her death brought into their home in Illinois while still in his teens. They had pretty much raised him from then on, and looked on him as an extra son. Ellen, nine when he was born, had carried him home from the hospital. Jack had met Clarence for the first time—Clarence had punched him in the stomach—when Clarence was not quite seven years old.

"So, how's the movie business?"

"I've got some posters for David and Liz. They're in the car. Remind me to bring them in before I leave."

"So, how you feeling?"

"My back's bothering me a little, and I think I'm getting a cold." With that, Clarence sneezed.

Ellen announced, "Dinner's ready."

"I'll call the kids," Jack volunteered.

Clarence ate as if food were about to be banned, as much as a pound and a half of Ellen's homemade lasagna. After dinner, they would all probably play Trivial Pursuit, Clarence and David and Ellen on one team, Jack and Elizabeth on the other. Somehow, Jack knew, that was supposed to make it fairer, a more even match, which was not entirely true. Both Clarence and David followed professional sports, Clarence more so. Jack Naile had seen two broadcast television football games in his life and had no idea how the scoring was figured beyond the obvious thing that a touchdown was good.

After dinner, and saying the obligatory but sincere "Anything I can do to help?" Jack steered David and

Clarence into the rec room, while Ellen put things away and Elizabeth helped her.

Jack had the photograph on the coffee table and showed it to Clarence.

"I agree that the photo is an interesting coincidence. That's all that it is," David announced, as if forming Clarence's opinion for him.

Clarence, six foot two and named after his fourteen-inch shorter grandfather, plunked down on the far end of the sectional sofa. "It's interesting. It's also creepy," he added with a laugh.

Jack leaned back into the center of the sectional, feeling very pleasantly full, and lit a cigarette. "Creepy in what way, Clarence? You mean that it might actually happen?"

"He doesn't think that. Do you, Clarence?"

"No, David. No. No, Jack. I mean, the same name thing."

"He's right, Dad. Nothing more to this than two men separated by almost a century who happen to have the same name. God knows, the guy who sent the picture to you could have doctored it just as a joke. There's nothing to it."

Jack Naile supposed that it was only fate that one member of the family had to be sensible.

Jack sat at his desk, but his eyes weren't on the screen of his computer, nor did his fingers stroke the keyboard. In his hands, he held one of his most prized possessions, a Colt Single Action Army .45, a second-generation gun made in the early 1970s, worked on for him by the world's fastest draw, and one of the finest trick shooters in history,

Bob Munden. The revolver had originally been nickel plated, but after Bob's work on it, the Colt was sent to another old friend, Ron Mahovsky, who had Metalifed it over the nickel, making it look like brushed stainless steel but more impervious to rust. The original checkered hard rubber grips were replaced with black buffalo-horn two-piece panels from Eagle grips.

The barrel was seven and one-half inches long. The trigger pull was fourteen ounces. It was the perfect Colt.

Jack Naile set the single action down on the desk and picked up the telephone.

"Hi. This is Jack Naile again."

Jack recognized the voice on the other end, and the woman belonging to the voice recognized his. "Arthur Beach is back. I'll connect you, Mr. Naile."

"Thanks."

After a moment, there was a voice announcing itself as that of Arthur Beach. Unlike the mental image Jack Naile had formed of a historian in a small Nevada town, someone old and perhaps a bit stodgy, Arthur Beach sounded barely thirty and seemed quite intrigued at the call. "When they told me about your calls, I did a little digging, Mr. Naile."

"Ohh, wonderful! Who was this guy Jack Naile?" Jack asked.

"Well, understand I haven't really been able to look into this too thoroughly yet. And, if you'd like, I'll get you more information."

"Anything you can dig up, yes. A photograph would be great, if one exists."

"I'll do my best. But here's what I can tell you so far about your namesake, Mr. Naile. The original Jack Naile was a prominent citizen, not only owning the store but a large ranch as well. After a time, he became very influential behind the scenes in Republican politics within the state and at the national level. Jack Naile's store became a Mecca for people from all over the area, people interested in the highest-quality products or just the unusual. As time went on, for example, Jack Naile's store was the first in the area to offer phonographs, radios and the like. In that respect, the store was more of a hobby for Naile. Naile grew to be one of the richest men around, with an uncanny ability to predict trends in public interest."

Jack Naile lit another cigarette. "What about Jack Naile's personal life? Do you have anything on that?"

Beach told him, "Well, Naile and his wife—I don't know her name off the top of my head—had two grown children, teenagers, I guess, when they first came to town."

"So none of them were born there, then."

"No. They just showed up in town one day, evidently coming from somewhere back East and en route to California. I understand that you're thinking about using this information as the basis for one of the novels you and your wife write."

"Yes, if we can dig up enough information," Jack Naile responded, keeping his cards as close to the vest as possible.

"I'll be happy to help all that I can. But you'll have to promise me an autographed copy of the book if you write it."

Jack agreed to that, he and Arthur Beach exchanged complete contact data and the conversation ended . . .

Ellen waited as long as she dared before the answering machine would pick up. Jack wasn't answering the telephone. She lifted the receiver, shook her hair back and put the receiver to her ear. "Hi. Can I help you?"

And Ellen almost passed out. It was their old agent, Lars Benson. A very nice guy, Lars had also been the most incompetent literary agent imaginable. "Jack around?"

"What's up, Lars?"

"I got you guys a sale, Ellen!"

Ellen Naile thought that she'd heard Lars Benson, who, in the first place, hadn't been their literary agent for more than five years and, in the second place, couldn't sell a space suit to a naked astronaut, let alone a book to a publisher, say that he had sold something.

"Let me find Jack, Lars. Okay? Hold on."

"Let me tell ya! I gotta tell ya!"

"Alright, Lars. Tell me." Sometimes, she wished that she still smoked. A Salem at this moment would have cleared her sinuses and given her something to think about besides how dear, sweet, honest and ineffectual Lars had gone off the deep end. "What did you sell, Lars?"

"Remember when you guys wrote *Angel Street*?"

Ellen wanted to say, "No, I forgot." Instead, she answered, "And?"

"One of the majors in Hollywood—and I don't mean an indie—wants to option it for a western."

Ellen Naile almost said, "shit" but didn't. "Lars," she

pointed out, "that book was set in the present day—at least the present day in the mid-1980s."

"Don't you get it, sweetheart?! They're movin' it to the 1880s. Or somethin'. We could be talkin' the Austrian Oak here makin' his first western, or—"

"He made a western with Kirk Douglas and Ann-Margaret. It's really funny, like a cartoon with people in it. It was intended to be that way."

"Well, I don't know who the hell's gonna be in it, but they're talkin' twenty-five large up front—"

"You've gotta stop watching *Miami Vice*, Lars."

"Twenty-five grand, alright?! And if they exercise the option and decide to lens it, we're talkin' major bucks city here, a hundred grand extra and a piece. A little piece, for sure . . ."

"Ohh, for sure. I'll get Jack, Lars."

Ellen pushed the hold button and shouted at the top of her lungs, "Jack! Pick up on line one! Now, Jack!"

Ellen had been on the kitchen telephone and ran toward the office, her fists under her breasts because she wasn't wearing a bra underneath the loose-fitting T-shirt.

Jack was on the phone as she came in and they exchanged glances. His eyes mirrored her thoughts—poor Lars had finally gone off the deep end, withdrawn into a fantasy world.

"*Angel Street*," Ellen whispered barely aloud as she sat down at her desk. As a western? *Angel Street* had been a book Jack had liked a lot more than she had. The hero of the story had been a hard-as-nails P.I. named "Angela Street" who takes a charity case, going after the drug lord responsible for the death of a teenage runaway.

The P.I. is closing in on the drug lord, about to get the goods on him, when the drug lord's gang ambushes her and kills her.

An actual angel—her guardian angel—appears and offers Angela Street the chance to return to life long enough to get the drug lord and his gang. Angela agrees. The angel—a very good-looking male angel—stays with her, helping her. It is a risk for the guardian angel, because, in order to help her, he must take on human form. And, should something happen to him while in human form, he would die, would be unable to return to life as an angel. He'd be dead-dead. Angela and her guardian angel fall in love—which Ellen had thought was way too predictable. More predictable had been the ending. Angela Street triumphs against the drug lord, of course, and the guardian angel gets fatally shot. As he dies, she kisses him and, somehow, she doesn't die as she should have.

Angela Street doesn't know if she's on borrowed time or has had life actually restored to her. But with whatever time she has left on earth, she'll fight on the side of good, against the bad guys on the street. "Yada yada yada," Ellen said aloud.

Jack, still talking with Lars, just looked at her uncomprehendingly. She smiled back and shook her head, hopefully signaling that she'd meant nothing.

"Okay, Lars. So, when do we see the contracts?"

Evidently, Jack had been sucked into Lars' fantasy.

"FedEx today?" There was a pause. "Yeah, Ellen and I'll read the contract as soon as it gets here and call you right away." There was another pause. "Of course I've still got your phone number, pal." Another pause. "Okay! Take it easy, buddy."

Jack said to her, "Did you get the part about the twenty-five G's?"

"I'll believe it when there's a check in my hand. Actually, that's not true. I'll believe it after the check has cleared the bank."

"Come here, kid! Gimme a kiss!" But Jack didn't wait for her to come to him. He was out of his chair like a shot and pulled her up out of her chair and kissed her so hard that her teeth hurt. "Twenty-five grand!"

"Wait to order the pizza at least until we've seen the contract, Jack," Ellen advised.

They'd signed three copies of the contract, faxed one up to Lars Benson. He'd been a ten percent agent, but wanted fifteen, more currently fashionable. They gave it to him, feeling he deserved it just for breathing—all that he had actually done, in fact, to get them the deal. Lars was agent of record for a book that hadn't sold very well at all; the rights had reverted from the publisher less than a year prior to Lars' phone call the previous day.

Ellen had the Express Mail envelope with the signed contracts on her lap, her right hand clutching the seatbelt.

"This is great, isn't it, Ellen? I mean, *Angel Street* as a western!"

"So, they'll turn the drug lord into a corrupt town boss or rustling king-pin, Angela Street will grow testicles and become Tex Wannabe, bounty hunter, and the guardian angel sex changes, too."

"Pretty much the way I figure it. A good, basic story has

a lot of inbuilt versatility to it," her husband told her. "Write that down, will ya?"

"Soon as we get home, Jack."

Jack made the left and slipped the Suburban into one of the diagonal spaces in front of the post office. Ellen grabbed her keys and climbed out. She couldn't quite figure out why, but for some reason she'd worn a skirt. Maybe it was because the weather was too warm for long pants, but not warm enough for shorts. The checkbook was in her left hand, her keys in the right patch pocket. An older man—she recognized his face, didn't remember his name . . . if she'd ever known it—held the door for her and she smiled.

Inside, she went first to the post-office box. "Crap," she said as she looked through its contents. Among the bills, the advertisements and the usual junk mail, there were three things that would grab Jack's attention. One was the Museum Replicas catalog, full of swords. Jack liked swords. Another was the A. G. Russell knife catalog. Jack liked knives. What had prompted her single-word remark was the third item, a legal-sized envelope, its return address label revealing that it was from Arthur Beach.

Ellen closed the door to the post office box, went to the counter and didn't even have to wait in line. The pleasant woman behind the counter weighed the Express Mail package and Ellen wrote out a check and left.

"Anything exciting in the mail?"

"Well, Museum Replicas and A. G. Russell."

"Great! Let me see."

Ellen Naile passed them over. "And an envelope from Arthur Beach in Nevada."

"Open it, kid."

"Priority Mail. Why does the post office have to be efficient when you don't want them to be?"

"Ellen!"

"This is really very creepy, Jack. This whole thing. For the first time in our lives, unless Lars really is whacko, we're going to have some real money, and there's this thing."

Ellen opened the envelope. There were copies of documents, and newspaper articles and a copy of a photograph, just a Xerox, but remarkably—damnably— clear. It was a photograph of Mr. and Mrs. Jack Naile and their two (unnamed) children.

"This has to be an elaborate practical joke, Jack."

"Lemme see, princess."

She handed it to him. She didn't need to look at the picture anymore. It was burned into her mind forever and she'd probably see it in her dreams—the kind called nightmares. Despite the age of the photograph and the fact that it was a Xerox, the resemblance between the Naile family of nine decades ago and the Naile family of the present was enough to make her want to throw up.

Her own counterpart, and that of her daughter, wore their hair piled up beneath feather-festooned picture book hats. They wore long, uncomfortable-looking dresses, their hands clasped in front of them at their obviously corseted waists like singers about to hit a high note at the opera.

The older of the two men wore a black hat, its shape identical to Jack's, even the hatband looking to be the same. He wore a vested suit, but it was, somehow, still casual looking. His mustache was identical to the one Jack had sported since he was twenty-two. He'd grown it because Ellen had always liked the look of Omar Sharif's mustache.

The younger man, clean shaven but with a noticeable five o'clock shadow—David always had that—was the epitome of male fashion for the period, from derby to cravat to spats. David always looked as if he'd stepped out of the pages of G.Q. Ellen had helped her husband with enough firearms-related articles to spot a concealed weapon, and there was a slight bulge at David's left side, as if his coat covered a handgun worn crossdraw.

And the older man also was armed, a gun on his right hip, what was perhaps the butt of a second one protruding from beneath his coat.

The gunbelt/holster was a Hollywood rig of the type worn in '50s and '60s television westerns, a style which didn't exist almost a century ago. Ellen Naile had even recognized it as one that Jack's friend Sam Andrews had made for him around 1990.

She'd been looking out the Suburban's open window. She turned her gaze to the other items from the envelope. There was a summary of its contents typed on an old-seeming machine, Arthur Beach's name scrawled at the bottom. She read it aloud to her husband. "'The Naile family arrived in town in 1896. The Nailes were apparently on their way to California for some new business when their wagon suffered an accident and was destroyed. They were unhurt, according to accounts. Reduced to only a few personal belongings, the Nailes seemingly had considerable financial resources. There is no material yet available to me mentioning the fate of their descendants, nor concerning how or when Mr. and Mrs. Naile eventually died. The county medical examiner's office burned to the ground in the 1940s, and all death certificates archived there were destroyed as a result. I'll keep looking.'"

"Holy—"

"Tell him to stop the hell looking, Jack!"

"Startling resemblance, that photograph. I'll say that."

Ellen nearly retched as she said it, but she said it anyway. "Jack, it's you and me and David and Elizabeth, and the fucking picture was taken almost a hundred damn years ago! Get me home before I throw up!"

The Suburban lurched into reverse, which didn't help.

CHAPTER
❖ TWO ❖

Jack picked up the phone and tapped out the number from memory.

"This is Arthur Beach."

"Yeah, Arthur, this is Jack Naile—the one in the present," Jack added lamely.

"Did you get my envelope yet?"

"That's the reason I called. Yeah. We got it. And thanks for being so helpful. Listen. Do you have any way of finding any more photographs of the Naile family? And getting them copied? Within reason, I'll pay whatever it costs. I could use a better copy of the photo you sent us, too."

"Before I forget, I uncovered some more information on the Naile family, Jack. And, even though Jack Naile was a businessman, he seems to have gotten himself a reputation for being handy with a gun. It kind of reads like some kind of a western movie," Beach added, laughing. "But, yeah, I think I can get some copies made of the photos. See any family resemblances?"

"Yeah—a little bit, at least." Jack lit a cigarette, his gaze fixing on the photograph of Richard Boone, long-barreled single action drawn and pointing at him.

Ellen sat beside Jack at the table. Unlike some of the higher-profile writers attending the science fiction/fantasy convention, she and her husband had no scheduled mass autographing, but their readers caught them at the beginnings or endings of panel discussions or merely stopped them in the lobby.

Ellen saw Elizabeth signaling from the back of the room that she'd wait for them outside, and Ellen shot her a wave. David hadn't come, having to work instead. But in a way, he was with them in spirit; they'd borrowed his Bondo-mobile Saab because the hotel's underground garage was too low for the Suburban.

Jack passed a copy of their latest novel over to her. He was still talking with the reader who'd brought it. Ellen signed and dated the frontispiece under Jack's signature. She closed the book, handed it back to Jack, and they exchanged a few more words with the man and his wife. Jack returned the book. The man and his wife smiled and walked away.

"You all set, Ellen?" Jack asked, starting to get up.

Jack pulled her chair for her. As Ellen got up, a good-looking young man in his late twenties or early thirties, a little boy of about four in tow, approached the table. An interesting thing about cons was that one got to recognize a lot of the faces of the attendees. And Ellen

Naile recognized this man—yet she had no idea from where or what.

Somehow, the beard that the man wore didn't look usual for him, nor did the glasses.

"I was wondering if you guys would mind autographing your book for my son here. I'm a big fan, and I'm sure he'll love your stuff, too—soon as he's old enough to read, anyway."

Jack laughed. Ellen smiled as Jack accepted the book and started writing in it. Even the voice sounded familiar, somehow. Ellen signed the book as well. Jack was joking with the little boy. He was very cute, with curly red hair and an almost pugnacious smile.

The young man offered his hand, and he and Jack shook. He offered his hand to Ellen, and she took it. "Your little boy reminds me of our son, David, when he was that age." And Ellen extended her hand to the little boy. Like a little man, he shook hands. Ellen laughed.

"Do I get a handshake, too, pal?" Jack inquired. The little boy seemed a bit reluctant, but shook hands.

"It was really great meeting you guys. My little boy will cherish this book and so will I. God bless." The young man swept his son up into his arms, smiled and walked away.

"What was his name, Jack?"

"He wanted the book autographed to his son. James was the name."

"Didn't that little boy remind you of David?"

"His father reminded me of David. Come on, I'll buy you and Elizabeth a drink."

They linked up with Elizabeth in the corridor,

Elizabeth immediately told them, "That little boy and his father? Wasn't that little boy cute?"

Ellen smiled.

Almost ten days after Jack's conversation with Arthur Beach, Ellen Naile found herself being reminded of the Norsemen, their belief that at the moment of birth the skein of one's life was woven by their equivalent of the Fates. The warp and woof seemed to be quite apparent.

Elizabeth, not seriously dating yet, was to go out with three of her friends, but one of them—the one old enough to drive—had to work instead.

David was to have been out with a few of his buddies from school, guys with whom he'd been on the wrestling team and the tennis team, most of them friends since kindergarten. But their plans fell apart; Ellen didn't know why.

Clarence had called and accepted their standing offer to come up from Atlanta and spend the night.

At the post-office box that morning, there had been another package from Arthur Beach, this one quite a bit thicker.

Ellen and Jack had opened it together in the car. Considering the age of the originals from which the copies had been made, the photos were remarkably clear. The likenesses of the Naile family of nearly a century ago to the Naile family of the present were not just uncanny, but unmistakably identical.

She could have lied to herself that the queasy feeling she had was because her period had just started, but she didn't; the reason was in an envelope on her lap.

The day had passed quickly—too much so—and, almost before she knew it, the entire family, such togetherness an increasing rarity, was seated around the kitchen table.

Perhaps to keep her mind off the photographs and their scary implications, Ellen Naile had done something that she rarely did—she made dessert. Lars Benson had called during the day, telling them that he had the advance check for *Angel Street* and that he'd have the disbursement check in their hands by the following day, Friday. Because of that, Ellen went to the grocery store and bought T-bone steaks, one of Jack's favorites.

The check was to arrive by Federal Express, meaning that it would be there in time for deposit. Because of that, Ellen was not surprised when she caught a weather report predicting severe thunderstorms throughout the Southeast. The storms would obviously be so severe that flights incoming to Atlanta's Hartsfield Airport would be delayed just enough that their check would not arrive until after two p.m., meaning that the deposit wouldn't be credited until the following Monday.

But she bought the steaks anyway.

The steaks consumed, she suggested, "Why don't we wait a few minutes before dessert, guys?"

Elizabeth stood up from the table, came over and felt her mother's forehead and cheeks. "Doesn't have a fever or anything."

"Mom must be sick, though," David cracked.

"So, fine, I made a dessert. It's got broccoli in it—don't worry."

"Did you check the ingredients?" Clarence asked.

Her nephew obviously knew that she'd checked the

ingredients. Although the rest of them kidded Clarence about it, his allergy to peanut oil was no joke. "Yes. It's cherry cream-cheese pie. I made the crust from graham crackers, and I checked the box for ingredients. Liz double-checked it."

"Well, you know I've gotta be careful."

Jack cleared his throat, got up, said, "Be back in a second," and walked into the hallway.

"What's up with Daddy?"

"Yeah. Dad seems awfully quiet," David declared, agreeing with his sister.

"It's not some more of that stuff about that other Naile family," Clarence began. "When I was up here the last time, I went home and didn't get to sleep for a couple of hours, and I had some really yucko dreams."

"Well, saddle up for some more of them, Clarence," Jack said. He stood in the kitchen doorway, both of Arthur Beach's envelopes in his left hand, a cigarette in his right. "Exhibit A." Jack placed the earlier package at the center of the table.

David picked it up and opened it. "Like I told you before, Dad, this is some kind of a sick joke." But David didn't take his eyes from the Xerox of the Naile family of the past.

Jack leaned against the kitchen counter, next to his ashtray. He passed the second envelope over to David, then returned to his ashtray. "Check out what's inside, son. Pass things around."

"No. I was just going to stare at the envelope, Dad."

"There's no reason to get pissed off," Jack told him. "Well, maybe there is, but wait until you've looked at all the new stuff, and then get pissed off. No sense doing it twice."

Elizabeth and Clarence were studying the Xerox from the first envelope. "Dammit!" Clarence exclaimed. "This is some kind of nutball jerking you guys around."

Ellen kept her voice calm. "When Jack and I did that book where we had this guy framed by his boss to look like a Russian spy? I did a lot of research about altering photographs. If these photographs were faked, they were done on equipment beyond state-of-the-art. And look at Jack's holster." Jack had obviously planned to mention the holster as well, because he disappeared into the hallway for a moment and returned with the black Hollywood rig, his pet Colt Single Action Army in the holster. "It's empty, right?" Ellen asked perfunctorily. Jack carried a gun almost every day of his life and he never passed around a gun that was loaded.

"Yeah, but show everybody."

Humoring her husband, Ellen removed the gun from the holster and opened the loading gate "C-o-l-t, right?" Ellen asked.

"Stop after you hear the O," Jack said.

Ellen drew the hammer back to the second click, spun the cylinder—empty as promised—drew the hammer back the rest of the way and lowered it, closed the loading gate and returned the gun to the holster, placing the loop over the hammer. "Look at the holster in the Xerox, Clarence, and look at the holster on the table."

"Want me to get my hat?" Jack asked.

"We get the idea, Daddy." Elizabeth was taking the photos from the second envelope as quickly as David passed them to her.

Ellen studied her son's face for a moment, not liking

the expression that she saw. David had inherited bull-headedness from her side of the family, and David was not going to choose to believe this, no matter what he saw.

"This is a load of crap," David announced as if on cue. "You've had that holster in a bunch of your gun articles, the single action, too. Somebody could have lifted the image, maybe."

"I don't think so, Davey," Ellen announced.

"You didn't really make a dessert," David said, getting up so suddenly that his chair almost fell over. "This is just to keep us from wanting one." He stormed out of the room. If she hadn't known better—and maybe she didn't know better at all—she might have thought that David was fighting to hold back tears.

"I'll go after him," Jack said, starting for the hallway.

"No! I'll go after him, because maybe all David wants right now is to be left alone, not reasoned with." Ellen pushed past her husband and ran down the hallway toward the front door. She half expected to hear the Saab starting up, or screeching out of the driveway, but as she reached the front porch, she saw the glow of a cigarette from the darkness.

Always more than a little night-blind, with great care she ventured out onto the darkened front porch. There were flashes of lightning in the clouds off to her left, and from behind the house. The storms were supposed to come in from the west and start to swing north. As yet, there was no thunder.

"It's still far away," David said, his voice sounding a little strained.

"You got another one of those cigarettes?"

"You quit years ago, remember?"

"Every once in a while, I take a drag on one of your father's cigarettes."

"It's a Marlboro, not a Camel."

Ellen Naile heard the first distant rumble of thunder. "Give it to me, and I'll break the filter off."

David shook loose a cigarette and Ellen took it, broke off the filter and asked, "Light?"

David lit her cigarette with a Bic, and then lit another one for himself. "You're not in one of the photos."

Ellen felt herself wanting to cry, wanted to say "Give me a hug," but instead told him, "Probably because I was taking it, if this whole thing is real."

"It can't be real, Mom."

Ellen exhaled through her nostrils. The nice thing about having given up smoking was that when she occasionally did take a puff—maybe six times a year or so—she could really enjoy it. "You ready to go back inside, Davey?"

"In a couple of minutes."

"Smoking's bad for you, you with your bodybuilding and everything. Don't want to cut down on your lung capacity. You'll be one of the top players on the tennis team next year."

"If there is a next year. Why don't you say that?"

"Because I don't know what's going on any more than you do. You know your father likes Sherlock Holmes, and there's something Holmes says about when you've eliminated everything that's probable, no matter how improbable what's left might seem, it's the answer. We haven't eliminated everything yet. So who knows?" Ellen took one more drag on the cigarette and tossed it off the porch, onto the sidewalk.

The promised storm hadn't come just yet, either literally or figuratively.

Clarence was saying, "In that one picture of the three of you guys, where's Ellen?"

As Jack started to answer, he saw his wife in the doorway. "David'll be in here in a couple of minutes."

"Did you hear what I was saying?" Clarence asked her.

"Momma was probably taking the photo, like she usually does," Elizabeth volunteered.

"Either that or I'm dead by then," Ellen said cheerlessly.

"Oh, gee, thanks!" Jack snapped. "Don't you ever, ever say anything like that again, Ellen!" His wife's eyes hardened, and she'd be angry with him, but Jack Naile didn't care. "There's a logical explanation. Elizabeth is probably right."

Clarence—who looked more agitated than Jack had ever seen him—said, "Logical my ass! None of this is logical at all! This is a load of bullshit! Maybe it's that guy from Arizona who was sending you all the hate mail."

"Nope," Jack said. "Not him."

Ellen added, "The typewriter used to write the note that came with the page from the magazine was a different machine. Every time I open something strange that comes in the mail, I always check. Not him, Clarence."

"Well, all I know is that some son of a bitch is messin' with your minds! That's what it is! If I find out who it is, David and I'll go beat the living shit out of him! We'll make that bastard wish he'd never been born."

"What are you volunteering me for?"

Jack looked toward the kitchen doorway. David stood there beside his mother. Jack's and Ellen's eyes met for an instant, and she didn't smile at him.

Jack's attention was drawn back to Clarence, who was starting another wave of vituperations. "Nobody messes with my family! No damn way! Whatever the hell nutball is doing this is—"

"What if nobody's doing anything, Clarence?" Elizabeth began. "Y'all. Listen. I mean, this is impossible, right? But the pictures look real. The photo from the magazine looked real. Dad's talking to the guy at their historical society—chamber of commerce, whatever—and he's real. All I know about time travel is when we used to watch *Dr. Who* on Channel Eight on Saturday nights, but it looks like us in those pictures. So these are either terrific fake pictures or, or—"

Elizabeth didn't say anything else, but started to cry.

Jack came over and dropped to one knee beside her chair. Ellen was beside them in the next instant, stroking Liz's head and whispering, "It'll be okay. Just calm down. Take a deep breath."

"It's not going to happen. Time travel isn't real. Period," David said, his voice emotionless, flat, almost leaden.

Clarence walked out of the room, sounding like he was starting to cry as well.

"Well, it looks like dinner has been a really big hit, Jack. Shit," Ellen said, going over to the wall and slowly, rhythmically hitting it with her fists.

Jack Naile's hands shook with rage or fear or exhaustion—maybe all three. He shook his head, lit a cigarette.

"That's your answer to everything? I don't think so,

Jack! You're just giving yourself lung cancer or something. Fine, we all go get time-transferred or zapped or whatever, and you die! What happens to the rest of us?!"

Ellen stormed out of the room, sounding as if she was starting to cry; and, after a second, Jack heard her running up the stairs, heading for the bedroom to cry or the bathroom to throw up.

Elizabeth cried even harder.

David just stared.

"Fucking wonderful," Jack said under his breath. He turned on the kitchen faucet and put his cigarette under the spigot.

The thunderstorms were upon them. Ellen holding his hand, Jack Naile stared at the lightning. "I'll try and cut down."

"That's the only good thing if this time-travel thing really happens. You would have had to roll your own in those days, right?"

"I guess."

"And you're too clumsy."

"Right."

"You going to fly out to Nevada?"

"Before Clarence went to bed, he told me he'd fly out there with me, at his own expense even. This is really shaking him up."

"I think David's going to start to plan for this, as a defense mechanism so he can keep himself from thinking about what happens if it really happens," Ellen almost whispered.

It was nearly midnight, the rain lashing at the front porch

from the northwest. Jack started walking toward the part of the porch that was getting soaked, Ellen beside him.

"You didn't help things with that bit about maybe you were dead and that's why you weren't—"

"David had been thinking that, and I figured that everybody else was. Sometimes the best way to deal with something is to get it said, get it out in the open." Ellen took her hand from his and wrapped both her arms around his left arm instead. "I bet I know what's at the back of your mind, aside from being able to play cowboy."

They could read each other, sometimes, it seemed. Jack Naile laughed a little. "My Dad?"

"Um-hmm. If that one photo was taken in 1903 and we didn't look too much older than we do now—you looked like you had a little more gray—but, you could go back to Manchester, New Hampshire, in 1908 and somehow see your father."

Jack Naile's father had died at age sixty-three, before either of his grandchildren had been born. "Yeah. I'd like to do that, but it'd be neat to meet him when he was old enough to talk to and talk back. Maybe that time when he flipped the fence and broke his elbow when he was maybe twelve or whatever."

"If we went back tomorrow to 1903, and—help me with the math here," Ellen said. "How old are you? I can never remember how old I am."

"This month you'll be forty-four, and five days later I'll be forty-six."

"So, if you were forty-six in 1903, you'd be fifty-one when your Dad was born. When he was twelve, you'd only be—" And Ellen stopped talking.

"The same age he was when he died from his first and last heart attack." Jack Naile's initial impulse was to light a cigarette, but he decided against it.

Jack had refigured the dates as they related to his father, remembering that Arthur Beach had found out the Naile family had first arrived in Nevada in 1896. If Jack Naile waited for his father to reach age twelve, he'd be seventy years old when he met his dad. If Jack Naile died at sixty-three, as his father had, he would be dead when his father was only five years old.

As Ellen Naile had predicted, FedEx shipments to their part of Northeast Georgia were running late because of the particularly violent thunderstorms the previous evening. Arrivals at Hartsfield were delayed.

Their check—a very nice big one with lots of lovely zeros on the left side of the decimal point—arrived at precisely five minutes after two, meaning that to deposit it before Monday morning would be an exercise in futility.

Ellen sat at the kitchen table with a cup of tea, the supermarket kind; she rarely bought any of the fancier variations because sometimes, when checks were late, the saving of a few pennies here and there made a difference.

The photo taken in 1903 was still on the kitchen table. She looked at it, realizing the irony represented by the photo and the house in which she sat while viewing it. Their house was built in 1903, perhaps under construction at the very time the photo—which hadn't yet been taken, but had been taken—was being taken.

Jack was right (something which Ellen certainly would

not admit to him); just thinking about the anomalies of time travel was enough to give anyone a headache.

"Headache," Ellen murmured aloud, just as Jack entered the kitchen.

"You have a headache, kid?"

"No, but I was just thinking. Let's say we do wind up moving to Nevada, but almost a hundred years ago. We'd be reduced to boiling down bark from a willow tree in order to get aspirin to knock out a headache."

"On the plus side, think of all the money we'd make if we preinvented liquid Tylenol!"

"I'm serious, Jack."

Jack sat down, lit a cigarette; he had cut down quite a bit from his usual daily consumption. "We really do have to start to plan," Jack said.

"So, we're going to figure out some way to get a washer and dryer back to the past with us?"

"I don't think we can manage that," Jack told her, smiling, running a hand back through his hair. It was mostly still brown, and no less full than when they'd been in high school. "But it appears as though we arrived in Nevada with some items we had today. Even with knowledge of the future, we would have needed money."

"That would go along with the gun-on-the-hip thing?" Ellen suggested.

"No, silly. It meant that they brought it with them—the money. And the wagon story could have been a ruse."

"A ruse?"

"A ruse," Jack repeated, so that the word sounded as if it had been said by Peter Sellers in the persona of his dim bulb French police inspector. Jack persisted with the accent—not doing such a bad job, really—as he continued. "It would be, I think, trés easy to 'ave the—'ow you say thees word?—wag-on?, thees wag-on 'idden away, no?"

"Shut up and be serious, Jack."

"*Je suis 'Jaques,' mon cher*—" Ellen hit Jack on the top of the head with her open palm—not hard—and he shook his head and wiggled his lips like some sort of cartoon character struck by a falling anvil. "Thanks. I'm better now."

"You're not thinking that somehow we'd be able to take the Suburban back in time with us?"

"I can't say for sure, but if we all get sucked back in time together and we all stay with the Suburban, there's a chance, right? We take out the rear seat and leave it. I take the Suburban over to the Chevy dealer and get them to put a roof rack on it and add an auxiliary gas tank. We get four additional tires—"

"Those ones from Sam's Club have held up real well."

"Right. Get four new wheels—we wouldn't be able to remount tires. If you did the research and got Lizzie to help you, we could get everything we needed to know on microfiche. Hell, we could probably get *Encyclopedia Britannica* that way. Medical and dental info, and the stuff we'd need for basic field surgery, dental care, like that. Learn how to fabricate nutritional supplements. You've always had a green thumb."

"There are lots of books we could get, and probably on microfiche—"

"Or get them put on microfiche, which could be kind of expensive, but worth it."

"And what are *you* going to be doing?" Ellen asked her husband. "Learning how to brand steers and—"

"No, I'm serious. I'll find out what we'd need so that we could keep some semblance of twentieth-century civilization going, even though we were a century in the past. Evidently, the Naile family lived there for quite some time, which means they built or bought a house, probably had one built. We could have one room that we could electrify if we brought the wire and the switches and the circuit-breaker box."

"How will we get electricity?" Ellen said.

"We build near a stream or river, set up a sophisticated waterwheel, or windmills—solar would be too cumbersome. We couldn't pack enough stuff to make it work. So, Lizzie could still listen to CDs, we could still have an electric clock—"

"A microwave—no, we wouldn't need it. But a hair dryer."

"A toaster!" Jack supplied.

"When was the last time we used a toaster? And electric can openers never work. But a small, conventional electric oven and a flat four-burner electric stove."

"There you go!" Jack enthused. "Stuff that would make life more livable. We could have electric lights. If we did the research, we could figure out a way to step down the voltage so that we could use the bulbs that Edison had already invented by then, and we could have a couple of fluorescent fixtures and replacement tubes and starters and everything so that we could have really serious light occasionally. Hell, with the right research and the money to get the work done, we could have somebody build us new fluorescent tubes in a couple of years. We could build another house and have the whole interior just like a modern place and nobody'd be the wiser. And running water? Hey, the Romans had running water. All we need is some PVC and gravity and—"

"I get the idea, Jack. That's all going to fit into the Suburban?"

"Yeah. I don't see why not. If we pack carefully. It's not like we're going to need a lot of clothes, because modern clothes would be a dead giveaway."

Ellen leaned back in her chair. "Nothing I'm going to like better than wearing twenty pounds of ankle length clothing everyday. Want a cup of coffee?"

"Sure."

Ellen stood up and went to the stove, pausing as she turned on one of the electric range's burners. "You really think we could do that? Keep a modern life, kind of?"

"What? The electricity and plumbing and stuff? Yeah, if the Suburban comes back with us. And the microfiche— we'd need two readers and a really ample supply of batteries, and we never let the case with that stuff out of our sight. We sleep with it, so even if we didn't get the Suburban back, we'd be able to reconstruct most of the stuff we'd need from things available a hundred years ago. It's just all in knowing how."

"What about your gun collection? The guns and the ammo will take up a lot of room."

"I've already been thinking about that," he told her.

Ellen had assumed as much. "I bring everything I've got in .45 Colt. There's going to be plenty of .45 Long Colt ammo available a century ago. I'd need a serious rifle. Maybe an 1895 Marlin in .45-70 and get a Vernier tang sight installed. A couple of knives made with modern steel. Everything else we can get when we get there. We sell the rest as quickly as we can and the money from the guns and stuff goes toward the electrical and plumbing stuff and the microfiche and shit like that. What do you think?" Jack picked up a cigarette, but set it down, unlit . . .

The cheapest way to get to the small town in Nevada devolved to flying via Las Vegas and over to Reno. Clarence, despite more than six years in the Air Force, hated flying and made no secret of it. Jack rented a car in Reno; Clarence talked all the way as they drove. "Ellen was really worried."

"Not after I reminded her that all four of us were in that one photograph and the Nailes arrived as a family of four. So, some of us aren't going to get time-zapped and the others left behind. We'll be fine. Relax, Clarence." Jack Naile's main problem was that he was too relaxed, about to fall asleep, the terrain different from Georgia's insistent greenery, but just as repetitive. He'd had the window open earlier, but Clarence didn't like open windows in cars, so Jack had closed it. But Jack started cranking the window down again. "I've gotta open a window, Clarence, or I'm gonna fall asleep."

"Why don't you turn on the air-conditioning? Or let me drive."

"It's cold with the air-conditioning. Fresh air is good for you, Clarence, keeps the lungs in shape. We've been breathing canned air on two airplanes. Time for some fresh." Clarence might bitch about it some more, but Jack Naile really didn't care and kept the window down about two inches.

"That photo with only you and the kids scares the crap out of me, Jack."

Jack Naile lit a cigarette. "I go with the theory that Ellen took the photograph. The composition is good. It looks like her work, with a modern camera. So that's why Ellen wasn't in the photograph."

"This is a pile of bullshit, right, Jack? I mean, there's gotta be some damned logical explanation for it."

"You think of one, let me know, Clarence." The two lane road was well maintained, but seemed to go on forever, the terrain surrounding them a cross between high desert and low rolling hills, as inviting as lunar landscape.

"You really see yourself and Ellen and the kids living here? David would never make it!" Clarence declared.

"Why would David never make it? He's ridiculously physically fit, smart—"

"Think about it, Jack! For God's sake, David has to have the newest and the best of everything," Clarence continued, chuckling. "And he doesn't even like going to a rodeo! You really think he's going to ride a horse? No way."

"Well, I tell you, Clarence. He'll either ride a horse, drive a wagon or walk until automobiles get out this way. You remind me of Cleopatra."

"What? Are you nuts?"

"That's beside the point, son. You remind me of Cleopatra after her barge sunk in the river—you're in de Nile."

"Yeah, you just go ahead and laugh! But you're buying into a load of shit," Clarence growled. Jack had long ago decided he'd fight the man who criticized Clarence for having a short temper, but that wouldn't mean that Jack wouldn't agree with the guy. "This is just fuckin' trick photography and some elaborate scheme of some fuckin' nutball, and you're buying into it. Time travel doesn't happen, Jack. We both know that."

"Looks like it's about to," Jack informed his nephew. "See, I don't particularly care to wind up in the Old West of a hundred years ago, either. Think about it, Clarence. If this movie actually gets made, it'll open the door for a lot of our other stuff to get made into movies, maybe. And just maybe we'll make enough money we can relax a little, do some good things for the kids, for you. Remember how Ellen and I've always said that the day we got a really big check in would be the day we had a nuclear war or a meteor struck the planet or something? Much as I wish it weren't, this time-travel thing looks like it's not only a meteor, but a fucking nuclear meteor, and aimed right at us. And there's not a damned thing I can do about it except try to make the best of it. We're going to miss you, Clarence, and you're going to miss us, but I can't change it," Jack concluded.

"Bullshit, Jack! Fuckin' bullshit!"

"You want me to turn around, and you can fly back to Atlanta?"

"Fuck you—no, dammit!"

"Then relax, okay? You'll live longer. We don't want to leave you in the present while we go into the past, but, if this happens, it doesn't look like there's a whole lot of choice." There was a green-and-white information sign coming up on the right. "See what that sign says, Clarence."

Jack already knew what it said—"Moment of truth upon

you in four miles." His hands sweated on the steering wheel, and the pit of his stomach felt like somebody had just turned on a blender.

Practically the first words out of Arthur Beach's mouth had been, "My God, you look just like the Jack Naile in those old photographs!" Because of this, Jack realized, Clarence had taken an instant dislike to Arthur Beach.

Atlas, Nevada, looked nothing like it had in the photograph that started the whole thing, Jack Naile mused. It looked modern, normal. There was a strong breeze blowing in from the desert, gradually intensifying; the occasional dust devil was the only thing that made the blacktopped street look like something out of a Western town.

"That's where Jack Naile's store once stood, Mr. Naile," Arthur Beach announced, pointing a well-manicured finger across that street.

"Remember, Arthur? Call me Jack. Mr. Naile's what they call my son."

"Right."

"That law office?" Clarence asked.

"Only the foundation is original, Mr. Jones. The building-commission people and the historical-society people were almost one and the same, husbands on the building commission and wives on the historical society. So when downtown was redeveloped, the wives got the husbands to save as much as they could, which is why this street looks like it's part of another town or something by comparison to the rest of downtown."

The "rest of downtown" wasn't all that much, really.

The old main street, where they stood, ran a distance of a long city block. The old foundations and some old facades, many of the buildings vacant, lined both sides of the street. At three of the four corners were short blocks which, Arthur Beach had told them, were part of the downtown-development project. The fourth corner was nothing more than where the highway did a right angle and went on past Atlas, across higher desert and toward the nearby mountains. A convenience store, an ordinary gas station that offered mechanical work and a diner that advertised it had slot machines and also sold ammunition were the only businesses there.

The old main street—which was called Old Main Street—was admirably wide. At eleven in the morning on Sunday, there was no traffic at all. Jack Naile stepped off the curb and started across the street.

The sun wasn't quite overhead yet and its angle allowed Jack to see his own reflection in the plate glass window of the law office. The wind coming in off the desert blew his longish, still mostly brown hair across his forehead. He noted that the corners of his mouth were downturned under his salt-and-pepper mustache. Was he as wary as he looked, he wondered absently, or was this just a face he turned toward Clarence—who had been pissing him off—and Arthur Beach, who was so cooperative that it made him wonder if Beach had some ulterior motive?

Jack stepped up onto the far side curb and stood in front of the window. He stood just a little less than six feet, and his shoulders looked broad within the A-2 bomber jacket. Since he'd stopped drinking beer and started drinking white wine, his waist was back down to a thirty-four, with not too much of a droop at the belly. Not bad for mid-forties, he reassured himself.

Jack thrust his hands into his pockets, his eyes glancing at the foundation below the plate-glass window. What did he feel? Did he know those bricks? Or would he? What he felt, really, was that he wished Ellen were with him, standing beside him. And he felt naked—because he'd flown, he'd left the Seecamp .32 in the gradually self-destructing glove compartment of Clarence's Honda. Jack Naile was so used to the feel of the little gun in his right pants pocket that its absence was something of which he was keenly, continually aware.

He looked back into the plate-glass window. Clarence, a big guy but looking that much bigger beside the slightly built Arthur Beach, was crossing the street. Jack lit a cigarette.

"Do you want to see the ranch? I mean, what's left of it, Jack?" Arthur Beach called out.

"Yeah, let's see the ranch."

As he'd lit the cigarette, Jack Naile had noticed the bronze plaque set into the foundation, assumedly by the local historical society. It read Jack Naile—General Merchandise. He noticed that his hands were trembling and thrust them into his pockets.

Clarence refused to enter the ruin of the house and stayed by the car. Jack stood within what had obviously once been a quite large home. Whether the structure had been claimed by fire—his own faulty electrical work?—or wind, there was no way to tell upon casual inspection. All that remained was a meticulously fitted stone-and-mortar chimney, most of the mortar gone, the chimney jutting defiantly upward from an extraordinarily large hearth of the same construction.

The land on which the house was built was almost a terrace, as level as if graded by modern equipment. The lot was separated from a stream by the distance of what would have been the width of an ordinary backyard, its far edge abutting the sloping bank. Fast moving, ideal for hydro-electric power, the stream's waters emerged from deep within a forest of pines, its boundary perhaps a hundred yards distant. A double rank of the trees broke away from the woods, arced downward and across the opposite boundary of the level terrace and onward, nearly intersecting the single-lane wide dirt track that had led them up toward the house from the highway. The highway was eight or ten miles back, perhaps two hundred feet lower in elevation.

The drive from the highway had been less boring than the last leg of the drive from Reno to Atlas, the terrain rolling up through foothills and into the mountains, mountains that would have been visible from a porch here, had one still stood.

"Who owns this property now?" Jack heard Clarence asking Arthur Beach.

Beach answered, "I don't know. I'm still trying to find out. Some corporation, it looks like."

"Find out, Arthur," Jack Naile called back over his shoulder without turning around. "I'd really appreciate it."

On the drive from Atlas to what had been the Naile ranch, Arthur Beach had asked about the book that Jack had told Beach was being written. Jack had given truthful answers about the progress of their research and the general plotline, never mentioning that with each detail that was uncovered, it seemed more and more frighteningly obvious that at issue was not a book, but an inescapable trip through time.

"You know, if you and your nephew would like, I can arrange for you to get some help if you want to go to Carson City, to the State Historical Society. It's not too far below Reno. Do you have the time?"

Jack Naile looked at Arthur Beach, then at Clarence. "What do you think, Clarence?"

"You let me drive, we'll get there with time to spare."

Clarence was an excellent driver, but Jack Naile didn't like being driven by someone who seemed frequently inclined to exceed speed limits, as Clarence had exhorted him to do while they'd crossed the desolate expanse that was the final leg of their trip to Atlas. When necessary, Jack could speed with the best of them, but never otherwise. He'd developed that habit—trying to attract as little attention as possible to his driving—when he and Ellen had lived in the metropolitan Chicago area and carrying a gun was seriously illegal.

Jack started walking toward Arthur Beach's white Jeep Cherokee, resigned to the fact that Clarence, who wore a thirty-six leg length, would get the front passenger seat again. "Let's see what time it is when we get back to town. And then I might get you to make that call, Arthur. I can't thank you enough already." Getting into the Jeep's back-seat was bad enough, but getting out of it made him feel like a cork getting tugged out of a wine bottle.

✳ ✳ ✳

"The reason we learned nothing new in Atlas was because there was nothing new to learn—it's a pile of crap." Variations on that theme had liberally laced Clarence's end of the conversation for the entire length of the trip back to and past Reno, toward Carson City. There had also been several remarks about Arthur Beach being "in" on whatever "it" was. Their overnight motel reservations—they would be flying back to Atlanta the following morning—were in Reno, and, after the visit to the State Historical Society, they would be retracing part of their route.

Finding the State Historical Society using Arthur Beach's directions was effortless in the light Sunday traffic, though finding a space in which to park the rented Ford proved somewhat challenging. Once inside, however, the first person they approached turned out to be the woman Arthur Beach had phoned and asked to assist them. Mrs. Hattie Lincoln, mid-sixties and a little plump, with a pinkish face and cheeks that indicated high blood pressure, heavy alcohol intake or too much blush, had already assembled mounds of materials for their review.

Jack told Clarence what to look for, and they split the work, Mrs. Lincoln popping in on them several times in the office she'd let them use. If Ellen had been with them, the research would have been smoother and more productive, Ellen being the best and most meticulous researcher Jack Naile had ever encountered. Yet even without her, with time running out before the facility closed for the day, Jack unearthed several documents, which Mrs. Lincoln cheerfully copied for them.

Atlas' single newspaper from shortly after the town's

birth as a mining camp in 1861 until the last issue came off the presses in 1933 was the *Atlas View*, and copies of the weekly's every issue from 1877 until 1933 were on file. Jack had majored in English in college—which, in part, accounted for his phenomenal (lack of) economic success—but had been a course or so short of a major in History. And, it took little historical insight to discern that the *Atlas View* was staunchly Republican, as Nevada had always been in those days, some even suggesting that Nevada's comparatively quick and easy shot at statehood had been because of that.

With more and more sucking up in the general media about the Democrats and the wonders of their presidential candidate, Jack Naile found the old newspaper's politics remarkably refreshing.

After thanking Mrs. Lincoln—no relation to *the* Lincoln, she told them when Clarence asked—Jack Naile climbed behind the wheel of the rental car. Clarence settled into the passenger seat beside him, and remained stonily silent for the duration of the drive back to Reno.

The aircraft an hour outside of Atlanta, Clarence started talking. "It pisses me off that you guys are going to disappear on me. You're about ninety percent of the only family I've got." Jack didn't bother to correct the math, just let Clarence talk. "I don't know if I can hack it, Jack."

Jack Naile took Clarence's hand for a moment; if the other passengers thought they were gay or something, he didn't care. "Look, Ellen and the kids and I love you, too, Clarence. You've always been like another son to us. You know that. But, if this crazy thing happens, I can't change

it, alter it so that you can come along. Anyway, I understand they cooked with peanut oil a whole lot in—"

"Knock it off about my allergy."

"Look," Jack continued. "From everything that's
stacking up, I don't think Ellen and I can stop this from
happening." Sometimes, however awkward, there was no
time like the present. Jack cleared his throat and told
Clarence, "When we first made out wills—"

"For God's sake—"

"Let me finish, son. When Ellen and I first made out
wills, when the kids were little, we named you as our
contingent beneficiary."

"I get all the bills, huh?"

Jack forced himself to laugh, and so did Clarence. "No.
No bills, but the house is worth a good chunk of dough.
We have other assets, like royalties off books, and there
might be more money off this movie deal."

"I don't wanna talk about that now."

"Fine. Later." If there would be enough later left.

Jack had barely walked into the house when the phone
rang. "Take it, Jack; whoever it is will want to talk to you
anyway," Ellen told him as she kissed him on the cheek.

"Right," and Jack took the receiver from Elizabeth's
hand. It was their "agent." "Yeah, Lars. What's up?"

Lars' voice betrayed his excitement. "They're starting
principal photography on *Angel Street* in six weeks, Jack!
Six weeks and they write a check for pickin' up the option!
Hey! And, they want you guys out there—all expenses
paid—the day they start shooting! Some publicity thing or
something. Wonderful, huh!?"

Jack shook his head, incredulous at the news. "Hold on a second, Lars." He pushed the hold button and told Ellen, the kids and Clarence, "Nothing wrong or anything; just the opposite. They're starting principal photography in six weeks, we get the money in two weeks and they want us out wherever the hell they're shooting it. All expenses paid."

"I can't leave my job," David said flatly.

"Summer-school session one will be over the end of next week, David," Elizabeth interjected. "You can work your days off to give you a four day weekend."

"David'll need more time than four days. We're going to have to drive out there with our stuff. Can't risk being separated from each other or what we hope to bring." Jack punched back on with Lars, Ellen automatically handing Jack his cigarettes and lighter and pushing the ashtray nearer to the phone.

"Lars, how can they have a script? It hasn't been more than a couple of weeks."

"This is the sweet part, Jack. This screenwriter I never heard of liked your book, wrote the script and then took the script to his agent and the script was the reason they optioned your book. The only reason it's taken this long— imagine!—is because they had to nail down the male lead. Some guy I never heard of, but he's big with kids. Got some TV show that's really up there."

"You remember his name?"

"Naw. I'll get it. Hey! Did Lars deliver or what, man! I'm gonna get you guys more deals like this! Wait! Just wait! Look, Jack, I'll get back to you with more details. Gotta fly!"

"Yeah, Lars. Have a nice flight. Thanks." Jack Naile hung up the telephone, wondering why—knowing why—he was depressed even though he was about to see more money in one chunk than he'd ever seen in his life.

"He's flying somewhere?" David asked.

"No, just trying to sound cool," that's all," Ellen said as if reading Jack's mind. "At least there's the money you were anticipating we'd have, Jack."

Jack nodded to his wife as he said to David, "You're the best businessman in the family. Do it tomorrow. Get on the horn and find out about diamond prices."

"Diamonds?" Lizzie asked.

"Why diamonds, Dad?"

"I know you don't want to accept the fact that this is going to happen, and no one wants it to. But if we're going to have money when we get there, we can't use folding money that was printed in the twentieth century. Gold—we'll have to have some—would be too heavy. Diamonds are portable. Can you use the Internet at the library to research diamond prices, find a source for buying in quantity at the best prices, and determine what type of stone would have had the greatest value a century ago? Stuff like that, David?"

"I suppose, but it's a waste of time."

"Humor your father," Ellen advised.

David nodded his assent.

They had never gotten a computer that was capable of going online, merely older machines from mixed parts that were used for nothing more than typing. Jack Naile supposed that now they never would.

❈ ❈ ❈

Jack's mother had always made lists, and Jack made lists. For that reason, aside from shopping lists for the grocery store, which Ellen grudgingly composed for Thanksgiving and Christmas, she never did lists at all.

But there was an exception to every rule. While Jack typed furiously—she reflected that *wrote* was a kinder word—on their latest novel, Ellen sat at the other computer and worked up a list in outline form.

Everything from electrical and plumbing skills to animal husbandry to pattern making for clothes to passive solar hot water heating to composting toilets had to be considered. Although microfiche would comprise the bulk of their traveling library, there were certain books they would try their best not to be forced to leave behind.

Jack believed very strongly in God. Ellen, whom Jack insisted was an agnostic and not the other *a* word, was the only one of the two of them who had read the Bible. Neither of them went to church, but a Bible should be brought. And, for philosophical comfort, they would want to bring Ayn Rand's *Atlas Shrugged*. Scrap books with family photos were a must for sanity's sake, lest they forget who they really were and where they had come from.

Ellen returned to the portion of the list dealing with household-related problems. Before the children were born, when she'd worked outside the home, she'd made quite a bit of her own clothes. She had always intended to show Elizabeth how, but never had the time. Soon, despite the fact that any sewing machine they would eventually acquire would be hopelessly primitive by comparison to its modern counterparts, she would have the time.

Ellen liked to garden, rarely for flowers, mostly for

vegetables. In recent years, there had been little time for that. A century away in the past, raising vegetables might not be a necessity, but would be quite practical.

There was a second list Ellen was making, one playing off the other. It was a listing of books she must read, despite the fact that they would be archived on microfiche. If circumstances forbade the use of the microfiche as reference material, she would still have her mind.

Certain entries on this second list were for Jack to read, books on reloading cartridges—he seemed to be the only firearms writer there was who didn't reload—books about caring for livestock (which she would read as well), works on electrical wiring and plumbing skills, woodworking without power tools (he'd always said he wanted to build furniture, if he ever retired), books on horsemanship—the list seemed unending for both of them. Yet it was imperative that Jack's list be appreciably shorter for two reasons. Most of this end of their current novel was in his hands at the present, so he would have less time. Secondly, she was the speed reader of the family.

In her high school days, Ellen had been clocked at twenty-eight hundred and fifty words per minute, with excellent retention. Nowhere near that fast anymore, she could read five books or more in the time it took Jack—whose IQ had measured one hundred fifty six at age twelve but who was a painfully slow, maddeningly thorough reader—to get through just one.

As David Naile had begun using the Internet to research the quality, characteristics and values of diamonds at the turn of the century, a thought occurred to him. On the off chance that this time-travel thing actually did take place—which was thoroughly stupid even to consider—there might be other data from the past that could prove useful as well.

Despite his youth, he had been working for several years, with his parents' help, passing himself off at times as older than he was. Although he'd worked in plumbing and landscaping, and had learned to drive a tractor before driving a car, sales had always been it for him. At seventeen he was the youngest assistant manager in his current company's history, while still a full-time student.

If this time transfer thing really should take place, then there was ample reason to assume that, however unlikely it seemed, they were to have a retail store, as indicated in the original photograph. According to the data his father had gleaned from this Arthur Beach jerk, the store proved quite successful and innovative in its marketing approach.

Clearly, his father would have had little to do with that sort of achievement. His father would be packing his six-gun, wearing his cowboy hat and living some sort of Western gunslinger/gentleman rancher fantasy. His mother would groove on vegetable gardening, cooking, raising cuddly farm animals, all the things she would have normally done in the present if she hadn't had to help his father make a living. And his sister—she was a very nice girl, but she'd probably just meet some cowboy with no interest in economics and start having babies in a few years.

If financial success was to be theirs, it would be his responsibility. And if he could research gemstone values from the previous century via the Internet, what was to prevent him from discovering who the movers and shakers were in this hick town in Nevada? What bank would be strongest? What locals would make good credit risks? Whose financial dealings would prove disastrous?

What products—goods and services—would become popular, with high consumer demand in the years following the supposed transition into the past? How would the overall national economy be doing? What companies, in which stock shares or ownership interests could be obtained, were destined to grow and prosper? Which would fail?

If he could enter the past armed with information from the objective future and a thorough knowledge of financial trends in the past—granted, he was only using a computer at a high school library, and there was, perhaps, little time remaining—he could position his family to accumulate true wealth and the capability with which to manipulate businesses in such a fashion as to increase this wealth almost exponentially.

If this time-travel thing actually did take place, he would be prepared with forward credit checks, market trends and everything else he could find.

Elizabeth slid open the mirrored doors of her closet. If the time-transfer really happened, everything in her closet would be useless to her.

In the summertime, instead of shorts and a T-shirt, she would be in long dresses. In the fall, as opposed to pants and nice tops, she would be in long dresses. In the wintertime, long dresses again. In the spring, long dresses. There would be no need for softball uniforms, tennis skirts, bathing suits—just long dresses and, perhaps for variety, scratchy, high-necked blouses and long skirts. Not to mention the world's supply of useless underwear and tightly laced corsets, which helped to induce fainting.

She was to enter her sophomore year, would be old enough to drive in just a little over six months—drive a wagon. "Shit," Elizabeth said under her breath.

A final adjustment to the strain insulator for the primary cable, and Jane Rogers was ready to tweak the anode plate's alignment with the control grid.

At seventy-three years old, prudence had cautioned her to be slightly more cautious in movement and diet, but these were her only concessions to age. Her mind, as she herself was able to judge, and—unless they were incredibly polite—everyone with whom she interacted seemed to concur, was as sharp as when she'd been the first woman in her alma mater's history to take a PhD in physics. Her judgment, Jane Rogers flattered herself, was appreciably better.

And her eyes—despite a lifelong and insatiable appetite for the written word—were just as keen, if a little less brighter blue. Ever so slightly, Jane Rogers re-aligned the anode plate once again.

The hardware was ready.

She had been born in the wrong era, that conviction and the death of her husband twenty years, two months and twenty-seven days before the only things which marred her contentment—if one discounted the tantalizing yet incomplete degree of success of her experiments in plasma electricity.

As a graduate student, and later as a degreed physicist, because of her sex she had always been someone's assistant rather than a project leader in her own right. Some things, admittedly, were determined by sex. When she was introduced to Albert Einstein, Jane Rogers found herself speechless and very nearly collapsed into a faint—and she was not a fainter, never had been. When she met and married the man of her dreams, she had aided him in his work in particle physics, abandoning her passion for electricity, no matter how much the work and its potential intrigued her and her own calculations confounded her.

Dr. Einstein had almost certainly thought her to be a ninny with an empty head. But her Frank had never thought that, she knew. All of the time before meeting Frank, she had worked with men who didn't do science nearly as well as she; Frank did it better, and she found this as irresistible as the curly hair he tried to beat into straightness with his military brushes, as the shy gray eyes he shielded behind rimless glasses he didn't really need to wear for anything but the most exacting detail work.

To have remarried—she was only fifty-two when Frank, ten years her senior, died—would have been unthinkable, was something she never once considered. But with Frank's death, Jane Rogers' attitude toward herself changed quite radically.

She concluded the series of experiments at which Frank had been laboring for the past eighteen months, perhaps more rapidly than Frank himself could have achieved the same results. Then she donated his notes and equipment to the graduate school of the university with which Frank had been affiliated since his own grad school days.

When Jane Rogers returned to the study of plasma and how it could be used to achieve the dreamer's dream, the transmission of electricity through thin air, her decades of work with Frank in particle physics had proven to be of greater help to her than she had ever realized they would.

At the time of Frank's death, they were far from his beloved university, plying their background in particle physics for the United States government as part of what well over a decade later would become the Strategic Defense Initiative. Then, as in the present, her notion reinforced by the continuation of SDI after the dissolution of the Soviet Union, she had believed that there was more to particle physics weapons research than just the means by which to get a leg up on the Russians. But if so, she was out of that line of work and no one would have volunteered information to her in any event.

Jane Rogers had come to be known as "strange" because of the common wisdom that anyone who labored in her particular corner of physics research had to be a poor scientist or have her bubble more than a little bit off plumb. No one had ever accused Jane Rogers of being a poor scientist.

After Frank's death, Jane made the decision—one she had never regretted—to remain in Nevada, but quite a bit more to the north, in order to escape the heat. Remaining in Nevada enabled her to be within relatively easy driving distance of the smallish cemetery where she had placed her husband's physical remains.

Jane Rogers supposed that she did honestly have one more regret. Frank, like the main character in Hemingway's *The Sun Also Rises*, injured during the war—but a different war than the one whose horrors were supposed to end all war.

The experiments she had been conducting for the last eight years—begun at age sixty-five when anyone with sense might think of retiring—had the sole purpose of generating a stable electrical field that could be precisely aimed across great distances on a laser carrier beam. When it reached its target, the electrical field would be as strong as it had been at point of origin. She would be able to broadcast electrical power to anywhere in the world with an appropriate receiver, transmit the modern age to the most remote corners of the globe.

"Jane?"

Jane Rogers realized she had been standing still, just staring at her apparatus. Hearing Peggy Greer call her name brought her back from her thoughts. "Just thinking about Frank and everything else, and what we're doing here. Are we ready, darling?"

"I've run everything on the computer so often I've almost got it memorized, Jane. The video monitoring equipment has been checked and rechecked. If everything holds up, we're more ready than we've ever been."

"Good. Good, darling. Now, Peggy dear, we may as well get started."

Jane Rogers walked toward the open rear doors of the GMC Suburban, where Peggy Greer was inspecting the screens of various pieces of monitoring equipment. She seemed to be paying particularly intense attention to the oscilloscope which they had modified for their purposes.

Peggy announced, "Screen's smudged. Got a tissue, Jane?"

Jane knew that she did not and said so. "Sorry."

Peggy merely shrugged her little shoulders and whisked the green scarf from her head, attended to the smudge on the screen and began retying the bandanna over her hair. Her hair was just past shoulder length, so bright a strawberry blond that it was nearly red. Despite the almost constant sunshine and Peggy's thorough dislike for any sort of hat that might shield her face, Peggy's mid-twenties complexion was pale, very pretty, a perfect setting for her sparkling green eyes.

Jane had taken to wearing a flat-crowned cowboy hat, new when Frank had bought it for her but long since battered and faded. Sun brutalized her face, given half the chance, always had. Even when she was Peggy's age, sitting poolside or at the beach, she'd always worn a hat, admittedly something more feminine in design. More than once, someone had likened her weathered Stetson to those worn by John Wayne in his myriad westerns. She hoped any physical resemblance ended there.

The wind was picking up, whistling down from the mountains and toward the desert. Jane hoped that—this time—her carrier wave would reach back into the mountains, where she and Peggy had positioned the receiver.

If it did, the light array set there would, at least, flicker. That had already been established. The solitary flicker their experiments had produced lasted so briefly that, had she blinked, she would have missed it. Yet witnessing it—nine months and six trials ago—was the first sign of hope since her experiments had gone from strictly controlled laboratory conditions into the field: the solitary glimpse of practical success since her work had begun.

Jane would be pleased if she and Peggy could duplicate it, ecstatic if they could better it.

"Ready, Jane?"

"Fire her up, Peggy."

"Right!"

A casual glance over her shoulder at the equipment was all Jane allowed herself before stepping to the tripod-mounted refracting telescope. Peggy knew her stuff, didn't require supervision.

Jane looked into the eyepiece, focus already achieved, nothing to do but pray that the objective lens sheltered within its sunshade cap would catch a flicker of light, showing that the carrier beam had done its work.

The generators hummed from the bed of the pickup truck parked a few feet from the Suburban, one generator to produce the electricity which the laser beam, powered by the second generator, would hopefully carry to target.

"On my mark," Peggy called out. "Five . . . four . . . three . . . two . . . one . . . Mark!" The humming of the generators was, for a moment, like the sound of a hive of angry bees. A crackle, more crackles. A hum, louder than the others, at a different frequency. There was a popping sound, a microsecond later a sound like a clap of thunder. Would there be a second one?

Jane's hands shook, and she dared not touch them to the telescope through which she peered toward the mountains.

But there was no second noise like thunder, there was no illumination—however brief—from the lighting array that was wired to the intended receiver.

There was nothing.

Jane looked away from the telescope. The humming from the generators was already subsiding. Peggy's monitoring equipment had already announced their failure.

"It didn't work. Were we any closer this time, Peggy?"

"I can't tell, Jane, not until I run the program check. I can do it here. We don't have to wait until we've traveled all the way—"

Jane cut off her young friend in mid-sentence. "That's it!"

"What's it?"

Jane Rogers ran toward Peggy, grabbed the girl by the shoulders and turned her around. "You have given us the answer, girl! It's the traveling! That's what it is! It's the damned traveling, Peggy!" Peggy's usually intelligent eyes stared blankly back. Jane hugged the girl, kissed her cheek. "You don't see, do you?"

"I don't under—"

"When we had our glimmer of light nine months ago?" Jane Rogers took the package of cigarettes from the pocket of her smock as she spoke. "Remember what happened? The cable—"

"The cable we used to connect the receiver to the lighting array had been chewed on by something and we substituted a piece of cable that was a foot shorter."

"So?" Jane prodded.

"So if we shortened the cable still further, there'd be less distance—"

"Less distance for the electrical charge to travel. If we're right, Peggy," Jane said, hands trembling as she lit a cigarette with her husband's old lighter, "when we had that flicker of light nine months ago and actually broadcast electrical energy, we had it right. If we go back to our figures from nine months ago and duplicate the experiment to the nth degree and use as short a cable as possible—"

"And better insulated than what we've been using," Peggy interrupted.

"Exactly! And better insulated. Shorter and better insulated. Yes! If we do that and we duplicate all the settings—"

"And atmospheric conditions, too. Wait for a day with the right humidity—"

"Yes, weather conditions. If we duplicate that day as closely as humanly possible, with the shorter—"

"And better insulated!"

"And better insulated," Jane agreed. "Shorter and better insulated cable and close to identical atmospherics, we should be able to get more than a damned flicker! We'll light up the array!"

"Yes!" Peggy threw her arms around Jane and hugged her so hard that Jane thought one of them would surely break a bone.

It was at once frightening yet miraculous that time could go by so quickly. Through some artful finagling—Jack was very good at that sort of thing, Ellen readily admitted—instead of getting their movie money at the commencement of principal photography, as per contract, they had the check in their hands twelve days before the cameras would roll. Part of the deal to get the money early involved an intentional misdirection—not a lie, of course—that the entire family would be taking a much anticipated trip, perhaps within days of the film getting

under way. There would be no time to put the money to
work for them. In exchange for the production company's
acquiescence, Jack promised that, before the commencement of principal photography, he and Ellen would have
found a way to cut eight pages from the last third of the
script. Successful shortening of the script had, so far, eluded
the professional writing staff assigned to the screenplay.
Without it, the film would be at least one million dollars
over budget, before it was ever started.

Their current novel—and, quite probably, their last,
certainly written in the present—was, finally, complete. In
the morning, they would set out by car for California.
David, surprising both Ellen and her husband, suggested
something quite bizarre. "Why don't you guys continue
writing once we've entered the past—I mean, if there is
anything to this goofy time-travel crap. But on the off
chance it does happen, you guys should think about it. You
guys could be the next Jules Verne, right? What did Verne
have? He imagined things like nuclear submarines and
stuff like that," David had gone on, answering his own
question. "You guys wouldn't have to imagine a damn
thing! Just use your imaginations to come up with some
science fiction story line and throw all the stuff from our
present day into the story. Like microwave ovens, compact
discs, personal computers—stuff like that. Even a trip to
the Moon and satellites orbiting the Earth. You guys
would still be able to do what you like and make a lot of
money."

Elizabeth had pointed out, "But they can't do that,
Davey. Because they didn't, or else those books would
already exist, just like the photograph of the store exists. It

might be a terrific idea, but for some reason or another, they won't do it, because the books you're talking about would have been published already, see?. Right, Daddy?" And Elizabeth had turned to her father, who was sitting at his computer, all the while staring at her almost worshipfully as she pelted her brother with the logic of time travel.

"You're a hundred percent on the money, babe. The reason the photo which started this whole thing—alerted us to it in the first place—exists is because we had already built or bought the store and put up that sign: Jack Naile—General Merchandise." Then Jack looked at David. "The reason those books will never be written—or published at least—is because they haven't already been published, David."

"So, Dad, you're saying that everything we do once we get to the past—if this stupid thing happened—is predetermined, written somewhere."

Ellen said it. "Written in time, David. It's already written in time, and if something did change that, the consequences would be incalculable. You'll probably start carrying a gun, for example. You were/will be in that photograph. If you had to shoot somebody and you killed a person or you didn't kill a person, but in the past you had already not killed or killed that person—"

"I don't follow you," David volunteered in a moment of rare candor.

Jack chimed in. "What your Mom's trying to say, David, is that if something any of us were to do were somehow something we hadn't already done—from our perspective now—we could screw up the present and the future. The smallest thing that would alter the past might have enormous consequences in years to come."

Elizabeth had offered an example, and a very good one Ellen had thought at the time. "Like if Hitler had been killed in some kind of accident when he was a little boy, then maybe World War Two might never have happened, but some guy who was killed during World War Two might have lived instead and fathered a child who blew up the world or something and none of us would be here right now. Right?"

"Exactly," Ellen agreed.

"Okay, how do we know what to do and what not to do, then?" David asked, slipping into sarcasm. "Do we just do only the things we know the Nailes did—and we don't know much of that—and the rest of the time sit around afraid to leave the house or whatever because we might screw up the future?"

"No, we just try to behave rationally," Jack said, "and we hope for the best."

"We do what this family has always done," Ellen declared. "We fly by the seat of our pants. And at least you and your father will still be able to wear pants," she added.

CHAPTER THREE

By the time they reached the hotel outside Bakersfield, California, near the site where principal photography on *Angel Street* would begin the next day, they had driven over two thousand miles, carried the attaché case with the diamonds and their modest supply of gold in and out of seven motels and nearly twenty restaurants, taught Lizzie how to drive quite well and eliminated a little over nine pages from the screenplay. Regardless of whether or not those pages stayed out of the script, their obligation to the production company was officially fulfilled.

Jack Naile had always considered himself somewhat anal retentive (convincing himself that attention to detail was prudent thoroughness, therefore a virtue rather than a psychological quirk). Consequently, he felt perfectly justified getting up a few times each evening, going to the window of whatever hostelry happened to be their abode of the moment and checking that the Suburban was as it should be.

The contents of the Suburban were vital to their success in the past. Certainly, it would be possible to survive without these items, but impossible to maintain any semblance of a normal late twentieth century lifestyle.

"Come to bed, Jack. The Suburban's just fine."

"Coming, kiddo."

"What's bugging you, Jack?"

"I'm just hoping that we didn't forget something. And I don't mean movies on videotape. It's like that kit we thought of that we can install so we can run the Suburban on grain alcohol."

"That was a good idea, seeing as we didn't have enough money or time to get a diesel engine put in."

"Yeah. With the right filter, we could have run the car off the equivalent of home heating oil."

From the semidarkness of the bed, Ellen said reassuringly, "There will obviously be some things that we forgot or couldn't anticipate needing, Jack. That's just the way that life is."

"What do you think the kids are talking about?" They were in the next room, an unlocked adjoining door connecting to it.

"David's probably sleeping. If he doesn't get his eight hours, he's a grouch. Liz is probably watching a talk show or a movie and keeping the sound low so she won't awaken David."

Jack Naile nodded, glanced once more at the Suburban and then walked back to the bed. The attaché case with their stash of gold and diamonds was beside the bed, between it and the nightstand. In front of the nightstand, abutting the leading edge of the attaché case was an aircraft aluminum case, larger and heavier. Inside it were all but one of the personal sidearms he had brought for their anticipated travel into the objective past.

All but one. The long-barreled Colt Single Action Army, five chambers loaded, rested on the nightstand.

Jack got into bed, his right arm curling around Ellen's bare shoulders. "Wanna make love? Might be our last chance in this century."

"What a come-on line, Jack! You ought to save that one for a book!"

"Well, it might be."

Ellen rolled into his arms and brushed her lips against his. "But just think how romantic it will be making love in the past, before we were even born. Do you want the little guy to be all tired out? Don't you want to save up until—"

"He's getting bigger by the second. He won't get tired out, and I don't need to save up. I make more all the time. Even when I'm sleeping, I'm always working, making more just for us. I'll get pimples. You wouldn't want me to show up in the past with a zit or something. Have you considered that? I think not" Jack Naile's left hand cradled his wife's face and he kissed her hard on the mouth. The zit thing almost always worked . . . .

The movie set looked just like something out of a movie, with several cameras—one of them on what looked like railroad tracks—and lights and canvas-backed folding chairs with names or titles stenciled on them and bunches of people. Half of them just milled around and seemed to be doing absolutely nothing, while the other half walked or occasionally ran. The frontier "town" consisted of a wide street lined on either side with clapboard commercial buildings, flat-roofed adobe huts of varying size, corrals and a big red barn at one end of the street, smallish houses with white picket fences at the other. What Elizabeth could see from standing near the catering truck and something her father had called a "generator truck" indicated that about half of the commercial buildings were not buildings at all, but merely facades, with nothing behind them.

The purplish gray mountains off in the distance—to the east?—were wholly real, she assumed.

Her father and David—David reluctantly—were off somewhere with the armorer, the property man in charge of the guns, while Elizabeth and her mother stood beside a long table stacked with stainless steel coffee urns, white Styrofoam cups and every imaginable kind of donut or breakfast pastry. There were bottles of water, too, representing several different brands. Bottled water, Liz had always thought, tasted pretty much like bottled water, regardless of what label it carried.

Holly Kinsey was someone Elizabeth had been reading about almost since picking up her first pop-culture magazine, watched as a presenter or recipient on innumerable awards shows, seen in every movie the woman had made. Attired in an ankle length, velvet-looking robin's egg-blue dress with a high lace collar, her usual shoulder-length brown hair hidden beneath a wig of cascading curls reaching to her waist, she walked straight toward them and stuck out her right hand. Her pansy eyes sparkled as she spoke. "I'm Holly! You must be Elizabeth. Hi! And you're Mrs. Naile?"

"Ellen, please."

"Ellen, then."

Elizabeth shook Holly Kinsey's offered hand. "I never thought I'd ever get to meet you, even when Mom and Daddy said you were one of the stars of the movie. I've seen every one of your movies. My favorite was *Sweetheart's Revenge*."

Holly Kinsey flashed brilliantly white teeth as she smiled and said, "That was my favorite, too. But I think your mom and dad's movie is going to be just terrific. The raspberry danish are really good, and there's orange juice and soft drinks, if you don't like coffee, or I can send out and get you something."

Elizabeth was aware, on one level, that the thread of conversation continued for a moment, then passed her and resumed, but between Holly Kinsey and her mother. Holly Kinsey was gabbing with her mother! Her mother! And, if this time travel thing really happened, she'd never be able to tell Keisha or Amelia or any of her other girlfriends about it! Life sucked . . .

Elizabeth would look beautiful, albeit a little nervous, Ellen guessed. Ellen, on the other hand, felt perfectly stupid. She'd never liked dressing up when she was a little girl, even for Halloween. And looking at herself in the mirror, dressed this way, considering what lay ahead of them, was extremely creepy. Her own hair was pulled back in a tight bun, some tendrils drawn out on either side of her face and made into curls by one of the makeup technicians. Holly had personally accompanied them to wardrobe after making the suggestion, "Would you guys like to be extras in the street scene? One of the AD's—assistant directors—can fix it up so the Guild doesn't throw a fit. Come on! It'll be fun! Especially for you, Liz!"

After that, Ellen Naile sank into what-can-you-do mode and agreed, figuring that Lizzie would have a wonderful time.

Wardrobe was full of enormous, uncomfortable-looking dresses and inane hats and clunky-looking shoes. Holly Kinsey shepherding them—almost smotheringly—every step of the way, outfits were selected and trailers were found and Ellen and Elizabeth went their separate ways. Damned if she'd wear a waist cincher, Ellen had squeezed herself into the dress and practiced her contortionist skills to get it closed up her back.

Hats were something Ellen Naile positively detested, and especially the one she wore. It had a broad brim, with lace trim banded around the crown matching the tight and itchy collar that felt like it was closing more tightly around her throat by the second. Remembering to catch up the enormous skirt and billowing petticoats under it, Ellen Naile opened the trailer door and warily navigated the trailer steps, her feet buttoned inside what had to be the ugliest cross between orthopedic shoes and combat boots ever conceived.

Settling her borrowed clothing, Ellen began looking for Elizabeth, after a few seconds and even fewer hesitant steps encountering her so suddenly that they almost bumped into one another, Elizabeth climbing down from the trailer next door.

"Oh, you look beautiful, Lizzie!"

"You look beautiful, Mom. You really do."

"I feel like an idiot." As if on cue, a wind blew up along the alley-width walkway between the rows of trailers and Ellen Naile felt her hat starting to go. She put her right hand, open palm, on top of it to keep it in place. "Having to dress like this every day is going to suck big time," Ellen declared.

Lizzie started to cry, and Ellen thought, "To hell with the hat," and put both arms around her daughter and just hugged her close while the wind kept blowing. But the wind from the mountains beyond the fake Western town wasn't the source of the chill that Ellen felt. The reason for the icy tingle that spread upward along Ellen's spine and stopped so abruptly at the crown of her head under the damned hat that her body shook with a paroxysm was something different. Both she and her daughter had glimpsed the reality that stalked their destiny, haunted their souls. They would be in a time when women were cared for and protected and sheltered and never, ever consulted, a time when everyday tasks consumed enormous amounts of time and a woman's intellect and desires weren't given a second thought.

"Kirk Douglas always believed—said so in print in his autobiography—that if he rode real erect-like in the saddle, he'd look like more of a horseman than he was. And he did."

Jack glanced down from the saddle into the weathered brown face of Elvis Wilson. "Are you saying I should sit up straighter in the saddle, Elvis?"

"Since you and your family got here ten days ago, and you connived me into teaching you and them some ridin', you've gotten a damn sight better, Jack. But until you get better still, sit erect. Remember Kirk's words, and you'll look good, at least."

The advice of Elvis Wilson was to be taken seriously. Some of the stuntmen on the set claimed Wilson was almost in the Ben Johnson class when it came to horsemanship. Once Jack Naile and his family had arrived on location, Jack had set out to find somewhere in the area where basic horsemanship could be learned.

It was Holly Kinsey who had said, "Elvis Wilson taught me and half the actors I know. He's good, and he doesn't expect miracles. And he likes kids, so he'd be great with Liz. Your daughter is just the sweetest and smartest girl in the world. And is your son David terrific-looking! He's so awfully mature." After thanking the actress for the compliments to his daughter and son, Jack had looked up Elvis Wilson, who was doing some stunt riding and a little acting in *Angel Street* when he wasn't supervising the horse wrangling. Despite Jack's insistence, Elvis Wilson refused to take money for his services, saying instead, "Everybody who's a decent person should learn himself to ride. Folks who aren't—decent, I mean—well, the horses are better off. Buy me a steak dinner or a bottle of scotch sometime, and we'll call it even."

David did not like horses. A natural athlete in every sport he'd ever tried, riding interested him not at all and chiefly because he openly ridiculed everything and anything which had to do with the Old West. This was, of course, because his father liked westerns, was a dedicated student of Earpiana and owned a cowboy hat and a Colt .45. Yet David agreed to the riding lessons without protest.

That only heightened Jack's already eerie feelings concerning their future in the past. Ellen, who loved horses but had ridden almost not at all, made steady progress, as did Liz, who admitted that she was afraid a horse would bite her. Of the Naile family's four students of equitation, it was David, of course, who was learning to ride so well that, with proper wardrobe, he could have served as a Mongol warrior under Genghis Khan.

Jack glanced down again into Elvis' weathered face. Wilson wasn't made-up; the scene in which Wilson was about to perform was one in which his face would never be seen. Wilson would be riding across a great barren expanse as one of fifty desperadoes on their way to wreak death and destruction. At Wilson's prompting of the second-unit director, Jack and David would swell that number to fifty-two.

"Nobody will see my face wearing some damn cowboy hat, right?" David had insisted when the idea was suggested a day earlier.

"Nobody will see you wearing a cowboy hat, son."

"Fine. I'll do it."

David, hat stuffed under his arm and leading his already saddled horse, walked out of the holding corral. "We ready?"

Elvis looked up at Jack Naile and winked, then went to get his horse.

It was hot despite the wind, or maybe because of it. The wind rustled the manes of the horses, tore at the hats of the men and necessitated squinting against driven dust. But it was the perfect special effect for the shot, and cost nothing. If Jack had learned one thing about moviemaking since they'd arrived on set, it was that free stuff was good.

"What did you say one of those camera trucks was called, Dad?"

"An insert car, I think."

There were two of them, whatever they were called, trucks with special suspension, each mounted with a movie camera, the cameras rolling. The second-unit director had just called "Action" and was getting the long shot of the head desperado turning around in the saddle and giving his cohort of nasties a pep talk about all the fun death and destruction that they could perpetrate upon the town. In another few seconds, he'd wave his sombrero and it would be the signal for everyone to start forward on their mounts, at little more than a canter at first, then breaking into a gallop.

"You up for this, Dad?" David inquired.

"Yeah. I'm not going to do anything dangerous. And you remember that, too. If the other riders start going a little too fast for us, we can rein back a little. Nobody'll notice. I mean, we're supposed to be bad guys, not cavalry in a John Ford western."

"Whatever."

The sombrero was waved, and, more to the point, the second-unit director signaled. Trucks rolled and mounted men started forward. "Kind of exciting," Jack Naile enthused to his son over the clopping of hoofbeats and the creaking of saddles and gun leather.

"Kind of dusty."

"That Holly Kinsey really seemed to like you, David."

Jack remembered to sit up straighter in the saddle, pulling his costume-department cowboy hat lower over his eyes against the rising clouds of dust.

"If I tell you something, promise you won't tell Mom?"

This was David's way of insulating himself from Ellen's direct criticism. David knew perfectly well that Jack would hold a confidence sacred from anyone except his wife. But prefacing the revelation as he was, David knew that his mother would never mention it, no matter what.

"Tell me." That was Jack's usual sort of response, non-committal.

"Tell me first. What did she say? Holly, I mean."

"That you were good-looking and seemed—yeah, mature. Holly said mature. Why?"

"I had sex with her the first time a little over a week ago."

"We've only been here a little over a week, David! The first time?! For God's sake! She's almost old enough—"

"I never dated anyone younger than I am. And don't worry—Holly's on the pill."

"Aww shit, son! Your mother and I never had sex with anybody but each other. Ever."

"It's the nineties, Dad, huh. You wouldn't buy one of these horses without taking it for a test ride, right?"

"I don't believe you!"

"We're lagging behind. One of the ADs is waving at us." And David leaned into the whipping mane of the bay mare he rode, the animal's pace quickening.

"I'm not through talking to you, Davey!" Jack Naile urged his buckskin ahead, the blunted rowels of his spurs raking the animal gently, as Elvis had instructed him.

"Put yourself in the horse's position, Jack," Elvis said.

That stud or whatever you're ridin' wants direction, control. No creature wants pain and meanness."

Jack cut the distance, pulled alongside David. "You're shittin' me, right?"

"I'm sorry I brought it up."

That was David's way. He sincerely wanted to be open and truth-telling, but he also had the uncanny ability to make anyone feel guilty about questioning his conduct or disagreeing with him in any way. "You're not shitting me."

"Let it go, Dad. I was just trying to be honest with you, and this is what I get for it."

"No, listen, son. I appreciate you telling me, sharing stuff with me." Jack Naile thought, *My God, he's doing it to me, making me feel guilty*. The insert cars were breaking off in opposite directions. In a moment or two, the second unit director would signal "Cut" and everyone would start reining in.

Movies were good. When the scene ended, that was it and life went on just as before.

"Our son did what, Jack?"

The suite of rooms the production company paid for was clean, comfortable and semiluxurious: huge bedroom with a king-size bed, couch and television; slightly smaller sitting room with another couch, several overstuffed chairs and an even larger television; bathroom with a large tub and great water pressure; a balcony overlooking the parking lot to the west and the mountains to the east. It adjoined a two-bedroom suite with a smaller sitting room and a bath, just as nice and with a better view of the parking lot, for Liz and David.

"You heard me, Ellen."

"I just don't understand him sometimes."

"Maybe it's good we're getting away for a couple of days." Jack was inspecting the contents of the attaché case, just retrieved from the production company's safe. The contents—the diamonds, the small amount of gold, the Seecamp .32, the only modern firearm he hadn't disposed of—seemed just as he'd left them. "Get David's mind off the girl. We can look around the old store, if the current owner doesn't mind, and check out what's left of the house, too," Jack told his wife. "It seems like we would have written something, left behind something. And if we could find out what we'd written, we might have an edge on what's going to happen." The mere contemplation of already having lived and died before they were born, having left notes or letters behind for their future selves in a past they had already lived but were to live again, was enough to induce insanity. Were they insane? All of them? How could this happen? Jack shook his head in momentary disbelief.

"Clarence called while you were getting the attaché case. He spoke with Liz for a while, and then got on the phone with me."

"You tell him we're all okay, kid?"

"Yeah, both physically and chronologically."

"Clarence doing all right?"

"He sounded . . . You know, I've never used this word to say it, but it fits. He sounded *distraught* and kind of depressed."

"Normal, huh?" Jack laughed. "I'm just kidding. I'm gonna miss him."

"The kids'll miss him. Speaking of the kids, where's David?" Ellen asked.

"Liz sleeping?"

"Yeah. I'm supposed to wake her up in about an hour. Where's David?"

"Riding."

"Oh."

"Not that kind. He's out with Elvis Wilson. David's conned Elvis into teaching him a Pony Express mount, and he wanted to polish it up before we left. I think he's thinking this might be it, or at least we're getting close."

"Or is it just that a Pony Express mount is a good bet for quick getaways?" Ellen suggested.

"Ellen."

"I'm sorry. No, I'm not. Are you going to talk to him about this thing with Holly Kinsey, since I'm not supposed to know about it?"

"He knows you'll know about it. And," Jack sighed audibly, "I really don't know what to say that I haven't said already. With one of the picture's stars out of—out of the picture," Jack said lamely, "for a few days with a dislocated shoulder, and the company shooting around him, we've got the time to get away and that may be just what David needs. It could be pretty overwhelming to a guy of seventeen to have a movie star tumble to him."

"Would you have done it, Jack?"

"No, but I'm not him, and we don't know the circumstances. Would a lot of guys do it if some hot babe who's an international household word came on to them? Probably would."

"That household word isn't hard to guess. It's got four

letters and the third one's a *u*," Ellen supplied. "And if you change that third letter to an *i*, that's what I'd just as soon do to Holly Kinsey's throat."

"Look at it this way, princess. Once this time shift happens, Holly Kinsey won't have been born yet and David will be living in a much less permissive era."

"And you just remember, Jack, that in those days the only way a girl could practice birth control was by keeping her knees together," Ellen added soberingly.

Driving across the Sierra Nevada Mountains was something that Jack Naile was certain he would never forget. There was the agricultural inspection station at the border; then, once out of California—Ellen was driving by then—they turned north toward Carson City, stopping there to stretch their legs, the Suburban cramped because of the load it carried. They grabbed fast food, tanked up the Suburban and drove on toward Atlas, reaching the little town in early evening.

"You were right, Jack. It doesn't look at all like it did in the photo, like it will for us," Ellen almost whispered as Jack helped her from the Suburban's front passenger seat.

"This can't be right, Dad," David declared, climbing out of the car and holding the middle seat door for his sister. "There's almost nothing left from the photo. Did the whole town burn down or something?"

"That's where the store was, wasn't it, Daddy?"

"Yeah, Lizzie, where that law office is now. The foundation is pretty much the only thing left of it, though, but maybe there was a cellar or something. It's too late to check it out today." It was after six, well after anyone who didn't have to kept office hours. But there was still plenty of daylight remaining, time enough for a quick drive to the ranch and an even quicker look at the remains of the house.

As there had been when Clarence and he had first stood on that street, alongside Arthur Beach, there was a strong breeze blowing in from the desert, dust devils appearing and disappearing.

They'd called for reservations at the town's only motel, eschewing the two bed and breakfasts because the rates seemed scarily low.

Jack looked down the main street to his right, back toward where the highway did its right angle and continued on, almost as if Atlas were merely an inconvenience to the highway department engineers as they pressed their road onward across the high desert and into the purpling mountains.

"Anybody need to make a pit stop?" Jack gestured toward the highway. "The restaurant's probably got decent johns."

No one volunteered.

The ranch was just as Jack had described it. Ellen stepped out of the Suburban and turned a full three hundred sixty degrees. Yes, just as he had described it.

Jack holding her by the hand, the kids fanning out at their flanks, Ellen walked across the surprisingly level ground that would have comprised a front yard for the ruined house. She wondered, fleetingly, what irreplaceable memorabilia might have been lost when the house burned. What memories were gone forever?

The bones of the house laid upon a terrace. More open land—about the same size as a suburban backyard—separated the house from a roaring stream that emerged from a higher, wooded area beyond. There were a great many pines, but other types of trees as well. When the season was right, there would be flowers in the meadow that lay like an apron beneath the tree line. She'd have to learn the names of the wildflowers and plants.

The farthest boundary of the backyard seemed some several feet above the stream, a good feature during times of heavy rains or snow melt-off; the ground sloped radically downward to the water. "You were right, Jack; this is a perfect place for using hydro-electric power—if we can rig it up."

"We can do it—we did it." and he squeezed her hand.

A line of trees, almost perfectly paired, reached downward from the woods toward the terraced lot, as if grasping for the dirt ranch road leading up to the house. The track was precious little wider than the Suburban.

"How far is it from the highway, Jack?"

"Just a hair under nine miles. But remember, on horseback we'd knock about six miles off between here and the highway. The highway follows a natural ridgeline and then dips into the valley, which is kind of a usual thing for roads dating from horse backing days. So that was probably the highway a hundred years ago, too."

The ride from the highway had been gradually uphill. Jack had said something earlier about the lot's elevation accounting for the swiftness of the stream as it coursed downward.

The kids closing in at their sides, Ellen stepped across

what was once the threshold, Jack beside her. Thankfully, he hadn't offered to carry her over it. Considering the fact that the house, in its current state, was like a dead thing, to do so would have been spooky in the extreme.

From the layout of the house, as best Ellen could discern, they stood within what had once been a combination of sitting room, living room and dining room, planned out in the shape of an L resting on its side, the long vertical leg forming the sitting room and living room, the short horizontal leg the dining room. There were indications that another room had been off to her right as she faced the rear of the house where there was evidence of still more rooms. "This is the layout of the first floor of the house in Oak Park, Jack. We always liked that arrangement of rooms. We built this place." And Ellen Naile shivered.

On closer viewing of the house, a fire might not have been the immediate cause of its destruction, but there had been a fire—afterward, perhaps.

All that remained essentially undamaged was an extremely nicely fitted stone-and-mortar chimney, the chimney thrusting upward into the deep blue of early evening from a hearth of inordinate size. "It's like the fireplace they had at that little restaurant in the Chicago Loop that we used to eat at."

"I thought that, too," Jack affirmed.

"Still no word on who owns the property in the present?"

"God knows. Maybe our great-grandchildren own it." Jack laughed softly. He might have been right. Ellen freed herself of Jack's hand and approached the chimney. "Whatchya doing?"

"If we were going to leave anything special in this house, considering there would have been no fire department or anything like that, and we knew that someday we might come back looking for it in the future, where would we stash it?"

"In the fireplace," Lizzie answered.

Ellen said, "That's my girl. David, start checking that side."

"But let's all be careful," Jack admonished. "With the mortar in its current state, we could get the whole thing tumbling down on us in a heartbeat."

Slowly, carefully, they began to inspect the hearth, Jack producing a Mini Maglite from his bomber-jacket pocket, the pale light from its beam helping considerably. If needed, there were more flashlights in the Suburban. Lizzie said, "I just remembered something," and produced a small light in the shape of a ladybug from within the bowels of her purse.

Thunder rumbled from up in the mountains and a flash of lightning freeze framed everything for an instant. "We've gotta hit the trail pretty soon. That road up here might be the kind that washes out during a heavy rain, guys," Jack cautioned.

"Just another couple of minutes," Ellen insisted.

"We can come back tomorrow and—" Lizzie began.

David interrupted her. "This stone almost wanted to come out by itself. Give me your knife, Dad." Jack took a folding knife from his pocket. David opened it one-handed. "I may hurt the edge doing this."

"I've got sharpening sticks in the Suburban. What have you found?"

"Just wait a minute, huh!"

"Take it easy, son," Jack responded. Ellen didn't say a word.

"Okay! Got it!"

David held a small metal box in his hands. Jack identified it. "Cast iron."

"Can we open it?" Lizzie asked.

Ellen tried raising the lid.

"Probably rusted shut," David announced.

"Let me have it, Davey." Jack took the box, set it on the ground at their feet and looked about. "There we go."

He stepped out of the light of the flashlights and back in the blink of an eye, holding a large rock of the type from which the hearth itself was constructed, probably the rock's origin.

"Here. Let me do that," David volunteered.

David took the rock and smacked it hard against the exposed single piano hinge at the rear of the box, then hammered against the front of the box, but knocking upward with the rock, trying to free the lid.

There was another flash of lightning. "If some Arab guys start chanting and we find the Ark of the Covenant, I'm leaving before we get to the part with the snakes," Jack informed them. Ellen realized that her husband was trying to break the tension; it didn't work.

When the rock hit the box lid, the sound was somehow different this time, and David got up from his crouch. "Got it!" Oddly, he handed the box to Ellen.

Ellen looked at Jack, and Jack nodded. Ellen lifted the box lid. Both flashlights bathed its interior in light. "A Ziploc sandwich bag, guys."

That was all. She took it out of the box, breathing a sigh of relief as she realized that inside the bag was a piece of paper. Carefully, uncertain whether or not the paper inside the bag might crumble, she tore open the plastic bag's seal. There were boxes of bags identical to these packed away in the Suburban. Could it be possible that the same bag somehow existed in two places at the same time? Ellen shivered and shook her head. Time-travel stuff was crazy, or enough to make one crazy just considering it.

The paper inside the bag seemed relatively undamaged by time. "Can I read it?" Elizabeth asked.

Ellen handed it to her daughter, who slowly, carefully, unfolded it, then read aloud.

"Dear Jack,

"Writing to oneself is probably like talking to oneself, an early sign of insanity.

"Anyway, here goes.

"Ellen and I pondered whether or not it would be wise to leave behind a record of this new life, and a record, too, of the future that we knew. If you were to read a record of this new life, would that change things? Were someone from your objective past, now the future, to read of the intervening years of which Ellen and I know, would such knowledge be for good or bad? Would such a record fall into the hands of some unscrupulous person who saw opportunity for wealth and power in changing the past to alter the future or the present?

"I don't think history is locked in bronze; or,

perhaps, graven in stone would be putting it better. Not now, not anymore.

"Ellen and I discussed this a lot, and she's less of a buttinsky than I am, as you well know. We finally agreed to let people know—before it was too late—what your today and my yesterday/tomorrow were/will be like. Ellen and I wrote. I became afraid. In frustration, I nearly burned all that we wrote, the videos which we taped, the still photographs. But I didn't.

"I don't know how to tell you to determine whether there's something odd about the world of your present, whether time seems out of order or something like that. When you enter the past, you'll have to make that determination for yourself, whether or not to leave a record.

"As I was about to burn our work, the records of everything, I came across where Ellen and I had noted that more than eight million Jews, not to mention the Poles and the Gypsies who also died, were killed by the Nazis during World War Two. If our writing could save only one of those innocent women and children, by alerting the future to Hitler's evil intentions, I couldn't pass up that opportunity and, instead, have even one of those deaths on my conscience.

"Once you've entered the loop, you and Ellen and David and Lizzie will have to determine such matters for yourselves.

"I am running out of time. If you are careful, you may have more of it than I.

"On the plus side, at least Ellen and I figured out why this happened/will happen. Maybe.

"There were/are/will be a lot of things wrong with the last half of the twentieth century. By changing events just a little—without trying— people who knew what was going to go wrong might be able, a little at a time, to make things go right.

"Maybe.

"Why is it us, the Naile family? Ellen and I don't have a clue.

"Our advice?

"We have no advice to give you, really.

"It would be wrong to tell you specifically what happens; or, at least, we think it is/was/will be. Anyway, just reading this will change your future in the past.

"I think.

"Suffice it to say, we can note three things which will hopefully ease your mind:

"1. Love does endure beyond the confines of time.

"2. Keep your faith in your family.

"3. Cheat time; you're good, but not as good as the knight of the sorrowful countenance. Bring the Seecamp.

"Point three is included because I believe that I am dying and wish for you to avoid that fate; there is still too much to do."

Lizzie looked up and there were tears at the corners of

her eyes. "It's signed 'Sincerely, who else but me/you?' He was—you—dying?!"

Ellen folded her daughter into her arms.

Jack cleared his throat.

The reference to the knight was, obviously, to Jack's fascination with Richard Boone's character in the television series *Have Gun—Will Travel*.

Jack, his voice little more than a whisper, said, "Shine the flashlight on my hand." David and Lizzie turned the two flashlights on the palm of their father's right hand. In it was the little pistol he had carried for so long and had thought about leaving behind: the Seecamp .32.

David moved the flashlight to shine on the palm of his hand. He held part of a wall outlet. "Just like the ones in the Suburban."

Lizzie was into full-scale tears. David—almost tentatively—touched at his sister's shoulder. Ellen felt Jack's head come to rest against her own.

CHAPTER
❖ FOUR ❖

There were two messages waiting for them at the motel. The first was from Arthur Beach. Jack read it aloud, raising his voice over the drumming rain cascading down on three sides of them from the covered portico where the Suburban was parked outside the motel lobby.

"I finally discovered ownership of the property in question. I can't imagine how you wouldn't have known, since, from the name at least, the owner would sound to be a relative. The listed ownership is Horizon Enterprises. Horizon is a corporation wholly owned by Alan Naile. Because of the similarity of names, I checked back on Horizon Enterprises. It was founded just prior to World War I by someone who bore the name David Naile. And get this! His father's name was Jack Naile, possibly the same Jack Naile who owned the store in Atlas! I'm digging for more information.

"I'll look forward to hearing from you soon."

Jack Naile handed the note to his wife through the open window of the Suburban.

"Note number two reads as follows: 'Call at once. Needed on set for rewrites. Dislocated shoulder is actually broken collarbone and production is stalled.' The director, the executive producer and one of the vice-presidents of the studio have their names at the bottom."

"Should we start driving back tonight?" Lizzie asked, leaning over her mother's left shoulder from the middle seat.

"I can drive," David volunteered.

"I know you can, son, but the weather would be with us for several hundred miles. It'd be foolhardy, David. But thanks for volunteering."

"Jack?"

Jack Naile looked at his wife. "What, kid?"

"They'll send a helicopter that would fly us to Reno or Sacramento, won't they?"

"Yeah," he sighed, instantly seeing the implication of his wife's words. They would have to leave the Suburban behind. It would have been smarter to go to their rooms, get the gear they needed out of the Suburban and sit down as a family and talk it out, where they could be warm and dry. Instead he asked, "What do you guys think? Should we just sit here and wait it out and leave the movie company stuck, or should we go on with our lives, and when this time shift or whatever the hell it is happens it just happens?"

David spoke first. "Well, since I now know the name of my company—Horizon Enterprises—if I can get to a computer, maybe I can find out what it's worth. Yeah. Let's do it. If this is going to happen, let's get on with it. On the plus side, we did get those wall outlets back in time somehow. And we do have a deal with the movie company. If this time shift thing doesn't take place for a year or so, we can't go pissing them off."

"David's right," Elizabeth chimed in. Her brown eyes looked sad, as best Jack Naile could make out his daughter's face in the diffuse light from the portico. "This is going to happen, whether we wait here or go back to California, to Bakersfield. Let's do the right thing."

Ellen's face glowed, Jack thought. He knew why. And, yes, she hadn't been thrilled about David and the actress, the thought of, along with her daughter, being time-shifted into second-class-citizen status was eating at her, and her whole world was about to change irrevocably. The reason for the look on her face was pride in her children—and, Jack hoped, in him as well.

"Let's show everybody we're smart enough to come in out of the rain, huh? David and I'll get you guys into the rooms and haul in the stuff we'll need. We can order a couple of pizzas—the guy at the desk said they deliver and the pizzas taste pretty good. Then I'll call Bakersfield. Agreed?"

No one disagreed.

Peggy Greer leaned back in her folding chair—the same one she used when they went out into the desert for their experiments with electricity—and stretched. The computer had yielded up all that she knew to ask of it.

The new cable was as short as possible, the added insulation enough to protect the wiring within from any conceivable loss.

Every item of equipment had been checked and rechecked, then checked again.

Jane Rogers entered the living room that was their makeshift office. The dining-room table was their indoor equipment-testing station. With every conceivable surface covered with printouts or gear or both, the TV tray Jane carried was practical in the extreme.

There were ham sandwiches on two plates, two small bags of potato chips—Jane liked the sour cream and onion variety, which Peggy could not abide—an open bottle of beer with a schooner beside it and a glass of white wine. Dinner.

Jane always brought a glass, and Peggy never used it, but Jane was from an era when a woman drinking straight from the bottle was on a par with a woman appearing in public with a cigarette hanging from her lips.

Huddled around the tray together, Jane asked, "How's the weather holding up for tomorrow, Peggy?"

"The rain should be gone by midnight or so. In the morning, meteorological conditions should be as close as possible to those prevalent on the day of our one brush with success, when the light array actually flickered. There's a second storm front like the one just passing, but it's stalled on the other side of the mountains, which goes to show that sometimes it really does rain in California."

Jane caught the musical reference and laughed softly.

"Maybe tomorrow will really be it, Jane."

"For a med student—"

"Hey, I have my degree!"

"You know what I mean, young lady. For a med student, you also happen to be one heck of a fine physicist."

"I'm a very tired physicist. And, with the rain, I'll take you up on crashing on your couch."

"Good. Then we can get a really early start in the morning." Jane nibbled at a potato chip, not yet touching her sandwich.

Peggy yawned, covering her hand with her mouth, then implored, "But not too early? Please?" And she bit into her ham sandwich.

"Where's the helicopter going to land, Jack?"

"Probably in that open area on the other side of the highway, if the rain has stopped and the ground isn't too wet. The production company will bring in a guy to drive the Suburban back. He's bonded. He's coming in on the helicopter. I'll have the guns and the attaché case and we'll be bringing two of the microfiche readers and the video camera. If it happens before we get the Suburban back, at least we'll have something. And we should have the Suburban back in under a day."

Jack rolled over onto his left side, and Ellen rolled over behind him, resting her right hand over his abdomen. Almost invariably, they slept naked, tonight no exception. Sometimes, when the weather was very warm, the heat from Jack's body could be a little much; but, with the rain, the temperatures had cooled enough that they wouldn't really have needed air-conditioning in the room. But they were both fanatics for fresh air and, failing the option of opening a window while they slept, on would go the air-conditioning. Ambient temperature in their motel room was close to frigid; tonight she was happy for the warmth of her husband's body, as Ellen knew that Jack was for hers.

"You catch it when Lizzie read the note?" Jack asked her.

"Eight million killed by Hitler and the Nazis? Yes, I caught it. Lizzie would have, too, Jack, if she hadn't been so caught up in reading it."

"Yeah, good old Davey. If it doesn't have to do with business, it isn't news. And if it's history, it's even less interesting, just old news. Catch the other thing?"

"You lost me," Ellen said honestly.

"He—I—didn't burn what they wrote. So if it didn't burn up with the house, somebody has it, and I'll bet that somebody is David's great-grandson who owns—what was the name of it?"

"Horizon Enterprises, or something like that. No. That was it. Horizon Enterprises."

"Which means Horizon has been operating all these years off knowledge of the future. And David—our David—will do the same thing."

"But consider this," Ellen suggested. "You know that six million Jews were killed in the Holocaust, not eight. And it can be assumed that the other Jack would have a similar knowledge of history, right?"

Jack rolled over and took her into his arms and she rested her head against his chest, tugged at one of the hairs there in order to get him to say, "Ouch! So, you're saying that maybe something that the Naile family did since the last time it traveled back in time and now was able to help lower that figure from eight million to six million."

"Maybe. So maybe David will be at least partially responsible for saving two million lives from extermination."

"My son the hero. Has a nice ring to it," Jack whispered.

"Horny hero. Sounds like a character out of a comic book." She added, "But Davey's a good guy. Hard working, aggressive, bull-headed."

"I wonder where he gets the bull-headedness. Certainly not from your side of the family. You and your dad—never bull-headed. We're blessed with two great kids. And they take after their mother, each in their own way. Great kids."

"Well, that's certainly true, but they have your eyes, Jack."

"I'm more interested in lips and other parts of the anatomy at the moment," Jack whispered, kissing her.

The trouble with being married to a wordsmith, Ellen was reminded, was that he was always looking for that special way to say things. Sometimes that annoyed her. Sometimes she liked that, liked that quite a bit.

Her fingers drifted across his chest as she kissed him back.

The helicopter had been able to land just on the other side of the highway, approximately two hundred yards from their motel rooms.

Jack made a last check of the Suburban, Ellen still inside their soon-to-be-vacated room, on the telephone with Clarence for what might be the last time. It would be a little before six in the morning in Georgia, Clarence probably not at his best. But if the time transfer were to take place without a last call, Clarence would be stricken. Clarence was a good man, a very good man and Jack realized that despite Clarence's often dour disposition, he'd miss him.

"David, you take the rifle case and that suitcase and the camera case."

"I can take the attaché case, too, Dad."

"Have you started carrying a gun, David? You haven't, so I hold on to the attaché case. Lizzie?"

"Daddy?"

"Grab what you can carry out of that pile, but remember that's what your brother and I are around for, so don't carry too much. Leave that one. It's very heavy." Jack Naile called his daughter's attention to the aircraft aluminum case with the two single actions and the derringer and a basic supply of ammunition for the three handguns.

"You're ready. You're really ready, aren't you, Dad?" David asked.

"What do you mean, son?"

"You're wearing your cowboy hat and your boots. I'll bet the gun belt Sam Andrews made for you is in one of the suitcases we're carrying."

Jack Naile grinned. "You win the bet, chief. Gotta be prepared."

Ellen's voice came from behind them. "If we were going back to prehistoric times, your father would have had Ron Mahovsky Metalife a custom club for him, and Sam Andrews would have made your dad a holster for it." Ellen reached for two suitcases and said, "Clarence was tired, upset, said he loves us and he won't like it without us being around. I told him pretty much the same, except for the parts about being tired and upset. I'm only upset."

It was a gorgeous day for flying, the sky clear, with only a few wisps of cloud to the south and east, the air cool without being cold. Of the four of them, only Jack had ever before flown in a helicopter. Although he didn't care at all for most amusement park rides and was a nervous commercial-airline passenger, the idea of being up in a helicopter once again excited him. The thought of leaving the Suburban and its precious contents behind mildly terrified him. "Hey, guys?"

His wife, his son and his daughter, all turned to look at him.

"I just wanted you guys to know, I love you all. And remember, we'll be together, whenever it happens." Jack looked away before any of them could respond and caught up Ellen's camera bag, the gun case and whatever else he could carry. There would be another trip back to the Suburban for him and David at least. Then they would be airborne.

As Jane Rogers did each time she conducted a field trial, she made final adjustments to the primary cable's strain insulator and triple-checked the anode plate for precise alignment with the control grid.

The generators hummed from the bed of the pickup truck parked a few feet from her Suburban, one generator to produce the electricity which the laser beam, powered by the second generator, would hopefully carry to target.

This had to be it, had to be the solution.

"Jane?"

"What is it, Peggy?"

"Listen carefully, to the west. There's a storm coming up over the mountains. I can hear thunder."

"Damn," Jane murmured. The front that Peggy had

said was stalled on the other side of the mountains had moved. "Can we make it, Peggy?"

"We might not have conditions so close again for weeks or months, Jane. What do you want to do?"

Was she being a bad scientist? Jane Rogers shook her head, took off her battered old flat-crowned hat. She stared toward the mountains. So far, no sign of lightning, just low rumblings of thunder. The storm could be taking its sweet time just beyond the highest peaks, enough time for the experiment. "Let's do it, girl!" Jane Rogers plunked her hat onto her head and approached the tripod-mounted refracting telescope. "I'm ready when you are!"

"On my mark," Peggy called out. "Five . . . four . . . three . . . two . . . one . . . Mark!" The humming of the generators seemed to increase almost exponentially.

Crackling sounds, so loud that they thrummed in her brain, then a different hum—the hum, with its unmistakable frequency. More crackling, the hum louder and louder.

As Jane Rogers peered through the telescope toward the distant light array that she prayed would fire, there was the anticipated thundering as the electrical charge was released along its carrier wave. But a microsecond—not even—after that, the array lit, and the most enormous lightning bolt Jane Rogers had ever witnessed in a life spanning nearly three quarters of a century flashed laterally across the sky. The array stayed lit, and a second, thunderous boom rent the air around her, the ground beneath her feet shaking.

"Shut down! Peggy! Shut down!"

As the lightning streaked across the sky, she had

distinctly seen a helicopter, with ball lightning crackling across the sky around it like electrons circling an atom. And then the aircraft just vanished, as if it had never been there, into a patch of inexplicable blackness. Then the blackness vanished, too.

The helicopter was out of control, and the pilot was almost certainly dead; Jack Naile was uncertain of the order in which the two events occurred. The single flash of lightning striking horizontally across the sky out of the mountains was as bright as the corona surrounding an eclipse, gone in an instant. In the same instant, the electrical systems within the helicopter's cockpit and all along the fuselage began to smolder, all lights and power gone. The pilot's body had stiffened. It lurched backward, hammered into the cockpit seat, the man's head falling at an unnatural angle to his right shoulder.

In the seconds that it took Jack Naile to shout, "Everybody hold on! We'll get out of this!" he realized that the pilot's body had snapped back with such force that the man's neck had broken.

The main rotor still rotated above them, but without power. The aircraft revolved more slowly beneath it, the sound of rushing air around the machine heightening by the instant.

"Jack! What'll we do?" Ellen's voice was even, under control, the look in her eyes one of determination more than terror.

"Just keep in your seats, brace yourselves, heads between your knees and fingers locked behind your necks!" Jack was already half out of his seat, David starting to do the same. "No, David! Stay with the girls! Do it! I'm counting on you, son!"

The blue that had been the sky was gone. Blackness surrounded them. The aircraft's only illumination was a pair of battery-operated emergency lights; they cast a yellow and flickering light, as if they, too, were about to fail.

The helicopter's sharply downward-angled nose coupled with the relentless twisting motion of the fuselage beneath the powerlessly spinning main rotor caused Jack's body to be slapped hard against the fuselage the moment he launched himself out of his seat. There were plenty of times that he had written about fictional characters flying helicopters. As he hauled himself to his knees, he recalled ruefully that there were even more times when the good guy would bring down an enemy helicopter with a disabling shot to the tail rotor, forcing the chopper to angle downward into the ground, to destruction.

There was no tail-rotor power.

The smoke from the burning insulation was thick, making the emergency lights seem even dimmer, stranger. Jack's eyes began to tear, and his throat began to close.

Jack half threw himself toward the cockpit. He landed hard on his knees, his head slamming against the head of the dead man with bone-jarring impact. Jack's vision blurred for an instant and the left side of his forehead began to ache. He shook his head to clear it. The only chance without power was to let the helicopter bring itself down, but in horizontal flight. Helicopter-pilot training included powerless landings, but somewhere at the back of his mind, from something he'd read or some expert with whom he'd spoken, he recalled that the key was to keep the machine horizontal and hope for a smooth, flat spot to land.

A helicopter's horizontal stabilizer was invariably located below the tail rotor. But finding the location of the control for the stabilizer was another matter—because his head ached so badly that he couldn't think clearly. The pounding in Jack's head, the roaring of the aircraft's slipstream in his ears, the realization that he had only seconds before the machine crashed—all of this was blocking him from thinking.

"Jack! Remember? Helicopters require hand and foot coordination, don't they?"

A smile crossed Jack Naile's lips.

There was no time to push the dead pilot from his seat, no time for anything but to wedge himself onto the console beside the pilot and get a hand on the joystick. The hydraulics might still work just enough to level the main rotor.

Ball lightning was everywhere around them, the sky still unremittingly black, everything above and below them black, except for what seemed like something viewed drunkenly in the very center of a kaleidoscope. And that was neither above nor below them, merely present, there.

He felt a slight change in the aircraft's attitude to the ground, but not enough. The nose was still dangerously low, and the helicopter's fuselage was pitched to starboard. The earth—treetops, boulders—was rocketing toward them, pouring out of the spot within the kaleidoscope lens, about to engulf them. There were pedals. Jack hit the seat harness' quick release and shoved the dead man from the pilot's seat and into the space between the seat and fuselage, hoping against hope that his brain was working and that the pedals were, indeed, linked to the horizontal stabilizer.

Jack worked one of the pedals by feel, eyes on the nose, not knowing which pedal he'd depressed. Simultaneously, he pulled back and left on the joystick.

"The nose is coming up! Hang on!"

The dead pilot's body was slipping forward, half covering Jack's left side.

Seat belt. Jack need to strap himself in. If he released the joystick, changed the orientation of his foot to whichever pedal it was, he might lose what little control he had.

No time.

"This is it! I love you guys—"

The aircraft touched the ground, bounced hard, and lurched violently, the dead body of the pilot hurtling forward, smashing out the windshield glass. A rock or tree stump punched through the fuselage undercarriage—something, Jack didn't know what—and started can opening the aircraft from the bottom.

The helicopter stopped as suddenly as if it had slammed into a wall of granite. Jack felt himself flung forward, flying, saw a blur of green and gray and blood red, then blackness.

Clarence Jones dropped the container of orange juice, spilling the yellow liquid all across his kitchen counter. A paroxysm raced across his spine, and he closed his eyes, a sadness unlike anything he had known since the death of his mother seizing his heart and mind.

"Jesus," he whispered. Somehow, it had happened and they were gone.

He left the orange juice and called the emergency number at the movie-production site. "This is the Nailes' nephew, Clarence Jones. Have you heard from them?"

The woman who'd answered the telephone said nothing for a long moment, and then asked if she could put him on hold. After several excruciating minutes, she finally came back to the line. When she did speak, her voice was choked with emotion.

CHAPTER
❖ FIVE ❖

"You'd be proud of your son, Jack," Ellen was saying.

Jack merely lay there, head cradled in his wife's lap as she knelt on the ground, hugging him.

"I thought you just might be dead despite it all, this time-travel thing. I thought you might be, but told myself you wouldn't be, and the time-travel thing has nothing to do with it."

Jack's own voice sounded odd to him. "I thought I was maybe dead, too."

"David couldn't get the fuselage door open and the cockpit was already in flames. Lizzie and I tried helping him. It was no good. The locking mechanism was jammed. He spotted a case bolted to the fuselage, opened it. It was some sort of survival kit. Anyway, there was an axe and a spare first-aid kit. He handed the first aid kit to Lizzie, told us to stand back, and he split the locking mechanism for the fuselage door with one swing of the axe.

"He got us out, used the axe to break into the cargo compartment and started getting out our stuff before the whole aircraft went up in flames or exploded. I told him to leave the luggage, that it wasn't worth the risk. He ignored me, of course, ignored his sister. We couldn't have tried to stop him physically, because we were already running toward you."

"But David's okay, right?"

"He's fine, Jack. Rescued the attaché case with the gold and diamonds, got all the luggage, your gun cases, even your cowboy hat."

Jack started to speak, but couldn't. He felt tears welling up in his eyes and his throat tightening, but not from smoke this time.

"David got away from the helicopter about thirty seconds before it blew up. He lit a cigarette as it happened. I told him he was a hero. Lizzie told him he was a hero. All David said was, 'Dad saved our lives. He's the hero.'"

Jack Naile lost it and wept uncontrollably.

Miraculously, it didn't seem as if Jack had broken anything, not even redislocated his right shoulder, something she had really expected from the position his body had been in when they reached him. Ellen had examined him to the extent of her quite limited medical training and when he seemed willing, encouraged him to try to stand up. The best way to get well was to act well, she'd always believed. And, with the afternoon waning, with no idea where they were except that their present location would have been an unpleasant one if a mountain lion or bear decided to get curious, there was little choice but to get in motion.

The weather was much colder than it had been when they'd boarded the helicopter, and the night promised to be colder still. If Jack could handle it, they had to get going somewhere, probably down and away from the mountains. At worst, they needed to find a sheltered area and water. Then David could use the helicopter's axe to cut firewood, and, if they found water, they could find a way to boil some for drinking purposes and stay by the fire for warmth as well as to scare away any wild animals.

When Jack did stand up, aside from being wobbly and visibly quite sore, he seemed to be all right. "You sure you can handle this? We can always wait a while longer if you like."

"I'm sore, but I'm cool," Jack told her.

"I'm going to have such fun counting all the bruises you'll have, especially if they're anything like the one on the left side of your forehead. You don't even have a bump, though. See, this wasn't any big deal."

"Sure. Everybody should be in a helicopter crash. Good for what ails you, huh?" Jack became more serious. "What about the pilot?"

Ellen's face grew somber then she shook her head. She checked her husband's vision to see if his eyes could follow a moving object, inquired about blurriness, nausea. The bruise on his head spelled the possibility of concussion, if nothing worse. But he'd displayed none of the obvious signs of which she was aware. When they reached some resting place, if either of the microfiche readers had survived without being shattered—there was an unsettling rattle from the case housing the video camera—she would probe more deeply into the symptoms of concussion.

"There's something I've got to do," Jack said. He leaned over and kissed Lizzie's forehead, then tilted her face up toward his and kissed her lightly on the lips. Lizzie hugged her father, and then Ellen put her arm around her daughter's shoulders. Slowly, a little unsteadily, Jack walked toward where David sat beside the cases and luggage.

Jack lit a cigarette. He offered one to David, who merely shook his head.

Ellen could hear David as he said, "'Jack Naile and his family were on their way to California, but there was an accident with their wagon.'"

Ellen watched as Jack leaned over and kissed David's forehead. David didn't pull away, but didn't help, either.

Ellen closed her eyes. Not a single aircraft had passed overhead. There had been not the slightest sound that could have been a truck engine or a chain saw. But the absence of such phenomena was unnecessary. As David had chosen to put into words, Ellen knew deep inside herself, no words necessary.

They weren't in the twentieth century anymore . . .

Despite his soreness, Jack Naile announced, "We've got to take the most direct route that we can to get out of these mountains. The highway—or the stage road along the ridgeline—whatever or whenever it is—should be easy enough to find. If we find—when we find—the road, all we have to do is follow it away from the mountains and we're bound to find a ranch or farm. Worst case, we'll reach Atlas in a day or so, whatever century it is. David?"

"Dad?"

They stood about one hundred yards downslope from the gutted helicopter.

"I need you to take that axe and mark some of the trees as we go along, so we can backtrack to this spot without much difficulty. We've got too much stuff to carry. So, before that, take the Winchester 94 and load it up, then look around the immediate area for a safe place to stash what we can't carry for maybe as long as a week or ten days. Use the axe to mark a path from the helicopter to where we leave the stuff. Lizzie?"

"Daddy?"

"Help your mom with organizing what we can't travel without and what we'll leave behind. The guns won't be in the cases, so we can use the rifle and pistol case for additional storage of anything that might be easily damaged when left behind."

"If we're not in the nineteenth century, Jack, being visibly armed won't be a good idea," Ellen supplied.

"Agreed. It might not be such a good idea even if we are, coming up on some little ranch house or something. David and I'll each carry a rifle. It's not going to look odd with two guys carrying lever action rifles. Each of you ladies carries one of the little guns in a pocket or something—the Seecamp and the derringer. Everything else gets thrown into a suitcase. And, remember, when you guys pack and separate, we can't carry too much ammo because it's too heavy, but we'll want just about fifty rounds of .45 Colt and twenty rounds of .45-70, plus what'll be in the guns."

"You want to bury the stuff or just cover it from view?" David asked, picking up the axe.

❋ ❋ ❋

Their trek toward some outpost of civilization wasn't anywhere near as long a one as she had supposed that it might be. And Elizabeth couldn't deny that the scenery was gorgeous. The farther down the mountain they went, the more abundant and luxurious were the trees, pine trees of astounding height, many as tall as or taller than those in their neighbor's back lot in Georgia, and those were taller than three- or four-story buildings. She recognized spruce trees, but that was the limit of her knowledge of evergreens (except for magnolias, which, unlike in the climate outside her bedroom window back home, would not grow here.)

The conifers, on the other hand, were either suffering some sort of blight or it was not only the year that had changed (if it had), but also the season. Leaves were everywhere, except in the trees.

Elizabeth had been hoping against hope for some sign of late-twentieth-century civilization, and her heart raced then sank with her first glimpse of the small house, lean-tos and two horse corrals still perhaps four city blocks distant. She had a case with a pair of her father's binoculars slung from her shoulder. She took out the binoculars, raised them to her eyes and adjusted the focus as she studied the landscape below. Beneath the shelter of one of the lean-tos was a wagon, what her father called a "buckboard" whenever he referenced one on those occasions when she could not escape watching a western movie. It looked not quite new, but not like an antique, either.

"If no one mentions hearing an explosion or seeing a fire, remember, don't mention it, either. Okay?" Elizabeth's mother told them.

"Gotchya," David agreed.

"And if somebody does mention it, let your father do the talking, and all of us will back him up. He's the word-smith, remember, so he tells lies for a living."

David laughed.

Elizabeth's father murmured, "Thanks a lot." Then he looked over his shoulder at David. "Hold that rifle with your hand over the receiver and keep the muzzle pointed toward the ground. That's the least threatening way."

"Right."

Elizabeth couldn't take her eyes off the ranch ahead.

Maybe half again the distance beyond the ranch house from where they were there were a few cattle, just grazing, with no fences that Elizabeth could see. A dozen or so chickens wandered aimlessly in the front yard, pecking at the ground. There was a windmill—she didn't know why she hadn't noticed that earlier—and it was mounted high on something that looked like a wooden version of one of the big metal-framed utility poles that connected one town's power grid to another. From what she had read of the period, knowing this time transfer was going to happen, Elizabeth imagined that the windmill's sole purpose had nothing to do with running electrical conveniences but was for pumping water instead. No wires of any type led into the house. There was no satellite dish.

They would be meeting people from the past for the first time, people who were dead before she had ever been born. Meeting people meant making first impressions. Elizabeth put away the binoculars and instinctively took stock of her clothes. The bib-front overalls that she wore were a little dirty and a lot wrinkled. Her jacket—"Daddy!"

"What is it, sweetheart?"

"We all have zippers on our jackets, and they didn't have zippers in the old days, did they?"

"Whitcomb L. Judson displayed a primitive zipper at the Chicago World's Fair in 1893, and the modern zipper was in use by World War I. Zippers weren't in general circulation until the 1930s."

David was laughing. "Aren't you glad you asked, Liz?"

"Point is," Elizabeth's father continued, "if the zippers get noticed, all we say is something like, 'Yeah, this guy named Judson invented them. They're really popular where we come from.' And we leave it at that, which isn't telling a lie at all."

"What about my deck shoes?" David asked, as if daring his father.

"It's like an Indian moccasin, but with a harder sole."

"Lizzie and I are wearing pants and bras," Elizabeth's mother threw in.

"Women were more physically modest—at least openly—in these days than in the time we come from. So nobody'll see your underwear. As for pants, after the accident with the wagon, with God only knew how long a walk over rugged terrain ahead of us, wearing pants like a man seemed like the only sensible choice for you guys. Try me on another one," her father dared.

"Ohh, ohh!" Elizabeth's mother exclaimed in an artificial sounding high voice. "How do men just ever stand wearing these terrible trousers?"

"That was a good one, Mom," Elizabeth proclaimed.

"Thank you, Lizzie."

"Okay, Dad," David volunteered, shifting his burdens and removing his wristwatch. "These things didn't come around until World War I, either."

"Good point, David. Make sure to keep your sleeves down so the paler skin where the watchband covers isn't visible." As he spoke, Elizabeth's father opened the bracelet of his Rolex and hid the watch in a pocket of his bomber jacket.

"I'm Tom, and this here's my wife, Mary. We're the Bledsoe's." The man was holding a rifle, but had a pleasant enough look about him.

"Pleased to meet y'all," Mary Bledsoe seconded, a shy smile crossing her pale lips, her hands bunched on the edges of a long white cotton apron.

A girl about Elizabeth's age approached hesitantly.

"Come on, girl. Come on up here and meet these folks." Tom Bledsoe waved the girl forward.

"Hey," Lizzie said, smiling.

No one could resist Lizzie's beautiful smile, and Jack Naile had that confirmed when the Bledsoe girl sort of half curtsied and said softly, "A pleasure to meet y'all folks. I'm Helen."

Jack Naile deduced that it was his turn. "I'm Jack Naile, and this is my wife, Ellen, our daughter, Elizabeth, and our son, David. We were on our way to California, crossing the mountains, when there was a terrible accident with our wagon."

"You poor things!" Mary Bledsoe blurted out, wringing her hands around her apron and then smoothing it as she went on. "Helen!"

"Yes, ma'am?"

"Go start puttin' food on the table while I find Mrs. Naile and her daughter something decent to wear. Scoot, child!" As Helen ran off—she had a good stride, skirts raised in order to accomplish it—Mary Bledsoe started gathering Ellen and Elizabeth to her, like a mother bird folding her wings about the babies. "It's terrible for you poor things."

Despite the fact that Mary Bledsoe seemed positively outraged that females—even strangers—were forced by circumstance to wear trousers, it was easy to see who wore the pants in the Bledsoe household. Jack Naile looked over at Tom Bledsoe. "David and I didn't know what we might bump into. Didn't want to put you folks off by walking up here with these." He gestured with the 1895 Marlin lever action that was in his right hand.

"Man'd be a fool for sure not goin' armed in these parts, critters with four legs and critters with two, and of 'em, the two-legged kind is the worse."

David asked, "Crooks—I mean outlaws?"

"Reckon y'all didn't pass through Atlas, didchya?"

Jack answered, "We were in kind of a hurry to get over the mountains into California, and we had all the supplies we needed, until the wreck, anyway."

Tom Bledsoe had long since lowered his rifle—a Winchester 1873—from a casual port arms to rest against his leg, the fingers of his left hand barely touching the muzzle to support it. "You'll need a hand fetching anything else from the wreck?"

"There's nothing left worth salvaging."

"That's a shame. You folks don't have much left."

"How far is it into town, into Atlas?"

"About two hours by wagon. My wife, Mrs. Bledsoe, her sister Margaret keeps school in Atlas, and young Bobby Lorkin rode out not more'n an hour back tellin' us Margaret was feelin' poorly and wanted Mary to look in on her. We reckon to set out early 'morrow mornin'. Y'all got people in Atlas? Well, reckon not if'n y'all didn't go a-stoppin' there. You can stay with us a spell."

Jack responded, "You and your family are very kind. If it's no trouble, we would very much like to spend the night tonight and take you up on that ride into Atlas. But I heard tell, I think, that there was a hotel in Atlas, or maybe we could rent a cottage."

"I never been inside no hotel, but it's a fact there is one. Ain't no cottages I heard 'bout. Lemme take some of y'all's possibles and let's go on up to the house." And with that, Tom Bledsoe grabbed up one of the suitcases in his right hand. "Never seen no thing like this afore. Travellin' bag?"

"That's what it is," David agreed.

"Leather, huh?"

"Special kind of leather called expanded polyvinyl," David told Tom Bledsoe, smiling.

Mary Bledsoe was Elizabeth's height, a little over five foot three. Mary had three dresses besides the one that she wore, four extra aprons (one with a bib front and lace trim all around it) and a solitary skirt.

Holding one of the dresses in front of her, Ellen realized that it was four inches too short, about the length that a young girl might wear. She opted to borrow the dark gray circular skirt and wear it with her own sleeveless top, but took the shawl Mary Bledsoe offered to cover the unseemly sight of bare arms. Elizabeth fared better, one of Mary's dresses—a lighter gray—was a perfect fit except for the bustline, which was tight. Young Helen provided Lizzie with a shawl.

"Don't have me much in underthings," Mary had confided to them.

"We'll be just fine, Mary," Ellen had told her, grateful not to have to wrestle with weird and uncomfortable underwear. By forcing the skirt down closer to her hips than her waist, it wound up at a respectable length.

Ellen and Elizabeth helped Helen set the table with very pretty plain white china, likely Mary's best. Mary finished the cooking. There was a potbellied stove at the center of the solitary large room, but the hearth was what was used for cooking. When it was cold, bricks would be heated on the hearth and placed in the beds in the two other rooms of the house. By comparison to frontier homes about which Ellen had read, the Bledsoe place was a condo on Chicago's Gold Coast, even boasting a well-fitted board floor.

When Lizzie volunteered to assist Helen with fetching water, the mere mention made Ellen Naile realize that she hadn't peed since a few minutes before boarding the helicopter.

Ellen Naile almost asked, "Where's the john?" Instead, she asked, "The outhouse?"

Mary Bledsoe's face flushed at the mention of something so intimate, so personal. "'Hind the house, o' course."

"Of course. Thank you."

The outhouse—complete with crescent moon cutout on the door, also handy for letting flies in during the right season—would have defied even Jack's powers of description. Pulling the skirt's waistband up to her natural waist, her face twisting into a grimace designed to limit oxygen intake through the nose, Ellen Naile stepped inside, for once in her life wishing that she were a man.

David had laughed at both of them when he saw them, and Jack had merely smiled, asking, "Having fun, darling?"

"Oh, peachy, Jack." Ellen was wearing an apron. After she had volunteered to help Mary finish preparing dinner, Mary had run to fetch one for her. Ellen, despite her sex, had worn an apron voluntarily perhaps half a dozen times in her adult life. "What have you guys been doing, Jack?"

"Tell her, David."

David sat down on the crate he'd brought in, evidently bidden to do so by Tom Bledsoe. There were seven for dinner and only six chairs in the entire house, including the rocking chair and one of those little fireplace chairs with a spatulate-shaped back, a heart-shaped cutout at its center.

"Well," David began, "Mr. Bledsoe kindly showed us his tack, let us see the horses and showed us the field he's going to plant next spring. He's got one fine manure pile, let me tell you."

"Gosh, menfolk have all the fun, don't they, Helen?" Lizzie lamented, wiping her hands on her apron.

Helen didn't say a word, only smiled enigmatically.

Dinner was a surprisingly tasty rabbit stew with a

number of overcooked and hard-to-identify vegetables, great-tasting dumplings and fresh wheat bread. David had always looked older than he was and was solicited by Tom Bledsoe to join him and Jack for a "snort from the jug and a chaw on the settin' porch" while the women saw to "clearin' and all."

Ellen Naile would have loved to be able to turn herself invisible and watch and listen in; but since she could not, she helped Mary, Lizzie and Helen make quick work of the dishes (in a way that made her shudder to think that she'd just eaten off of these same dishes). There was no mention of joining the men on the porch or having an adult beverage for themselves, but Mary put on the kettle for tea and showed off her latest needlepoint, confiding that there was always so much mending to do that she had little time for such frivolous activity.

Despite the unspeakable outhouse, clean as such things went, she imagined, and the awkward clothing and social status, Ellen Naile realized that she wasn't really having such a bad time. It had been years since they had dined in the home of friends.

Ellen and Lizzie were washing the breakfast dishes, helping Mary while she fed the chickens and collected the eggs and milked the cow. It was already late, according to something she'd overheard Tom Bledsoe saying. By Ellen's own reckoning, the time was about six in the morning. Jack and David were assisting Tom with hitching up the team and feeding and watering the rest of the stock.

"I think I felt a mouse near my foot last night," Lizzie confided, edging closer to Ellen at the wash basin.

"It was probably Helen's toe," Ellen reassured her daughter, thinking all the while that Lizzie was probably right. Lizzie and Helen had, at least, had a bed—Helen's. Ellen's own sleeping accommodations had been to share the bed with Mary Bledsoe that Mary normally shared with Tom. The bed had seemed clean enough, the mattress too soft, too uncomfortable, the bed's framework easily felt every time Ellen rolled over. Mary had only one nightgown, and it wouldn't do to sleep in twentieth-century underwear, so Ellen had slept in her clothes. In the morning, the once-unwrinkled skirt was no longer that way.

Lizzie was lamenting, "And that outhouse! Yuck! I just won't go, Momma!"

"A couple of hours riding along a dirt road in the back of a wagon with no springs will make you feel differently. Go potty!"

"They don't wash or anything!"

"You'll hurt their feelings. Think of it this way. Would you really want to use a bathtub set up in front of the fireplace? I don't think so."

"My hair's all greasy, Momma!"

"So's mine, so's your father's and so's your brother's. We'll find a way of getting clean once we get to town." Ellen Naile wished that she felt as certain about that as she hoped she sounded.

Ellen had spoken precious little with her husband since their arrival at the Bledsoe place, the way of things between men and women in this time. But in a brief moment Jack had told her, "Bledsoe says that things are a little wild in town, advised us to carry pistols if we had them. Make sure Lizzie's up on using a Seecamp, and you know how to use that derringer. Each of you carries once we start for town."

She'd given Jack a snotty "Yes, sir, Jack, sir," but realized that he was only looking out for them.

With the dishes through, she told Lizzie, "Hey! How's about this? We go out to the outhouse, and I'll use it first, then you'll be using it after me? Okay?"

"Yeah, dammit," Lizzie moaned.

"Ladies don't talk that way, now or anytime."

When they stepped together onto the front porch, the potential lethality of all of the unknown factors into which they were about to insert themselves hit her with the force of a rock. Jack was dressed in the same gray long-sleeved shirt and dirt-stained black Levis he'd worn the previous day. The item of apparel that was different was the gun belt, the black Hollywood rig that Sam Andrews had made for him, the gleaming, long-barreled Colt revolver sitting almost jauntily in its silver concho-trimmed holster.

When she noticed David, helping Bledsoe with hitching the team, the rock that had hit her struck again; but this time it had grown to boulder proportions. Her seventeen-year-old son had Jack's second Colt, the old blued one that someone had cut the barrel back on to an "unofficial" five inches. He wore it in the old brown-leather Arvo Ojala gunfighter rig his father had so proudly traded for years ago, which David had never worn, never even wanted to try on without being forced.

David had fired a gun under his father's tutelage for the very first time when he was only five. In this time and place, seventeen was a grown man's age and, if others were armed, it would be incumbent upon David to be armed as well. Dumb clothes and outhouses were an inconvenience; Jack and David facing an armed encounter every time they stepped outside into a street was frightening.

"Y'all look like one of them 'range detective' fellers Jess Fowler went and hired on," Tom Bledsoe remarked out of the blue.

"Range detective?" David asked from behind them.

"A euphemism for hired gunfighter," Jack told his son. "You remember Jack Palance in *Shane*?" Jack Naile dropped the idea, because, even though David had seen the classic film, he would have pushed it from his thoughts because it was a western.

"Jack who?"

"Famous guy where we come from, Tom. And *Shane* started out as a book."

"Can't say I read much, 'ceptin' the *Bible* and them catalogs down at the general store. Giddyup, there, Dusty." Tom Bledsoe flicked the reins to the team, Jack Naile noticing the man's perfect ease. Dusty was obviously the horse on the right side, and had been lagging behind the other animal. When the reins cracked, the rein on the right came down hardest.

The four women occupied the wagon bed, Ellen and Mary sitting facing forward, Lizzie and Helen facing back (which was probably making Lizzie a little car sick). David sat scrunched between Tom and Jack on the seat, his gun belt pulled around so that the holstered Colt lay over his right thigh.

"So, who's this Jess Fowler guy? Local big shot?"

"Don't rightly know a party'd call Jess Fowler that, but he owns half o' ever'thin' round these parts and has his damned eyes on—"

"Tom Bledsoe! In front of women to say such!"

"Sorry, Mary," Tom called back over his shoulder, but then turned to David and Jack, his voice barely above a whisper. "He's a sneakin' son o' a bitch for a fact." He spat tobacco juice and fell silent.

For once in her life, Ellen Naile wished that she had a fat butt. The added cushioning would have helped. While she and Liz were taking turns at the outhouse, they agreed to use the ride to pump as much useful information as possible out of the Bledsoe women, hoping that Jack and David would do the same as concerned Tom Bledsoe.

While the springless wagon bounced and jostled along what would someday become the highway their lost Chevy Suburban had driven/would drive over so effortlessly, they worked the "pump."

The actual year was 1896, but it was early fall rather than summer, the date September nineteenth. Atlas had not yet undergone the mining boom, which would be good news for David's financial empire-building. Real-estate values would be low and would increase dramatically.

Jess Fowler was the local rich bastard, and then some. Some of the "I never gossip none, y'all know" that Mary Bledsoe shared with them concerning Fowler, if there were any substance to it beyond rumor and hearsay, drew a chilling portrait of a megalomaniacal sociopath, like something out of one of Jack's old Hopalong Cassidy films—he loved them and thought that William Boyd was not only a fine actor, but had created an unforgettable character. Fowler owned much of the land and a substantial portion of the town which it surrounded, and he controlled much of the local government from behind the scenes.

Yet, more like a twentieth century rackets boss, Jess Fowler kept himself whistle clean with the law, letting his hired minions—the range detectives—do all of the dirty work.

Atlas, as an entity, was barely getting along. Fowler controlled the local economy with such a tight fist that he strangled economic growth or expansion, business dying unless it was his business. Ellen realized, sadly, that her family had done absolutely no research on the town in the years preceding the date of the photo from the magazine. That they could have been so shortsighted was, in the cold light of reality, beyond sobering.

The next few years, she realized, were a total unknown. Jack could have been killed, the store named by David after his late father. The possibilities were endlessly scary.

Mary Bledsoe, true to her sex, also craved information. She had pegged them as Easterners; Ellen confided that all of them had been born in Chicago and lived, for a number of years, in Georgia, not too far north of Atlanta. The combination of Chicago and Atlanta and having the apparent wherewithal to travel all the way to California seemed to have suggested to Mary Bledsoe that she—Ellen—and her daughter, who Mary evidently thought was older than fifteen, would have all the latest word on fashions of the day.

As Ellen and Elizabeth—quite valiantly, fantastic bullshitter that Lizzie could be—tried bluffing their way through talk of bustles, hats and hemlines, Ellen silently wondered if she would go mad here. A bustle would have been great at the moment, had she been able to sit on it; hats were something she wore with less frequency than aprons; hemlines, in the era from which she hailed, could be anywhere from the ankle to just south of the crotch. And Ellen Naile could not have cared less.

Ellen had a terrible thought. If the photo of Jack, Lizzie and Davey—her own image conspicuously absent—hadn't been taken by her, her being behind the camera the accepted explanation within the family, had she died of boredom? Or merely been institutionalized among the insane?

David was given a turn at the reins, and the only time before that he had driven a horse-drawn conveyance was when he had just turned eight. The occasion involved a horse-drawn carriage in New Orleans and a driver who had become fed up (albeit, good-naturedly) with David kibitzing his driving techniques. That David was nine years older and driving two horses this time instead of one did not inspire Ellen Naile with that much confidence.

Bledsoe and Jack were talking about manly stuff, most pointedly about Jack's revolver. "Yeah, a friend fixed it for me, Tom. And another friend refinished it. It has a fourteen ounce trigger pull."

"I'd admire tryin' it when we rest the horses, Jack."

"And I'd admire trying that thumb buster on your hip, Tom." Bravo, Jack! Ellen thought. Don't let that guy hold your pistol unless you're holding his. She was going crazy,

Ellen decided; aside from the fact that her thoughts could have been some sort of perverted sexual reference, they were certainly paranoid. The Bledsoe family had been marvelous to them and there was no reason to suppose that any malicious thoughts had crossed any of their minds. Still, caution was a good thing.

His father had been practicing, David Naile decided. Jack Naile, who had been writing about guns and shooting since 1973 (a ridiculous contradiction, of course, knowing that it was only 1896), had always, with admirable honesty, portrayed his own marksmanship skills as mediocre, which they always had been. That his father had taken steps to correct that was obvious.

Firing the seven-and-one-half-inch barreled Colt Single Action Army at a deadfall tree from a one-handed dueling stance, he had just placed five earsplittingly loud shots into a circle of about four inches at what David estimated as just a little less than fifty feet.

David looked back toward the wagon. His mother, sister and the two Bledsoe women were holding their hands over their ears.

When Jack Naile reloaded the revolver and handed it to Tom Bledsoe in exchange for Bledsoe's less spectacular looking and shorter barreled Colt, Bledsoe eyed the gun almost reverentially.

"Watch that trigger pull. Really light."

Bledsoe raised the revolver and the first shot went off into the air. "Dang! That ain't like nothin' I ever shot 'fore."

This time, the revolver was lined up before Bledsoe

even cocked the hammer. There was a reassuring mark on the dead tree. Bledsoe fired out the last three rounds and, David had to admit, wasn't as good with the gun as his father had been, but hit what he aimed at.

David watched as his father made to fire Bledsoe's revolver.

The gun barked, a puff of gray smoke emanating from the end of the barrel (his father would, correctly, call that portion of the revolver the "muzzle"). The bullet hit the dirt in front of the tree.

David's ears rang so badly that he was certain it would be hours before he'd be able to hear properly. He was used to wearing ear protection on those occasions when he did any shooting; ear and eye protection were safety considerations that his father and mother had always driven home with both him and his sister.

His father changed the way he held the gun: if memory served, it was called a "Weaver stance." He held the revolver in his dominant hand, pressing against his left hand, his left shoulder turned nearly toward the target.

The revolver discharged again; the tree was struck this time. Three more shots—David's ears felt hollow, somehow—and the dead tree was "killed" three more times.

David watched as his father and Tom Bledsoe exchanged revolvers, exchanged pleasantries concerning them. He could hardly hear much of anything.

Jack inspected his revolver briefly, drew the hammer back to second position—when a genuine Colt or one of the twentieth-century Italian copies was cocked, the sound seemed to spell "C-o-l-t"—and swung open the loading gate. He punched out the empty brass and reloaded with his modern ammo, slipping a cartridge into the first chamber, skipping the next, and then loading the remaining four. Drawing the hammer to full stand rotated the cylinder in such a way that the empty chamber was under the hammer. He lowered the hammer gently.

Had Bledsoe used cartridges from his own belt, they would have been filled with black powder and necessitated more cleaning of Jack's pet Colt than Jack would have liked. There were two thousand rounds of Federal 225-grain lead hollow points packed in the Suburban, which, somehow, Jack Naile couldn't quite give up on seeing again. In what was now the objective future, the remains of a late-twentieth-century wall outlet had been found in the ruin of the house they would build. Unless things had already changed, that modern outlet had to get into the objective present somehow, and there were four dozen such outlets packed in the Suburban.

In another hour or so, they would reach Atlas. Ellen and Lizzie would need to acquire proper clothing for the period at once, which meant exchanging some of the gold in the attaché case. The diamonds would have to wait.

"Reckon y'all and the boy there oughta 'member this. My Mary," Bledsoe said suddenly as the most remote edge of Atlas came into view on the horizon, "she's a handsome woman, I always considered. Y'all's women are right beautiful."

"Thank you," Jack Naile told him.

"Ain't the point, Jack, David. Jess Fowler's range

detectives been known to'up'n start a pistol fight over women was a whole lot less favored than y'all's. What I mean t'say is, hope y'all's as good at a'jerkin' that fancy pistol down on a man as shootin' at that ol' dead tree."

With genuine sincerity, Jack Naile almost whispered, "Let's pray that we don't have to find that out."

CHAPTER SIX

Talk drifted to politics while the buckboard creaked and groaned across the mile or so remaining of the flat and comparatively barren expanse at the end of which lay the town of Atlas. David Naile, not interested greatly in politics per se, liked that kind of conversation nonetheless, because politics and business could be inextricably linked.

Tom Bledsoe spat every time he mentioned the word *Democrat*, making Bledsoe's own political bent obvious.

Atlas, like most of Nevada in the post Civil War period, was a Republican stronghold, but Jess Fowler had thrown his weight to the Democrats in the state government. Because the Democrats were a minority who wished to improve their lot, Fowler could figuratively—and literally—get away with murder as long as he provided financial support. As a result, Atlas was, effectively, rendered an island in a hostile and violent sea controlled by Fowler.

Steve Fowler, a notorious bank robber and killer, was

often seen out in the county, roaming about unmolested between his murderous rampages of lawlessness, occasionally in company with his older brother, Jess, and the county sheriff.

Republican loyalty was the reason that Nevada was a state and not a territory, statehood having been rushed through in the aftermath of the Civil War. During the War Between the States—"In Georgia, where we come from," David interjected, "some people still refer to that as the War of Northern Aggression."—Nevada had supplied the Union with much of the financial capital needed to keep Mr. Lincoln's armies marching and winning. Because of the rush to statehood, Nevada was in many ways still wild and untamed.

"Reckon y'all weren't ol' 'nough to fight," Bledsoe said to David's father.

David smiled as he heard his father's response. "I'm forty-six and this is 1896. An eleven-year-old wouldn't have gotten too far trying to join up." His father had just given the impression that he was born in 1850, without actually lying and saying that he was.

"What caused Yankees like y'all t' move t' Georgia there?"

"Well, I make my living as a writer, and Ellen and I just got tired of the hard winters in Chicago right around the time Lizzie was born. So we moved south." That was all true. Brilliant, David thought. Then David's father laughed a little conspiratorially. "I never did push the idea that I was a distant relative of President Grant's vice-president, though." True again.

Bledsoe laughed out loud. "Dang, ain't y'all the smart

ones! Yeah, them ol' Rebs for fact woulda wanted t' skin y'all's hide."

"We found the people in Georgia to be pretty much like people everywhere: lots of nice ones and some few not so nice. It's a good place to live—Georgia."

"I've got a question, Mr. Bledsoe," David interrupted.

"Ask away, boy."

"How is it that a man who spits when he says the word _Democrat_ and calls Southerners _Rebs_ has what I'd call a Southern accent?"

"Pa was born in southern Illinois, and Momma's people had come out from the Carolinas. A whole mess o' families from them parts moved west to Kansas and, lemme tell y'all, boy, soundin' Southern weren't no good thang in certain o' them parts o' Kansas in them times."

"'Bloody Kansas,'" David's father interjected.

"It were that fo' sure. Yeah. It were that." And, abruptly, as if lost in some unpleasant reverie, Tom Bledsoe fell silent.

Bledsoe turned the wagon and, stretched out before them, in all its lack of splendor, lay Atlas, Nevada.

The town was one long street of clapboard buildings, mostly whitewashed, some painted gray or slate-blue. Corrals—each with one or more lean-tos—were set at the near and far ends of the street. Beyond the farthest of the buildings and the respective corrals lay a half-dozen or so smallish tents and one larger one, these all faded khaki in color.

The Bledsoes' wagon turned right midway along the main street—it was as broad in the past as it had been in the future—and into what was the beginning of the residential street Jack remembered. In 1896, there were but a few houses, no more than a dozen. These were also clapboard, some with nicely maintained white fences and smallish front yards, all of the houses looking to have been built from the same simple architectural plan, to have been coated from the same lot of white paint.

As if proudly wearing symbols of defiance, one of the houses had green-painted window shutters. These brazen badges of nonconformity were slatted, as usual, but, rather than the upper edges being mere unadorned one-by-two, their tops rose several inches upward, forming almost a heart shape. There was a cutout of a heart at the center of each of these crown pieces. It reminded David of the small chair by the fireplace.

"That your sister-in-law's house, Tom?" Jack asked.

"Them shutters, right! Y'all got the eye, Jack."

"You made those?" Without waiting for a reply, Jack declared, "You're one hell of a good carpenter, especially with hand tools."

That was a slip up, and David mentally noted it.

"Y'all know o' some other kind o' tool?"

"I just meant that carpenters' tools require a great deal of skill and patience."

"Learnt carpentry back in what y'all called Bloody Kansas when I was a sprout. Pa was right smart at it, and they was a lot o' call fo' pine boxes and such, if'n y'all get my drift."

The era of fighting between pro- and anti-slavery factions within Kansas had precipitated some of the most prolific bloodshed in the history of the United States, and schooled the country for the conflict to come. John Brown was that school's most infamous alumnus, graduating to the raid on the arsenal at Harper's Ferry. David's father had made them watch the Errol Flynn movie *Santa Fe Trail,* and Raymond Massey's portrayal of John Brown was so scary David actually remembered it.

"You've had a rough life, Tom," Jack Naile said, sounding like he meant it.

"Ain't we all."

"And you're a bit of a philosopher, too."

"I ain't no what-you-said; I'm a Republican."

"That, too, then," David supplied, imagining his father was about to go into a lengthy explanation of the meaning of the term *philosopher.* Instead, the buckboard stopped.

Margaret Diamond was a smallish woman, quite pretty and refreshingly well-spoken, her house neat in the extreme, except for piles of books and sheaves of writing paper. Mary looked, by comparison, old enough to be her sister's mother, if, in fact, there were any family resemblance. There was none apparent, except that both sisters had the same color hair and eyes; brown and brown.

The meeting with Margaret Diamond was brief, the woman obviously feeling quite "poorly." With admirable politeness, she had offered to prepare tea and vouchsafed that she had some little cakes, but Ellen had declined on their behalf. "We really have to get some clothes and find a place to stay."

Margaret seemed somewhat disconnected, one minute suggesting Mrs. Treacher's boarding house as the best of available accommodations, especially for ladies, then in the next breath switching subjects to lament that her pupils at Atlas' one-room schoolhouse would fall behind in their studies. Then she offered to make tea again, evidently failing to remember her earlier invitation.

Mrs. Treacher's boarding house was back on the main street, and Tom Bledsoe drove them there in his buckboard, accomplishing a U-turn with it in front of his sister-in-law's house. "She gets a fever now and again; ain't bad like the last time, I reckon."

Ellen, alone with Lizzie in the back of the buckboard, asked, "What sort of illness is it that Miss Diamond has?"

"Don't rightly know, ma'am, and that's fo' fact. Last time Doc Severinson was in Atlas—"

"Doc Severinson?" Jack repeated, incredulous.

"Y'all heard o' the Doc?"

"Forget it, Jack; it'll only confuse things," Ellen cautioned.

Jack nodded silently as Tom Bledsoe went on. "Leastways, ol' Doc tol' Margaret she oughta get herself down t' Carson City for a good looksee with the docs they got down there. But, Margaret, she don't cotton much t' leavin' her students fo' no week or two."

Ellen volunteered, "Maybe we can help, Lizzie and I."

"I'll tell Margaret, then, if'n y'all like."

"Sure," Lizzie volunteered.

Each "survival kit," aside from things like aspirin, acetaminophen tablets, antiseptic cream, bandages, water-purification tablets and a good knife, contained a small gold bar. Ellen, Elizabeth and David each had such a kit. Within the attaché case were the diamonds and three additional gold bars. Converting one of these to current United States money at the general store—which, somehow or another, Jack Naile realized that they would come to own—provided them with enough cash for their immediate needs and then some.

A "suite" of rooms at Mrs. Treacher's rented for the princely sum of twenty dollars a month, including clean linens, breakfast and dinner, which was called "supper." Mrs. Treacher was, at one time in an apparently quite distant past, British. She was a well-spoken woman, but her speech was very plain, and her usage was peculiarly stilted. As a guess, Jack Naile assumed that she might have spent her younger years "in service" to some household in England or in the eastern United States, following a husband west. She wore a simple silver wedding band, but there had been no mention of a Mr. Treacher. Short, plump, rosy-cheeked, she reminded Jack Naile of some movie version of a "typical" Swiss or German hausfrau.

With accommodations arranged for the immediate future, there were other pressing concerns, funds or the lack thereof fortunately not among them. The ample gold supply that the Naile family had brought with them into the past would carry them through, as David gauged it, for more than a year, providing sufficient opportunity to eventually bring the diamonds to San Francisco and convert these into serious money.

No one thought to be hungry, and by afternoon Ellen and Elizabeth were back at the general store acquiring clothing and other necessities.

There was little in the way of ready-to-wear, most

women apparently making their own clothing or engaging the services of the town's solitary dressmaker.

Jack and David fared little better, finding themselves faced with two alternatives: poorly cut, boxy-styled vested woolen suits or heavy, canvaslike work clothes. "It's a cinch Roy Rogers never would have shopped here," Jack remarked to his son. They were trying to determine if any of the suits would be close enough in size to be a decent fit.

"I'm not going to wear shit like this for the rest of my life," David announced.

"I know you've never thought a great deal of my sense of sartorial resplendence, but we can't start the first Nevada nudist colony, so pick some threads that'll make do for the time being. We can get down to Carson City after a while and find something better. We can order out of a catalogue, maybe. Anyway, once we own this place, we can stock it with clothes we'll all like—or at least tolerate."

David groaned, taking the most expensive suit of the few available. It was twelve dollars.

The Naile family's "suite" consisted of two bedrooms— surprisingly clean—and a small sitting room. The outhouse was behind the boarding house, of course, but there were chamber pots ("Who gets to clean these?" Lizzie asked the moment Mrs. Treacher had left them). There was a room at the end of the second-floor hallway with a large bathtub. Lizzie was given first dibs on the tub, but said she wouldn't use it unless her mother sat outside the door. Ellen agreed, but insisted on Lizzie doing the same for her.

Jack bathed last. It was safe to wear his Rolex on his wrist since no one could see him, and he smudged soapy water from its face to read the time. He'd reset the watch to local time shortly after they'd reached Atlas, and the luminous black face read nearly nine in the evening. All his life, Jack Naile had hated baths, seeing the concept of sitting in a bathtub as nothing more than simmering in one's own dirt; but there was no such thing as a shower to be had in Atlas, all the more reason to move forward on acquiring the property where they would have their house built. Even without the amenities packed within the Suburban, a shower could be rigged, a good one.

After a bland dinner at Mrs. Treacher's table, and conversation generally even more bland with a corset salesman, the traveling dentist (who had commended them on the apparently fine condition of their teeth) and a gun salesman, Jack had taken David with him and gone off to arrange a carriage for the following morning.

Upon their return to Mrs. Treacher's, the gun salesman had been seated on the boarding-house front porch smoking a cigar. His name was Ben or Bob something, and he was a tall man for the period, about five nine or ten, and wore a plain gray three-piece suit. His hair was blond and straight, slicked back over a high forehead that seemed to be gaining ground in a battle against his hairline. Jack judged the man's age at close to forty, but he seemed quite fit and trim. After a moment, David went inside and Jack lit a cigarette. "You're from back East, though I can't say I've seen prerolled cigarettes."

"They're much more convenient this way," Jack told him, his voice a little shaky sounding to him. He'd almost used the disposable Bic lighter from his pocket to fire the cigarette but had remembered at the very last second to strike a match against the porch rail instead. "So, what's a Colt Single Action Army revolver sell for these days?"

"I can get you a nice blued one for eighteen dollars. Nickel—but it will last longer—costs two dollars more. You'll see 'em higher, but not lower. That's sure a nice lookin' one on your hip."

Jack didn't offer to show it to the man, lest he notice that the gun hadn't been made yet and wouldn't be until 1971.

"Didn't figure you'd show me your gun, Mr. Naile."

"And why is that?"

"Me, as a salesman, I'm good with names. Bob Cranston's the name, and guns are my game." He laughed as he pulled a business card—one of the old, square kind, larger than its late-twentieth-century counterpart—from his vest pocket.

Jack took the card. "Thanks."

"I've never seen a man with a gun like that who didn't use it for making his living. You don't strike me as one of Fowler's range detectives, so that means you must've been a lawdog somewhere, back the other side of the Mississippi, maybe. Bein' a salesman, I got a good ear for the way people talk. Only two places from around here you and your wife and family could be from, and that's San Francisco or Denver, but I'd say Chicago's more like it. Policeman back there?"

"We're from Chicago originally, but we lived in Georgia for a while. And, no. I've never been a policeman. You'll have to excuse me. It's been good talking with you."

Jack had left the porch. He found that David was using the bath. Twenty minutes later, with water that was more cool than hot, it had been Jack's turn. He'd washed his hair first, and then bathed.

Jack checked the Rolex again; he'd have to find some way in which to wear his watch without attracting attention. He stood up, slowly dousing himself head to foot with the last pitcher of fresh water.

Definitely. Build a house, take a shower.

Mounted on a rented bay mare, Jack rode in comparative silence beside the carriage, which only sat three people. David sat on the far right side of its solitary seat, near the brake and the rifle, his hands holding the reins. Lizzie sat on the opposite side, Ellen in the middle.

"This is more comfortable than that buckboard thing Mr. Bledsoe drives," Lizzie declared with an air of finality.

As best Jack Naile could recall the terrain, and judging from the map and his modern lensatic-compass bearings, they were nearing the site of what would be/had been their home here.

On the way out of town, as they passed the larger of Atlas' two saloons, he had spotted what he assumed were some of Jess Fowler's range detectives. A quick glance exchanged with his wife had confirmed that she had pegged the men as Fowler's minions also. Jack was, of course, armed, as was David, David having donned the old Hollywood rig so that the holster was on his left side, the gun butt forward, the cartridge loops across his abdomen. However David carried a gun, Jack sincerely did not want his son to have to use one against another human being, and especially against someone who was evidently quite skilled at killing as a trade.

The stream's water sparkled clean and cold and ran fast, just as it had/would in the future (only almost certainly cleaner).

"Hey, guys," Jack Naile suggested. "How about you ladies taking a dip in the stream? Closest thing we'll have to taking a shower until we get one rigged up."

"It's going to be cold, Jack." Ellen scrunched her nose, but eventually agreed. While the ladies took a quick dip, Jack and David watered the horses downstream and out of visual range. Sooner than Jack would have expected, Ellen found them, her hair dripping wet and the skirt of her "storebought" green dress clinging to her legs. "I never would have done that if I'd thought about not having towels, Jack. Watch the rocks. They're slippery. But even though it was a little cool, it feels so good to be clean."

Jack Naile looked over at his son, "Just like the YMCA pool in Athens, huh? Come on!"

Once they hit the water, Ellen's description of the water temperature proved woefully inadequate. "This is freezing!" Jack shouted as he stepped into the stream.

"Yeah! Isn't it though!? Didn't you wonder why my lips had turned blue, Jack?" Ellen called back from the other side of the carriage, where she and Lizzie stood out of sight.

"Lips are not what's turned blue on me!"

"You shouldn't talk that way in front of your daughter, Jack! You and David have fun. If you're good, maybe we won't hide your clothes."

Five minutes by the face of the Rolex was all that Jack could take, and David was out of the water in three minutes flat. David was rubbing his naked arms and legs to shed excess water, glaring as Jack emerged from the stream. "This was a dumb idea, Dad."

"We'll get used to it, son!" But Jack hoped they wouldn't have to get used to it for long. On the return trip to Atlas, Ellen and Lizzie sat huddled in their shawls, their bodies still shaking a little. Maybe David had been right, Jack Naile mused. It had been a dumb idea.

It was very nearly dusk as Jack was handed back his deposit on the buggy and the horse and saddle. He'd dropped his family in front of the store that would, if this round of history proved out, someday be theirs. Rather progressively, considering that the time was after five, the store had still been open. David had taken the rifle with him, Jack keeping charge of the all-important attaché case that contained the family fortune.

Jack lit a cigarette, his second of the day, remembering to use a match rather than the Bic. He was down to one pack remaining and, after that, it would be learning to roll his own, smoking cigars or quitting.

He felt lighthearted, more so than at any time since their abrupt and potentially deadly arrival in the past. The property where the house would be built looked even better than it had/would. If they could rig it up and find something to use for wiring, the stream would provide more than enough hydroelectric-power potential. And despite the water temperature, the dip in the stream had been fun. Had the children been elsewhere, it would have been more fun, with Ellen's body up against his in the water and wanting his body's warmth once out of the stream. Yet those times would come. All too soon, he realized with each day that passed, the kids would be grown, on their own, he and Ellen alone with memories of a past that was a future that had not happened yet, but somehow had.

As Jack approached the boarding house from the opposite side of the street, he wondered absently if Ellen, Lizzie and David had already gone up on the little porch and continued inside.

The corset salesman, looking weary beyond endurance, sat in the solitary rocking chair. Jack couldn't remember his name. "Let me guess. The axle for your wagon still isn't fixed."

"You're right there, fella." The corset salesman shifted his bulk—he was pushing three hundred pounds if he weighed an ounce—simultaneously with shifting the stump of a cigar from the left side of his mouth to the right side. "I needa be on my way soon. Got customers to see."

"Corsets a big business?"

"Big. Future's in corsets." Jack laughed silently at that. "Someday every woman in this here great land o' ours gonna be wearin' one o' my corsets. See, I don't just sell 'em, neighbor. My brother-in-law and me, we own the factory back in Chicago what makes 'em. I cover the West and he covers the East."

"Sounds like he's got the easier job, friend."

"Future's in the West, neighbor. And your average woman, well, she wants to have what other women have, and that's a corset. If'n you'll pardon the word, 'virgin' territory. That's what the West is for corsets. Virgin territory."

Jack Naile shrugged his shoulders. "Where I come from, most of the women who wear corsets aren't exactly virgins. Say, you see my wife and son and daughter come in?"

"That wife o' yours—and I mean no disrespect—but her and your daughter, you might wanna get 'em some of the Night Thrush corsets. They're top o' the line. Top!"

"My girls aren't the corset type, friend; but, I'll ask them. So, they went inside?" Jack pressed.

"Ain't seen 'em, neighbor, and I been on this here porch since . . ." He tugged a big gold pocket watch from the confines of his nearly bursting vest. "Since half-past four."

Jack licked his lips, simultaneously snapping away the butt of his cigarette and thumbing the hammer loop off his revolver holster.

"Thanks, friend!" Jack shouted, grabbing up the attaché case as he broke into a dead run through the gathering darkness, toward the store, his right hand on the butt of his gun lest it pop out of the holster.

Jack heard indistinguishable voices from the narrow breezeway to the side of the store. The store's lights were still on. He passed the store at a dead run, glancing through the near window, the double doors and the far window as he ran. The aproned, balding proprietor was sweeping up, no sign of customers.

The sounds coming from the breezeway were definitely voices, male and female.

Jack stopped, his hand still on the butt of his Colt, his palms sweating.

"Lookee heah, gals. Don't matter no mind to me an' Lester whether you hitch up them there skirts y'selves or we go an' do it fer ya. Less'n ya like gettin' on ya knees and doin' us that way. And don't go lookin' to the boy. If'n he wakes up, it won't be for a long time, and that's fo' fact."

"Go to hell, you son of a bitch."

It was Ellen's voice, and Jack, stepping into the mouth of the breezeway, announced, "And I can send both you assholes to hell real quick."

The only light in the breezeway came in broad pale-yellow shafts emanating from gaps in the curtained windows above. The general store had a false front, but the building beside it had a true second floor, the rooms there serving as a cheap rooming house for cowboys and drifters.

Ellen and Lizzie, all but lost in shadow, but obviously scared, stood shoulder to shoulder, their backs against the side wall of the Merchants Café. The men bracing them, on the general-store side of the breezeway, were more readily visible in the weak light from the café's second-story windows.

David lay sprawled on the ground, mostly in shadow, and Jack couldn't tell his condition.

"Lester" and the man who'd declared his foul intentions wheeled around to face Jack. They had the look of Fowler's range detectives about them, broad-brimmed slouched hats, leather stovepipe chaps, each of the men with a six-gun at his right hip and a second one butt forward at his left. Jack noticed one of them had a third revolver, probably David's.

"They mess with you or Lizzie, Ellen?"

"They don't have the balls, Jack. One of them—that piece of shit, Lester—" Ellen stabbed an accusatory right index finger toward the man with David's revolver in his belt—"he slugged David from behind while David was beating the crap out of the other one."

Jack Naile wanted a cigarette very badly. "If you harmed my son, guys, you're in deep shit."

"Back y'all's play an' fill y'all's hand!" Lester of the three revolvers shouted, the gun at Lester's right hip springing from his holster as if levitated by David Copperfield.

Jack felt his body moving, his right leg snapping out and forward, his right shoulder dropping as his right knee slightly bent and the fingers of his right hand closed around the butt of his Colt. Something whistled past Jack's right ear—probably a bullet.

The sound of the Colt firing from the hand at the end of Jack's extended right arm shocked him into awareness of what he'd been doing only by reflex action. The single shot from Jack's Colt struck Lester somewhere between the dark wild rag over Lester's Adam's apple and the belt buckle above Lester's chaps. Lester fell back against the wall of the general store.

The unnamed man, who had threatened Jack's wife and daughter with rape, had a six gun in his right hand and was grabbing for Lizzie with his left. Ellen punched him in the face. He let go of Lizzie and seemed perplexed for a split second, stepping more fully into one of the shafts of yellow light. Hit the woman or shoot the man?

Jack didn't wait for the range detective's decision, triggering a second shot. The man's right eye and cheekbone seemed to collapse, as if sucked into his face, his pistol discharging into the ground near his boots. His body sprawled back along the wall of the general store.

"My God, Daddy," Lizzie murmured, just loudly enough that Jack could make out the words over the ringing in his ears. And he heard something else. The voices of men behind him, cheering, applauding.

Jack felt suddenly nauseous, but suppressed the reaction, dropping to his knees beside David. Ellen and Lizzie were already at David's side.

Lizzie was crying, hugging David. Ellen said something like, "He's alive." So far.

The town's occasional doctor was, of course, not in town, but the traveling dentist who had been so impressed with the Naile family's dental hygiene was among the cheering crowd of well-wishers who surrounded Jack in the aftermath of the shooting. In lieu of a medical doctor, the dentist had volunteered to examine David and treat, as best he could, any injuries David might have sustained. The two men Jack had shot needed no treatment.

Jack was rather out of it, and Ellen took over. "Yes, please, examine him." David was starting to come around. Western movies and detective novels notwithstanding, any blow on the head could be serious, and one which resulted in unconsciousness, however fleetingly, could be deadly.

After an almost too-quick examination to ascertain that David's neck or back had not been broken from the range detective's blow with a pistol butt, two of the townsmen made a chair seat of their locked hands and carried David to Mrs. Treacher's, ensconcing him in the parlor.

A large crowd had gathered on the porch, with more gathering in the street.

Jack, still seeming numb, knelt beside the couch as the dentist—his name was Joel Lowery—looked David over more carefully. Lizzie held an oil lamp for Dr. Lowery while Ellen held David's hand. Ellen felt oddly reassured when David jerked his hand from hers.

"How many fingers am I holdin' up, young fella?" Lowery asked, raising three fingers of his right hand.

"Three."

"Good. Now, focus on my index finger and follow it with your eyes as I move it."

"I'm following it just fine."

"I'll be the judge of that. Any double vision?"

"No."

"Headache?"

"Yeah."

"Good. A headache is logical to expect after a blow like you got. There's a bruise on the right side of your neck. The polecat missed your spinal column. Good thing. Must have just grazed your skull behind the right ear. Here. Listen to my watch." He placed his pocketwatch beside David's right ear, gradually moving it farther and farther away. "Can you still hear it?"

"Yeah."

"Keep listenin' and tell me when—"

"I can't really hear it now."

"You've got good hearin', young fella. Get a good night's rest and take it easy for the next couple of days, and you should be fine."

"Thank you," Ellen said sincerely.

"We're in your debt, Doctor," Jack volunteered, his voice barely above a whisper.

"No. I don't charge for doctorin' unless I gotta cut somebody open and dig out a bullet or like that. Dentistry is my trade. And you folks could sure help me by tellin' me what it is that you use on your teeth. The young fella, here, looks like all his teeth are perfect. That's not too surprising with a good diet, and the same with your daughter. But you and your wife gotta be near twice their ages and your teeth look just as good."

"Not quite," Ellen confided.

"Can you analyze something for chemical content?" Jack asked.

"Daddy!" Lizzie cautioned.

Dr. Lowery said, "I can send it back east."

"Good. I'll give you a sample of what we use on our teeth, and you can check it for yourself."

"I push baking soda."

"Baking soda is good," Ellen told him, hoping he'd forget about Jack's offer to give him a sample of late-twentieth-century toothpaste.

"Your boy looks like he's gonna be right as rain," a booming, jovial-sounding voice from behind them volunteered.

Ellen looked up toward its origin. The man was about her height, over two hundred pounds, somewhere in his late forties or early fifties, a derby hat clutched in both hands as if shielding the classic male potbelly behind it. He had thinning blond hair with a hint of gray and a high forehead over a broadly set face.

"Hope you're right." Ellen smiled up at him.

"Looks like a healthy young man to begin with. And Dr. Lowery makes a right good sawbones when he has to."

"Thanks, Tom," Lowery said. "Folks, this fella is Tom Berger, mayor of Atlas."

Jack stood up, then offered his hand to Ellen, helping her to her feet. Her shoes were caught in the cheaply made hem of her dress, and she shook it free as she stood. "What can we do for you, sir?" Ellen asked, always suspicious of authority, especially since it was appearing in the immediate aftermath of a double killing. There had been no law enforcement of any kind so far. Was the mayor also the marshal?

"I wanted to talk with your husband, ma'am."

"You can talk with us both," Jack said flatly.

"Lizzie—stay with your brother. Keep him on that couch resting a while," Ellen ordered.

"Would you folks step out on the porch with me?"

Jack picked up his hat in his left hand and took Ellen's elbow with his right. The attaché case was under his left arm, and David's revolver was tucked into the front of his gun belt. "Sure. Crowded out there, isn't it?" Jack observed.

"Citizen's Committee—"

"If it's about—"

"Is and it isn't, sir. Don't fret. You neither, ma'am. Nobody's angry 'cause some of Jess Fowler's trash is dead. We just wanna talk is all."

The mayor held the door for them. Jack paused to assess the porch, then ushered Ellen through the doorway a step ahead of him. As men saw her, they removed their hats entirely or at least tipped them. Someone pulled up the porch's solitary rocking chair and offered it for her to sit down. Gathering her skirts about her, she took the offered seat, waiting, almost holding her breath.

"With you folks new to Atlas and all," Mayor Berger began, "it's like as not you don't know what's just happened."

"I killed two scumbags who assaulted my family and were about to . . ." Jack let the obvious hang as Mayor Berger and some of the other men—some in business suits, some in work clothes—cleared their throats and shuffled their hats nervously in their hands.

Jack rested the attaché case across Ellen's lap. Her eyes settled on Jack's face, trying to read it. As the mayor began to speak, Ellen's heart began to sink. In her mind's eye, she saw Jack looking not like Jack at all but like Errol Flynn. And she was Olivia deHavilland, overhearing the good citizens of Dodge City asking Errol Flynn to take on the job of town marshal.

"Jess Fowler won't try anything in the open, Mr. Naile," Mayor Berger was telling them. "But his range detectives won't rest until they've done settled the score with your family, sir."

Ellen Naile had a sudden picture of Jess Fowler as a young Bruce Cabot, with Victor Jory cast in the role of Fowler's chief evil minion.

"But," Mayor Berger continued, "Jess Fowler would be less likely to loose his dogs of war against the family of the city marshal. If you'd take the job even for jes' a little while, that'd give us the time to find ourselves a career peace officer. You saw tonight firsthand what having no law in town can bring about."

"Mayor Berger," Ellen interjected, looking up from the rocking chair. "My husband isn't a lawman. He's a writer by trade. He was just defending his family."

"I never killed anyone before tonight and I hope to God that I never have to again." That Jack made this statement amidst a crowd of well over a dozen armed men was a credit to his honesty and his nerve, Ellen reflected, proud of her husband for his courage.

A voice from the back of the crowd—she recognized the gun salesman—chimed in. Lizzie had said she thought he was handsome. "I don't live here, it's true. But you folks might be interested in knowing that the famous Wyatt Earp of Tombstone had killed a man only once before that big gunfight they had down that way. When I was just gettin' started as a gun salesman and I was workin' over Colorado way, I sold Doc Holliday a nice little nickel-plated Colt with birdshead grips. I bought him a drink or two, and we talked for a while. I'll never forget it. But Doc Holliday's the one what told me that, and there was no reason that he would've lied over it."

"Look, guys," Jack said in earnest. "I'm not Wyatt Earp, and I'm not Doc Holliday."

"All I know, Mr. Naile," Mayor Berger persisted, "is that you happen to be the first and only person to stand up to Jess Fowler's gunmen and not come away with a beatin' at best or jus' plain shot dead."

"You never had a peace officer here?" Ellen asked.

"Had one up until two months ago," Mayor Berger admitted, his manner quite suddenly subdued.

"Dead?" Jack inquired.

"No. Fowler's men ran him off. Them two from tonight

and four others. Forced Marshal Bilsom to unbuckle his gun belt if'n he wanted to live. Then they figured they'd up an' see how far they could go. Made him take off his clothes, right there in the middle of the street in front of the general store. By that time, Bilsom had lost any nerve he had. They tied him on a horse stark naked—beggin' your pardon, Mrs. Naile. Don't know what possessed me to speak that way in front of a woman."

"It's all right, Mayor Berger," Ellen reassured him.

"Anyways, a bunch of us lit out after Bilsom, brought him clothes and a gun and seventy dollars and tol' 'im adios."

"And none of you made to help the marshal when he was up against six gunmen, professionals?" Jack queried, a poorly disguised tone of disgust edging his voice.

"Weren't that way," another of the men on the porch said.

"Still. No excuse," Mayor Burger declared passionately.

"I still don't understand," Ellen said calmly. "Would you please just explain what happened so that I can understand, Mr. Mayor?" Men liked to feel intellectually superior to women, and sometimes the best way to get a man to divulge something he was reluctant to say was to feign ignorance, interest or both.

"When Bilsom came to town, he made himself off like a professional, a good hand with a gun. Said he'd deputied for Bat Masterson's brother over in Colorado. And he was the best trick shot I ever seen! Could blow out the pips on a playin' card at twenty feet fast from the holster. We all seen him do it. Bluffed his way along for two years, never drawin' that gun o' his 'gainst nobody, but always doin' trick shots, like they say Wild Bill used to do back in the old days in Deadwood."

"He was no Wild Bill," one of the men on the porch suggested.

"He was yeller," Mayor Berger confessed. "Pure and simple. When he first took on the job, he insisted that the first time anyone interfered with him as he enforced the law, he'd quit. No matter what, didn't want nobody t' help him. By the time we realized he was a charlatan, a liar, a coward, if'n any of us had gone to help, Fowler's men would've killed 'im. We'd a been jes' as hoosiered up, and Bilsom woulda been dead in the street. We been advertisin' for fillin' the marshal's position since Bilsom left town."

Ellen felt a chill along her spine. Jack had always been a sucker for hard-luck stories, and this was the hardest. A whole town at the mercy of killers because their only lawman had been a jerk. "What about the county sheriff?" Ellen insisted.

"In Fowler's pay. Won't do nothin' without Fowler tells him to."

Ellen looked at Jack, again imagining herself as Olivia de Havilland and Jack as Errol Flynn. But there wouldn't be any Guinn "Big Boy" Williams or Alan Hale, Sr., to stand and fight at his side. She almost told Jack out loud, "There's no little boy who's going to die on the way to the Sunday school picnic. You don't have to do this." But Ellen merely said, "Do what you think is best, Jack."

"Only until you get a regular peace officer, and only if I'm assured of the fact that all or any of you will back me if it comes to that. Even a half-dozen professionals won't stand against a whole town united. I'll take the damn job, but only that way and no other."

The townsmen assembled on the porch sent up a cheer, and Mayor Berger pumped Jack's right hand, smiled down at Ellen, handed Jack a shiny silver-plated star, pumped Jack's hand again and clapped Jack on the shoulder.

There should have been a crescendo of music and a quick montage sequence of Jack cleaning up the town. Warner Brothers Pictures would have done it that way.

But there was none of that, only the smell of tobacco as some of the men lit cigars and Jack lit a cigarette—the match was struck for him by Mayor Berger.

The only other thing was the hollow, scared feeling Ellen Naile felt in the pit of her stomach. Ellen closed her eyes, letting reality fade to black.

CHAPTER
❖ SEVEN ❖

The helicopter wreckage, although only weeks old, looked to have been where it was for decades. The twisted metal of the rotor blades was rusted well more than half away. The upholstery for the seats was rotted to near nothingness. Clarence had demanded that the FAA officials show him photos of the pilot's body (found buried in a shallow grave near to the wreckage site, a pile of stones used as a marker). These were Polaroids showing the open grave. There was no corpse, only bones—bones stripped clean by what could only have been decades of rot and decay. Even the dead man's watch was covered with corrosion, Clarence was told. The pilot's horsehide leather flight jacket, the FAA official admitted in strictest confidence, had been more rotted than unpreserved leather gear from World War I.

The condition of the wreckage and the solitary body were "inexplicable."

Clarence Jones had flown to Nevada within hours of being notified by the film company that the helicopter carrying his aunt, his uncle, his niece and his nephew was missing. He'd taken the Chevy Suburban—Jack and Ellen had left him with the paperwork giving him power of attorney, and he'd always had a set of spare keys—and driven as close as he could to the approximate crash site, a one-hundred-twenty-five-square-mile area, mostly mountains and woods. He'd joined the state and local authorities in their search for the downed aircraft, working with them from dawn until dusk each day, the search slowed by unseasonably heavy rainfall in the mountains on the Nevada side.

After two exhausting weeks, the search had yielded nothing and would, in days or less, be called off. Clarence had already determined that he would not give up the search, no matter how long it took. But, on the afternoon of the fifteenth day of the search, a private pilot reported spotting something that could have been wreckage. Despite the fact that the area had already been searched, it was searched again.

Clarence found himself seventy-eight miles away from the crash site when it was finally, positively, located. He connived a ride with a volunteer helicopter pilot.

By the time he had reached the crash site, the pilot's grave had been discovered, the body exhumed, gone.

But the Polaroids were enough—almost—to finalize the treatment his digestive system had suffered from the helicopter ride. Yet he held it in, realizing that it was hard to cry and throw up at the same time. He cried.

That the Suburban was left behind signified that something had gone terribly wrong for his loved ones.

Lighting a cigarette, staring through his tears at the helicopter wreckage, the nearly bare metal frames that had once been seats, evidence of catastrophic fire damage abundantly clear, Clarence Brown told himself that if anyone could have somehow escaped death here it would be his aunt and uncle. And David and Lizzie were tough, competent, smart survivors, taught to be so by their parents.

If they were alive in the past, they would need what they had somehow been forced to leave behind—the contents of the Suburban.

The search was continuing, looking for four more bodies.

Clarence's search had ended.

His family had made it through the barrier of time, somehow. They were alive and well in the past, somehow, and needed his help. And they would get that help. They had never abandoned him. He would never abandon them.

It would take money, because he would have to quit his job. He was barely holding on to it even as he stood there, gone from it for more weeks than he had vacation time or sick leave. Despite the fact that it would take quite a long time for Jack and Ellen to be declared legally dead—no bodies, and there would be none—his power of attorney would enable him to utilize their remaining assets to help him to help them.

With intelligence work, when there was a blip or a sound that didn't belong, there was always the means, however convoluted, of somehow identifying what had caused it. Thinking back to one time in Greece, he appended that to "almost always."

But, here, specific things had taken place. The helicopter had left Atlas, Nevada, at a specific time, filed its last radio transmission at a specific time. Whatever other extraneous events had occurred, he would discern them, ascertain their effect. He would find a way.

The sounds and the blips were different, and he would not be reading an O-scope, consulting volumes of material, have precise logs to peruse. But the problem was the same.

If one time-travel incident were possible, then it could be duplicated—somehow.

By parlaying his old comrades in arms, he could make contacts in the Federal Aviation Administration and National Transportation Safety Board, gain access to the analysis of the downed aircraft's black box, its flight recorder. There had been no cockpit voice recorder.

Clarence shuddered as he lit a cigarette, exhaling smoke through his mouth and nostrils, shivering in the mid-morning chill as NTSB technicians started to move the wreckage.

His family was alive, he almost verbalized. No remains of their belongings had been discovered. Jack never traveled without a gun unless aboard a commercial aircraft. That would have meant that, had they died, the gun's rusted remains would be discovered.

No such remains would be discovered.

There would be no dead bodies found miles away in the deep woods, no bones along the side of some animal trail.

Clarence looked hard at the helicopter's wreckage, his heart filled with hatred for it because it had failed. Through clenched teeth, he swore an oath. "You didn't get them, you fucking piece of aircraft shit! You didn't get them! Not them! I'll find them and I'll come back here or wherever the hell the FAA puts you and I'll piss all over you! Hear me!?! I'll shit on you, dammit! My aunt and uncle and my niece and nephew aren't gone, damn you!"

Clarence stood there a moment longer, noticing only peripherally that all of the law-enforcement and FAA and NTSB personnel and volunteers were staring at him, fear in the eyes of some.

"Hey! Listen up, dammit! They're alive. They're fuckin' alive, and I'm gonna find 'em, go after them, find them! They're fuckin' alive, and no fuckin' helicopter crash is killing them! Hear me? They're fucking alive, and I'm fucking finding them, and I'm gonna piss all over this fucking helicopter and anybody who fucking tries to stop me!"

Clarence lit still another cigarette and walked away. He had work to do.

It had been almost a year since their first significant success with the transmission of electrical power through the air, many flickers of illumination from their lighting array, but none so brilliant as when the storm had so suddenly struck.

Sometimes, at night, Jane Rogers would awaken, haunted by a question she could not answer. The terrible helicopter crash about which she had read, had seen the aftermath of on the television news, seemed to have occurred at roughly the same time as that so-successful experiment. There was no reason to suppose that it had, but what if her experiment had somehow contributed to the deaths of five people, wiped out an entire family of four?

The driving force behind her research was to help mankind, not destroy.

Each time that she and Peggy Greer had returned to the high desert and, once again, attempted to project electricity on a laser carrier, a secret fear had consumed her, the fear that all scientists had at one point or another in their lives: Had her work, somehow, unintentionally, innocently, caused the loss or degradation of human life?

On several occasions, Jane Rogers had discussed this very trepidation with Peggy Greer. "It couldn't have been anything that we did, could it?"

"You're looking for assurance that I cannot give, Jane. Logic tells me that the answer is no, and logic tells you the same, but that's not good enough to put your feelings to rest, is it?"

"No. Not really."

"Do you want to stop the experiments?"

"No. Not really."

"What if something else unexpected should happen?"

"I don't know. Is it ego, dear, ego that drives me?"

"Ego drives us all," Peggy answered.

At such a juncture, Jane Rogers would say nothing more than a pleasantry, perhaps good night, perhaps something else. The reason was that ego, of course, drove all men—and women—drove all who strove to do the undoable.

Such troublesome thoughts bothered her progressively more and more with each venturing into the high desert, with each equipment setup, with each test.

This day was no different.

As she began her by-rote examination of all data and equipment preparatory to another trial, another test, there was, this time, something different. It was not a dust devil, but a cloud of dust from some large vehicle coming toward their location.

"Do you see that?" Peggy asked her.

"Yes. I do."

"You don't think it's some biker gang, like that time almost two years ago?"

"It looks like a small truck or a big car. See? It's battleship gray, I think, or maybe blue. But it's only one vehicle."

"Who do you think it could be?"

Jane Rogers imagined that they would soon find out, so she made no response.

The vehicle proved to be a Suburban, similar to theirs, but with a fold-down rear deck as opposed to double doors. It seemed packed beyond endurance, even the front passenger seat loaded.

A man stepped from the driver's side. He was quite tall by any standard, dark haired, with a drooping black mustache and several days' growth of stubble on his cheeks and chin. He was dressed in white track shoes, blue jeans, a well-worn olive-drab military field jacket (the shadows of military patches subsequently removed were noticeable) and a black cowboy hat. Beneath the jacket, the tails of a light blue snap front cowboy shirt were visible.

"Right out of the pages of *GQ*," Peggy Greer whispered beside Jane Rogers' left ear. "But still kind of cute."

He was somewhere in his early to middle thirties, Jane guessed. And if the military jacket was his originally, his last name was Jones and his first initial was C.

As he approached, he removed his sunglasses. The dark eyes beneath frightened her for an instant, a look of desperation and intensity in them that was most disconcerting. It was a look that she had seen in her own eyes when she had realized that her husband was dying and there was nothing that she could do to save him.

"I came to talk to you about the helicopter crash that took place up in the mountains almost a year ago. My name is Clarence Jones, and the four passengers in that helicopter were my family. My aunt and uncle and their two teenage children." His voice was deep, but not overly so, and quite pleasant.

"I'm very sorry for your loss, Mr. Jones. I assume that you know our names, since you've obviously come looking for us. Nonetheless, I'm Jane Rogers. This is my friend and assistant, Peggy Greer. How is it that you think that we can help you?"

"I just learned—you know how the government misfiles reports and stuff, sometimes—that you two were the first to report a possible crash, contacted the state police."

"I didn't know that we were the first," Peggy volunteered. "But, yeah, we saw it, or we think that we did."

"How do you mean that?" the young man asked, a hint of a smile appearing for only a split second as he turned his gaze toward Peggy.

Jane kept quiet, letting Peggy answer him. This might

prove interesting. Peggy didn't have a beau, and hadn't been on a date for better than a year. She was pretty, personable, intelligent, just never seemed to meet men.

"Well," Peggy answered after a too-long pause, "I can't really explain it. We were conducting one of our electrical experiments, and there was a lightning strike at the same time. Jane saw the aircraft, and then it was gone."

The young man refocused the intensity of his gaze. "I read the police report. You said it was there one minute and gone the next. How did you mean that?"

Jane Rogers answered him. "Exactly what I said. I was looking through the telescope—that one over there near our equipment. It was set up in exactly the same spot, aimed at precisely the same place in the mountains that it is aimed at today.

"There was a sudden electrical storm," she went on, "and our experiment was already in progress."

"What kind of experiment?" Clarence Jones asked.

Maybe she would show him later, if he remained pleasant. For the moment, she gave him a basic explanation. "We generate a laser beam, and we generate electricity. We're trying to use the laser beam as a carrier wave for the electricity, to broadcast the electricity, as it were, through the air. We have a lighting apparatus up in the mountains. The laser carrier is aimed at a receiver near the lighting array. If we have success with a particular trial, I can see the lighting array fire through the telescope.

"On the day of the helicopter crash," Jane Rogers continued, "there was a clap of thunder just as we fired the carrier beam. In answer to the question which you are bound to ask, the laser beam could not have struck the aircraft carrying your family. Had it done so, the lighting array would never have flashed to indicate that we had broadcast electricity for a few microseconds or so. As I was looking for the light array to fire, I saw an aircraft—it turned out to have been the helicopter, from everything I understand. It was there one second, then gone the next. And just before it vanished—"

"The word you used," Clarence Brown began.

"It vanished," Jane Rogers reiterated. "But there was something more."

"What?" the young man asked.

"The lightning streaked across the sky and my eye just naturally followed it, but the lens of the telescope was locked into position, so I couldn't turn the telescope. It was the brightest, biggest flash of lightning I'd ever seen in my life. I would have remembered it even without what happened next. I caught sight of the aircraft, as I said. Simultaneously with all of that there was a clap of thunder, extremely loud, and I saw the aircraft. Then the aircraft vanished into something black, blacker than night, and there was another clap of thunder, possibly from the earlier lightning bolt. The black thing, whatever it was, vanished. And there was nothing in the sky where the aircraft had been. It was as if the aircraft had gone into some sort of hole, and the hole closed up around it." Jane laughed in disbelief, "Which is, of course, almost certainly impossible."

"Don't black holes suck things in?" Clarence Brown asked her.

Peggy answered, "If there were a black hole close enough for us to see with the naked eye, Mr. Brown, we wouldn't be seeing it. All light and time and matter would be distorted, falling into it. Just because something is a hole and it's black doesn't mean that it's a 'black hole.'"

"Then what the hell was it? Because it distorted time, was an opening into the past."

The young man, despite his nice looks, had to be demented, Jane realized. What a pity. She wondered if he might become violent.

"You think I'm crazy," he offered unbidden, echoing Jane's thoughts. "I've spent almost a year investigating this thing. When I learned about the electrical storm around the time of the helicopter's disappearance—"

"It was found, Mr. Jones," Jane insisted.

"It disappeared from this time, Dr. Rogers."

"What an interesting notion. But, we have work to do, my assistant and I, Mr. Jones. So if you'll excuse us, we—"

"I thought it was just the electrical storm. But when I learned what you were doing out here, it made sense."

"It makes no sense at all, I'm afraid, young man."

"Yes, it does. Are you aware of the condition of the helicopter when it was found?"

Jane felt uncomfortable. She'd heard rumors, like something out of a supermarket tabloid.

Peggy told him, "Metal can be oddly affected by extreme heat, Mr. Jones—"

"I've read the FAA and NTSB reports, Dr. Greer. The wreckage was in a condition indicating prolonged exposure to the elements."

"That proves nothing, sir," Jane declared, starting to

feel at once angry and stupid—angry with his imbecilic notion about time and black holes and stupid for continuing the conversation.

"The pilot's body? The best forensic pathologists the government could find examined it and, despite the fact that such a thing had to be impossible, independently they all reached the same conclusion. The body had been in the ground for nearly a hundred years."

"Then they unearthed the wrong body," Jane told him.

"Same watch, same crucifix and old military dog tag around his neck. His wife identified his wedding ring and belt buckle. The body was clothed in a rotted horsehide bomber jacket. His wife got it for him in 1990 for a Christmas present. All that stuff was on the body they dug up, the pilot's body which had been dead for a hundred years, even though the incident took place just weeks earlier."

"What do you want from us?" Jane asked.

"I've got copies of the FAA and NTSB reports and the pathologists' photos and their reports."

"What is it that you want from us?" Jane insisted.

"I want to recreate what happened. I want to join my family."

Jane felt a tear start at the corner of her left eye. Perhaps Clarence Jones wasn't crazy, only very, very sad and terribly lonely. She knew the feeling well.

David Naile had found the thing that would change their lives for ever, alter their expectations and destroy their hopes. He had found it by accident only that morning. His father, still wearing the badge of town marshal after well over a year, did not know of it yet. Neither did Liz, nor their mother.

There had been no claim to the property on which they gradually built their house. They'd filed a claim and ridden out to Tom Bledsoe's place, asking if he would help with the carpentry—there was no such thing as hiring a construction company out of the telephone book. Phones existed, patented in 1876, but they did not exist in Atlas.

Work on the house went slowly, and by design. Because they had discovered a solitary wall outlet when they had visited the ruins of the house almost a hundred years in the future, they all clung to the notion that, somehow, the Suburban and its contents would magically time-warp to them. In turn, because of that, they slowed the construction process in order to be able to accommodate the electrical wiring and outlets to come.

Hope sustained them, electricity only a part of that and a very small part, but a symbol of normalcy. Hope translated as meaning some semblance of what had once been their reality, their life: light, music, videos, a few modern conveniences, a jump up on the primitive amenities of the world around them. The battery in the video camera was long since drained and dead. It was impossible to recharge it. The record which they had hoped to make—for themselves to find in the future?—consisted of two hours or so of tape. From what David had read, even stored with great care, the tape would likely be useless after fifteen years or so. All plans to continually copy the videos until they could be transferred to film were dashed. And what did it matter, anyway?

Hope meant having some of their own carefully selected

things, treasures packed away in the Suburban. For his mother, that would be cherished photos of the family, and the memories those photos recalled.

For Liz, photos, too, but also something as silly as her two-foot-tall brown teddy bear, a possession she had kept on her bed since childhood. Liz was a grown woman of sixteen, the town's substitute school teacher for Margaret Diamond, who was increasingly more frequently ill.

David didn't quite know what it was that he wanted from the Suburban, and the issue had become instantly academic. If this were a continuous time loop from which they would never be fully extricated, as his father theorized, the Suburban would never come because it had never come.

The solitary electrical outlet that had become the talisman upon which their future was based had traveled with them into the past by accident, and that alone accounted for its being discovered in the ruins of the house in the last decade of the twentieth century.

Fate.

Fate had caused them to discover the outlet when they had surveyed the ruins of the house in 1992, and Fate had made David Naile drop the charred outlet into his pocket. Fate had made him wear the same jacket on the day of the helicopter crash that he had worn that day when they inspected the ruins. Everybody in the family had always razzed him about having so many clothes, jackets in particular.

There was a hole in the pocket of the jacket, and the outlet had slipped through the hole and into the padded lining, never to be found until he had taken the coat out of the trunk into which it had been placed, never to be found until this very morning when he had decided to wear the jacket when he rode off to practice his shooting.

His mom was experimenting with what, for 1897, was a modern camera. His sister was filling in for Margaret Diamond once again, as she had for the last week. His father was patrolling the town, perhaps for one of the last times—the services of a professional peace officer for Atlas had finally, it seemed, been engaged.

Instead of riding out of town to practice his marksmanship with the old blued Colt .45 (which would not actually be produced at the Colt factory until 1957, sixty years in the future), he'd put on his city clothes, left the tiny house they'd purchased down the street from Margaret for a mere eight hundred dollars and gone to look for his father.

The wall socket was in his vest pocket.

Jess Fowler's men still came to town, their eyes and holsters hate-filled. Whenever they spied any member of the Naile family, they would walk away, robotlike, as if their actions were programmed into them. But there had been no repercussions from the night more than a year ago when his father had killed the two men who had accosted his mother and sister and left him unconscious.

The only tangible results of the encounter were his father wearing the town marshal badge and David's own pursuit of heightened marksmanship skills. Had he been as good with a gun then as he was now, he might have taken both of Fowler's range detectives himself, and his father might not be wearing that badge.

David turned onto the main street and walked past the general store. Its balding proprietor, Carlton Smithfield, had agreed in principle to a deal for his store. As David passed the open double doors, Smithfield smiled and said good morning. David, who didn't like Smithfield at all, smiled back. "Good morning, sir. A beautiful morning, yes."

David was searching for his father and in no mood for useless chatter. He passed the breezeway where his father had shot to death Fowler's two range detectives. David walked on, along the board sidewalk and under the porch roof which shielded the windows and doors fronting the Merchant's Café. He opened the near door and looked inside. Two of Fowler's men, drinking what passed for coffee. Dave, the waiter. Dave was a good guy, if not too terribly bright. No sign of his father.

"See my dad around, Dave?"

"Yeah, Dave! He was walkin' up the street not more'n fifteen minutes ago. That ways!"

Dave the waiter always called David "Dave" and seemed to get a kick out of that. David liked to be called "David," tolerated his parents occasionally calling him "Davey" as a sign of affection. But Dave the waiter was an exception to the rule. "Thanks, pal. Catch you later."

There was a nasty look from the two Fowler men. David gave a nasty look back, closing the door and pacing off toward the edge of town.

After walking half again the length of the street, David finally spied his father. Jack Naile stood, leaning against the corral on the same side of the street along which David walked, essentially invisible from a distance. Maybe this was the first speed trap, David wondered absently.

"Marshal Jack Naile," David said under his breath. "The Law East of the Sierras. Shit."

The clothing problem had pretty much been solved via catalogue, his mother and sister having decent, albeit uncomfortable-looking, dresses. They were getting into making their own, almost as a means of self-defense. He and his father had also found a source for attire that was, at least, more acceptable than that found at the general store. But that would change. As it had been in the future and continued to be in the past, David Naile's taste in clothes was far more sophisticated than that of his father.

Jack Naile wore his black Stetson from the twentieth century, one of his half-dozen black on black vested suits and black cowboy boots with a medium heel. Visible above the collar of his jacket was the collar of a white shirt. He would be wearing a black tie, knotted just as it would have been a hundred years or so in the future.

The only jewelry he would be wearing was his gold wedding ring and the gold chain he had acquired for his Rolex.

His father had solved the wristwatch problem uniquely. The town blacksmith also repaired tack, making him the closest thing to a leather worker. Jack had removed the Rolex from its wristband and commissioned the blacksmith to cut and sew a pouch that would hold the Rolex in securely. A small brass grommet was affixed to the top of the leather case. With a gold watch chain added, the Rolex would pass for a period piece unless given more than a casual glance by someone who really knew watches.

"I heard those boards in the sidewalk creak when you walked across them," David Naile's father announced, turning around quickly, his right hand not reaching for his revolver, but near it.

It seemed as if this fall would be cooler than the last, and a brisk breeze cut along the main street out of the high ridgeline of the nearer Sierras, across the plain and toward the low mountains beyond Atlas. "I've gotta tell you something, Dad."

"Everything okay?"

"Everybody's fine. Look at this." David reached into his vest pocket, extracted the wall outlet and tossed it to his father. Jack Naile had always been pretty miserable when it came to catching things, and David actually felt proud of his father for catching the object he'd thrown to him, albeit a little awkwardly.

"Where'd you get this?"

"You know what it means, Dad? That's the wall outlet that we found in—" And David glanced around them, to make certain no passerby could hear. "It's the one we found in 1992, in the ruins of the house. Don't you see? That's how we were able to find it in the house. I brought it by accident. The Suburban never gets here."

Jack Naile dropped the outlet in his coat pocket, taking the makings for a cigarette from his other pocket. "Shit," David heard his father say before turning away and looking off toward the mountains again.

Clarence had not worn a suit since leaving his job as a theater manager in suburban Atlanta a year and a half earlier. Thinking back, he could have worn a suit at the small memorial service held at the site of the helicopter wreckage, the memorial service arranged by the movie company. But he chose not to attend the service. To have done so would have been to tacitly accept the idea that his aunt, uncle and teenage cousins were dead, or at least gone from him forever.

Always somewhat claustrophobic, even when managing a movie theater, he had never particularly enjoyed being in one, always staying toward the back of the theater so that he could egress quickly.

It was, then, with considerable reluctance that he allowed Peggy Greer to talk him into going to see *Angel Street* when it hit the theaters. They sat in the very back row, Clarence sitting in the aisle seat, Peggy holding his hand. *Angel Street* was a bizarre western, a mixture of classic oater and occult suspense with a strong dash of mystery and romance. Professionally speaking, he thought the film was "okay" and little more than that. The male lead was a well-known supporter of liberal causes and the female lead simply didn't turn him on. The action sequences were good enough, but not as good as those from the old John Wayne movies, which he had loved since his boyhood.

At the very beginning of the end titles appeared a dedication, naming Jack, Ellen, David and Elizabeth Naile and the pilot, Evan Soderstroum, as the victims of a terrible tragedy and stating that all five would be remembered fondly.

That got Clarence to get up and walk out of the theater, Peggy Greer at his heels. "Didn't you want to see the end titles, Clarence?"

"No, baby. That just pissed me off. They're not dead."

"Even if they aren't, sweetheart, wasn't it kind of sweet that they dedicated the movie to them?"

"Let 'em dedicate something that's gonna make money to them, then. You watch and see. This thing is gonna bomb."

"You're angry, Clarence."

"You're right, Peggy."

As he later explained to Peggy, another one of the myriad things wrong with *Angel Street* was the music. Jack was a movie-music aficionado, had collected sound tracks. Jack would definitely not have liked the music. It needed the music of a Jerry Goldsmith or a John Williams, not some guy nobody had ever heard of. And, Clarence went on to explain, Jack would not have liked the gunfire. "Take *The Magnificent Seven*, for example. Jack explained it to me once, that the gunfire was too soft sounding. He didn't know for sure, but he guessed that they actually recorded the sound of the blanks and didn't edit in live gunfire with full-charge loads. He learned all about that stuff when he did one of those movie articles he wrote. Nowadays, they edit in the sounds of real gunfire." They'd talked throughout the evening about the film and about the work they'd been doing out in the desert. And about what lay before them on the following day.

For a little over six months, Clarence had assisted Peggy and Jane Rogers with their experiments, his background in electronic intelligence making the use of the equipment simple to learn. The math behind the experiments was something he only vaguely understood. He'd mastered trigonometry for his work in electronic intelligence, but it was Jack who had pumped fractions and decimals into Clarence's short term memory before he had taken his preinduction aptitude test.

The experiments now, almost routinely, would fire the light array for as long as a few seconds, that record achieved during a fortuitous thunderstorm with intense lightning activity. It was in the aftermath of packing up from that touch of success that Jane Rogers had announced, "Curse my age and stupidity!" She slammed shut the double doors of her Suburban. "There was something I had forgotten, that I saw just before your family's helicopter vanished. It was ball lightning."

"And what the hell is that?" Clarence had demanded.

The instant that he spoke, it began to rain, rain hard, but neither Clarence nor Peggy nor Jane made any move to get out of the rain. As calmly as a teacher in a classroom patiently explaining in simplified terms something quite complex to a group of dim students, Jane began, "Ball lightning is extraordinarily rare, so rare that no photos are known to exist which conclusively have captured it. The only time that ball lightning can be witnessed is usually in association with a conventional streak of lightning, the ball lightning found at or near its termination point. Like the conventional lightning bolt which I saw just as the aircraft carrying your family disappeared, ball lightning also moves laterally, at somewhere between five and six miles per hour, it's estimated. That was the first time that I had ever actually seen ball lightning.

"Those with more experience relating to the phenomenon have indicated that ball lightning has a number of extremely peculiar properties. It can enter a structure through a closed surface, for example, without precipitating damage to the surface through which it has passed. There is frequently sound accompanying the phenomenon, often described as like unto air slowly exiting a membrane through a tiny puncture.

"Considering that ball lightning is almost certainly superheated plasma gas," Jane continued, "it should, logically, rise in air, but it doesn't. It's of short duration, or seems to be, and as the particular manifestation of the phenomenon concludes, there is frequently the sound of an explosion accompanied by the smell of something burning in its immediate aftermath.

"Its physical appearance seems not to be confined to one particular coloration, but several. That may relate to temperature or other variables. Size is usually seven plus inches in diameter—close to the size of a regulation basketball, I should think. The duration of the phenomenon is a matter of several seconds only."

"About the same amount of time that we're able to fire up the lighting array when the experiment really works?" Clarence suggested.

"Yes, about," Jane agreed.

The rain beat against them and the ground on which they stood with the intensity of a high-pressure car wash. Still, none of them moved toward shelter, the equipment long since packed safely away and their bodies long since soaked to the skin.

"There is no universally accepted theory as to the exact nature of ball lightning, other than that it is composed of superheated plasma, as I believe I mentioned. Nothing, as of yet, satisfactorily explains its peculiar mobility or the source of its energy," Jane concluded.

"And you saw this stuff when the helicopter disappeared?"

"Yes, circling around the aircraft. I remember now thinking that it reminded me of electrons circling a nucleus. Most peculiar motion pattern for ball lightning. And they all vanished into the black spot into which the helicopter seemed to disappear as well."

"Then it's hopeless," Peggy Greer declared, raising her voice to be heard over the drumming of the rain.

"Why?" Clarence demanded.

"We can't make ball lightning, and the phenomenon occurs with such irregularity that we might have to wait indefinitely. Lightning experiments in laboratories produce pretty puny stuff by comparison to the real thing, and that's conventional lightning," Peggy went on. "And experiments of the type we'd need to conduct even to attempt to produce a laboratory equivalent of ball lightning, even if they were possible, would cost a fortune—a large fortune."

It was then that Clarence Jones had decided to find the owner of Horizon Enterprises, the company Ellen had told him, in their last conversation, owned the property in Nevada on which the ruined house stood—the company started by David Naile. One hundred percent of the stock in Horizon Enterprises was owned by a man named Alan Naile. Alan, if Clarence remembered correctly, was David's middle name.

Wearing one of his theater suits—he had almost a dozen of them, this one gray—Clarence waited with Peggy Greer in a side office for Alan Naile to arrive. The secretary, a pretty girl, but not as pretty as Peggy, had apologized, telling them, "Mr. Naile called on his cell phone that he was detained in traffic. He should only be a few moments. May I get you something?"

As neither Clarence nor Peggy wanted anything but information and help, and neither of those could be provided by the secretary, she left to go back to the outer office.

It had taken Clarence nearly a month to find the means by which to contact Alan Naile, evidently a very private person, and this only after utilizing his ex-military buddies once again for their information gathering talents.

Yet once he got a phone number where Alan Naile could be reached, it was almost as if Clarence had been expected and the appointment was arranged within days.

There was an ashtray. Clarence lit a Winston. Peggy didn't smoke, but didn't seem to mind it when he smoked.

In the instant that Clarence pocketed the Bic lighter, the door at the side of the room opened and Clarence almost dropped the lit cigarette from his mouth. It was David's face, David's height and build, but this David looked to be about thirty years old, immaculately and expensively tailored, the steel gray suit he wore an obvious Armani.

"I'm Alan Naile, Clarence. And, you must be Doctor Greer." Clarence stood up. Alan Naile offered a firm, dry handclasp to Clarence, then held Peggy's hand briefly, almost as if he were about to raise it to his lips. Peggy had remained seated.

Alan Naile had David's dark, wavy hair; but, unlike David, who habitually kept his hair short and brushed the waves as straight as possible, Alan Naile's hair was grown out to where it was brushed back above his ears and, at the neck, it went slightly over the collar of his jacket.

Alan Naile got right to the point. "I have debated with

myself since I first learned of the time anomaly when I was twenty-one whether or not I'd interfere with it someday, especially since, for the bulk of the time I would be running Horizon, I'd have no knowledge of future history. I even brought my oldest son—my youngest was born nine months ago—to an autographing session at a science fiction convention so that he could meet Jack and Ellen. I knew I look like my great-grandfather, David, quite a bit, so I prepared by growing a beard and getting some fake glasses. It would have been awkward to explain looking almost identical to their son. What was I going to say? Your son is my great grandfather?

"And you're here because you want my help, perhaps with those experiments Dr. Greer has been conducting with Dr. Rogers. You guys have come up with the same conclusion that I reached as soon as I learned that your experiments with electricity and the helicopter's disappearance may have been related. It could be done again—maybe."

Clarence realized that the cigarette was burning his fingers. He stubbed it out and lit another one. "Smoking's bad for you, Clarence. And please, don't mind my calling you Clarence, because we are related." Alan Naile sat on the edge of the desk for a second, and then stood. "Follow me, will you? We'll all be more comfortable in my office."

Alan Naile opened the door through which he had just entered, turned into a narrow, carpeted corridor with sconced bulbs providing the illumination. The hallway looked like something out of an old movie, the frosted glass covers over the lights having what his aunt Ellen would have called an art-deco look.

Halfway along the corridor, Alan Naile put a key into a lock and opened a mahogany-colored door. "Please," he beckoned, letting Peggy, then Clarence, inside ahead of him.

Alan Naile's office was large enough to hold an intimate dance party. There was a huge, dark wooden desk at the far side of the room that fronted enormous windows with soft-looking white sheers over them; the sheers diffused the sunlight, filtering it.

The desk itself was clearly one belonging to a wealthy and busy man. Several telephones, a computer monitor and keyboard, stacks of files and several notebooks littered the desk in patterns that seemed neither haphazard nor perfectly organized. Either his secretary knew Alan extremely well, or Alan maintained full responsibility for his own clutter.

Alan crossed behind his desk. "Sit down, guys. Can I have Cecily get you anything? Coffee, a Coke, a beer if you want."

"I'm fine," Clarence volunteered.

"Me, too," Peggy added.

"See this?" Alan picked up a Lucite block from the front of his desk and crossed around his desk again, showing it to them. "This is the first money that actually came into Jack Naile's General Merchandise. Ellen Naile saved it. Great-grandpa would have invested it." He laughed. "It's an 1853 half-dime. Can you imagine that? A half dime, contemporaneous, since it was still in circulation in 1897, with the nickel. Amazing. So, you want me to finance your trip back through time, Clarence, if it can be managed? Right?"

"You get right to the point, don't you?" Peggy Greer observed.

"I have to, Doctor. Anyway, it would seem, since there was never a mention of you in anything Jack and Ellen left behind, or my great-grandfather, for that matter, that you are a new element into the mix, Clarence. Perhaps your mother died during childbirth, or your father died before you were conceived."

"What the hell are you talking about?" Clarence demanded.

"Simple. Every time Jack and Ellen Naile make the trip—and don't ask me to explain it, because I don't understand it myself, only that it happens. But every time they make the trip, history changes a little. In documents they left behind the last time, the most glaring example is that eight million Jews were killed by the Nazis during World War Two. Yet we all know that six million were killed. Something that my great-grandfather did—likely the private-intelligence organization he put together— helped to alter history and save two million lives.

"Anything that any of us could accomplish would pale in comparison, I'm sure you'd both agree. Who knows? Maybe one of the Jews who didn't die did something that somehow in some way we could never figure out allowed you to be born, Clarence. Who can say?" He shrugged his Armanied shoulders, went back around his desk and plunked down into the insanely expensive-looking leather swivel chair.

"At any event, Clarence," Alan went on, "you're here in the first quarter of 1994, and you want to go back to there, which, judging from what they left behind, is probably the spring of 1898. That means that your grandfather, who was also named Clarence, is just a month or two old somewhere in New York, and his older sister hasn't taken up her profession as a madam in East St. Louis, just probably still is some cute little girl about to become an orphan.

"We could change history in a radical way here, Clarence, maybe for the better . . . or maybe we'll just fuck everything up. Your call."

"Oh, thanks a fucking lot!" Clarence exploded. "If I go back in time, I could alter history?"

"Of course. Jack and Ellen have gone back in history I don't know how many times, because the last time, they found a partially destroyed wall outlet in the wreckage of their house, which means that they had gone to the past before. This could be a time loop that never ends. Think about that for a while, Clarence, and see if you don't get yourself the gigantic headache that attacked Cleveland."

"'Those who don't learn the lessons of history . . .'" Peggy began.

"Perhaps that's why they and we are doomed to relive it. We failed to learn history's lessons or some crap like that. At any event, I'm not going to play God. My wife tells me that my ego is big enough already. No. If you go back, Clarence, you might bring about great good, you might bring about great evil, and you might break the cycle of the time loop. God knows and He isn't telling me.

"If you want my help," Alan said flatly, "you've got it to the limit of Horizon Enterprises' resources, and those have virtually no limit at all. We make more than a number of not-so-small countries, Clarence. I don't have the notoriety, because I don't want it, but I'm one of the two dozen or so wealthiest men in the world. Take all the time that you want and let me know, or tell me now. Whatever. Even though your mother was Ellen's adopted sister, I still consider us blood, which in fact, if not in hemoglobin, we are. So you name it and it's yours. I don't envy you the decision. And, it might not work, anyway."

Clarence looked at Peggy sitting beside him. She wore a pale blue sweater set and a dark blue straight skirt. Her hair was up. She wore makeup, which she rarely did. She was really way too pretty a girl, but he asked her anyway, "Would you go with me? I mean, marry me first?"

"Yes. Twice." And she reached out and took his hand and rested it over her thigh.

Clarence looked at his newfound relative and benefactor. "Let's try and book two passages into the past, Alan. What do you say?"

"I'll have my best people on it by tomorrow morning. Meanwhile, let me buy you guys the finest dinner in Chicago. Unfortunately, I won't be able to join you, but I'll see you guys tomorrow right here at eight a.m. I'll send a car around. Consider the dinner an engagement present. You guys are staying at the airport Hilton. Let's say a driver will pick you up in the lobby at quarter to seven, traffic and all. Now, let's schedule that dinner, shall we?"

CHAPTER
✳ EIGHT ✳

Peggy led the way, driving the Naile family Suburban, Clarence beside her in the passenger seat, his eyes on the side view mirror. There was no road, only the flat plain of desert. Trucks and more trucks, eighteen-wheelers all, two and three abreast, roared after them along the barren terrain, enormous clouds of dust in their wake. Some of the trucks bore oversized load banners, huge yellow generators mounted on their flatbed trailers.

Overhead flew helicopters, three of them, the lead machine bearing Alan, the other two packed with scientists and engineers.

The Suburban itself pulled a box trailer, both the trailer and the Suburban packed with additional items Clarence thought might prove of use to his aunt, uncle and cousins, as well as some few of his own belongings and Peggy's things.

There were myriad questions, all of them either too

complicated to answer or their answers subject to mere chance.

If the time-travel mechanism could be repeated, what if he and Peggy were thrust into some other time, before or after his family had reached Atlas, Nevada? Millions of years before, Nevada had been prehistoric woodlands, and before that submerged below an inland sea and before that even more savage jungle.

What if there were other time loops, or the series of time loops through which his family had traveled were somehow interwoven, and he and Peggy fell into a loop where Clarence had never existed? Would he automatically cease to exist because he had never been born? And, what, then, would become of Peggy? Rather than marrying him in the presence of his family, would she, too, cease to exist, because he had never brought her into the past? Would she somehow remain in the objective future? Or would she be doomed to survive alone in the past without him?

Could any of his fears be possible? How could Alan's scientists duplicate the effect of Jane's and Peggy's experiment that day when the very nature of ball lightning, perhaps critical to the time-travel soup, was not even understood, could not be explained?

"You know what Alan will eventually do, if the experiments are successful and he can get us back through time," Peggy said, her voice raised over the roaring of the trucks, the whirring of the helicopter blades. "You've told me yourself that Jack and Ellen always preached that enlightened self-interest was the most moral reason for action of any sort."

"And?"

"And, if Alan's scientists can send us back successfully, what reason is there to suppose that Alan won't send equipment and fuel along the same time loop? In theory, if that could be worked out, reversing the process by means of which we would travel back would allow people to travel forward."

"A time machine?"

"Not a bit," Peggy told him. "Just a portal, a doorway. I don't think anyone envisions what we're hoping to do here as building some sort of time machine. All we're doing is duplicating a natural phenomenon which we don't understand and don't even have sufficient data to rationally theorize about. If it works, all we'd have would be a two-way corridor, ninety-six years apart. Just think of the implications. I'm not saying that Alan is unscrupulous but, if anyone who were should gain control of the process—assuming that we succeed—the entire twentieth century could be molded to that person's will and benefit.

"History would be changed irrevocably," Peggy declared, "everything unraveling. Think of the original event like a small pull in a sweater, which leaves the tiniest tuft of yarn visible above the surface. If you ignore that pull, it will slowly, inexorably, alter the sweater with time. If you tuck the pull back in, the sweater may wind up not being damaged any more at all. If you start to tug on the pull and keep tugging on it, the sweater starts unraveling. The hole that was that time rift would become larger and larger until nothing can be done to save the sweater and everything has come undone. I'm not getting cold feet, Clarence. I'm with you forever, wherever that takes us. But I wanted you to know what we might be doing."

"Remember what you said I've told you about Jack and Ellen and enlightened self-interest? Well, Jack and I would always argue, because I'm a fatalist. If we have the means to go back in time," Clarence told her, lighting a cigarette as he spoke, "and we choose to go back in time, that means that, in the greater scheme of things, we were supposed to go back in time and nothing we do will change the outcome." And he forced a laugh. "If the way of duplicating the original event presents itself, we're fated to go back, and what will happen will happen anyway."

Clarence told himself that he believed his words completely; if he didn't, at least they sounded good.

"Think of it this way, Peggy. I know you've felt guilty over the prospect of leaving me, ever since you agreed to go with Clarence. But you shouldn't."

"But I love you so, Jane. It's like thinking about leaving your mother and knowing that you'll never see her again."

Jane stood up, walked around to Peggy's side of the smallish table and folded her arms around the girl, cradling her head against her breasts. "And you've been like a daughter to me; you are the daughter I've never had. I love you with all my heart, dear."

Jane heard muted sobs. Peggy's arms encircled her waist, hugging her.

"Think about the possibilities, Peggy. If history really can be changed, and the present changed because of that, think what an honors graduate of one of the world's top medical schools could do to alleviate suffering and advance the cause of medicine in the fight against disease."

"But that would be intentionally changing history,

Jane," Peggy insisted, looking up at her. Peggy's eyes were rimmed with tears.

Jane leaned over and kissed the girl on the top of the head, then took a handkerchief from her pocket and offered it to Peggy. "Blow your nose?"

"Mmm," Peggy nodded, sniffed, taking the handkerchief. the sound of her blowing her nose something more like Jane would have associated with a child than an adult.

Jane's health was, after so many years, beginning to fail her, in simple but persistent ways. She got out of breath more easily, controlled her breathing less easily. She would feel tired for no reason or melancholy for no reason, either. At times, she would be giddy with happiness, at other times wanting to cry.

The cause of her sadness sat before her, sniffling into the handkerchief, forcing an embarrassed smile. Jane would truly miss Peggy Greer, friend and confidant, and truly the daughter she had never had.

What happiness Jane felt was derived from the astonishingly rapid progress that had been made with her experimental program. After all these years, all it had required to validate her hypothesis was the aid of some of the finest electrical engineers, particle physicists and meteorologists in the United States, plus the expenditure of more millions of dollars than she could bring herself to imagine.

In a little over three months, the wave pattern of their first successful experiment on that day, nearly two years earlier when the helicopter had crashed, had been identically matched, amplified and boosted in power and field. An orange, a potted geranium, a frog, and then a rabbit had been caused to vanish—into time? How would they ever know without sending back a human being she had wondered.

It was Alan who had suggested the obvious. He had a small sphere constructed, at its core a radioactive isotope with a well-established rate of decay. The reading of the isotope was taken; the sphere was whisked away—really through time?—and, in less than the blink of an eye, it reappeared exactly where they had placed it. Only it was partially covered with dirt and had to be dug free. The metal showed surface corrosion. When another reading of the isotope was taken, the numbers almost identically matched the theoretical prediction of decay for the passage of somewhere between ninety-four and ninety-eight years. Several more animals, another, different radioactive isotope—all were sent into the past. The recently euthanized body of a rabbit, secured within a stainless steel box, was transmitted into the past, the box reappearing in the next instant, the stainless-steel showing considerable surface corrosion. When the remains of the rabbit were subsequently examined, the veterinary pathologist declared that the animal appeared to have expired a century ago.

Finally, it was time for a human experiment.

One of Horizon's scientific advisors had suggested recruiting the services of some terminally ill medical patient with mere days to live, offering a million-dollar financial estate to the person for the service to be rendered and equipping the volunteer with two items. One would be a hypodermic syringe with an especially lethal cocktail that would render him or her almost immediately unconscious, death ensuing within minutes. That was to be used at the volunteer's election after he or she performed one vital function. A stainless-steel sphere would accompany the volunteer, the sphere fitted with a key to be turned right or left, toward the words *yes* or *no*, the key then to be withdrawn and discarded.

When the sphere reappeared, if the position the key had been turned to indicated the selection *yes*, the volunteer would have signified that there were no perceived ill effects from the time transfer. If the key was not turned, whether removed or not, sound evidence would exist that the timetransfer process had killed the volunteer. The *no* option was merely to give the terminally ill volunteer peace of mind—if he or she were dead, actuating the key would be impossible—or indicate that what was perceived as fatal injury had been suffered during the time transfer.

Jane had felt proud of both Alan and Clarence when they insisted, almost simultaneously, that such an experiment would be cruel in the extreme, regardless of how much money would inure to the terminally ill volunteer's estate.

After much consideration and debate, it was determined that, indeed, it was time for a human experiment—and the subjects would be Clarence and Peggy. They would, of course, have with them a stainless steel sphere, to be left behind before they ventured off through their new time. Inside it were to be stored immediate observations, remarks concerning perceived aftereffects or the lack thereof and any other information that they might think useful. The sphere would also contain, of course, a radioactive isotope with a precisely established rate of decay. If the experiment was successful and time-travel were achieved, the sphere would appear in almost the same instant that Clarence and Peggy and all of their gear vanished into the past.

The idea of Peggy and young Clarence—Jane had become nearly as fond of him as had Peggy, but in a different way, of course—allowing themselves to be human guinea pigs at once frightened and repulsed Jane.

An idea, which had been hauntingly formless, suddenly took shape, became perfectly clear.

Jane would not share with Peggy or Clarence the nature of her epiphany but if Clarence was somehow right about Fate being inescapable, then this was why her body had been slowing, beginning to tell her that time was running out at last.

She smiled at the thought. Rather than time running out on her, if Alan would see her logic, be her enabler, she would run out on time.

The principal personnel who remained at the site all or most of the time had motor homes. Alan's motor home was a palace on wheels.

The vehicle was as large as a cross-country bus, yet had sleeker, more modern lines. There were four of what Jane Rogers had learned were called "bump-outs" adding extra roominess to the vehicle's interior. Considering that Alan was only on-site for important meetings and actual experimental trials—which averaged about ten days out of every thirty—Jane secretly felt that the motor home was egregiously elaborate and, despite its tasteful decor, in the poorest taste.

There were armed guards with sentry dogs surrounding

the work site, standing watch over equipment and personnel, but nothing, presumably, would impede her from knocking on Alan's front door.

Her watch showed the time to be a little after eleven in the evening, but there were lights on within his motor home. She hoped she was not disturbing him, but her thoughts had to be shared with Alan as quickly as possible.

The door opened. There was a portable phone to Alan's ear, and he was talking into it. He smiled, gestured her into the sanctum sanctorum. He picked up a bottle of wine, gestured with his shoulders and eyebrows, then nodded his head toward the bar.

"Yes," she almost verbalized. She could use a drink.

Jane Rogers poured herself a small glass of single malt scotch, added water to it, then dragged her old bones onto one of the bar stools.

The decor was art deco, chic, expensive, real wood, real marble, real crystal and real leather in abundance. Naile's bedroom door was open (she'd accompanied Peggy and Clarence to dinner here when the experiments had only recently gotten underway). She hoped that the bedroom was unoccupied, but for all his brusqueness and cocksure attitude, Alan did not strike her as someone who would cheat on his wife. He had a strong sense of family, and she liked that.

At last, Alan took the phone from his ear and pushed a button. "Hong Kong and Tokyo on that conference call. How can I help you, Jane? That scotch looks good; I'll pour myself a glass and join you." Jane Rogers started to speak, but didn't get the chance. "I've been given reports that you haven't seemed to be feeling so hot over the last few weeks. Everything okay? Sure hope so. I bet I know why you're here. Let me guess."

Jane decided to let him guess. She couldn't get a word in even if she tried. As he poured two fingers of scotch, then added a few ice cubes from the bar refrigerator's dispenser, he told her, "You're worried about Clarence and Dr. Greer taking their trip the day after tomorrow, aren't you? And you've hit on a handy solution. Stop me if I'm wrong. You've been feeling a bit less than in top shape and you've decided that if any life is to be risked traveling into the past, you're the one to do it. Right? If it works, Clarence and Peggy could be there with you within an hour, because we can charge everything up and be ready to go again in half that time. And, if it doesn't work, we'll know because you'd leave a sphere behind like the one that one of my people suggested with that stupid idea about hiring some poor terminally ill schmuck to be a human guinea pig. Well, if you want to do it, I can't talk you out of it. If it works, you'd be with Peggy and Clarence until the end of your days, which you probably figure isn't too much longer. If it doesn't, you would have saved their lives. Right? I know, I know that you're wanting to do this out of love. If we try it, and it fails, Clarence will be mega-pissed with me. Knowing him, he might try to beat me to death. But, if that's what you want. Want another drink?"

Alan probably put it down to awe of his personage and that was why people were so reticent around him.

Everything possible had been taken into account to compensate for almost two years having passed between the initial incident and the experiment to be undertaken this day.

Vagaries in atmospheric electrical charge, potential effect of nearness to solar maximum, relative position of the Earth in its orbit and, of course, the weather.

Ball lightning had, as expected, proven impossible to realistically duplicate, but somehow, Horizon's physicists had worked their way around that, learning to generate an electrical field that was generated of such enormous proportions as to compensate for whatever effect the ball lightning might or might not have had. Firing the light array for as long as ten seconds was routine. All evidence indicated that the power created by the bank of enormous industrial generators was enough to send large objects back in time.

Jane waited quietly, sitting in a chair beside the control truck. Rather than resting, and to avoid conversation with Peggy and Clarence, she had driven south on the day after her late-night one-sided conversation with Alan, driven to the small cemetery where the remains of her late husband were buried, gotten down on her knees to be nearer to him, lain atop his grave and whispered that she loved him and, if there were an afterlife, would join him sooner or later, perhaps much sooner.

Crying, she had driven back to the site and lain awake all night, wrestling with every detail of the experiment.

In the morning, Jane ate a very small breakfast (it wouldn't do to get motion sick inside an armored stainless-steel capsule), showered, washed her hair extra well, dressed in her favorite comfortable clothes and set off to rendezvous with her coconspirator, Alan. Her backpack was filled but not stuffed with some essentials, should she survive. She used no special medications, and, if she survived, when Clarence and dear Peggy joined her in the past, she would have the services of a fine physician at her disposal. The essentials, rather than the usual things women of her somewhat advanced age might bring along, consisted of two favorite books, the small leather photo album with pictures of herself and her late husband, two changes of underwear and stockings, a long nightgown (in preparation for mixed company until everyone was settled), a flashlight, extra batteries, a Swiss Army Champion with every sort of blade imaginable, a topographical map of the immediate area and a lensatic compass, bought as G.I. surplus.

Alan had met her at the control truck, asked her if she'd like to come in—she declined—and helped her to the canvas-backed folding chair in which she sat. He had told her, his voice held to a conspiratorial tone, that he had contrived a wild-goose chase for Clarence and Peggy, so that they would not be in the area when the time transfer experiment took place. Jane Rogers thought that quite wise.

Lost in reverie, she was vaguely surprised when Alan was by her side again and asking her a question.

"Did you just ask if I wanted a gun?"

"Well, there are wild animals in these mountains, even today, and more so a century ago. And in the past, of course, you might encounter some disreputable person and—"

"Alan, I have no quarrel with persons who choose to own, use or even carry firearms. It is a Constitutional right, as it is my right to profess total ignorance of the use of firearms. So, were you to insist that I lugged along such a contrivance, it would be of little use to me, unless it were shaped like a softball bat or a frying pan, both of which I know how to use in my own defense."

"I see."

Alan had excused himself to attend to some technical details, he said, but was gone for fewer than five minutes. Upon his return, they set out toward the capsule.

The capsule was roughly the size and shape of the space capsules utilized by the Mercury astronauts in the early days of the United States space program, but would be more comfortable. The interior was littered with precious little instrumentation, merely two television monitors with which to view the surroundings of the capsule at almost any angle, a blood pressure and heart rate monitor and an oxygen tank and mask.

"Who ordered the oxygen tank!?"

"I thought that it might be—"

Jane was determined not to let Alan outtalk her. "If the Naile family arrived alive, they did so without oxygen tanks and masks. However, from the wreckage photos, it appears that there was some sort of fire, perhaps electrical. A fire extinguisher, yes. Oxygen! I should say not! I have no wish whatsoever to be incinerated, young man."

"Yes, ma'am." And he shouted over his shoulder toward the knot of technicians, "Deep-six the oxygen, guys!"

The day was bright and clear, the sky a perfect blue punctuated by marvelously fluffy white clouds and higher, thin wisps of cloud, these in long, graceful tendrils stretching in series almost like protein chains from horizon to horizon.

Alan, handsome lad that he was, suggested, "I think, Dr. Rogers, that it might be best to get started."

"Time is money," she told him, thinking herself mean-spirited for saying so.

"Not at all. I merely want to make certain that we're well underway, at least, before Clarence and Peggy might return. Clarence's temper, you know."

"Of course. I meant no slight. Will you see that the results of my initial studies and the work of your personnel are properly documented and published?"

"Documented, to be sure. Published? Perhaps not advisable, unless you want 1898 to get awfully crowded."

"Well put, young man. Well put."

"May I kiss you, Dr. Rogers?"

"Are you that afraid for me?"

"Either way, it is good-bye, and I hate saying good-bye to a beautiful woman. Always a failing of mine and a worse failing with my great-grandfather."

"Really—"

"Please? Not to be mercenary, but you wouldn't be here on the threshold of discovery without my help."

"Really!"

"Then, as a memory of a voyage I shall never take?"

"Do you always get your way with women?"

Alan smiled wolfishly. "Actually, you probably wouldn't want to know."

"Shame on you. Yes, a solitary—"

Despite the difference in their ages, Jane Rogers almost fainted as this marvelously handsome young man folded her into his arms and all but crushed her lips under his. She wanted to protest, but was embarrassed because she liked it. As Alan raised his mouth from hers, he whispered, "That will be something I will always treasure as a memory. My great-grandfather wasn't much for a belief in God when he set out for the past, but he learned otherwise, and the habit has stuck with the family since. So, in all sincerity, God bless you." And he kissed her hand as he ushered her into the capsule.

Jane Rogers' heart was fluttering.

Inside the capsule, she found an aluminum softball bat and a cast iron skillet. She felt a smile cross her lips. He was a very nice young man, Alan Naile, and she was not surprised at all that he had his way with women, whatever that way might be—and she didn't want to know.

A very intelligent and very pretty blond-haired girl named Mary Cole—blonde jokes notwithstanding—was in charge of the capsule's systems. In this capacity, Mary Cole was also in charge of the last minute check. "Now, Dr. Rogers, all you have to do is sit tight and relax. With this one control, you'll be able to check any of the video." She placed the remote in Jane Rogers' hand, and then took an instant to refix her ponytail. "The reason, once again, that this is not a wireless remote is that we don't want to risk any signal disruption as you travel. Actually, as we've discussed, you should be there in the blink of an eye, or less. This is the primary control for blowing the hatch. Remember to flip the guard away. As with everything aboard, there's a backup and a redundant backup. God bless."

She leaned over and gave Jane Rogers a soft little peck on the cheek and stepped backward out of the capsule. Jane also had a panic button that she could hit if, at the last minute, she got cold feet. She had no intention of using the panic button.

Instead, she played with the buttons on the remote. There were redundant backup screens, and she watched all of them, each flashing the same picture as she switched from one camera's perspective to another then to another. Although she couldn't hear the generators through the walls of the capsule, she could hear them perfectly over the monitors. Should sound become a problem during the time transfer, the pickup microphones in the cameras would automatically cut out until a safe decibel level had been reached.

Everything seemed just as it should be.

Jane Rogers felt like she had to piss, but that could wait ninety-six years. It wouldn't be the first time that she had squatted in the woods. She looked around at her surroundings again. First-aid kit mounted on the bulkhead. Emergency rations in a small chest mounted to the deck. A survival kit, which she imagined held some sort of firearm and, more useful, a flare gun.

Her backpack was secure in a chest about the size of the rations chest, this mounted to the deck on the opposite side of the capsule.

Jane Rogers wanted to look at her watch, to see if time actually would move backward. But she did not want to miss the show for something that unlikely.

She checked the seat restraints that Mary Cole had checked, and then leaned back, trying to relax.

"This is capsule control." Mary's voice cut out the ambient audio. "Time transfer attempt will commence on my mark. God bless, Dr. Rogers. Ten . . . nine . . . eight . . .

seven . . . six . . . five . . . We have full power for lightning stroke and carrier beam. Four . . . three . . . two . . . one . . .

"Discharge! Mark!"

Jane forced herself not to blink. There was a blinding flash of light, the cameras unable to take it, she presumed. The screens whited out, the sound of thunder rumbling all around her. The screens went black. In less than a second, the high desert surrounded her again, the monitors revealing no trucks, no generators, nothing but sand, rocks and a view of the mountains, the same view she normally saw through her telescope, but seeming farther away because she saw it through the television screen, unaided by magnification. The only difference was that the mountains had a great deal of snow on them at the higher elevations.

Was this it? Had she traveled through time?

After a review of live video from every camera, Jane deduced that this was most likely exactly the same set of coordinates that she had left, except for the time, and hopefully that was 1898.

Jane flipped the guard back and actuated the button to blow the hatch. The rush of air that entered the capsule was cold. She was glad she'd brought a good, warm sweater.

"You let her do *what*?" Clarence Brown hammered his fist down on the capsule engineer's desk; Alan was perched on its edge.

"We had the test capsule, she wanted to go and she had the best motive— to save your lives," Alan told his cousin many times removed.

"And you're sure she's all right?" Peggy insisted.

"The capsule reappeared the instant after it vanished. The interior of the capsule was fully intact, the exterior covered with dirt and moss and lots of surface corrosion. It seemed to our people that it was extremely likely the capsule had been exposed to the elements for a century or so. And look, you guys, she made the noble gesture, and it worked out. Anyway, I don't think she wanted to be left behind. You guys are her family," Alan supplied. "Look at the note."

The note was encased within a special, hermetically sealed plastic pouch, a superexpensive version of a Ziploc bag. When Clarence held it properly to lose the glare, he could read the words through the plastic. Clarence read aloud.

> "Dear friends,
> "I have traveled successfully through time, I think. There is snow in the mountains; so, if you come, remember to bring warm clothes, as it is rather nippy.
> "I seem to have suffered no ill effects.
> "Love and kisses.
>
> "Jane"

"She was in great spirits when I did the last minute systems check with her. Relaxed, really." Clarence looked across the desk at Marc Cole, as the man re-ponytailed his long blond hair. And, Clarence had the oddest sensation that there was something different about the person in charge of capsule command. But Clarence just couldn't put his finger on it.

❋ ❋ ❋

The capsule in which they would travel through time was more like a gigantic steel crate with fold-down ramp doors at either end. It looked nothing like a movie time machine and, in fact, wasn't. As Jane had explained to Clarence and Peggy, time-travel had not been "invented." What they were doing was merely slavishly duplicating the effects of an anomaly. "Think of it this way, Clarence," Jane had told him. "When Sir Isaac Newton identified gravitational pull with his famous—and likely apocryphal— dropping of the apple, he didn't invent gravity, but merely took advantage of it. The phenomenon existed. He didn't float through the air, because gravity disallowed that. Neither did the apple. It's rather as if we were living on the edge of a lovely pool of water in the shadow of some enormously high precipice, and a rock fell—all by itself, due to forces which we could not understand—from the lip of the precipice and the rock struck the pool of water, making the most beautiful rippling effect anyone had ever witnessed. Now, we wish to see that gorgeous ripple effect again. So we dive into the pool and retrieve the original rock. Then we question everyone who witnessed the event, trying to ascertain the exact spot where the rock struck. We have certain givens, for example, in that we have the original rock, know precisely from whence it originated and know that the rock accelerated at a speed of thirty-two feet per second as it fell. Therefore, we can calculate its speed as it struck the water, given that we can deduce the precise height of the precipice utilizing basic geometry.

"Now," Jane Rogers had gone on, "for some reason, we

can't climb the precipice, cannot actually repeat the original event. But we can go up above the pool in a hot-air balloon or a helicopter or whatnot, and even though we can't get as high as the precipice, we can increase the launch speed of the rock in such a manner that, as it accelerates, it will have precisely matched the speed it had when it struck the pool naturally. If we do all of that just right, and just the right portion of the rock makes the initial strike into the pool at just the right angle, we'll get that same marvelous ripple effect as before. We still can't climb the precipice and throw down bigger rocks or smaller rocks or strike other parts of the pool. We can't travel through time willy-nilly, only simulate the effect, and do a trick without understanding why it works. Do you see, Clarence?"

Clarence had always disliked driving the Suburban because it was so large, and with the trailer attached to it, the vehicle seemed more the "fucking bus" than it had to him when he'd dubbed it so after Jack and Ellen had first driven it home on New Year's Eve, the last day of 1988.

The crate—or "capsule"—was merely to protect them and what they brought with them through time from whatever forces might be exerted against them. And, like the solitary capsule in which Jane Rogers had travelled, it served the function of an observatory from within which the occupants could witness what transpired around the capsule as the time-travel process occurred.

Clarence doubted that they would see anything strange or even interesting unfold. He sincerely believed that in one instant they would be in the autumn of 1994 and in the next in the last month or so of 1898. If he blinked, he'd miss it.

Cole walked into the crate-shaped capsule, two other technicians with him. Alan had accompanied them.

To reduce the size of the capsule, once the Suburban and its trailer were inside, there was very little room on either side. The driver and passenger doors could be opened, but it was a squeeze to get out. Because of that, the video monitoring array was set on an armature which could be raised and lowered by means of something similar in appearance to a VCR remote control. The technicians, squeezed on either side of the Suburban's hood, were guiding the arm downward to rest just forward of the windshield wipers. Marc Cole—his long blond hair in a single braid—was working the remote. Alan stood next to the driver's side window. "Remember to leave word for us in the capsule, Clarence, like Jane Rogers did. That'll help. But it's really important for you guys to use the camera afterward. And then seal the film just like we worked it out. There's a good chance that the film will survive a hundred years, and we'll have an indisputable record of what's about to transpire."

"But it'll go no farther than you and your people," Clarence insisted.

"He's right, Alan," Peggy Greer cut in. "If this process got into the wrong hands—"

"Hey, guys, I know," Alan agreed. "I mean, this isn't some 1950s sci-fi movie, right? This is 1994, almost 1995. We have state-of-the-art security. Nobody's getting this technology. What I intend to do is have my top people perfect the means by which this process can be used both ways, like a doorway. That way, if Jane or you guys should wish to come back, you can. You leave a note, as agreed, and it'll appear inside the capsule immediately after you leave. And we'll be able to come and get you. I'm sure that we can work out how it'll be possible. I mean, I know it's not as simple as reversing the process literally, but it should be close to that.

"Anyway," Alan went on, as he seemed to do so remarkably well without even pausing for breath, "that is the only reason for perfecting the return system. Maybe a hundred years from now, there'll be a practical and safe use for time-travel technology, and this experiment we've begun will lead us to that technology's full fruition. Right now, it'd be too damned dangerous."

"What we're doing right now could have already had repercussions," Alan concluded.

Marc announced, "We're ready, people!"

Clarence felt Peggy squeeze his hand . . .

The device Clarence held in his left hand and aimed out the Suburban's window was an ordinary, if expensive, garage door opener, whereas the device that Peggy held in her lap was considerably more sophisticated. "Hit it, Peggy!" There was a sound like a small explosion from in front of them. The seal on the forward hatch was blown. Clarence pushed the button on his remote, and the front door of the crate-shaped capsule started to fold open and downward, forming a gently sloping ramp across which they would drive.

"There's her capsule!" Peggy barely whispered. "But I don't see—Oh, my God! You don't suppose that our capsule appeared on top of her and we crushed her to—"

"Odds of that happening in anything outside of a Warner Brothers cartoon are extremely remote," Clarence reassured her.

As Clarence had anticipated, the journey through time was a non-event, at least from the standpoint of anything at all remarkable to see. There was a brilliant flash of light and the video monitors went to fuzz. Yet these were state-of-the-art pieces of equipment, and, sooner than Clarence would have thought possible, picture returned to the monitors. Despite the insulation of their carefully engineered capsule, thunder boomed loudly all around them. In the instant that the monitors returned to visible picture, the cacophonous rumbling ceased as well.

The monitors showed the same landscape the capsule had just left, except for notable differences. The only trace of the hand of man was the smaller, one-person capsule that had transported Jane here only a few hours earlier. The terrain seemed little, if at all, different. The wooded areas along the mountain slopes seemed the same, the shape of the peaks themselves subtly altered by mounded snow.

There was sand, rock, some vegetation, mostly scrub brush.

"Let's elevate the video array and power down," Clarence suggested.

"Powering down monitors," Peggy answered back, working the wired control panel on her lap. "Raising array."

Had the remote controls for blowing the hatch and

opening the forward door not functioned, the first backup system involved getting out of the Suburban and activating the controls manually. Getting out of the Suburban would have been challenging in the narrow confines of the capsule, and Clarence silently blessed technology.

The array was fully raised on its arm, adequately above the Suburban's roofline, even with the added luggage rack. Clarence felt stupid ducking his head as he started the Suburban. He was relieved that the engine fired. Very slowly, Clarence started the Suburban down along the ramp which had been the capsule's forward door.

The luggage rack was not the only retrofit to the Naile family's Chevrolet Suburban. Alan Naile had volunteered to purchase a brand-new one, but Clarence had felt that, somehow, Jack and Ellen would feel heartened by seeing their own vehicle again. Bowing to Clarence's perception of Jack and Ellen's wishes, Alan had contacted a friend at General Motors and made arrangements for GM's resident engineering expert on the Suburban to be flown via one of Horizon Enterprises' corporate jets to oversee the improvements to the Naile family's Suburban.

The short block was pulled, replaced along with every belt and hose, gasket and seal and fitting. The vehicle was converted to on-demand four-wheel drive. The task of a unique parts replacement conversion kit for the Suburban that would allowed it to run on grain alcohol Alan Naile assigned to a team of Horizon's best minds, these men and women working with the engineer from GM. Fuel economy would be terrible—in the extreme—but under the circumstances wouldn't matter. A spare-parts kit containing everything from serpentine belts to a spare gas cap to oil, gas and air filters was made up. The transmission was pulled, replaced. Under the supervision of Horizon staff, every scintilla of information about care and maintenance of the vehicle was collected, recomposed into layman's language and a full tool kit assembled that would aid the Naile family in everything from changing a battery to recharging the air conditioning.

The Suburban, as Clarence Brown put it in park and shut off the engine, was newer than new, the final touch a paint job.

Clarence opened the driver's side door and stepped out into the brave old world.

Peggy was suddenly beside him, holding his hand. "Did you ever see the old movie *When Worlds Collide,* when the survivors from Earth prepare to set foot on the new planet?"

"Jack conned me into watching it. It was one of his dad's favorite movies. Yeah. It is kind of like that. Right down to having our own little ark." Clarence nodded toward the Suburban.

"Jane!" Peggy called out.

"Dr. Rogers! It's us!"

Peggy tugged at Clarence's sleeve and he looked down at her. "Yeah?"

"Well, who else could it be but us?"

Clarence shrugged his shoulders. "You made your point." He raised his voice and this time just shouted, "Dr. Rogers!"

"Why don't you get a gun, Clarence?" Peggy suggested.

Clarence Brown had nothing against guns, was, in fact, a staunch supporter of the Second Amendment. On those rare occasions when he had fired a handgun, he had proved to be a reasonably decent shot. He'd had no problem qualifying with the M-16 for the Air Force. He didn't own a gun, had no desire to own one and, if a weapon were called for, considered rocks and paving stones to be more than adequate. For genuinely serious matters, a softball bat was all he could see himself ever requiring. Usually, fists and feet were more than enough. "We don't need a gun."

"Get a gun, Clarence? Please?"

Clarence shrugged his shoulders and reached into the Suburban, opening the center console between the front seats.

The were six Colt Single Action Army revolvers in the Suburban, all of them custom tuned by Bob Munden, then refinished for durability by Metalife Industries, just like Jack's pet long barreled Colt. All six had four-and-three-quarter-inch barrels and two-piece wooden grips. Two of the Colts were packed into the center console. Clarence took them out of the butterfly-style zippered pistol cases, verified that each had five rounds loaded, lowered the hammers over the sixth (empty) chamber and walked back to rejoin Peggy. "You look like the two-gun type. Here you go." Clarence rolled both revolvers over his trigger fingers and closed his palms, the butts of the guns presented toward his fiancée.

"I've seen western movies, Clarence. You're going to try and twirl them around and—"

"Jack taught me that; called the road-agent spin and no, I'm not going to do that. You want 'em?"

She took both revolvers into her hands. "Jane?"

"Come on. She can't have gone far." Clarence picked up a rock about twice the size of a baseball, hefted it and closed his right fist around it.

Jane Rogers' frail little body looked like that of a rag doll which someone had tossed away. As Clarence ran toward her down the long, narrow, gravelly defile, he thought that certainly the old woman must be dead. He called back to Peggy, "Be careful—there's something weird goin' on!"

Looking from side to side as he ran, almost slipping and falling more than once on the loose gravel and sand, he saw nothing out of the ordinary. But as he neared Jane Rogers, his eyes flickering to the ground, checking his footing, he spotted the clear impressions of horseshoes in the dirt. Feeling as if he should say something Jay Silverheels-esque like, "Uhh! Many horses, riders travel fast. White men. Indian ponies no wear shoes," he thought better of it, and he was too out of breath anyway.

Still holding his rock, Clarence dropped to his knees beside Jane. "Dr. Rogers? Speak to me. Jane?"

As he started to gently raise her head, Jane Rogers opened her pretty eyes. "Is he alive?"

"Who?"

In the next instant, Peggy was kneeling beside Clarence, the pistols on the ground beside her, her hands starting to explore Jane Rogers for any sort of wound or injury. "Are you in pain, Jane? What happened?"

"Is he alive?"

This time, Peggy asked the question. "Who, Jane? Is who alive?"

"That handsome blond-haired cowboy who tried to save me from those hooligans who robbed me."

"Robbed you?" Peggy repeated.

"Look," Clarence said, gently raising Jane's left wrist. It was heavily bruised and there was a small cut, but no wristwatch. Inspecting more closely, he realized that her wedding ring was also gone. It had been a simple gold band, worn from the years, narrowed by time to little more than a heavy thread of metal.

"Which way did they go?" It was such a cliché, and he realized it as he said it.

"They—they rode off, and he followed them into the trees and there was shooting."

Clarence stood up, Peggy cradling Jane's head in her lap. Clarence's and Peggy's eyes met. Her gaze flickered toward the pistols on the ground beside her. "Keep 'em. I'll be back." And Clarence ran toward the treeline, scrub pines at its edge, the trees wide enough apart that a man on horseback could easily have ridden by. His eyes spotted more hoofprints. He quickened his pace.

The ground rose again. Clarence was familiar with its contours, the same terrain as it would be/had been almost one hundred years in the future. He passed the boulders where the light array would be/had been. Clarence climbed up along their craggy surfaces to find a vantage point from which he could survey the landscape beyond.

He was making himself a potential target and he knew it, but if there was some man out there injured, a man who had tried to help Jane, Clarence would find him.

And he did.

There was a body perhaps a hundred yards distant,

posed at an unnatural angle over a slab of upthrusting gray-yellow rock. Hatless.

Clarence climbed down from the boulders, nearly losing his balance, then starting forward again, the rock which he'd picked up to use as a bludgeon still clenched tightly in his left fist.

He lost sight of the hapless figure for a few seconds, and then broke through a patch of low conifers into open ground. Clarence could move more quickly, the footing more reliable. And he could see the body more clearly. There was a gun belt about the man's waist, but the holster was clearly empty. The man's feet were stockinged only, the boots taken, too. No horse grazed nearby—stolen, of course.

Just in case the man were alive and had some other weapon, Clarence called out to him as he approached. "Hey, man! I'm a friend of the old lady you helped back there. I want to help you."

The man's head rose slightly, and his lips moved, but Clarence could hear nothing.

Narrowing the distance to the apparently injured man, Clarence dropped the rock, showing his open hands. "I don't mean you any harm, man."

This time, the man's head did not rise.

Cautiously, lest this was some sort of trick of the men who had robbed Jane, Clarence approached the prostrate figure. As he did, he could see something he recognized quite clearly from military first aid films—the man had a sucking chest wound. Clarence bent over the man, the boulder he was laying on at approximately the height of a table. There was a bandana around the man's neck and

Clarence untied it, placed it over the wound. "Look, pal, my girl's a doctor. I'll get her and you'll—"

"Old lady—how is she?"

"Good," Clarence responded, thinking he was probably lying. Jáne had looked pale as death, and her breathing had seemed labored. And this man was clearly beyond any help short of a fully equipped modern hospital and a blood bank; his clothes were saturated with blood, and blood had puddled on the rock beneath him. The bullet had gone through and the man was bleeding from both sides of his body, the blood dark, which Clarence thought he remembered meant it was arterial. But Clarence kept compression on the chest wound despite the fact that the bandanna—Jack would have called it a "wild rag"—was already saturated. "What's your name, friend?"

"Al Cole. Look. Ya ever meet up with a Jim Cole—looks just like me. We's twins, twin brothers. Tell 'im he should go 'n' marry up Clarisse. She loves us both. An' me, I'm outa it fer good, an' that's plain fact. I'm killed by them darn devil range detectives workin' fer Jess Fowler."

There was a rattle from deep within the man's chest as he tried to say something else and failed. His eyelids fluttered, remained open, and his head lolled back. Blood trickled across his lower lip for a second or two, onto his chin. Then the blood flow stopped.

It was creepy in the extreme, but Clarence forced himself to touch the dead man's eyelids and push them down, having no idea if they would stay that way.

Clarence stepped back, stared at the man for a moment longer. He paused to pick up the rock he'd dropped, thinking that he might need it. At a quick jog trot, he started back toward where he had left Peggy to care for Jane, fearing that he might just be in time for another death.

Making his way rapidly along the route over which he had come, passing once again the rocks in which the light array had been/would be placed, Clarence quickly rejoined Peggy and Jane.

He had missed death, arrived only in time for its sorrowful aftermath. Clarence took Peggy up from her knees and into his arms and simply held her while she cried, Jane's body resting on the ground as if peacefully asleep.

Would her soul join that of her late husband, although he had not yet been born to grow up, meet her, live and work beside her and unwillingly abandon her through his death?

Time-travel, Clarence had realized from the moment he'd learned of the fate potentially in store for Jack, Ellen, Lizzie and David, was fraught with questions, scarce on answers.

But he suspected that he knew one answer. There had been something that struck him oddly about the mission supervisor, Marc Cole. It had been as if he had never met Marc Cole before, albeit that he had worked with the man for six months. And the cowboy, Al Cole, with the twin brother, Jim. And the girl—Clarisse had been her name— who had loved them both but, evidently, was to marry Al, who was dead. Had/would she marry Jim Cole instead? Had there been something different about the mission supervisor with the long blond hair before Jane had been inserted into another era? Had Al Cole not been killed, gone on to marry Clarisse? Was that it?

The answer, he knew, was that he would never know the answer, only wonder. If there had been something different about Marc Cole, the mission supervisor, Clarence could not remember what it was. And that infuriated him.

Another question nagged at him. Jack had once recounted a science fiction time-travel novel that he'd read as a boy. Clarence had never thought about it until now. In the story, when one of the time-travelers died in the past, it was as if they had never lived. Clarence believed in Fate, but not even Fate could be quite that cruel. But if it were, he would never know. He wanted to hit something, pulverize it.

That would have to wait until he met up with "them darn devil range detectives workin' fer Jess Fowler." Jane's wristwatch would be a novelty, the sort of thing a psycho might hold on to because of its uniqueness, as a kind of trophy.

Whoever this Jess Fowler bastard and his fucking range detectives were, if Clarence ever saw that "trophy" in the possession of one of them, he'd beat the man to death with his fists and enjoy every minute of it.

CHAPTER
✳ NINE ✳

Liz Naile didn't like her hair. Without the use of a hair dryer, it always looked flat. It reached to her shoulder blades. If she cut it short, as she'd worn it sometimes, drying it would be easier, but women in 1898 didn't wear short hair, and she would only draw more attention to herself.

Once, while substitute teaching for the frequently ailing Margaret Diamond, as she did periodically and more often than she cared to, she'd remarked to one of the students— a pretty girl of thirteen with really gorgeous hair—that the girl's hair always looked so perfect, she reminded her of Marsha Brady. Since television hadn't even been invented yet, and *The Brady Bunch* wasn't even in first runs let alone re-runs, Liz had quickly made up some little piece of bullshit to cover the slipup.

On another occasion, when the class had been studying a unit called "History of The World," and the closest thing to a textbook for twenty students had been one beautifully illustrated two-volume set with the same title, she had compared Genghis Khan to Adolph Hitler. She'd covered that by telling her students, "You'll study about him a lot later on."

That night, Lizzie asked her father and mother the dates for World War Two, realizing that, indeed, it would be much, much later on that anyone would hear of him. Her father had told her, "Hitler should be about nine years old right now."

"What if we went over to Germany—"

"Austria. He wasn't born in Germany. But what if we went over there and killed him?"

Lizzie thought about it and then said, "I guess we'd still be killing a nine-year-old boy and not a dictator, because he hasn't even heard of Nazis yet, right?"

"History," her mother began, "is going to present us with a lot of dilemmas, Liz. And a lot of opportunities. We're just going to have to decide on a case-by-case basis if something we do is going to screw up history and do more harm than good. Lots of times, it'll be a compromise."

As Liz stared at herself in her makeshift bedroom's mirror, compromise was exactly what she saw looking back at her. She wore her high school tennis-team T-shirt under a sweatshirt that had Calvin Klein emblazoned across the front, all of this over an ankle-length full skirt, the toes of her solitary pair of track shoes poking out from beneath its hem.

If someone rode up to the house, she could always lie and say something like "Uncle Calvin likes to personalize his gifts" and scrunch down a little so her skirt would cover her shoes completely.

She quit her room and started toward the front door along the wide corridor. One side of the house—where they had been living most of the time for the last six months—was completed, her father and mother still holding off on finishing the rest of the house in the—she considered—vain hope that somehow they'd find a way of electrifying parts of it. Liz had about given up on that. And David, who spent most of his time in town running the store, didn't seem to even think about it.

As she exited the house into the early December morning—it was nearly noon, but sleeping late when she could was one part of her old life she'd been able to hold on to—she saw her father. There was a chill in the air but, in spite of it, he was shirtless. He wore a gun, as he always did, but not his fancy one in the fancy black gunfighter rig, just a plain one he'd bought in town, worn crossdraw in a plain brown holster on a plain brown belt. Jack Naile was using a posthole digger, and she knew that he'd be expecting her—and her mother—to help him after a while. And she would. Despite her sex, she'd always had a great deal of upper-body strength; with David rarely home because of the store, more and more she'd found herself filling the function of surrogate son. She just thanked God that her body type didn't get big muscles from doing that sort of stuff, like guys did.

Her mother was down by the stream working with the cereal box-like camera and tripod she'd ordered from St. Louis. David brought it out on his last visit from town. Ellen Naile, all her adult life forced by necessity to take photos of little else but guns and holsters and knives in association with Jack Naile's magazine articles, was determined to actually do something she wanted with a camera; wisely, saving the film she had brought with her for special occasions, she was attempting to master the equipment currently available. Her mother was into compromise as well, Liz thought, smiling. For as long as Liz could remember, her mother had always preferred pants in the fall, winter and spring and shorts in the summer, only wearing a dress or skirt when the occasion called for it. Now Ellen Naile wore a long, dark blue skirt and a light blue long-sleeved blouse. The sleeves of the blouse were rolled up past her elbows, the collar of the blouse was left unbuttoned and the back of the skirt was drawn up between her legs, its hem tucked into the skirt's waistband, forming something like baggy legged pants. Her mother flat-out refused to wear an apron as so many women did as part of their regular attire.

Liz sauntered over toward the stream. When her dad saw her, he waved and she waved back, which gave him an excuse to stop using the posthole digger and roll a cigarette. He smoked much less than he had before they'd traveled back in time, but took a certain pride, she thought, in having learned to quite deftly roll a cigarette, even outside when it was a little breezy, as it was this morning.

Her mother was looking through the camera lens, and Liz could hear her snarling, "What a piece-of-crap lens!"

"Hey, Momma."

"Hi, sweetheart," her mother responded. "I'd be better off with Dad's mother's old Box Brownie. You know, I'm not into fancy cameras. That 35mm of mine we bought at J.C. Penney's back in 1975, I think. And I almost never used the wide angle lens. But this thing really sucks!"

Liz had started to hitch up her skirt just like her mother's as she asked, "Isn't there a better camera available? Maybe from Europe or someplace!"

"I don't know."

Liz was about to say something reassuring as soon as she could think of it. As she tucked the hem of her skirt into her waistband, she caught sight of a cloud of dust coming from the direction of town and the higher mountains beyond. "Who's that? It must be a big wagon or something?"

Her mother turned the camera around and leaned over it. "I can actually see something through this lens! You're right. That's a big dust cloud. Go tell your father."

Lizzie ran toward where her father was building the new corral, on the other side of the house from the stream, where the ground was flatter. "Daddy! Daddy!"

Her father had, apparently, just picked up the posthole digger again, the cigarette hanging out of the corner of his mouth. "What's the matter, princess?"

"Look! In the direction of town!"

She stopped running, about halfway between her mother and her father, her hands fumbling with the hem of her skirt to pull it out of her waistband so she could hide her 1990s track shoes from 1890s eyes.

"Lizzie. Go up on the porch and get that new Winchester shotgun David brought up from town. It's loaded, but the chamber's empty. Be careful."

Liz ran toward the porch, nearly tripping on her skirt. The shotgun—her father had told her what it was called, but she didn't remember—was leaned beside the door frame, its butt resting in a notched piece of wood her father had chiseled out for it, then nailed to the porch floor, the muzzle in a similarly contoured piece of wood. The shotgun was big and heavy.

Her father and mother had both gravitated toward the porch. She joined them, giving the shotgun to her father.

The cloud of dust was bigger, definitely nearer, but she couldn't see what was causing it. "Hey, guys? You think it's a stagecoach?"

"No stage line passes this way. No freight line, either. Whatever it is, whoever's driving it is coming to see us."

"You don't think it's Fowler's guys, now that you're no longer filling in as town marshal?" Ellen asked.

"A wagonload of range detectives? Doubtful. But be ready to get up on that porch and into the house and grab a gun if it looks like trouble." As he finished speaking, Jack seemed to weigh the shotgun in his hands. "Ellen? Lizzie? This shotgun was first used by the United States military as a trench gun during what will be World War I."

"Now is not the time to play *Jeopardy*, Jack."

"It's a '97 Winchester Pump. And if you have to use it fast and at close range, anchor the buttstock against your hip, work the pump and hold the trigger back. Peculiarity of '97s. As long as you hold the trigger back, the gun will fire as soon as the action closes. There's buckshot in here, and at close range—and I mean pretty close, like from here to the porch—you'll do a lot of damage. Just a good thing to remember."

"Right, Jack. We'll remember that. Won't we, Liz?"

"Oh, yeah! You bet!" Lizzie remembered the '97 part was what the gun was called, her attention elsewhere, on the still growing cloud of dust.

"'A fiery horse with the speed of light, a cloud of dust—'"

"It's probably not the masked man and his faithful Indian companion, Jack."

"Just trying to lighten things up a little bit, ladies."

"Don't try and lighten things up, Daddy. Just try and see what—"

"It's the Suburban!" Ellen Naile exclaimed.

"You've got good eyes, kid," Jack Naile declared. "Not only can you see through a cloud of dust that's more than a mile away, but you can see a hundred years into the future."

"Look! When the dust parts a little, Daddy," Liz said. "It's big and kind of gray—"

"Holy shit," Jack Naile hissed. "It is the Suburban, I think."

By this time, the horses, which were tethered to a sturdy rope picket line while the corral was being built, were starting to react, at first to the gigantic dust cloud. Soon they would see, and then hear the Suburban. The horses were hobbled, so they couldn't run.

Lizzie had to urinate, but that could wait.

So this was the legendary Naile family, minus the one that Clarence talked about more than any of the others. Clarence often quoted Jack or Ellen, talked unendingly about how wonderful and pretty Lizzie was—and she was beautiful, certainly—but he talked about David's capabilities as if David were some sort of "wunderkind" who was, somehow, beyond the ordinary human.

Peggy had stood off by the Suburban, the tethered horses seeming skittish but not terrified as the initial greeting, the reuniting of this oddly mixed family, took place. She'd smiled, was hugged by Lizzie, had shaken hands with Ellen, shaken hands with Jack, too, then was hugged by Jack as Clarence had mentioned, almost in passing, that they were engaged and had waited to be married until the family was reunited in the past. At this, Lizzie not only hugged her again, but seemed on the verge of tears of happiness. Ellen only looked at her, at once warmly yet oddly. Jack had said, "Welcome to the family, Peggy."

There were several exchanges about what was in the Suburban, in the trailer, some of the most genuine enthusiasm she had ever seen when Clarence reassured all and sundry that he'd brought all of the electrical wiring. There was the perfunctory man thing when Jack inspected the handguns, selected a "brace" of them, as he called them, and shoved them in his belt. She'd noticed that he was already wearing one gun and holding another in his hands as they'd approached.

There was a quick exchange between Clarence and Jack Naile about "How'd you get here?"

Clarence ended it by telling his uncle, "Long story. Tell you about it later."

Jack Naile stood about an inch or so under six feet tall, had a broad chest, a surprisingly narrow waist with little trace of a middle-aged gut. His arms—he was shirtless at first, but donned a shirt as they entered the house—were long, muscled with reasonably well-defined triceps. His hair was reddish-brown, with plenty of silver-gray, especially at the sides, though not yet at the temples. His mustache had the mottled look of both his hair colors and held a hint of yellow from his smoking. He'd lit a cigarette—rolling it first; Clarence kidding him about it—as they stood outside and talked. He had brown eyes and his hands—bony, with the knuckles and veins prominent—looked as though they should have belonged to a pianist, a violinist or a surgeon. He was, of course, none of these. According to Clarence, Jack had a really good singing voice but was too fumble-fingered to play any instrument requiring more manual dexterity than a kazoo. Clarence had told her, on more than one occasion, that Jack would say, "I was going to be a brain surgeon, but I couldn't complete my studies because of the expense. It was those custom-made surgical gloves with ten thumbs."

The hair on Jack Naile's chest, particularly the right side, had significant white in it, and there was some beginning trace of white hair on his shoulders. He had a lot of hair on his back, and she didn't like that, although she imagined that some women probably found it sexy.

Ellen Naile, who was forty-six, Peggy knew, looked barely thirty. With the right clothes and makeup—and she didn't seem to be wearing any makeup—she would have looked younger still. There was a gray hair or two visible when the sun caught her just right, but her hair—a dark auburn—was beautiful. Parted down the middle, sixties fashion, or what kids in the 1990s called a "butt cut," Ellen had hair almost to her waist. Ellen's features were prominent without being at all sharp. With the right makeup, her cheekbones would have looked like the kind a model would have envied. Ellen stood about five seven, discounting the period shoes she wore which added another inch or more to her height. Her eyes were what some would call hazel, gray and green without being either or both. They were very pretty.

Jack's voice was baritone, at once soothing and commanding. Ellen was a perfect alto.

The much-spoken-of Lizzie immediately struck Peggy as the warmest, sweetest person she had ever met. Her features more closely followed those of her father than her mother, even to his eye color, and she shared his hair color. And her hair, without any part, held back by an anachronistic plastic headband, fell just past her shoulders. Dark-eyed, with the most genuinely, sincerely engaging smile Peggy had ever seen, Lizzie somehow had her mother's look about her, even though there was no particular feature or combination of features that could at all be compared.

With a more amply endowed bosom than her mother, Lizzie stood perhaps five-three or five-four. Like her mother, Lizzie was also alto-voiced.

Lizzie seemed to convey her mother's femininity and confidence, while mingling it with her father's apparent strength. She was an interesting girl, complex yet somehow seeming to be one of those people about whom it was said, "What you see is what you get."

After they had all entered the house, Ellen offered drinks, apologizing for not having any sort of refrigeration. There was only wine, whiskey, water, coffee or tea. Clarence announced, "We brought a bar refrigerator, Jack!"

"Bless you," Lizzie declared emphatically. "Now we can have ice."

Clarence took a glass of water. Peggy had a glass of

wine, as did Jack and Ellen. Lizzie had water, complaining that it tasted like nothing at all, only wet.

Clarence smiled as he held out a package of unfiltered Camel cigarettes to Jack and said, "I've got a dozen cartons packed in the trailer."

"Which nut you want me to cut off, the left or right?"

"Daddy!"

"Sorry, princess. I was overcome by emotion."

Emotion was, it appeared, the watchword here. Ellen had merely given Clarence a light hug and a peck on the cheek when they first arrived. But that she loved Clarence was obvious from everything about her. Jack had hugged Clarence as if Jack and his nephew were two bears about to get into a wrestling match. Lizzie had hugged Clarence around the neck and given him several kisses on the cheek, then held his hand for a while.

"Anybody want some lunch?" Ellen asked, as if desperate to do something.

"I'll help," Peggy volunteered.

"The kitchen's awfully small at the moment. With no refrigeration, we've been eating a lot of pasta. I make it myself. Liz helps me." She looked at Clarence, "I hope that's a pretty good-sized bar refrigerator, or we'll be eating smoked turkey for Christmas. How soon before you guys can get some electricity in here?"

"Ahh—"

"Think about those devilled eggs you like, Clarence, before you give me an answer. And, Jack, you think about that cherry cream-cheese pie Lizzie makes. You don't like smoked turkey, remember?" Ellen smiled and walked off, presumably toward the kitchen.

The house—what was completed of it—was remarkably (and uncharacteristically for the period) bright and airy, with large picture windows about the size of what might be seen in a jewelry store. The furniture was quite plain, simple. It looked less than half-finished, but when it was done, its size would be impressive.

The homemade pasta was good, but Ellen apologized for it. "You can't get most of the herbs and spices to make a decent spaghetti sauce. In the spring, I'm finally going to start a garden."

The water for the pasta was boiled over the hearth, the room slightly warmer than comfortable, but the fire was gradually diminishing. How could any woman who had been living and working in the late nineteen hundreds ever live here, Peggy Greer wondered. No stove, no refrigerator, probably no running water. "There may be a chance for you guys to escape," Peggy blurted out.

Jack and Ellen both looked at her. Without shifting his gaze from her face, Jack said, "Clarence—it's about time you told me how you guys were able to get here."

Clarence started, Peggy chiming in with some of the scientific details, assuming that Jack and Ellen and Lizzie might understand at least some of the process, pleased that they seemed to grasp it quite well. When Clarence recounted Jane's tragic death and the death of the cowboy, Jack Naile offered an explanation of just who Jess Fowler was and the nature of his range detectives.

"Daddy killed two of Jess Fowler's range detectives when they tried to assault Momma and me. David was fighting one of them off, but the second one hit him from behind. When Daddy was town marshal, Fowler's men left us alone. Now, though . . ." Lizzie let the sentence hang unfinished.

"Clarence told me something," Peggy Greer volunteered. "It's important. There was a tech guy—head guy, really, like the mission-command guy—and his name was Marc Cole. I didn't notice it, but Clarence thought that Marc Cole seemed strange somehow, familiar but not. And the young cowboy was named Cole. He was a twin, and he and his brother were in love with the same girl. Now, suppose that because Jane Rogers came into the past, the young cowboy's life ended when it shouldn't have. What if Marc Cole was somehow different? I mean, there's no way to tell from this end, but if we could get back, and we found out that Marc Cole's great-grandfather was the young cowboy's brother, what if that's the reason Marc Cole struck Clarence as somehow odd, something wrong with him? What if Marc Cole, as we knew him just before we left, was different because the young cowboy should have been his great-grandfather and Jane changed all of that?"

"So," Jack Naile posited, "we know that Ellen and the kids and I were supposed to come here, into the past. But anyone else, like you guys, could alter history in little ways or big ways."

"Like when I suggested going to Austria and killing Hitler!" Lizzie enthused.

"Hitler?" Clarence repeated.

"Yeah, he's about nine years old now," Jack said dismissively. "Where we came from, though, the little shit grew up—nobody killed him while he was nine. On the surface, if you get around the moral problem of killing a nine-year-old who hasn't become a mass murderer yet and won't for another three-plus decades, you've gotta basically ask yourself if playing God could cause more evil than it prevented. The point I think you're making, Peggy, should have dawned on you guys before you came here in the first place.

"I'm ecstatic over having the contents of the Suburban," Jack Naile went on, "especially the electrical wiring—"

"And the cigarettes," Ellen supplied.

"And the cigarettes—right. And, we don't have to tell you how much we missed you, Clarence, and how happy we are to know that you and Peggy are getting married. But if Alan Naile was right that there was no historical record of you being with us in the past, then you've altered the time loop. Even if you guys go back—and you have to explain how that would work—the damage—" He lit a precious Camel cigarette. "'Damage' is too harsh a word. Let's say the change could already have radically or subtly altered the future. Maybe for the good, or maybe for the not so good."

"Going back is simply a matter of figuring how to reverse the process, if it can be done," Peggy volunteered.

"And if it can't be reversed," Ellen Naile said, "you and Clarence can't go off and be hermits, never interacting with anyone."

"Well, shit!" Clarence swore.

"Clarence," Lizzie said, "you'll just have to do your best to, well, do your best. And rely on that to get you through and not cause anything bad to happen that wouldn't have happened already. You're a good man, so the chances of you doing good are greater than the chances of you causing something evil or terrible to happen."

"Well put, kiddo," Jack Naile told his daughter.

Peggy wondered if she had—somehow—done something which would unravel history, merely for her own selfish ends. And, if the process couldn't be reversed, if they couldn't even at least communicate with the future, they'd never even know . . .

"It's so damned obvious!" Alan declared. "God, I'm stupid," he told Marc Cole and Morton Hardesty. Morton Hardesty was his chief scientific advisor, privy to anything that had to do with Horizon Enterprises and technology. They sat in Alan's trailer, the note Clarence and Peggy had left inside the crate-shaped capsule on a round table around which they all sat. "It's a fricken mailbox to us, the capsule, but we can send stuff out by express. We can communicate with the past and the past can communicate with the future. They still use the capsule as a mail drop. What we do is periodically send smaller capsules back, with mail from here."

"You know what it costs, Alan, every time we send something back?" Morton Hardesty queried.

"Yeah, and I bet you do, too, Mort. Hell, it's worth it. We can pass messages through time." Alan looked at Marc Cole. "Did you find out if your great-grandfather had a twin brother who died?"

Marc Cole ran his fingers back through his long blond hair. "I got my mom on the phone and she called my aunt Clarisse, who was named after my great grandmother.

Great grandpa Jim had a brother named Al. Al turned up missing a year or so before the turn of the century."

"My God, what have we done?" Alan murmured, not expecting a direct, immediate answer . . .

Bethany Kaminsky paced back and forth in front of her enormous and spotless desk, her hands thrust into the pockets of pleated, loose-fitting, charcoal-gray slacks. She wore a silk blouse with long, full sleeves and deep cuffs with multiple buttons covered in the same material, the blouse nearly as dark a gray as her slacks, unbuttoned to her cleavage, a solitary—and large—diamond visible, pendant from a thin gold chain. This and a Jubilee band Rolex—he couldn't see it, but she always wore it, even in bed—were her only jewelry.

Morton Hardesty couldn't take his eyes off her, hadn't been able to take his mind off her since their first clandestine meeting six months earlier. In all that time, this was the first time they'd met in her penthouse office at Lakewood Industries' world headquarters. Because it was Sunday morning, she had insisted that it would be safe.

Bethany Kaminsky's blonde hair formed a perfect bell shape, barely touching her shoulders, moving as she moved, thick, gorgeous, beautiful, in control, as she was. Her blue eyes sparkled under a brow that was knit in concentration and—he'd seen the look before—anger. "So," she said at last, looking at him, "you cannot bring them back from here."

"I don't think so, Bethany."

"You either think or you know, Mort! What is it?"

"Given current technology, I know that we can't. See, as

I've told you ever since Lakewood Industries approached me about this, Dr. Rogers didn't invent time-travel. All she did was unwittingly participate in an accident, and her equipment kept a nearly perfect record of what transpired. She would have been the first person to tell you that time-travel, given our current level of technology, is impossible, if it would ever be possible. All she wanted to do was broadcast electricity without wires. On the plus side, we're close to achieving that; maybe another decade's worth of work and Horizon Enterprises will be able to bring electricity to every corner of the globe. Or," Hardesty digressed, "if you keep paying me, Lakewood Industries will beat Horizon to the punch and get the patents and the loot that goes with them.

"All that we did when we sent inanimate objects and the like into the past," he explained, "then eventually sent Dr. Rogers and the Nailes' nephew, Clarence, and Dr. Greer with him into the past was to artificially duplicate the energy waves Dr. Rogers had accidentally created during the thunderstorm. Horizon Enterprises still doesn't have a clue as to why it works. We've gotten really efficient at duplicating the process, however, like a dog that just keeps getting better and better at performing the same popular trick. But all that we can do is send someone or something back in time a period of ninety-six years, sixty-eight days, four hours, twenty-three minutes and sixteen seconds. We can only send someone or something to the same place and nowhere else. The whole thing is probably a research blind alley as far as real time-travel might be concerned. No way to tell."

"So, if you time-traveled somebody from my office—"

Bethany Kaminsky almost sprang onto her desk, crossing her legs Indian fashion like a child sitting on the floor, waiting for someone to tell her a story. But she was doing the talking. "So, if you time-traveled me right now, I'd wind up in exactly the same place."

She had such tiny feet and tiny shoes. "Which," Morton Hardesty pointed out, allowing himself to laugh a little, "would be very bad for you, Bethany. Ninety-six years and sixty-eight days ago, Lakewood Industries hadn't yet built a high-rise office building in the Chicago Loop. Therefore, you'd wind up in the air hundreds of feet over turn-of-the-century Chicago, and you'd fall to your death."

"I get the point, Mort. What's the exact problem with making it a two-way street?"

"Okay, Bethany, you're not a physicist, but this is the general idea. We can't reverse the wave pattern fully unless we have equipment in place at the point of origination for the persons or things that we wish to bring back."

"You mean there, there, ahh, back in the past."

"Bingo! In theory, if we were to send duplicate equipment ninety-six years back in time, and we had it perfectly synchronized with the equipment here in the present day, we could probably do it."

"Then why hasn't Horizon done it? What's Alan Naile afraid of?" Bethany Kaminsky lit a cigarette, climbed off the desk and took an ashtray from the glass coffee table in front of the couch. She set the ashtray on the desk and resumed her cross-legged seated position, this time kicking her shoes halfway across the office. She wore semi-transparent black stockings. He wondered if they were pantyhose or if she used a garter belt.

"A couple of things. First, Alan's afraid he'll fuck up history. I told you about the thing with the dead cowboy and our mission control guy, Cole. We don't know if it happened, but if it did, the consequences of any further deaths in the past might prove devastating, people disappearing all over the place and we'd—for the most part, at least—never even know they were gone, because they never would have been here . . . in a way, at least. You need the damn math to even talk about this, Bethany. This is—"

"What else?"

"That's the principal thing," Hardesty told her. "As much as he'd like to get Clarence and Peggy Greer back, and Alan Naile feels he needs to before history is further disrupted, there's an even bigger problem."

"Which is?" Bethany Kaminsky lit a second cigarette from the glowing tip of the first. He could almost taste her lipstick on the filter.

"To do it—and we never really shared this point with Dr. Rogers—we needed a small nuclear-powered generator. We were extremely careful and nothing ever happened out of the ordinary. To bring them back from the past, if we could, we'd have to ship the identical apparatus, about which I spoke a moment ago, into the past. Including a duplicate nuclear-powered generator. If something went wrong and we lost control of the device, we could be responsible for something incalculable.

"You have to remember," Hardesty continued patiently, "that there were whole bunches of really sharp scientists around ninety-six years ago. Once we shipped the equipment into the past, there'd be no way of retrieving it, since the equipment itself would be needed to transport the equipment. Somebody would have to stay behind, and then there'd still be potential problems, maybe worse than those that Clarence and Peggy Greer might cause or have caused already. And, if some really good and creative scientists from 1898—well, it's 1899 there, now—got hold of that generator, instead of the first atomic bombs coming at the end of World War Two, hell, a nuclear weapon might have been dropped— Here," he said, motivated by a flash of inspiration. "Let's say that all of that happened and the right German scientists got their hands on fissionable material. Instead of everybody slogging back and forth through the mud of no-man's-land in France during World War One, the Germans could have used biplanes to fly cover and dropped a nuclear weapon over Paris or something, out of a dirigible, or smuggled a nuke into London to force the British out. Hell, when America joined the war in 1917, the Germans could have sent a bomb to New York or Washington and cleaned our clocks for good.

"Alan is right, I'm afraid," Hardesty concluded. "There's just too much risk in this thing for any rational person to take."

Bethany Kaminsky seemed unfazed, and Hardesty was more than slightly unnerved at the thought. "So, if we went back in time to—1899 now?—to 1899, and, let's say, we set up the initial equipment at a spot somewhere in present-day Germany or England or wherever, we could ship all the equipment we needed back in time to that same spot in Germany or England. And we could just travel back and forth between now and the past, however we wanted, like going through a damn revolving door.

And, if we had a cadre of personnel armed with state-of-the-art modern weaponry, nobody back then could hope to win against us and seize the stuff. Right?"

"In theory, yeah—but, Beth, you can't—" And Morton Hardesty suddenly shivered, because he realized that what he feared was exactly what she was thinking.

"Think of the possibilities, Morty. Hmm," Bethany purred. "The reason Horizon Enterprises has always been a jump ahead of Lakewood Industries isn't because the Nailes were such sharp business people. No! Hell, no! They knew what was going to happen. So, what if we went back and made a deal, long before Horizon Enterprises became anything more than a fucking fancy variety store and a pissy little ranch? We offered the future's technology to the three countries which would have the capability and the balls to use it, the manufacturing infrastructure to make it happen to our specifications. The United States, England and Germany. The only three contenders, with France a distant number four.

"Whichever one came out as the best deal," Bethany enthused, "gets us under contract with a shitload of money and real power in exchange for us giving them the tech stuff to take over the whole fucking world. And they can't double cross us, because we still control superior technology that they want and we can use to crush them like fucking bugs if we have to. And they'll be terrified we'll make a deal with their enemies. It's perfect. It's a marriage made in Heaven, Morty."

"Look, Bethany. I'm nuts about you. You know that. But you're talking crazy stuff now. What you're proposing could just as easily be a marriage made in Hell."

"Well, if the fucking's good, who cares, right?" Bethany didn't glare at him, only smiled. "By the 1920s, we'd be the ultimate power in the whole world, Mort. By now, 1995, we'd flat-out rule the whole fucking planet."

"You might obliterate your own existence, too, Bethany. Or you might destroy the whole population of the planet with just one mistake."

"Then again," Bethany smiled almost wistfully, "I might pull it off. We might, Morty," and she drew her feet up under her then, catlike, and sprang from her desk. She crossed to his chair in two long, easy strides and sat down in Morton Hardesty's lap. Bethany Kaminsky's hands grabbed his face roughly, and her mouth crushed his lips under her own.

CHAPTER
❊ TEN ❊

The *Nugget*, Atlas' optimistically renamed newspaper, had dispatched its top-flight photographer—who was also the editor, the copy boy, the reporter and the paper delivery person—to take their picture. "All of you should remember that this photo will help build business for Jack Naile—General Merchandise, so you should smile because of all the money you'll be bringing in."

This was the photo, her daughter and herself with absurd picturebook hats, hourglass-waisted long dresses worn over heavy-boned corsets, David in a pinchback suit, spats and a derby, Jack wearing a black vested suit, white shirt and tie and the black Stetson he'd painstakingly shaped to match the one worn by Richard Boone. Jack and David were armed, of course. And this was the photo Arthur Beach had sent them in the future, confirming that an impossible set of ircumstances was about to alter their lives forever, an impossible set of circumstances that had become their lives.

Ellen Naile had watched this scene in countless western movies she'd seen on television on Saturday afternoons with her father (when Jack Brickhouse wasn't doing play-by-play for a Chicago Cubs game), seen it also in western movies her Jack had talked her into watching over the years of their life together. Given their present circumstances, the threat of watching a western movie had passed; she lived a western movie, instead.

The photographer's left hand was raised high, holding the long flash-powder tray, his right hand controlling the shutter; his head vanished under the camera's black cloth shroud. Perhaps it was just the desire to stay in character for the period, or perhaps it was something deeper than that, an unexpressed fear that, when the flash powder detonated, they would all be blown to bits. But they stood rigidly, waiting, and waiting, and waiting.

There was the flash, and the photo was made. Ellen leaned up to whisper in Jack's ear, "I'm going into the back of the store to change and get rid of this stupid hat and this damn corset."

"I'll help you, at least with the corset part," Jack gallantly volunteered.

"I bet you will."

Ellen entered the store, expecting that Lizzie would be right behind her, expecting that Lizzie would be just as eager as she to change into more comfortable clothing. But, as she looked behind her, she saw that young Bobby Lorkin, the boy who did odd jobs and messengering, was outside, trying to make conversation with Lizzie. He was sweet on her, Ellen knew the look well, remembered it from the mirror when she'd had that look in her own eyes after first becoming aware of Jack as more than just one of the guys in high school.

Lizzie did not have that look for Bobby Lorkin, hadn't yet had it for anyone. And Lizzie was waiting for that look. Lizzie wanted a marriage for love, not convenience.

Ellen walked on through the store, toward the back room, where she would change. David hadn't yet turned the store into a supermarket, but it was a little reminiscent of a convenience store. Stock was arranged to facilitate traffic patterns, to allow customers to inspect goods at closer range than over a counter. The self-serve supermarket was not to be "invented" for quite some time yet, the credit for that innovation reserved for Piggly Wiggly stores. Yet David had displays, was using his merchandising skills to pitch product rather than merely waiting for a customer to ask for something by name. Since so much ordering was done from catalogs, David had catalogs arranged on a smallish desk the height of a bar, with three bar stools next to the desk, the setup almost identical to that used with pattern books in some stores in the late twentieth century.

Closing the storeroom door behind her and wedging a chair under the door handle in order to avoid having someone walk in on her while she was changing, Ellen began to undress, the ridiculous hat the first thing to go. The hairstyle that went with it would be rectified later. She started getting out of the dress. For a woman to properly dress, with all the requisite undergarments of the period, could take the better part of a half hour. Undressing was quicker, but not anything near what one might call convenient or quick.

But, all told, things weren't so bad. They had working plumbing and could shower and wash hair as regularly as they had in the future. A large, central room of the house—for privacy's sake a room with no windows—was relatively fully electrified. They could listen to music, watch a video, run a hair dryer, almost live like normal people. Admittedly, washing dishes without a dishwasher was a total drag, and cooking on a wood stove, albeit the best multiburner model available from back East, was not only a chore, but sometimes quite an adventure.

By rationing her supply of modern 35mm film and mastering the antiquated equipment of what was the present day, she'd been taking some of the best pictures she'd ever taken, and had been forced by necessity to get into developing, something she had always avoided (just as Jack, firearms aficionado that he was, had always shied away from hand loading ammunition).

She had created a small scandal in town by taking on a few writing assignments for the local newspaper, pieces which had nothing to do with church socials, recipes or women's fashions.

Although David, through skillful ordering, could obtain many comparatively modern products for their use, to get a decent shampoo still required brewing their own. Other personal items demanded innovative approaches as well. Lizzie and Helen Bledsoe had become great unlikely friends. Theirs was an improbable friendship because Elizabeth, with the vastly broader range of experiences to which she had been exposed, was savvy and sophisticated. Helen was wildly naive. Whereas Helen was grounded, by and large, in only the homely skills and her knowledge of the world was, by any standard, parochial, Liz had traveled much of the United States, had rubbed elbows with the famous, stayed in some of the finest hotels and dined in some of the best restaurants. Through books, magazines, newspapers, television and radio—even school field trips—Liz had a knowledge of the world around her and its possibilities, even in this time. She knew that men would walk on the Moon in three-quarters of a century, would perform open-heart surgery, and would cross the United States coast to coast in hours rather than months. Yet more importantly still, Liz had been raised with the idea that "The only thing a man can do that a woman can't is piss standing up without getting his legs wet." For a woman to compensate for the superior physical strength and endurance of the male simply meant—usually—the substitution of brain for brawn, even if that meant recruiting a man to do the strength-related task for her, such as twisting open a stubborn jar lid. Elizabeth was very much the traditional female, but realized that her horizons could be as broad or nearly so as she worked to make them. Helen was schooled in the idea of achieving full contentment and realization of personal abilities in keeping a clean home for a husband who was the ultimate authority and had the final say-so in every aspect of life, to raise their children so that the boys would be as he was and the girls would, however such meekness might not be to their liking, acquiesce, serve, obey.

In discussing this concept of female second-class-citizenship with their daughter once, Jack had described the arrangement in a manner at once bizarre, yet painfully accurate. "However much a man might care for a woman, genuinely love her, in certain societies at certain times—even today—a wife was/is expected to be a love dummy which does not require inflation, yet is capable of house-cleaning and cooking."

Despite a chasm of differences between the two girls—and, sometimes, Ellen imagined, to Helen's mother's consternation—Lizzie and Helen were pals, buddies, and Lizzie, Ellen aiding in the conspiracy as often as she could, was regularly and conscientiously planting the seeds of independence in Helen's life, the idea that in order to have a free will and the intelligence to use it, testicles were not required.

Clarence's wife, Peggy, a medical doctor possessing knowledge of which the finest doctors in the age had not the slightest inkling, would be considered an oddity, nearly a freak, merely because of her sex. So far, at least, Peggy had hidden her skills; Ellen doubted Peggy could perpetuate so distasteful a charade.

That Lizzie would someday move to a large city, where a woman's role could be less constrained if she had the brains and the talent, was obvious to Ellen. Lizzie would still only be in her thirties in the 1920s, when skirts shortened and minds broadened—at least a bit.

But the thought of Lizzie moving off sometime was very depressing, would leave a hole in her own heart and in Jack's.

Ellen buttoned her blouse, rolled up her sleeves, cursed her hemline and left the storeroom.

Soon, David and Clarence would be off to San Francisco, "sin city" with its enticing Barbary Coast brothels, its ruthless press gangs shanghaiing the unwitting and its vile opium dens where a night on the pipe was some men's glimpse of paradise—their only glimpse. David's and Clarence's mission was to convert a modest quantity of the family diamonds into coin of the realm, the remodeling of the store and the completion of their house having seriously depleted the family's cash reserves.

However, there was a plus to David and Clarence being gone; she would be so worried about them she wouldn't have much time to fret over Lizzie moving away someday and how lonely Jack and she would be.

And, in it all, Ellen found herself unable not to smile. Jack, ever the fan of Richard Boone's immortal black-clad gunfighter, had instructed David and Clarence, "Whatever you do, if there really is a Hotel Carlton in San Francisco, get me a piece of hotel stationery or something. Okay, guys?"

David and Clarence, who had once obtained a Texas Ranger badge made from a Mexican peso and framed it with fake Texas Ranger identity papers as a gift for Jack, enthusiastically agreed to humor him this time as well.

Titus Blake swung down off the same big chestnut mare on which he'd ridden into Atlas when he'd come to assume the job of town marshal. Ellen remembered that day very well; Blake's arrival had meant that Jack would no longer be filling in as the only peace officer in Atlas. She had never been fond of the idea of Jack being a cop (although Jack and she had several good friends in law enforcement in the future they'd left behind); Jack being the town marshal—a cop by another name—had been fraught with the potential to shatter their life together.

When Titus Blake rode down Atlas' wide, dusty Main Street that first time, there'd been little gear on his saddle, merely a canteen, a rifle scabbard and a pair of saddle bags that had looked all but empty. The second horse he'd had in tow wore a pack saddle with what, she'd assumed at the time, were all of Titus Blake's worldly possessions.

This time there was no packhorse. Blake's saddlebags bulged, and a bedroll covered by a faded yellow slicker was lashed to the saddle as well. The rifle scabbard was there, its mouth just beneath the right saddlebag, the butt of a lever-action Winchester poking out from inside it. A shotgun with double barrels and exposed hammers was secured in a second scabbard on the left side of the saddle, near the horn. Ellen remembered Jack calling such a firearm a "Greener."

Titus Blake looked ready for a gunfight and not some showdown at high noon with a lone gunman. But for the moment, all he did was remove his high-crowned, broad-brimmed gray Stetson and ask, "Miz Naile, Jack home?"

Ellen Naile inquired, "What seems to be the problem, marshal?"

"Ain't for no woman's ears, ma'am, lessen your husband thinks it's proper. But I can say this. I need his help."

"Come inside," Ellen said without further hesitation.

"Ma'am?"

"Yes?" She turned around and looked at Titus Blake. "What is it?"

"Reckon I should remove my spurs?"

Ellen Naile could never remember the names for different styles of spurs, whether they were "jingle bobs" or whatever, but the marshal's spurs had big rowels with spikes. "If you're careful, Marshal, I don't think they'll be a problem."

"If you say so, Miz Naile."

Ellen forced herself to smile. Exaggerated politeness to women generally pissed her off. Ellen Naile opened the front door and went inside, Titus Blake's spurs jingling after her. "You can leave your hat on that table, if you'd like."

"Thank you kindly, ma'am."

Ellen led him into the parlor off to the left of the short entrance hallway, the civilized side of the hearth to her right. The hearth in the kitchen, on the other side of the wall, shared a common chimney with this one. Sometimes, pleasant kitchen smells wafted their way into the room and imparted a cozy atmosphere she would have never thought she would enjoy, but did.

"Would you care for a drink, Marshal?"

"Right kind of you, Miz Naile, but I ain't got a lot of time."

Ellen took that as meaning he wished she'd shut up and go get her husband. "Please, take that chair by window. It's quite comfortable."

"Standin' is just fine, Miz Naile."

She nodded to Marshal Blake, gathered her skirts and walked out of the room and down the side hall, stopping at the door on her right. Very faintly, she could hear something that sounded like a car chase, punctuated by gunfire. She opened the door quite quickly and just wide enough to slip through, closing it even more rapidly behind her. Jack was listening to a CD, but wearing headphones while cleaning a revolver partially disassembled on the smallish table in front of him. It was the audio from the Mel Gibson videotape that Lizzie was watching on television that Ellen was afraid Marshal Blake might hear. How could she ever explain the sounds of gunfire, incidental music and high-speed "horseless carriages" coming from inside her house? Ellen had never thought that she would ever utter such words, but she said, "Turn off that Mel Gibson movie, Lizzie! Now!" Her daughter's eyes registered naked shock.

Jack stood in front of the cold hearth, his right arm outstretched along its mantle, his right foot on the hearth's elevated brick apron, his knee bent. He smoked a cigarette he'd just rolled.

Titus Blake, hands resting on the butts of the Colts at his hips, cleared his throat as if about to make a school recitation. His prominent but tiny Adam's apple bobbed up and down. "I need a man who's got a good hand with a gun and a cool head, Jack. There's gonna be killin', I reckon. You sure it's all right for Miz Naile and Miss Lizzie to hear this?"

Ellen was sometimes very proud of Jack. "You said that time was of the essence—very important, Titus. If you feel uncomfortable talking about this in front of my wife and daughter, it'll just take that much longer if I help you, because I'll have to take the time to repeat to them everything you've told me. Ellen's a grown-up. So's Lizzie. We have no secrets around this house."

"As you say, Jack. By mornin', news o' this will be spread all over the county. We get a passel o' armed folks don't know what they's doin' chasin' all over the countryside, there could be some real problems.

"Tom and Mary Bledsoe's place was attacked by a bunch o' no-goods with their faces hid behind bandannas and such. Tom caught two bullets in the leg. Ain't bad shot up, though. Miz Bledsoe's got herself a bunch o' bruises and maybe a broke wrist. Brave woman," he editorialized. "Drove the wagon in with that wrist o' hers, she did, Tom laid out in back with a tourniquet on his leg. They're bein' tended to. But them sons o' bitches—forgive me, Miz Naile! I wouldn't blame your husband if'n he felt like horsewhippin' me sayin' words like them in front o' you and the young lady."

"I've heard worse, and so has Elizabeth," Ellen told him truthfully. "I've even said worse. So has Elizabeth."

"Yes, ma'am. Anyways, them owlhoots hauled young Helen away screamin' an' all, throwed her over a saddle and rode off west with her, toward the mountains. Miz Bledsoe thinks she counted eight o' them men. We gotta get little Helen back 'fore any of them eight men tries a, . . ." Marshal Blake let the thought hang.

"Having their way with her?" Jack supplied.

"Yes."

Jack turned away from Titus Blake and walked toward where Ellen and Lizzie stood just inside the entrance to the room. "No need waking Clarence's wife, but when you get the chance, mention what happened and see if she thinks it might be a wise move to just casually check out Tom Bledsoe. Not until I get back. The three of you will be safer here, together. When I hear *tourniquet* mentioned, I start thinking damaged blood vessels and infections and stuff. You guys know I've gotta do this."

"I wish I could go with you," Ellen whispered only loudly enough for Jack and Lizzie to hear.

"Me, too, Daddy."

"I know you guys do. When in Rome, huh? So, you guys gotta stay here and be extra alert. Keep guns handy, more than usual. We've never had any repercussions from Jess Fowler's range detectives, and there's no reason to be paranoid and think they've got anything to do with this. It never really hurts to be paranoid." And at that, Jack looked over his right shoulder at Titus Blake. "I'll get my gear. If you want a fresh horse, you're welcome to one."

"I'm fine."

"As you say." Jack nodded. As he left the room, he shot Ellen and Lizzie a wink.

It was nearly nightfall as she looked beyond the corral and toward the mountains to the west, their peaks obscured by heavy clouds. But regardless of the cloud cover, the flashes of lightning that had been visible in the mountains for the past several evenings could still be seen.

Elizabeth Naile had the upper-body strength to throw the saddle on her father's horse, but at three and one-half inches over five feet tall, she had to stand on her tiptoes as she did it. Her mother was making sandwiches for the men to take with them, her father changing into trail clothes and packing his gear. With David away, the job of saddling the big chestnut mare with black stockings, mane and tail had fallen to her.

As she tightened the cinch strap, she remembered her

father's explanation as to why he had named the horse as he had. "Most of the horses on television and in the movies had really manly kinds of names. Silver, Scout, Victor, Trigger, Champion, Razor, Buckshot—even Joker is a guy name. But with a mare, it'd be kind of dumb to have a name like that. I needed something to call her, and I was thinking about it, and for some reason I remembered when you were little and used to play with dolls."

"You're not going to name her Pretty Pony, Daddy!" Lizzie had interrupted.

Her father had laughed. "Good idea, though. I decided to call her Barbie."

Lizzie led Barbie out of the corral and brought her to the hitching rail in front of the house and tied her there beside Marshal Blake's horse.

Her father stepped onto the porch in company with Titus Blake in the next instant. He wore his black hat with the concho band, a dark gray cotton pullover shirt with the buttons that went halfway down its front left open. He wore his fancy gun belt with the long-barreled Colt over a pair of black woolen slacks, boots, of course, but no spurs. A pair of brown saddlebags was over his left shoulder, a slicker-wrapped bedroll, a jacket and his .45-70 rifle in his hands. Lizzie took the rifle and slipped it into the rear-mounted scabbard on the right side of Barbie's saddle while her father tied the saddlebags and bedroll behind the cantle.

Her mother emerged onto the porch a moment later, carrying a white canvas sack and a blanket canteen. Lizzie took the canteen and slung it to the right side of the saddle horn, her mother looping the sack on the other side. "The sack's got six big sandwiches—nothing that should spoil too easily—extra makings for cigarettes, extra matches and a hundred extra rounds of .45 Colt ammunition, just in case."

"Thank you." Her father kissed her mother's forehead.

"Much obliged, Miz Naile."

Elizabeth's mother smiled back politely at Titus Blake, and then looked up into her husband's face. "You were worried about Jess Fowler and his men. I'm still wondering about the lightning flashes we've been seeing. I'm not going to tell you to be careful, but why is it that guys get all the fun?"

"You know, I saw George Montgomery and Dorothy Malone play this scene once in a western movie. So don't worry. He came back after he got the bad guys." Her father swept her mother into his arms and kissed her, then kissed her again and still again.

He pulled on his coat, slipped the knot on Barbie's reins from the hitching rail and swung up into the saddle. Cocking his hat back on his head, he leaned off the right side of his saddle and took Lizzie's face in his hand, saying, "Gimme a kiss, kiddo."

She kissed her father's cheek, her arms closing around his neck and shoulders for an instant. He kissed her head. Then he leaned down off the left side of his saddle and kissed her mother again.

Lizzie mounted the porch, her mother stepping up beside her. Her father took off his black cowboy hat for an instant and replaced it, but pulled down low over his forehead. "Let's do this, Titus." Barbie wheeled left under her rider's urging knees and heels and started off toward the mountains.

"Riding off into the sunset," Lizzie's mother said, her voice sounding a little strained.

"Daddy'll be all right."

"I know. I was just thinking, though. Here's your father riding off into the sunset after the bad guys, and it has to be overcast." Lizzie caught the irony.

The bundle of rags on the ground wiggled. Jess Fowler eased out of the saddle, walked over to the bundle and reached down into its center. He tugged at one corner of the old grain sack, pulling it away. Helen Bledsoe's face looked dirtier than it was, he supposed, because her tears had left long, uneven streaks down her cheeks. Despite the darkness, her eyes squinted shut, likely just from the glare of the lantern he'd picked up and held over her.

The bandanna tied into her open mouth looked soaked through. Her clothes were torn, the left shoulder of her dress ripped away and its sleeve just hanging there on her forearm, its skirt torn partially down the right side, nothing left of her apron but the waistband, which was still tied.

Her wrists were knotted together, drawing her hands up tightly between her barely noticeable breasts. Several coils of ropes secured her hands there, wound round her chest and waist, while another coil of rope passed through her elbows and tied at her back, keeping her hands and arms totally motionless, locked against her. Her ankles were bound as well.

"She's gonna look so pitiful, Jack Naile won't be able to pass up the chance. He'll see her and he'll come on a runnin' right into where we want him. For icin' on the cake, before we set it up, one of you men take that spool of barbed wire off the pack horse and wrap some wire around her. And loosen the gag so he can hear her moan. That'll suck in that son of a bitch for sure."

He looked at the eight range detectives who stood in a circle around him and the terrified girl. "The man who brings in Jack Naile slung over a saddle gets himself a fifty dollar gold piece and can do whatever he wants with the girl here. Any questions?"

There were none.

Jess Fowler draped the sack over the girl's head, set down the lantern and went back to his horse, more work ahead of him this night.

It was a nice evening to sit on the front porch, and just being inside the house without Jack being there gave Ellen Naile a mild case of the creeps. Jack's lever-action Winchester was in the niche beside the door, and a pair of Colt revolvers was on the seat of an empty chair.

Peggy sat on the rocker; Ellen, Lizzie beside her, on the steps. "Daddy was telling me something last night."

"What, honey?"

"Today's August fourteenth. You know that Charlton Heston movie that Daddy really likes?"

"He likes a lot of Charlton Heston movies. Let's see," Ellen mused. "1900. I know! 55 *Days At Peking*. Right?"

"And August fourteenth, 1900 is when the different troops rescued everybody from the embassies."

"I remember that well," Ellen kidded Lizzie. "Charlton Heston and David Niven were down to their last few rounds of ammunition. Got pretty hairy." She hugged her daughter, proud that Lizzie had listened well enough to

Jack's mental meanderings to remember. "You're a good kid. You know that?"

"I'm nineteen, Mom. We've been here just about four years."

"If you're nineteen, that makes me—Well, let's change the subject."

As if on cue, Peggy spoke. "That's one of Clarence's favorite movies, too."

Ellen was about to turn to look at Peggy, but there was a particularly bright flash of lightning in the mountains. "What do you think all the lightning's from, Peggy?"

"I've been thinking about it a lot, guys. I mean, this is a good time of the year for thunderstorms late in the day, but where's the rain? And storms move. Those flashes are always in the same place.

"I don't want to be an alarmist," Peggy continued, "and that's why I haven't said anything. I wish your husband hadn't gone up into the mountains."

Ellen stood up, waited at the edge of the porch steps, and just looked at Peggy.

After what seemed an interminable period of time, Peggy went on. "What if the time-travel mechanism that was developed to slip Clarence and me into the past was being used over and over again?"

"You guys were up at the capsule two weeks ago. You didn't say you saw anything strange. You left a message. What if they're trying to send back a response?" Ellen queried.

"Not all those flashes. What if, instead of lightning, it's electricity of the kind that we generated to duplicate what happened to you guys?"

"What do you think is happening?" Lizzie asked, the exasperation in her voice undisguised.

"If the flashes are man-made, associated with the time-travel phenomenon, the only reason I can think of for so many of them would be to bring back equipment or manpower or both. The only reason to do any of that would be if they worked out a way of making something like a doorway, or a portal."

Ellen's mind raced. As if Lizzie had read her mind, she asked, "You mean like a revolving door, so that people or things could go back and forth between here and the future?"

"Well, I mean they'd just be experimenting," Peggy told them. "You see, there was no way in the world that we could actually do what we did any other way than the way we did it."

"What?" Ellen snapped.

"I mean, real time-travel? Like a time machine thing? It's been four years since you guys made the jump. Two years ago that we did. In two years, they weren't going to discover time-travel. All we did was duplicate with technology what happened by accident the first time, when you guys came here. We didn't understand it! All we were able to do was duplicate a set of conditions that propelled somebody or something ninety-six years into the past to the exact same place they were in the objective present. That's why Clarence and I didn't wind up in Cincinnati or Topeka or Paris or Moscow—or in the middle of Antarctica! We showed up two years after you showed up here because two years had passed in both time periods."

"And?" Ellen prodded.

"Well, we had the exact data that we needed to send things ninety-six years, sixty-eight days, four hours, twenty-three minutes and sixteen seconds into the past—no more, no less. It's not like the first person who figured out that putting a bandage on a cut stopped the bleeding understood the circulatory system, guys! He just discovered a trick that worked and could be repeated. It was mathematically possible, theoretically possible, too, that we could figure out how to do the trick backward. Like removing the bandage from the cut."

"And, if they'd come to let you and Clarence know they could retrieve you, take you back," Lizzie said very quietly, "they would have let you know two weeks ago when you checked the capsule because they'd know you guys check it and could have left a message in it for them to check."

"Alan would have done that, yes," Peggy said hesitantly. "I'm sure he would have."

Ellen thrust her hands into the pockets of her dress. "So you're suggesting, Peggy, that somebody might be doing time transfers up there in the mountains, and, if it were Jack's and my great-great-grandson, Alan, he would have let you guys know, right?" Ellen didn't wait for Peggy to give an answer. "So if somebody's doing time transfers up in the mountains without telling you—shit!"

Ellen took Lizzie by the shoulders and made eye contact. "Help me get stuff together, then saddle a horse. I'll need two pistols, a lot of ammo, food, water. I'll need one of your dad's knives."

"The rifle?"

"No. You guys keep that and the shotgun and the other

handguns. I've gotta dig through your father's closet and find some clothes. If I look like a man from a distance, there's less chance of trouble. Peggy?" Ellen glanced at Clarence's wife. "You help Lizzie. And find me some binoculars. Let's hurry it up. Jack could be riding into God knows what!"

As soon as she was through the front door, Ellen reached around behind her and started undoing the buttons down the back of her dress.

Alan had never felt guilty owning a Ferrari. As one of the richest men in the world, he could choose to drive whatever he wished. Someone had once said to him, "I pity a man like you, Mr. Naile. Rolex watch, fancy car. How many houses do you have that you never stay in more than a couple weeks at a time? How many homeless people could live in them? I ask you that!"

Under agreements of strict anonymity, Alan had donated tens of millions of dollars to various causes, all from personal funds. Horizon Enterprises actively sponsored a wide range of charitable endeavors, some openly, others quietly. No one shamed him into giving, because he had no obligation to help his fellow man; it was his choice to make and he chose to do so, because giving people a leg up when they needed it, donating to medical research and the like was something he liked to do. It was not his obligation to give; it was his privilege to do so.

When he'd first realized what Morton Hardesty had done, Alan Naile called his wife, told her his discovery. He had asked her, "Wasn't I paying Mort enough? Why did he sell out to Lakewood Industries? To get into Bethany

Kaminsky's pants? I mean, I just don't see why . . ." There had been no answer. There could be none.

Alan usually took his wife's advice.

Morton Hardesty lived in Hubbard Woods, in Winnetka. Alan had taken his private elevator to the parking garage, gotten into the Ferrari and started to drive. It was nine in the evening and traffic was light, everybody in Chicago apparently celebrating an October Indian Summer night in ways that didn't involve congesting the Kennedy Expressway.

Alan Naile's wife had advised against confronting Hardesty, at least until the following day. Against his usual wont, Alan Naile ignored his wife's advice.

The Edens was even more deserted, and Alan Naile did something he rarely did, despite the muscle his car possessed. The top was down, and Alan Naile let the Ferrari do its thing, settling in around eighty-five and feeling the night air rip across his face.

"Shit!" Alan Naile roared the epithet into the slipstream. Lakewood Industries was the dark side mirror image of his own company, exploiting everyone that it could, profiting from the misery it created. Bethany Kaminsky, his opposite number at Lakewood, apparently never listened to her connscience . . . if she even had one.

The rivalry between their firms had begun in his grandfather's time, when his grandfather had run Horizon with the advice and consent of David Naile, who had started it all, built the business from a small ranch and a smaller general store in Atlas, Nevada, into an economic and technological empire.

There had been strong evidence to suggest that, at least

prior to World War Two, Lakewood Industries had worked closely with Nazi Germany. Alan's own father had told him once, "My dad felt that Lakewood kept some of its ties with the Nazis long after Hitler invaded Poland, even after the Japanese bombed Pearl Harbor. There wasn't any way to prove it. We profited from the war, but legally and ethically. Lakewood profited any way that it could. If old man Kaminsky hadn't had certain members of Congress in his back pocket, more of it would have come out. There's a lesson to learn here, Alan. We're capitalists and damned proud of it, son. We're out to make money, and that's called self-interest. Enlightened self-interest means that you have a moral grounding. You'll work hard for a buck; you'll sacrifice time that you could be using just to have fun or whatever. There are some things you won't do for a buck or a million bucks or a hundred million bucks. It's called having a sense of personal and professional honor. I want you always to remember that."

Alan Naile remembered it now.

He wanted to rip Mort Hardesty's head off and crap down Hardesty's neck. Instead, he'd try to reason with Hardesty, ascertain how far along Lakewood Industries had gotten in the pirated time-travel experiments and put Horizon Enterprises into full overdrive on damage control.

"Shit!" Alan Naile shouted out again into the night. He so much wanted to pound Morton Hardesty's face into a wall, his hands were shaking.

Ellen Naile reined back on the Appaloosa, legs braced

against the stirrups. Still in the saddle, she reached into her left saddlebag and took out the Maglite flashlight she'd thought to bring at the last minute. Batteries were precious, even the rechargeable kind, but time might be even more precious. It was full dark and still overcast, and her night vision had never been anything to scream about.

Ellen flashed the beam ahead, and then trailed it back along the ground. As a young girl, her favorite cowboy hero had always been Clint Walker. He could read trail sign like an Indian, she remembered, and she wished he were with her now.

She saw what might be hoofprints on some of the softer looking ground. "What the hell," she murmured, shutting off the flashlight and hoping the Appaloosa could see in the dark better than she did as she dug in her heels and gave the horse its head . . .

Alan Naile wanted to break down the door, but he rang the bell instead.

Morton Hardesty's house was a large red brick bungalow. Architectural styles were something Alan Naile had never really learned, but the house looked nice, vaguely English, with ivy trailers growing up along the front and low steps leading to the doorway. Mort had inherited the house from a maiden aunt some years ago, its entire complement of antique furnishings and old oriental rugs part of Hardesty's legacy as well. He'd had a housewarming party shortly after moving in, inviting all of his coworkers and the corporate management staff.

Alan had cut short a brief stay in New York and flown back at midday from a conference out on Long Island in order not to miss the occasion. Like his wife, like his parents, like his grandparents, he had never been much for parties, but to have missed Hardesty's soiree would have appeared snobbish, and Alan had never wanted the image of something he personally found disgusting.

As he prepared to ring the doorbell again, a nervous-looking Morton Hardesty opened the front door, his eyes shifting right and left. Other than that physical manifestation, Hardesty appeared as he always did: bland.

Hardesty wore a long-sleeved knit shirt, the buttons of its front plaquette closed to the throat. The shirt was gray or green—Alan Naile was marginally visually color challenged; but Hardesty wore slacks that were clearly blue, so, unless Hardesty was even more color blind than he was, Alan Naile assumed the shirt to be gray.

"Alan."

"Mort. I need to talk with you—now."

"Is there something wrong?"

"You know what's wrong, Mort."

"Ahh, yes. I do. Not much of a porch, is it? Why not come inside?"

"How far along is Lakewood with the time-transfer process, Mort?"

"Pretty far along, Alan. They've established a base in 1900 up in the mountains not far from the Naile ranch. And, of course, we've worked out all of the kinks in making the trip forward in time, so, essentially, we can enter the past and return to the present whenever we wish. Why don't you come in?"

"Why did you betray me, betray us, Mort? Wasn't I paying you enough? You could have told me that and I would have paid you more. What was it? Bethany Kaminsky?"

"I find her irresistible, I don't mind admitting. A woman like that, Alan, and a guy like me? Well, I had to bring something else to the table. Bethany has a certain vision that's daring, to be sure, but intriguing. If she's successful, who can say? You might cease to exist in the next few seconds because you were never born. I don't pretend to understand time. If your great-great grandparents die, well, you'd still be here. But if your great-grandfather dies, well, before your grandfather is born, that could be a whole other kettle of fish. But if you had never existed, then the time process wouldn't have been developed, so your great-grandfather would have lived and you'd still be here. It's confusing as hell to talk about, but if you'll come inside, I can explain it better mathematically. But you're not all that good at higher math, are you, Alan? Only bottom lines."

"Fuck you and the horse you rode in on, Mort."

Morton Hardesty smiled. "See, I was already here, Alan, and it seems that you're the one who 'rode in' with that flashy Ferrari of yours. And as to being fucked, well, I'm the one who gained, and you're the one who lost. Why not come inside and maybe we can work this out, Alan?"

Alan could feel something—almost genetic, it was so deep within him—telling him that he should get out of there. He hadn't taken his wife's advice, and perhaps he should have. But he wasn't going to ignore an instinct that seemed to come from so deep within him. "Tell you what, Mort. Instead of coming inside, I'll have my attorneys burn some midnight oil instead. Trust me. You're the one who's fucked."

Alan turned to start down the steps and back toward the curb where the Ferrari was parked. He stopped when he heard Bethany Kaminsky's voice. "Alan. All this toilet talk in front of a lady! Really! Actually, depending on how one uses the word, Mort really did get fucked." Alan Naile reached the bottom of the steps and turned around, looking at Bethany Kaminsky. She was barefoot and wore a man's bathrobe, the fingers of her right hand straying through her tousled hair. "I just fucked him. And, later on this evening, I'll fuck him again. Actually, I fuck his brains out, sometimes two or three times a day.

"You know me," Bethany Kaminsky continued. "I'm always right there to squeeze the last penny out of a buck. Mort's great. Doesn't give two shits about money! Just wants his brains fucked out on a pretty regular basis, and even old Mortie here beats a vibrator!" She clapped Morton Hardesty on the shoulder almost like a man would, then leaned up on her bare toes and kissed his balding forehead. "But in the figurative sense, Alan, you're the one who is fucked. We have a time base in 1900. We're going to take over the world, but we'll keep your great-grandfather alive if Mort says we have to, so we don't screw this up. And you, my old rival, are about to really get fucked, in the figurative sense, although it might be fun in the literal sense. But, hey, we'll always have Paris."

"What the hell are you talking about?" Alan asked her. "You and I never had Paris or Pittsburgh. I'd be afraid of catching a disease."

And, at the small of his back, Alan Naile felt something that he had never felt before, but instinctively recognized: the muzzle of a gun.

"Have you two guys met, Alan?" Bethany Kaminsky asked, the tone of her voice something more suited to a casual introduction at a cocktail party than a confrontation. "Alan, meet Lester Matthews, Lakewood's security consultant. You and Lester will have a lot of time to get to know each other on a very intimate level before we take you back in time and kill you. Isn't that a great idea, Alan? The classic problem of what to do with a dead body instantly resolved. And even if someone ever suspected, the crime will have taken place almost a century ago."

"There's no statute of limitations on murder, Bethany," Alan announced matter-of-factly, the forced calm in his voice belying the churning in his stomach and the perspiration coating his palms.

"Say! That is true, isn't it? Well, we'll just have to be doubly careful, then," Bethany told him, smiling.

As a boy, Alan had gone to camp several summers. The summer that he was twelve, instead of camp, he'd spent three weeks staying with his best friend's family, their guest at a compound on Lake Superior near the border with Canada. The last ten days of the stay with his friend Brad's family had been the most exciting, because Brad's grandfather had come up to join them. In his sixties then, the grandfather, Alan had learned, was a veteran of the OSS, World War II's Office of Strategic Services, the organizational predecessor to the CIA.

The older man was delighted to learn that young Alan had a genuine interest in those stories of wartime service which could be freely discussed. With only seven days remaining of Alan's stay, Brad's grandfather had come up to him after breakfast and asked, "Would you like to learn a few things?"

In those last seven days, Alan learned the basic uses of detcord (blowing up a few old tree stumps), a few hand-to-hand combat maneuvers, how to throw a *Ka-Bar* knife and certain means by which one might disarm an armed opponent. Alan tried one of those techniques in the instant that the recollection sprang to mind, realizing full well that he hadn't practiced it since that summer more than two decades ago. With as much fluidity as he could muster, reassuring himself feebly that Bethany Kaminsky really wouldn't want to run the risk of a shooting on a public street in a Chicago suburb, David smashed the heel of his right foot downward against what he hoped would be Lester Matthews' right instep, throwing his body weight back and arcing right. The muzzle of the gun was hard against his back for a microsecond. With his right forearm, he swept the weapon to the gunman's left, his body twisting to the man's right. Alan's balled left fist hooked upward and across, catching Lester Matthews full in the right side of the mouth.

The gun—some kind of automatic—clattered to the concrete, and Lester Matthews' body sagged at the knees, off balance and falling.

Alan sidestepped and started a dash toward the Ferrari, getting two strides into the run before a blurred shape smashed into him from his right side, knocking him down. His head struck the sidewalk. Alan shook his head, trying to clear it. He pushed himself half to his feet, and something hammered the base of his skull in an explosion of pain.

Staggering to his feet, he reached for the throat of the man who'd knocked him down. There was still another man, something shaped like a blackjack at the end of the man's extended right arm. The blackjack arced downward.

Alan didn't feel the impact, but blackness was flooding over him. He tried dragging his right knee up and into the groin of the man with whom he grappled, but before he could tell if he'd connected or not, the blackness engulfed him.

CHAPTER
❖ ELEVEN ❖

Most nights, since the electrical wiring in the central room had been completed and the water-powered generator brought on-line, Elizabeth would spend an hour—rarely more or less—reading through the microfiche of *Britannica III*.

Progress was slow, because she would most times find herself reading the shorter entries in the first volumes and going to the more detailed references in the latter volumes. One really didn't start at "A" and methodically work one's way toward "Zwingli."

This night, however, she decided to forego her usual pastime and keep Peggy company on the porch.

The acquisition of knowledge had not been a consuming passion for her prior to the trip backward in time. Somehow, that experience had forever changed her outlook. David's obsession was business and the acquisition of money that could be turned into wealth. If Elizabeth had an obsession, it was to be happy. Knowledge, in this time and place, might be the needed key to that; plus, she enjoyed the acquisition of knowledge for its own sake.

Looking across the plain from the front porch, toward the mountains, the flashes were still visible at regular intervals. "If they are building a base here in this time," Liz said, thinking out loud, "they can't be accused of laziness."

"What? I'm sorry. I wasn't listening."

"I was just thinking that if those flashes are from a time-travel mechanism like the one which brought you and Clarence here, they're not letting any grass grow under their feet. Are they?"

"I guess not."

"Do you still want to go back?"

"Say again! Go back? Of course! Wouldn't you, Lizzie?"

Liz shrugged her shoulders under her shawl. "I don't know. If I do, we'll change history, and maybe for the worse. Oh, you know what I mean! I'm not into altruism. That sucks! But what happened to us piled a lot of responsibility onto our shoulders, too. You know?"

"You really think I should wait to go into town until your father gets back? Tom Bledsoe's wounds might not wait. If he's treated improperly after a tourniquet was used, he could develop gangrene."

"I've been praying for the Bledsoes, especially Helen, taken away by those men. There are only the two of us here, Peggy. If something happens, we'll be hard-pressed to make a fight of it. One of us wouldn't stand a chance. You should stay. That's what Daddy wanted you to do. That's what Clarence, or David, for that matter, would want you to do. What if Momma gets to Daddy, and Daddy or Marshal Blake was wounded? As a doctor, you might be the only chance either one of them would have. Please stay, and for your own sake, too.

"You never took to horseback riding that much," Liz went on, "so you'd have to take the buckboard, stick to the road. It'd take a while at night, and be awfully dangerous. On horseback and dressed in men's clothes, Momma has a chance of avoiding trouble if it's out there. You wouldn't. In the morning, why don't we get out by the stream and do some target practice? You could use the practice, and we've got plenty of ammunition. God knows, we might need it. And if there is something going on and we're being watched, showing whoever it is that we can shoot and have ammunition to burn might be a good idea, don't you think?" Liz pulled her shawl more tightly around her shoulders and fussed with her apron while she waited for Peggy's reply.

After several more seconds, Peggy sighed audibly, then said, "Fine. I'll stay. At least until Ellen gets back."

Liz smiled at Peggy and got up from the rocking chair, taking up the pistol and the rifle which they'd kept with them on the front porch.

Liz opened her eyes, the luminous face of the big Westclox windup alarm showing that she had been asleep for three hours or so. Before falling asleep, she had thought about her conversation with Peggy, about whether or not she would ever go back to her own time if she could. There, she had been purposeless, without direction. In this time, even though she was a woman and, perforce, a second-class citizen in many ways, she could do a great deal.

She heard a noise and realized it was the same noise that had awakened her.

Next to the alarm clock on her bedside table was a brace of Colt Single Actions.

Throwing back the covers, she found her slippers in the same instant that she stood up and the hem of her night-gown fell to her ankles. The sound she'd heard had been horses, several of them, certainly more than three. Only her mother, her father and Marshal Blake might be expected to be riding up to the house at two o'clock in the morning. No one else whose intentions Liz trusted should be nearby.

She retrieved the rechargeable flashlight that she found in near total darkness on the floor at the side of her bed, but didn't turn it on.

Lizzie grabbed up her wrap from atop the chest at the foot of her bed. It was the size of a Welsh nursing shawl and cocooned her from shoulders to well past her hips. Shielding the flashlight within her shawl, she turned it on. From the nightstand's drawer, she grabbed a long straight pin, its head in the shape of a cross. Closing her eyes, she turned off the light and pinned the shawl closed a few inches below her throat. She picked up the revolvers. Peggy did not sleep with a gun in her room; Clarence used a gun only with great reluctance, feeling he didn't need one for protection and Peggy echoed his sentiments.

The noise was a constant in the few seconds since she had left her bed, the ever-loudening drum of hoofbeats. A half-dozen horses or more were fast approaching. Lizzie didn't kid herself that they might be riderless. There was a double-holster rig hanging from a peg beside her bedroom door. She set the pistols on the chest of drawers near the door, took the flashlight from under her arm and did the same with it. When her father had insisted on a gun belt for her, "just in case," she had humored him. Under the circumstances, it seemed quite practical.

The rig had two holsters, right and left, the holsters slid over a cartridge belt looped with dozens of rounds of .45 Colt ammo. On the left side of the belt, behind the holster, there was a sheathed knife.

Lizzie buckled on the gun belt at her waist, letting it settle to her hips. She holstered the revolvers, picked up her flashlight and went to rouse Peggy.

"This is too easy, Titus," Jack proclaimed as he stood up. Periodically, one or the other of them would dismount to search for tracks, lighting a few matches or a candle for illumination, finding the hoofprints or dislodged stones largely by feel, the night's overcast not helping them. "I never hunted much; had to get up too early for it where I come from," he said honestly. "But I've read a great deal about reading trail sign. We're able to follow these guys in the dark, and it's not that tough. With kidnapping a young girl in this day and age, they have to figure there'll be angry people chasing after them. It would be easy enough to wipe out their tracks or go to higher ground where there's more rock and less dirt and following tracks would be a lot tougher. This is a setup, I'm thinking. You're the professional, Titus. What do you think?"

"I don't think—I jus' know we gotta get 'em. But the

horses is plum wore out. We should take us some sleep for a few hours, I reckon, then light out after 'em 'fore daybreak."

"Camping out under the stars; one of my favorite things, Titus," Jack said sarcastically. He'd always liked Gene Autry's theme song. As a kid, the part of the lyric about sleeping out every night sounded appealing. As an adult, it left a lot to be desired.

Ellen rubbed down her horse. The night was cool and the animal drenched with sweat from being pushed as hard as it had been. While she worked, she debated with herself about building a fire. A cold camp was unappealing, but a fire might attract the two-legged kind of predator. Yet it would frighten off many of the four-legged variety.

When the first raindrop touched the tip of her nose, she made a decision: a fire it would be, a sandwich from her saddlebags and a shot from the flask of whiskey. With daylight and her horse fresh, she could make better time.

When Tom Bledsoe had seen her father's rough drawing for the front porch of the house, he'd asked, "Why not just rails and spindles?"

The drawing called for solid pieces of hardwood punctuated at varying distances and levels with heart-shaped cut-outs, the wood to be two inches thick and kiln dried, meaning that the wood had to be imported to Atlas.

Lizzie's father had dismissed Tom's query. "I always wanted a front porch that would be truly versatile, Tom, useful under a variety of conditions." The heart shapes, her father had explained to them earlier, were firing ports, and the reason for the thickness of the wood was in the hopes of stopping or dramatically slowing the big, lazily paced lead bullets of the period.

Lying flat on the porch floor, elbows propped up, the barrel of a Winchester protruding through one of the heart-shaped cutouts, Liz truly hoped that her father had been right about the wood offering some protection against bullets.

Her father's anachronistic pet .45 Colt Model 94 saddle ring carbine lay beside her, the rifle in her hands one of six .30-30 Model 94 Winchester lever actions. Peggy had one, too.

The riders had stayed back about a hundred yards from the house. Doubtlessly, her father could have hit a man-sized target at that distance, and perhaps she could have, too, but she wasn't going to risk it.

The riders would have seen her and Peggy exiting the house, two women in their nightclothes, probably frightened out of their wits and, if not terrified by the mere sound of a gun going off, almost certainly poorly skilled with firearms. In actuality, from her readings, a great many women on the American frontier had developed quite satisfactory skills with a firearm, particularly a rifle or shotgun. Hopefully, these guys hadn't heard of that.

"Remember, Peggy. Hold the front of the rifle so that it doesn't beat itself into the top of the firing port when you trigger a shot. Keep the butt of the rifle solidly tucked into the pocket between your arm and your shoulder. It'll be loud, and you've never heard a real gunshot without hearing protection, but don't worry—I have. Your ears will ring. Hang tight, huh?"

"Right. What do they want?"

"Probably some of Jess Fowler's men, and they want to kill us, or they're some of the same gang that kidnapped Helen Bledsoe and they've come for us."

"I wish Clarence were here."

"I even wish that my brother were here! Can you believe that? But they're not, and neither are Mom and Dad. It's up to us. Their bullets probably can't punch through the wood we're hiding behind," Lizzie declared with more confidence than she truly felt, "and they won't expect us to offer organized resistance."

"How many of them are there, do you think, Liz?"

"Not too many," Lizzie returned, hoping that her tone sounded upbeat, optimistic. "Once we shoot a few of them, the rest of them will ride off," she added, hoping that she was right, realizing that she very well might not be.

"I don't know if I can take a human life. Can't we just shoot over their heads? I'm a doctor. I'm supposed to save lives, not take lives."

"You aim for the center of mass, Peggy! Don't do anything different. Shoot into the biggest target possible. If you shoot one and he falls off his horse and starts to crawl toward us, shoot him again."

"I couldn't harm someone who was injured!"

Lizzie swallowed hard, keeping her voice as steady as she could. "We're both young and try to look pretty. We're wearing nightgowns. What do you think they're going to do to us if they get their hands on us? If you don't shoot at them and they overrun us, I'll make sure that the last shot I fire kills you. And not to protect you, but to get even. Be ready." As she glanced into the distance, she worked the Winchester's lever and added, "Here they come." Her front sight was shaking.

There were thirteen of them, and Lizzie sincerely hoped that there was something to the superstition about triskaidekaphobia, at least as far as their attackers were concerned.

Despite the night's heavy overcast and the soft drizzle that had started only a split second before the men began riding toward them, she was certain that she recognized Jess Fowler; she'd seen him several times when they'd lived in town, always from a distance, as now.

The men rode in a single rank, Jess Fowler at their precise center, their horses—somehow very big-looking—walking forward slowly, easily.

Jess Fowler's horse was tall and black, white stockinged with a white blaze in its face. Fowler and his mount looked like something out of a nightmare, Fowler's dark colored duster fanning out behind him like Dracula's cape, his broad-brimmed black hat low over a face that she remembered as skeletally well-defined, set with eyes that somehow didn't seem to be there at all.

All of the other men had weapons drawn, a few with rifles, one or two with shotguns, the rest with handguns. Fowler—there were two handguns at his hips—held nothing in his hands but the reins to his horse.

As if Jess Fowler had a marvelously evil sense of horrific drama, he signaled his men to an abrupt halt. The next instant, he started forward alone. His hands—they seemed huge—were gloved in black leather, the color matching his boots, his gun belt and his clothes, rendering him all but invisible in the darkness. He held his hands out at his sides, not even holding the reins of his horse, merely guiding the animal with his knees. "I wanna parlay, women!"

Lizzie called back to him, "I love your French, Fowler! It sucks!" The crack was lost on him, she knew, but it made her feel better. "Try anything, and I'll shoot you out of the saddle!"

Fowler laughed.

Lizzie shivered.

Fowler's mount walked slowly forward.

About three or four car lengths away from the front porch—she couldn't help herself; she still thought in the terms from the period in which she had been raised—Jess Fowler's horse stopped and lowered its enormous head. .

She could see Jess Fowler's cadaverous face quite clearly, somehow.

"How many of you in there, girl? Talk up fast and true or it'll go harder on ya'."

"Would you believe a Swiss mountain battalion? How about seventeen highly motivated ice-cream salesmen?"

"What the hell you talkin' all crazy about, girl?! Tell me now, dammit!"

"We are ladies, and we've never heard such foul language before, sir! I do declare!"

"I'm warnin' ya!"

"Kiss my ass! But get off our property first, or guess who stops lead before anybody else!" Lizzie really regretted having worked the Winchester's lever and already chambering a round. The dramatic effect would have been great. She was scared shitless, but pissed.

"Fair enough, women! Lord knows I tried bein' civil!"

"The Lord knows you're about to be judged by Him if you don't haul ass and take your pansy buddies with you!"

Somehow, Lizzie knew that ticking off Jess Fowler couldn't worsen their situation; maybe it was in her genes to be a smartass. Suddenly, Lizzie just wished that she were taller. She could afford to waste the round already chambered, so she worked the lever as rapidly as she could, hoping the noise would be loud enough that Fowler heard it.

He heard it, she realized.

"Suit yourself!"

He turned his horse and started back toward the line of his men. Lizzie fired the Winchester, a little too quickly. Jess Fowler's horse went down, and she couldn't tell if she'd hit him or the animal as Fowler tumbled from the saddle and the horse whinnied and foundered.

"You shot that man in the back!" Peggy nearly shrieked.

"God save us from liberals," Lizzie muttered, racking the Winchester's lever and firing again.

"Kill the bitches!" Fowler shouted, scrambling to his feet, his horse doing the same. Lizzie thought that she detected a limp, hoping that her second shot had connected with Fowler rather than his horse.

"I can't stand this noise!" Peggy shouted.

"I can't stand people who can't stand stuff! Fire that damn rifle and complain later!"

As if on cue, the rain increased as Lizzie made to fire again. And, on the same cue, Fowler's twelve range detectives opened fire and scattered for cover.

❋ ❋ ❋

Jack raised the lean-to he'd constructed out of his slicker and peered out through the steadily falling rain. "Sleeping out under the stars! Shit! What stars?" With his booted right foot, he gave a sharp kick to the butt end of the log, pushing it deeper into the hissing flames of the campfire. A handful of crystallized pine resin from his saddlebags had helped the fire to get a rapid start, despite what was then only a modest drizzle. Since it hadn't rained for a quite a while—Nevada got very little rain—the wood that he and Titus Blake had found was bone-dry below the surface.

The log had been a stroke of good fortune, a half-rotted piece of deadfall pine about four feet long and six inches in diameter. Using some forked twigs, Jack Naile had constructed a shelter over his saddle and blankets, keeping most of his body and his gear dry.

He and Blake had consumed some of the sandwiches Ellen had packed for them. Then Blake promptly rolled over and appeared to sleep. Jack had lit a cigarette and taken his hip flask from one of the saddlebags. The Suburban had contained a single case of a luxury item Jack Naile had not wanted to be without: Myers's Rum, the dark kind that looked like a fine whiskey and heated the body on a cold night with enough warmth to resuscitate the cryogenically frozen. He'd sipped at the rum several times, but made it appear that he'd drunk nearly the entire contents of the flask. This was for two reasons. First, he had no wish to share the single flask of rum with Titus Blake; secondly, it might be advantageous for Titus Blake to think that his campmate was less than sober.

Jack Naile kicked at the log again. When Kirk Douglas

and Burt Lancaster, as Doc Holliday and Wyatt Earp, had camped out awaiting an ambush in *Gunfight at the O.K. Corral*, the weather had been decidedly better—a greens set on a soundstage, to be precise. Yet the most important difference between their experience and his own was that Wyatt and Doc had each trusted implicitly the man in the other bedroll.

Jack Naile's rifle was secure and dry, his gun belt well up under the shelter, the long-barreled Colt .45 conspicuously holstered. But underneath his blanket was the extra Colt with a four-and-three-quarter-inch barrel that Ellen had insisted he hide in his saddle bags. Intentionally, rather than leaving just the charging hole under the hammer empty, he'd left the next one empty as well. If he awakened from a deep sleep and didn't come instantly alert, loading the revolver that way could avert an accidental discharge. And if it was grabbed from his saddlebags and not checked, the first time someone went to fire it, nothing would happen. That could buy a precious second or two, which could mean the difference between life and death.

The hem of her nightgown bunched in her left hand, Lizzie crawled across the porch floor, toward the open front door. Peggy was just ahead of her. Lizzie's bare knees ached against the pressure of the hardwood floor. The holsters at her hips slapped lightly against her as she moved. The Winchester 94's buttstock regularly tapped against the floor with each movement. All in all, crossing from the porch to the central room with their late-twentieth-century conveniences was arduous in the extreme, but she dared not stand and make a run for it.

Jess Fowler's men were dismounted, had taken what cover they could, and so far their indiscriminate gunfire had shattered windows at the front of the house, ventilated furniture and pockmarked the wall over the large mantle against which her father had leaned when he'd spoken with Titus Blake.

But neither Peggy nor she had been hit, and Lizzie intended things to remain that way.

At last, after what seemed an eternity, they reached the doorway leading into the hidden room. Beneath a rug was the trapdoor entrance to a tunnel. The tunnel's main purpose was to obscure from view the water pipes leading from the stream and the electrical cable leading from the waterwheel that served as their generator. But the tunnel led to the stream, and there was a means of egress before actually reaching the water. Her mother had put it best. "I don't think your father is expecting an Indian raid or anything, but it would be silly to have this perfectly nice tunnel and not be able to take advantage of it, just in case something happened." Knowing her father, Elizabeth Naile figured that he might very well have fantasized a group of "renegades jumping the reservation and out looking for scalps" or something like that but now, she was quite thankful for the tunnel.

As soon as both she and Peggy were inside the secret room, they were able to stand. Once the seriously heavy door was closed and bolted behind them, she put down her rifle and the boxes of ammunition she'd carried basket-fashion within the fabric of her bunched up nightgown. She set to work pulling the rug out of the way and prying up the trapdoor.

❊ ❊ ❊

Lizzie crouched in the down-pouring cold rain beside the tunnel's escape hatch. Bricked around to form a frame, the actual door was crafted of teakwood, so as to be resistant to weather. The doorway was about twenty yards from the stream, well below the level of the house, out of sight of the men Jess Fowler had brought with him. Peggy crept out next, proclaiming the obvious in a loud stage whisper. "It's raining!"

"Come on, Peggy." Lizzie was no more enthused about getting soaked to the skin than was the girl she considered a sister-in-law, her cousin's wife. But there was work to be done before they could come in out of the rain. Liz had already decided that if they survived, Peggy could have the first hot shower, but she promised herself she'd beat Peggy to death if she used up all the hot water. "Keep the muzzle of your rifle out of the dirt so you don't get a bore obstruction." Her father would have been so proud of her, she thought.

Liz had appropriated a linen tablecloth from the large round table on which incriminating late-twentieth-century framed family photographs were displayed in the secret room. Tying the ends together, she'd formed a sack in which she could more easily carry the spare ammunition for the rifles.

Creeping along the base of the drop-off that paralleled the stream, Lizzie issued orders sotto voce. "I want you to find a good spot and stay there. I'll be moving. All you need to be able to do is keep firing in the general direction of the bad guys. Don't expose yourself trying to get an accurate shot. I want them firing toward you. They'll have to expose themselves in order to do that with us being behind them. As they do, I'll pick them off and keep moving. You'll be the only fixed target, so you have to stay well within cover. Just shove the muzzle of the rifle around or over whatever it is you're hiding behind and keep firing. That's all you have to do. I'll do the rest." As a whisper only she herself could hear, Lizzie added, "God willing I don't get shot."

The volume of gunfire pouring toward the front porch had largely subsided, which meant Fowler's men would soon plan on advancing against the house.

That would make things even better—maybe.

Peggy was well hidden behind an outcropping of rock above the embankment leading up from the bank of the stream. Only the most impossibly ricocheting shot could have a chance of hitting her if she stayed down and fired from one side of the outcropping or the other, but not from over it.

Leaving Peggy with an extra fifty or so rounds of .30-30 Winchester, Liz went farther along the base of the embankment in order to come up well behind and to the side of Fowler's men. Her father's pet rifle with the pretty walnut stock and the gleaming Metalife finish was just inside the front door of the house, unceremoniously stuffed under a chair. The wiser move had been the one she'd chosen—take the rifle that fired a rifle cartridge rather than a revolver cartridge. One of the ordinary blue steel Model 94s in her hands in what her father would have called an "assault position," she slogged her way onward through the increasingly sticky mud. Water was washing down over the embankment, the rain so heavy that she could barely see.

But that was also good.

If she was able to shoot a few of Fowler's men, considering the cold, the rain and the darkness, only the most dedicated of Fowler's minions would elect to continue shooting it out.

The toe of her shoe caught in the hem of her ruined, soaked-through nightgown, and Liz nearly fell. She stopped, stood, caught her breath and told herself that it was time to get up the embankment and get to work.

With visibility as limited as it was, the darkness nearly absolute in the downpour, Liz more carefully inspected the embankment as she walked slowly onward. After another minute or two, she found a spot less steep and with outcroppings of rock that might provide some sort of purchase for her hands and feet.

The rifle had no sling, and she could not hold it and climb at the same time. But the pistols she wore would be useless at any true distance, at least in her hands. "Think," Liz exhorted herself. She had to make a sling. There was a ruffle at the hem of her nightgown. Unsheathing the knife from her gun belt, she cut into the ruffle where it was sewn to the gown, found the seam and tore.

The ruffle came away relatively cleanly. The knife resheathed, Lizzie tied one end of the ruffle to the muzzle end of the rifle just forward of the handguard, the other to the butt just behind the lever. If she had to, before removing the improvised sling, the rifle could still be fired.

Adjusting the sling to be a tight fit across her back, Liz

Naile attacked the embankment. With the first step, she fell, slid, soaked her upper body in mud. On her feet once more, pulling the shawl more closely around her, she tried again. By almost digging the toes of her shoes into the mud, she was able to reach the first outcropping, clinging to the cold, wet, slippery rock for an instant before going on.

It seemed an eternity, but was probably less than five minutes, and she was just below the top of the embankment, wedged against an outcropping lest she slide downward. Slowly, cautiously, Liz peeked up over the lip of the terracelike mound.

She was about fifty yards or so from the house, Liz guessed, realizing full well that she'd never been very good at eyeballing distances. It could have been a hundred yards.

At about two-thirds that distance, whatever it was, Jess Fowler's men, backs obligingly turned, crouched in muddy depressions, behind tree trunks. One of them was behind a horse that looked dead.

Before leaving the porch for the tunnel, Lizzie thought that she might have killed or wounded two of Fowler's men. Her initial observations indicated that instead of thirteen men, Fowler included, there were only nine. That could have meant that two healthy men took two wounded men off for medical attention. At least, she hoped that accounted for their absence and that they, too, had not thought to come up on their opponents from behind.

There was no way to know.

Her eyes scanned along the ground. If she could make it into the pines, the trees would disguise her position and provide some cover as well as concealment.

Running twenty yards or so across open ground wasn't something she wanted to do, but to climb back down the embankment and walk more of its length, then climb back up again would take too long and was just more than she wished to attempt.

Cra vling up over the lip of muddy ground, she lay perfectly flat, barely raising her head to peer along the expanse. She spat muddy water away from her mouth. As far as she could tell, she hadn't been noticed.

Lizzie got to her feet in a crouch, caught her tattered nightgown up to her knees and ran. Twice she slipped and nearly fell on the wet ground, but she reached the tree line without incident, collapsing behind a pine trunk. If she'd been one of those ninety-eight-pound girls who looked like walking corpses, the tree would have fully protected her from returning fire. As it was, it afforded partial cover, probably adequate. She was about to test the hypothesis.

Undoing the improvised sling and stuffing it into the corner of the tablecloth with the sodden boxes of ammunition bound inside, she thumbed back the hammer of the Winchester, a round already chambered. Bringing the rifle to her shoulder, she found her first target. In her father's and mother's books, whenever the good guy was in a fight with more than one bad guy, he always shot the bad guy closest to him, the one with the greatest chance of returning an accurate shot.

It was Lizzie's intention to do the same.

There was a man with a dark hat, high crowned like something out of an old movie. He wore chaps, a belt with two six-guns and a knife, and he clutched a rifle in his hands. He was crouched behind a rock. His left shoulder blade was a perfect target.

Despite the rain and the darkness, she could make him out clearly enough. Water was beaded in her rifle's rear sight. She blew it away like blowing out a last candle on a birthday cake.

The rifle's sights were lined up. Tears were welling up in her eyes, and her nose was running. This was more murder than self-defense, at least in a way. Sniffing, correcting her sight picture for the last time, Lizzie opened fire.

The man fell over in a heap.

In the next instant, gunfire came toward the trees. Lizzie was already in motion, running along the length of the tree line, just deep enough inside the woods to keep trees between her and the men trying to kill her. She slipped on pine needles, fell to her knees.

Crawling up behind the nearest trunk, she raised up to her knees, worked the rifle's lever. Lizzie found another target. He wore a lighter-colored hat, low-crowned, and had a big, light-colored wild rag tied around his throat. A rifle was up to his shoulder. He was turned a quarter of the way away from her.

Lizzie fired, and must have hit him somewhere, because he fell down and dropped his rifle, which discharged before it left his hands.

At last Peggy's rifle opened up.

Lizzie ran for a fresh position, just like Anthony Quinn had done while shooting it out with Nazi soldiers in the movie of *The Guns of Navarone*, which her father had convinced her to watch. Quinn's character's purpose had been to create a diversion. Hers was more deadly.

As Peggy's wild shots kept coming, rapidly at last, Lizzie found another position. She fired, missed, fired again. Whether she hit or not, she didn't know. Return fire slammed into the tree trunk inches from her eyes.

Startled, she fell back, nearly dropped her rifle.

Shaking her head, sniffing back tears, Liz dug into the tablecloth sack, tore some cartridges free from their sodden box and reloaded as she drew deeper into the trees.

Two of Fowler's men were at the edge of the tree line.

There was no time for anything but to shoot and hope to hit them. The rifle to her shoulder again, she knelt beside a tree trunk and fired at the nearest man. He had a shotgun, which discharged into the ground at his feet as he fell back and didn't move. Two pistol shots rang out toward her and missed. A good thing, she thought absently, since there wasn't any time to move. She fired, levered the action and fired again, the body of the man with the pistols in his hands jerking twice. As he fell back, the Colt revolver in his right hand jackknifed upward and discharged.

The tongue of flame from its muzzle was enormous and bright as the sun, it seemed to her. And the pain that suddenly consumed her left side burned like fire.

"Holy shit! I'm shot!" Lizzie exclaimed aloud.

In the movie, Wyatt and Doc had lain quietly, resolutely it seemed, awaiting the inevitable attack, staying awake into the early hours of morning, their campfire nearly out.

The real campfire mere feet away from Jack still sizzled in the heavy rain and he felt anything but calm. The phrase "scared shitless" came to his mind more than once, but there was nothing for it but to wait and see who tried to kill him first, the marshal he somehow had suddenly come to distrust or the kidnappers who had left a trail a blind man could have followed.

Despite the chill, his right palm sweated on the butt of the revolver he held clenched beneath his blanket. His back was sore from the hard ground. Everything was damp or plain wet.

With the crackling of the burning log and the thrumming of the rain, every sound, however slight, was somehow different, ominous.

He heard one of the horses whinnying. Perhaps the horses were just as disgusted with the weather as he was. Or perhaps the moment had come.

When a Colt Single Action Army was cocked, there were four distinct clicks.

Jack heard one, then another. Two more remained. The clicks had come from where Titus Blake lay. But, Blake could have sensed an impending attack and might not be intent on betrayal and murder.

The third click.

There was no way to know Blake's intentions.

Jack had to give Titus Blake the first move.

With the fourth click, Jack rolled from under his blanket, knocking down the tiny lean-to, the hidden Colt's hammer drawing back as Blake fired into where Jack's body had lain a split second earlier. Jack jerked the trigger, let it fall over the second empty chamber and held the trigger back, slip-cocking the revolver, almost like fanning it, but using only the shooting hand. At this range—fewer than ten feet—it would be hard to miss.

Jack's gun fired and he threw himself left in the next instant.

Blake's revolver fired, a spray of muddy water assailing Jack's face. Blake lurched back, hit.

Jack thumbed the hammer back on the Colt and stabbed it toward Blake, firing and striking Blake as Blake fired again. Jack felt something warm against his right ear.

Jack fired the third shot from the revolver. The bullet visibly impacted Blake's chest, snapping Blake's body back. As Blake fell, Jack could see his face clearly in the firelight. There was shock, what might have been disappointment—and there was terror.

Soaked to the skin, a hot trickle of blood along the right side of his neck, Jack shoved the almost-empty revolver into his waistband, reached under what little remained of the lean-to and snatched his long-barreled, hand-crafted Colt from its holster.

Jack dropped to his knees beside Blake and grabbed the man as roughly as he could, fingers knotted into Blake's shirtfront. It was wet, and Jack could not tell if the moisture was blood or rain—but it was probably both.

Cocking the revolver and shoving it toward Blake's face, Jack snarled, "Why!? Tell me now, Marshal—tell me now or there'll be no help for you. Back at my house, there's my nephew's wife. She's a doctor, more skilled than any doctor in the country. She can save your life," Jack lied. Blake was nearly bled out, the color drained from his face and the clear sound of a sucking chest wound in the man's labored breaths. "Tell me now, or the muzzle of this revolver is the last thing you'll ever see."

"The Bledsoe girl—really took her. Suckerin' you away

from your place so they can kill the women. They was gonna hit 'em hours ago. Count 'em dead."

The dialogue wasn't crafted for effect this time. "You fucking bastard!" Jack Naile almost pulled the trigger as he stabbed the revolver toward Blake's face.

"Figured if'n I killed ya', Jess Fowler'd pay up more than just' the gettin' ya out here. Mebbe ya got me, Naile, but them women is goners sure 'nough by—" And he died.

Marshal Titus Blake's head lolled back, rainwater falling into eyes that would not shut. Jack let Blake's body slump to the ground.

On his knees beside the dead man, the long-barreled revolver, rain glistening from its metal in the firelight, balled tight in his right fist, Jack Naile shouted into the darkness above. "Why, God?! Why?!"

In his old life, Jack had written of violence, never really tasted it, never felt the hollowness inside that a killing bred, that every killing nurtured. He had, at last, become the fantasy role model of his childhood, the triumphant gunfighter on the side of goodness and right. But death was death, and Jack had neither the taste nor the stomach for it; and, perhaps, neither had the real-life gunmen, the counterparts of the fictions spun from imaginations like his own. It started, it went on. It was a trap. And nearly all that was precious to him might already have been sacrificed because of his passion to play cowboy.

"God! Don't let them die! Please, God!" Jack rose from his knees.

Like the fictional heroes of his boyhood, there was a clarity within him, and he knew what he had to do. If his home had already been attacked, what had happened had happened and he would not rest until he found those responsible and took their lives.

But there was a terrified girl, a girl the same age as his daughter, less than a half-day's ride, perhaps only hours, away. Any way he judged it, she was closer to get to than his own family. Her life could still be saved, because she was being kept alive to trap him. That was obvious.

Jack partially lowered the hammer on his revolver, rolled the cylinder, then lowered the hammer onto an empty chamber. He buckled on his gun belt. If he left Blake's saddle, but took the dead marshal's horse, swapping mounts every hour or so, he could catch the men before they would expect him. It would take more than twice as long to reach his home. If his wife and daughter and Clarence's wife were dead, they'd still be dead when he got there, and the Bledsoe girl's death would be on his conscience as well.

Jack still had that: a conscience.

Soaked to the skin, chilled to the bone, he shrugged into his coat, its lining still dry, but not for long.

He grabbed up his saddle and walked toward the picket line where the horses were, away from the light.

Lizzie felt something shaking her, and she opened her eyes. "Fifteen more minutes?"

But it wasn't her mother's voice. Rather, it was Peggy's that she heard. "You're not home in bed. You've been shot. And you'll bleed to death if I don't get the bullet out. And I can only do that at the house, where there's light. I'm not strong enough to carry you, Lizzie. You've got to get up and walk. The ones you didn't shoot rode off, Fowler with them. It's safe. The house is alright, but I have to get you there."

"Just five more minutes? Wake me up at—"

"Get up and walk! Or you'll die!"

Liz mumbled, "If you're going to be all bent out of shape about it, then I guess—"

CHAPTER TWELVE

Ellen was up and riding before full dawn, the heavy gray clouds, high and moving fast, made blue in patches by the infusion of the first tentative rays of sunlight from below them. The morning was cool, the air clean. Despite being chilled to the bone—after decades sleeping beside Jack, she was ill-used to sleeping alone—and having to take care of the obvious bodily functions without even so much as a chamber pot, she felt refreshed. With the wind in her face as it was, its freshness stinging her skin, she could have felt no other way.

She'd wiped off her Colt revolvers and her knife, checked her tack, saddled up and ridden off. Neither Ellen nor her husband was usually a breakfast eater, and she hadn't wasted the time this morning, either. But when she made her first stop to rest her horse, her body was telling her that it was lunchtime even though it was merely a little after nine. She ate half a sandwich, the bread slightly damp.

Always a voracious reader since girlhood—she'd devoured all the great Russian novels before entering her teens—Ellen Naile had often found that some seemingly trivial detail she'd read in years past might be extremely handy to recall. As she spotted a string of horse turds on the ground ahead of her, she slowed and dismounted. Finding a stick wasn't the easiest thing to do in certain parts of Nevada, but in these higher elevations toward which she climbed there was ample vegetation. She was not about to use her fingers or even the blade of a knife for what she intended to do. Using her knife, Ellen Naile stripped an inch or so of bark from one of the twigs, then whittled the exposed wood into as abrupt an edge as she could manage. It would probably cut less well than a plastic knife at a picnic, but would be adequate to her purpose. Using the second twig to hold the largest of the lumps of equine fecal material steady, she cut through it with the sharpened twig.

Had it been the roasting hot days of summer, her experiment would have been easier to interpret. But the interior of the horse poop she examined was of essentially identical consistency to the exterior. Regardless of weather conditions, that meant that a horse had defecated here relatively recently. Considering the heavy rain of the night before, had her find dated from any time before morning, it would have been malformed at least, perhaps partially dissolved.

Ellen was following an animal that had passed this way since around dawn. Discarding the twigs and taking the reins of her horse from beneath her foot (where she'd held them secure while engaging in her research), she began walking forward, eyes scanning the ground. With the earth still damp, she didn't have to walk more than a few paces before finding what she sought: two fresh sets of hoofprints over hoofprints nearly washed away.

It seemed likely to her that she had intersected the trail of either Titus Blake or her husband, but not both, since one set of hoofprints was more deeply etched in the ground than the other, meaning that one horse had been riderless. Watching Clint Walker and Jay Silverheels on television—not to mention Gail Davis, always her hero as Annie Oakley—had taught her that.

Suddenly very chilled, Ellen grabbed up her reins, clambered into the saddle and rode forward.

Without the benefit of an X-ray machine or any of the tests that might routinely be performed in a late-twentieth-century hospital, Peggy still felt confident that Liz would enjoy not only a full recovery, but a rapid one. Fortunately, Peggy knew the blood type of every member of the Naile family, and it was even more fortunate that Lizzie was an A positive, as was she.

With a rifle across her lap, Peggy sat in a rocking chair—it was bullet riddled but still serviceable—on the front porch, watching for she knew not what. The front porch, like the chair, though shot full of holes, was also still serviceable. What did she really wait for? The return of Ellen and Jack? Certainly not her husband, Clarence, and David, Lizzie's brother. They would still be in San Francisco, assuming that they had arrived already. Did she expect Jess Fowler and his evil minions to sneak back for a second attack? More likely; that was why she clutched the rifle in her hands. But what would she do if they did try again? Could she take a human life, even in defense of Lizzie's life or her own?

The bullet that had struck Lizzie had precipitated considerable blood loss and three wounds, one largely superficial. The bullet's path was incredible to consider. The lead had apparently traveled at a slight upward angle. Perhaps it had been what was called a ricochet? Peggy didn't know very much about guns and wished that she knew even less. Regardless, the bullet had creased the side of Elizabeth's left breast, traveled upward and entered her body just slightly rearward of and below the armpit, exiting the lower shoulder without breaking bone, as best Peggy could ascertain. The entrance and exit wounds had been far more than superficial, producing considerable blood loss and pain.

Lizzie rested. Peggy would not allow this luxury to herself. She had gotten Lizzie—chilled—out of the sodden nightgown and into dry clothes, covered her with half the world's visible supply of blankets and positioned two late-twentieth-century hot-water bottles to flank the girl while she slept. Something for pain, a tetanus booster and an antibiotic shot rounded out the best care Peggy could provide her friend, given their primitive circumstances.

Peggy had been so busy worrying over Liz, she had forgotten to worry about herself. Once Lizzie was resting, she'd changed into warm, dry clothes—not daring to take a hot shower lest Fowler's men return and find her helpless, wrapped herself in a blanket and taken up her sentry duty.

Peggy was tired. It was falling off the adrenaline

express train, of course, and she had, after all, transfused Lizzie with about a pint of her own blood. The letdown from the terrifying rush and the depletion of her own blood—she'd nibbled on some crackers and consumed half a glass of red wine (the French method) by way of fortifying herself—made her feel exhausted. But she dared not doze.

The negatives of her present state, current potentially dire circumstances discounted for the moment, basically consisted of three factors in conflict with one another: she was female; she was a doctor; she had medical knowledge that far outstripped that of any other person on the planet.

To use that knowledge—demonstrable, easily provable as science rather than quackery—might alter the entire course of subsequent human events. The Spanish-American War was past, but World War I loomed ever closer over the horizon. The enormous death toll both from the military conflict and the lethal epidemic of influenza that followed/would follow it could be drastically minimized by the knowledge she carried in her head.

Which was the worse sin? To alter the future or to conceal lifesaving knowledge from mankind?

There was another issue.

Jack and Ellen, one evening, had spoken about their old home in Illinois, before they had migrated to Georgia. An older couple with whom they had become friendly had been survivors of World War II. The woman, much like Anne Frank, had been sheltered from the Jewish persecutions by caring Christians. Eventually, her identity as a Jew was discovered, and she had been captured and sent to the death camps. She'd survived, unlike six million others.

Foreknowledge of the coming Nazi storm might minimize or even totally avert its effect. Wasn't it the greater good, rather than preserving the brutality of the future, to alter it for the better? Perhaps one of those lost six million souls would discover the cure for cancer, or the means by which to achieve world peace.

In films and on television, in books of science fiction, the time-traveler was usually someone to be envied, flitting from one era's adventure to the next. But, the "awesome responsibility" of future knowledge was not a blessing; it was a curse, worse than that of any fictional demon of fantasy, more painful than those in mythology that some hapless hero had labored to expiate. Future knowledge was a sentence of moral death, the possessor of such foreknowledge damned whatever her choice might be.

The very procedure of blood-type matching in order to successfully transfuse blood was unknown in this time, such a thing as the Rh factor probably never even contemplated.

No physician in human history had ever had such an opportunity to alleviate needless suffering.

Peggy gripped the rifle, energized, standing, swaying back and forth, her feet tight together beneath the hem of her dress. Her oath was to alleviate suffering. She began to walk, pacing.

Peggy had decided, the clarity of the moment, an epiphany in the truest sense, coursing through her veins. She would be true to her oath.

Ellen had turned back, obsessed with knowing the fate of her husband, abandoning her search for a possible time base, backtracking the unevenly weighted sets of hoofprints, reasoning that the process wouldn't cost her that much time.

In under an hour, she was riding up on what had been the campsite presumably shared by her husband and Marshal Blake. She shuddered. There was something wrapped in a blanket on the ground near the ruins of a campfire; it was shaped like a man's body.

Lest the tableau be some sort of trap fabricated by the men her husband and the town marshal had set out to pursue, Ellen Naile restrained herself from jumping down from the saddle and running to the blanketed form. Instead, hands trembling, she walked her horse slowly, inscribing a rough circle around the campfire. She eased the revolver at her right side in its holster, the hammer thong tucked away, her fingers contacting the Colt's smooth wooden grips.

There was no evidence of an ambush.

Slowly, keeping her right hand touching the revolver, Ellen dismounted. Cautiously, Ellen approached the body as she drew one revolver, then the other. As she raised her eyes, she spotted something shining up at her from near her right boot. Holstering the revolver from her left hand, she crouched, picking up the shiny object. It was a cartridge case, big enough to be a .45. Her glasses were in her saddlebags, but when she held the yellow-brass case at just the right angle and distance, she could make out what Jack always called the "head stamp," and it read "FC."

Jack used commercially available ammunition from the period for some of his target practice, but refused to use anything but the Federal Cartridge ammunition in his special Colt, or any revolver he might carry for defense.

Jack had been shooting here, and had been well enough afterward to empty the spent cases from the revolver after he was through. Her heart leapt, but she'd always felt that she should have been born in Missouri rather than Illinois—she'd believe that Jack wasn't the body under the blanket when she confirmed the fact with her own eyes.

Dropping the empty case back into the mud, she walked toward the body. Just to be safe, she kicked the body in the side, where the hip would be. There was no movement. Again, she kicked it, in the ribs. Nothing.

Looking over her shoulder, glancing all about her, Ellen turned her eyes to the blanket-covered form and tugged the rough gray fabric from the face and downward.

"Oh, shit," Ellen gasped. It was the face of Titus Blake, blue veins tracing a map across gray skin, eyelids rolled back, eyes staring. She drew the blanket downward. Blake's torso was heavily blood spattered, the blood caked and brown. He'd been shot, at least twice, a careful inspection for additional wounds not something in which she had any interest.

The man leading the riderless horse was her husband; and, although she couldn't be certain, Ellen would have laid odds, whatever the reason, that the bullets inside Titus Blake had traveled down the barrel of one of Jack's Colts.

Pulling the blanket up, tucking it around the dead man as securely as she could, Ellen Naile took a deep breath.

Jack and Lizzie were the religious ones of the family,

but she shot a glance heavenward before grabbing the reins of her horse and holstering her revolver.

Helen Bledsoe, a heavy rag tied over her face, obscuring her eyes and mouth, visibly shivered. She was bound around her upper body and legs with—Jack Naile focused the binoculars more precisely—barbed wire. Her filthy, tattered dress was everywhere splotched with blood, some of it clearly dried, some of it obviously fresh.

The eight men who had set their midday camp in the cratered out depression of gravel and dirt, a poorly made fire at its center, were drifting up into the higher surrounding rocks, leading their horses, the cinches loose. Some of the men held their saddle carbines cradled in their elbows or swinging at the end of an outstretched arm.

The Bledsoe girl, Jack thought, was clearly the pathetic cheese in the mousetrap.

The plan, apparently, had been for Blake to lead Jack into the killing ground, Helen Bledsoe's plight so intentionally and obviously tragic as to force anyone with the slightest modicum of human compassion to fling caution to the winds in an attempt to aid her. Blake would likely have declared, "Jack—get her and I'll cover you," or something to that effect.

Jack was not short on compassion, but neither would getting himself killed help Helen.

From his observation point well over two hundred yards out at the height of a rocky defile, he meticulously noted the position of each of the eight would-be ambushers. He waited and waited some more.

An hour passed by the face of his leather-cased Rolex, then another and half of a third. The eight men were already shifting uncomfortably. At least two of them had dug cat holes to urinate. One man was nursing a pint bottle of whiskey. Still another had set down his rifle, turned his back on the scene below and pulled the ragged brim of his high-crowned tan hat low over his eyes, as if sleeping.

Jack had written countless times of stealthy heroes creeping up noiselessly on dull-witted but nevertheless dangerous sentries, dispatching them coolly with the thrust of a knife or a deftly placed karate blow. He had never done anything like that in reality. "First time for mostly everything," Jack reminded himself ruefully and half aloud. He left his vantage point in the rocks and started toward the horses, another hundred yards back.

Ellen remembered John Wayne's character in *The Searchers* admonishing Jeffrey Hunter to rest his horse rather than ride it into the ground in what would prove a fruitless attempt to intervene against a Comanche murder raid. "Right, Duke," she murmured as she reined in and slipped down from the saddle. Her horse needed rest, and, if it gave out, she might never reach her husband before he rendezvoused with whatever danger lay ahead of him. She tied the horse, loosened its saddle, got its muzzle into the feed bag. Sitting down on a flat rock, Ellen ate the second half of the sandwich from earlier, the bread not so soggy tasting this time. She wished, however, that she had a cigarette instead.

❋ ❋ ❋

The .45-70 Marlin with its flip-up Vernier-style tang sight was capable of considerably greater range than the pistol caliber saddle rifles and carbines—probably .44-40s—in the possession of Jack's would-be ambushers. He had spied Winchester '73s and Model 92s, but noticed not a single of the heavier framed rifle caliber 1894 Winchesters, nor any of their Marlin counterparts. So long as he could keep the distance between the muzzles of their long guns and himself at well over a hundred yards, he would be in little if any real danger except from what would—to him, at least—be an incredibly unlucky shot at the hands of a fine marksman.

In his younger days, he'd become friends with the great American marksman Art Cook, who had won/would win a Gold Medal in the 1948 Olympics. Jack couldn't even approach such skills, but hitting center-of-mass required considerably less talent and discipline than clustering holes into a tiny bullseye. And with the .45-70's impressive bullet weight and energy, one hit somewhere in that comparatively large target area would do the job.

As Jack settled in for his first shot, he congratulated himself on his common sense. Had he attempted a silent approach on these men, as one of the characters in his many books would have done, the endeavor would have proven suicidally useless.

Ellen realized full well that the pathetic sight of the bloodied and cruelly bound Helen Bledsoe was bait for a trap, a trap intended to be sprung on her husband. She also realized that, somehow, no matter how illogical that seemed, she had to have passed Jack, reached this spot before him. Otherwise, the jaws of the trap would have already closed. Either that, or Jack lay in ambush somewhere himself, ready to use his long-range Marlin rifle.

As Ellen replaced her binoculars in their case, she sighed. Jack would never allow her to do what she was about to do, but she felt that she had no choice.

Clambering up into the saddle again, her back more than stiff, her butt a little sore, she pushed her hat down from her head, letting it hang on its stampede cord. She shook her hair free. It was important to Ellen that the heartless shits who had done this to Helen Bledsoe would know that a pissed-off woman was coming to kill them, if she could. She positioned her gun belt so that it would be easier for her to reholster when her first revolver was emptied and draw the second one. John Wayne might have been able to handle a horse holding the reins in his teeth with a Winchester in one hand and a Colt in the other, but she could not.

The reins to her mount gripped tightly in her left fist, drawing a revolver with her right hand, Ellen screamed, "All right, you motherfuckers, let's see what you're made of!" And she dug her heels into her horse's flanks.

CHAPTER
❊ THIRTEEN ❊

Jack heard the words but couldn't believe his ears. There was no time for doubting his eyes. He'd caught a fleeting glimpse of his wife riding down from the rocks on the opposite side of the depression, her horse streaking toward where the ambushers waited.

"Shit," Jack snarled, squinting his eyes shut for a microsecond, then catching his breath as he opened his eyes and retook his sight picture on the most alert-seeming of the desperados. Three things happened simultaneously: the resounding crack of the .45-70 cartridge launching its bullet toward the target, the butt of the rifle punching his shoulder and the Marlin's muzzle rising slightly.

His ears still rang from the sound of the shot; despite that, Jack could hear pistol fire. That had to be Ellen firing at the ambushers. He didn't take time to look, a fresh cartridge already levered into the Marlin's chamber, his right eye picking up a target through the peep aperture of the tang sight. When he had a man's center of mass floating over the front sight, Jack fired again.

This time, as soon as he verified he'd hit his mark, Jack looked to his right and down into the depression. Ellen was swapping revolvers, still riding toward the ambushers.

It was almost a relief when the long-gun-armed men sheltered in the rocks at last returned fire. The first fusillade of gunfire poured down toward Ellen, clumps of earth and large pieces of gravel exploding on all sides of her, but neither she nor her mount seemed to be struck by a bullet.

While he'd watched the scene unfold, Jack had crammed two more rounds through his rifle's loading gate. Levering the action, he fired again. He caught one of the ambushers as the man stood, bringing a Winchester '73 to his shoulder. The impact of Jack's shot sent the wannabe murderer flying back against another of his fellows. That man's rifle discharged into the air. As it did, Jack levered another round into his own rifle's chamber and fired. He struck the second man somewhere in the chest.

Jack scanned the terrain to his right. Ellen was taking heavy fire from the remaining ambushers. Her horse, struck, collapsed under her. She jumped clear, landing hard, it looked like, as her horse raised its head once, then died.

Four of the ambushers were either dead or, at least, out of the fight; four remained.

It was time to draw their fire away from Ellen. Jack broke from cover, packing two more rounds into the rifle as he ran toward the next suitable spot where he could take shelter from enemy fire. He fired a wasted shot toward his enemies, baiting them to return fire. They did. The rocks just ahead of him seemed to explode with bullet impacts, but the range was still too much of a reach for anything but a lucky shot or a fine marksman.

Jack caught a glimpse of Ellen. She was slowly rolling onto her back. One of the outlaws was on his horse, racing down out of the rocks toward her, a revolver in his hand, firing.

Jack snapped off a shot, missed.

A man was riding down on her, his six-gun blazing. Ellen could barely breathe. Every bone in her body ached, but nothing felt broken. The revolver still holstered on her gun belt was empty, but the one she'd dropped as she fell from her horse had three rounds left in it. Her eyes swept over the ground, searching for it.

Ellen spotted the Colt Single Action Army half obscured under her dead horse, near where the cinch strap crossed the animal's belly.

By dint of willpower more than strength, she scrambled to her feet, half hurtling, half falling toward her dead horse, her right arm at maximum extension, grasping for the revolver. Her hand closed around it. Jerking it free, Ellen looked up.

The mounted killer was so close she could see the front sight of his six-gun and the flecks of yellow in his squinted green eyes. A bullet impacted the right hind leg of her dead horse, inches from her own left leg. Ellen stabbed the revolver toward her assailant and did the only thing that made sense: shot at the largest and easiest target, firing the Colt's remaining three rounds into the chest of the killer's oncoming mount.

The horse pitched forward, its knees buckling. As the animal rolled into an awkward-looking somersault, the green-eyed killer launched over his mount's neck and head.

Ellen scrabbled for cartridges from her gun belt, knowing that there wouldn't be time to reload if the fall hadn't killed or injured the man.

As she glanced toward him, a sick feeling chilled her stomach. He was unsteady, but he was on his feet, his right arm fully extended, the first finger of his right hand drawing back to trigger a round. Ellen snarled, "Fuck you!"

There was a click. The revolver's hammer fell, but no round discharged.

"Damn bitch," the man hissed. He let the revolver drop from his hand, then reached for the one holstered cross-draw. He drew it, cocked the hammer. Ellen threw the empty revolver at him, missing him but making him dodge.

There was a loud shot, then another. The killer's body twitched, then lurched back, falling spread-eagled to the ground.

Ellen raced toward him, picked up the still-cocked single action, which had fallen from his hand, then spun around.

"Jack!"

"Get down, kid! Behind the horse, just like in the movies!"

There were still more men in the rocks above them.

Bullets tore into her horse's body as she flung herself behind it. Jack was beside her in the next instant. He rolled onto his back, smiling at her as he reloaded his big rifle, pulling the cartridges out of a belt slung crossbody from his right shoulder to left hip.

As if reading her mind, Jack told her, "Three of them. All with rifles and revolvers. And horses. Hopefully, they'll use them—the horses—and ride off."

"What about Helen, Jack?" Ellen Naile saw the Bledsoe girl rolled up almost into a ball less than what she judged to be a quarter of a city block away from them. "If one of those guys up there decides to be a real schmuck, they'll shoot her just for spite."

"I've got plenty of .45-70s left, Ellen. If you can do this fast enough, we can make it." He took off his Stetson and shrugged out of the bandolier, then replaced the black hat, pulling it down low over his eyes. There was a spare revolver stuffed in his trouser belt; he drew it, rolled it in his hand and offered it to her butt first. "You keep them busy, like they used to say in the old westerns. Keep 'em pinned down. I'm going to go get the girl to cover."

Ellen warned him, "She's tied up in barbed wire."

"It won't cut up my hands so badly that I can't shoot."

"You bringing her back here?"

"Only place that's close enough. Fire the rifle once, then throw a few pistol shots at them while I run toward her. Save the rest of what's in the rifle until I'm on my way back with her. Only four shots total in the magazine. And remember, keep the butt of that rifle tucked tight into your shoulder or you'll hurt yourself." He drew the one remaining of her original revolvers from its holster and loaded it as he said, "This may also flush them out, which means they may rush us."

"Why did you leave me the cartridge belt with the rifle ammunition in it?"

Her husband smiled. "Just in case."

"You are not going to get yourself killed. Do I make myself clear, Jack!?"

Jack tipped his hat as he responded, "Yes, ma'am. But I wasn't exactly planning on doing that anyway."

"Jack?"

"Yeah?"

"When this is all over, are you going to make some profound literary reference, some quote, like Richard Boone always did on TV?"

Jack laughed. "I'll see what I can do." He kissed her, scrunched his hat down tight and low, drew his special long barreled Colt and ordered, "Fire that rifle shot now!"

Ellen brought the rifle to her shoulder, worked the lever and fired. The recoil slammed into her, and the rifle barrel rocked upward from where she'd rested it across the body of her dead horse. Why would anybody want to shoot something that hurt so much? she asked herself.

She looked behind her.

Jack had already started to run, keeping to a low crouch. He turned around once and snapped a shot toward the three bad guys in the rocks above them as he skidded to his knees beside the Bledsoe girl. He fired another shot, holstered his revolver and swept the girl up into his arms, running with her. Ellen fired out one of the revolvers, put it down, brought the rifle to her shoulder and fired, fired again.

As she prepared to fire a fourth shot, Jack was beside her, Helen Bledsoe between them. "Chamber a round yet?"

"No."

Jack grabbed the rifle from her hands, worked the lever and fired. Ellen Naile heard something that sounded like a man's scream of pain.

"Two left," Jack said flatly. It was when Jack turned around to reload the rifle that Ellen noticed his hands, covered in blood. His shirt was cut, blood oozing through in spots. "Lucky we've all had tetanus shots recently. She'll need one."

Jack seemed about to say something else, but a flurry of shots from the two men still up in the rocks interrupted him. Blood splattered them both as bullets thwacked into the body of her dead horse.

"Stay down!" Jack commanded.

Ellen did as she was told, but was able to peek around the neck of the dead animal. She spied two riders, barreling down from the rocks above, revolvers firing wildly toward Jack and her. Ellen looked to her left as Jack's rifle boomed, then boomed again, then again.

One of the riders tumbled from his saddle. Jack's rifle fired a fourth time. The last of the desperados fell from his saddle, but sprang to his feet like some sort of Hollywood stuntman. He reached for the pistol worn crossdraw at his left side. "Jack! Look out!" Ellen Naile shouted.

There were two shots, almost simultaneous.

The bad guy's knees just seemed to buckle, and he fell backward in a heap.

Ellen looked at her husband, his gleaming long-barreled Colt revolver held at full extension of his right arm.

As he holstered the gun, in his best deep voice, Jack intoned, "A wet bird never flies at night'—da-da-da-dum."

For a moment, Ellen Naile just stared at her husband, and then she started to laugh so hard that she almost pissed.

"Load your guns," Jack told Ellen, already loading his. He set his rifle down and, without missing a beat, set to work freeing Helen. Ellen joined in a moment or so later. "So, you guys were able to repel them when they came against you at the house?" Jack asked Ellen in a measured, conversational tone. The Bledsoe girl was whimpering with every movement as they began to free her of the barbed wire with which she was bound.

"Who? Who came against the house? Nobody—"

"Oh, my God," Jack whispered, looking suddenly frightened, visibly shivering, overwhelmed.

"Lizzie? And Clarence's wife? More guys like these that tried killing us? They were going to attack the house?"

"Blake told me before he died. Take care of her, of Helen, as quickly as you can, Ellen. Tell me what I can do to help." He cut away the last of the barbed wire with the Leatherman tool he carried in his saddlebags, then sat down and covered his face with his bloodied hands for a moment.

"I'll help you round up some horses. You take a couple of them. You can leave us out here alone. There is no choice but to do that. I'll get Helen back by myself."

Jack looked up from his hands. His eyes looked as if he were holding back tears. Some of the Bledsoe girl's blood was smeared on his face. "We'll pick up the best of the guns these guys lost, so you and Helen have plenty of fire-power if you need it." The Bledsoe girl seemed some-where between sleep and unconsciousness, had made no sound but those associated with pain. "Can you make it back with her?"

"She's not comatose, just really hurting. I can make some of that better, get her back to the house so Clarence's wife can take care of her. We'll be fine. We can load a spare horse with all the rifles and handguns we can carry. With my hair stuffed under my hat, from a distance I'll look like a guy. We'll be fine," Ellen volunteered again.

Jack nodded, mumbling something about getting his own horse as he jogged off.

The room was cold, kept that way, perhaps, to keep the computers—banks of them—running at peak efficiency. Alan Naile was freezing, but wasn't numb. Almost every inch of his body hurt. When he'd awakened tied to a straight back chair as a captive of Bethany Kaminsky's thugs, Lester Matthews had ordered, "Hurt him a lot, but not anything permanent yet. No bones or teeth. We're not a hundred percent sure of how we'll play this."

Expertly, two of Matthews' men began following their boss's orders with egregious zeal, their blows leveled at muscle groups, at the abdomen, the groin, Alan sinking beneath the waves of pain, awakening and, in the next instant, the administration of pain beginning anew. It went on like that—the brutalization—for what seemed to him an eternity. Pain, unconsciousness, more pain. The only way to judge the passing of time was by the faces of his tormenters. They had both had average five o'clock shadows in their hollow cheeks when the pain began. When at last it ceased, their faces showed at least another full day's growth.

They freed him from the chair and hauled him, still otherwise bound to his feet. He wet himself as he stood, but had done that already after they'd first started beating him in the stomach and groin. Matthews remarked, "You stink, Naile." Then Matthews ordered his men, "Clean him up a little before you bring him along. But be quick about it."

Cold water from a scrub bucket was thrown on him. His feet free, his hands—those were numb—still bound behind him and his arms bound at his sides with a rope tight around his chest, he was led off toward the door of the room in which he had been beaten. Before the door was opened, a dark blue pillowcase was pulled down over his head. One of his tormenters threatened, "Let out a fuckin' word, and I'll haul your ass back in here and put your nuts in a bench vise. When the pain gets too bad and you pass out, you'll fall, but your balls'll still be locked in that vise. You might even tear 'em off."

Alan said nothing, only nodded his head within the pillowcase. It was clear that the identity of the tortured prisoner was something to be kept secret. Why?

He was shoved along, walking for what seemed blocks, the pillowcase hood removed only after he'd been tied into another chair in this room filled with computers and high tech electronics.

Bethany Kaminsky's face had smiled down at him.

After she walked away, joining Matthews, Alan had begun his assessment of the room. A dozen computerwork stations, another room beyond with what was likely a supercomputer. But other equipment looked at once strange and familiar. As seconds dragged on into minutes, recognition slowly returned. What he was looking at—at least some of it—were upgraded versions of certain of the monitoring systems devised to duplicate the time-travel phenomenon.

Why was such equipment here? As he nearly verbalized the question aloud, Alan's consciousness was flooded over by a wave of bitterly cold realization. If the time base to which both Mort Hardesty and Kaminsky had alluded was, in fact, in the mountains in Nevada, then this equipment was for farther research. If Lakewood Industries' minions could travel back and forth into the past from one location, other locations could be established. Not in an office building in some Chicago suburb, he told himself. No, such equipment had to be for something else.

Kaminsky interrupted his thoughts as she called to him from across the room, then began walking toward him, Matthews—the left side of Matthews' face bruised from where Alan had punched him—at her side. "You're wondering what all this stuff is for? Right?"

"Research into time-travel?"

"In a way. The supercomputer in the next room is running permutations, as Mort calls them. If such and such event took place or such and such person ceased to exist or never existed, how would the present be affected? Like that. This is complex stuff, my soon-to-be-ex-rival. The actual time-travel stuff that we have is for plotting coordinates and polishing our technique.

"I always just loathe it in movies when the bad guy tells

the good guy his plans before killing him, don't you? But," Bethany went on, "in this case, it's a sure bet you're going to die. And if for some reason you escaped at the last second before death, you'll be almost a hundred years in the past. Who would you tell? What good would it do? Besides your damn relatives, everybody'd think you're crazy.

"So," she continued, obviously enjoying herself, "here's a kind of overview of the business plan, Naile. I want to control the world, but from behind the scenes. Women do it best that way—control things. For that, I need the cooperation of a country. Now, I'm as patriotic as the next gal—well, not really, but anyway—so, we'll give the good old USA a shot at things. And Germany and England. I left out the French, but I don't think they'd work out. They'd rather do everything for themselves."

"You're leaving out places like the Sudan, Iceland, Columbia, too? Gee! Need an industrial base at the turn of the century?"

"Now, isn't he clever, Lester!" Bethany Kaminsky enthused, throwing up her hands. "You can see why Alan Naile's a captain of industry! Right you are, Alan! Very good boy! At the close of the nineteenth and the beginning of the twentieth centuries, there were only four countries that could ramp up for the kind of technology I'm offering. But here's why I sort of figure the United States wouldn't be interested, and probably not the Brits, but, they might surprise us. Who knows? Right? Better yet, you guess, bright boy."

Alan didn't have to guess. "You're going to offer late-twentieth-century war-related technology to the highest bidder, enabling that nation to take over the world. Aerial dogfights with F-16s pitted against Sopwith Camels? Ground battles with modern tanks against horse-mounted cavalry, M-16 rifles against old bolt-action infantry weapons? You filthy bitch!"

Matthews grabbed Alan by what remained of his shirt-front, but Kaminsky waved him off. "By controlling the flow of technology, then playing the combatants against one another, I think I'll do well. No high-tech fighter planes like F-16s, but maybe the Korean War kind of jets. That sort of thing. One sale like that a hundred years ago would propel things along throughout the century to where Lakewood now would be the dominant financial power in the whole world. All thanks to your lovely family, the present is going to change very dramatically. Technology will leap ahead by a hundred years. If you could see what the present will be like, you wouldn't recognize it. The more high-tech military hardware I introduce into the past, the more technology will have to catch up. Progress, Alan. Progress! I'll own it all. You'll be dead. Your relatives back in the past will watch it happen and won't be able to stop it.

"Just think, Alan." Bethany stooped down in front of him, grabbed his testicles through his pants and whispered, "The dream of Caesar, Napoleon, Alexander the Great, Hitler—all of them, guys, couldn't do it. I don't have balls. I don't need them. And I'm the one who's going to conquer the whole fucking world."

Bethany stood up and ordered Matthews, "Take him back in time and shoot him with a period weapon with period ammunition. Then leave his body for the insects and the animals—and his loving family."

CHAPTER
❖ FOURTEEN ❖

Jack had taken his own mount, Barbie, Blake's horse and one other, heading back for the ranch to discover Lizzie's and Peggy's fates, essentially retracing the way he had come and as quickly as possible. With hard riding, he would be at the ranch by dawn.

For safety's sake—it was a way less traveled—and because the route would be easier on someone who was injured, Ellen had told Jack that she would take the slower course back, through the mountains.

With dusk approaching, early it seemed, and leading Helen's mount behind her, Ellen began a serious search for what would be their evening's campsite. Clayton Moore and Jay Silverheels had always found a convenient "grove of cottonwoods just outside of town," but there were no cottonwood groves to be had, and town—Atlas—was quite a long distance away. Ellen Naile settled instead, for what in other climes might have been called an oasis. In the barren expanse so high still in the mountains, there were few examples of vegetation other than scrub pines, but they happened on a reasonably flat tract perhaps a quarter the length of a football field and nearly as wide, an ideal mountain pasture except for its comparatively miniscule size. There was decent-looking grass for the horses, a pool of water from which she wouldn't be reckless enough to drink (without a ceramic filter) and pines that looked overall fuller and greener, less as if they were struggling for life. All told, the spot was as fine a campsite as she might have hoped for.

"We'll stop here for the night, Helen."

"Yes, Miz Naile."

"You can call me Ellen, sweetheart."

"Yes, Miz Ellen."

"Youth." Ellen shrugged and sighed under her breath. Albeit bruised, with abrasions and cuts all over her body— Ellen had treated them from her first aid-kit—the Bledsoe girl had bounced back remarkably quickly. Aside from her tattered dress beneath the blankets in which she was cocooned and the cuts that were obvious on what skin still showed, the Bledsoe girl's principal physical symptom was exhaustion. And she said little about that. The relatively stoic pioneer girl was mainly bone tired, but elated that her parents had survived.

"Helen," Ellen volunteered, continuing quickly before the girl could return some polite response. "I'm going to help you off your horse, then get you settled. If you want to nap, feel free. I don't need any assistance at all getting camp set up, and I really just want you to rest so you're feeling good when you see your mother and father. I'm going to make something warm to eat, and I want you to have plenty of it."

Eating—Ellen had yet to defecate since she'd set out after Jack and had no intention of doing like the proverbial bear in the woods unless such were unavoidable; she would eat sparingly.

In a way, Ellen felt liberated. After eating, the inevitable did, in fact, become unavoidable. She had gotten through it—less yucky an experience than she had thought that it would be—and felt confident that she was, at last, at home in the wild, could handle the rugged life. She laughed at herself. However successful the experiment in physical hygiene had been, she harbored no desire to repeat it.

Adjusting her clothes as she walked out of the trees and toward their small fire, Ellen wished again for a cigarette. Certain bodily functions just seemed to cry out to be punctuated with a smoke.

Looking past the fire and into the fast-advancing night beyond their campsite, Ellen spied flashes of light in the purpling darkness.

Barbie had settled into a long-strided trot after Jack Naile resaddled and remounted the mare. According to his leather-cased Rolex, the time was a few minutes after two in the morning. Judging from the terrain, at the current pace he could make it to the ranch by a little before six. At this stage, Blake's horse and the mount Jack had liberated from one of the dead ambushers were more a liability than an asset. He left them behind to show up on some spread nearby—perhaps even his own ranch—when they got tired of foraging for food and water and missed the security of the feedbag and the trough.

There was the matter of Blake's body, but the marshal's death would be easily enough explained. As a writer of fiction, Jack had occasionally referred to himself as "a professional liar," and covering for Blake being gunned down—especially in an age where forensic ballistics were all but unknown—wouldn't even be a challenge.

All that concerned Jack Naile was the safety of his family. He had already promised himself that he would kill Jess Fowler, had to before Fowler hatched some other plot. Soon, perhaps within days, David and Clarence would be back from San Franciso, having cashed in a portion of the diamonds brought back into the past as a portable and negotiable source of wealth. Once they were back, Jack was determined to do what he had to do.

Jack turned his horse on the familiar track toward the house, filled with trepidation. Vengeance had or would have little to do with the intent to kill Fowler, merely practicality. With Fowler dead, there would be no one left with a blood vendetta against the family.

Alan was packed aboard the Lakewood Industries jet which would bring him to a private airfield not far from Reno. He would then be spirited, by vehicle, to the time transfer location in the mountains near Atlas, Nevada. The Lakewood Industries time base was fewer than twenty miles from the sparsely guarded facility used by Horizon Enterprises, a single mountain peak masking its presence.

Once arrived, Lester Matthews would personally over-see Alan's one-way trip ninety-six years into the past, kill him, abandon the body and return to the present.

Standing outside the hangar from which one of her small fleet of business jets would soon emerge, Bethany Kaminsky gave Matthews his final instructions, her voice raised against the roaring intake of the jet engines. "Remember to kill him with that special gun."

"The revolver." He let his sportcoat come open, revealing the wooden-gripped butt of the handgun. "Use the .45 Colt caliber Smith & Wesson revolver so if Naile's body is found the bullet won't be looked at as being—what's that word you used?"

"Anomalous, Lester. Anomalous. And when you get back, work up some plans for me on how we could have some terrible accident wipe out every living member of Alan's family. Maybe if they have a bodyless funeral for him a few months from now, maybe then. I want all the descendants of David Naile and Elizabeth Naile killed, but artfully."

"Wipe out the whole fuckin' family. You're really into this vendetta thing, aren't you, Bethany? Blood vendetta. You woulda made one helluva mob boss during the twenties and thirties."

Bethany took that as a compliment.

"Just figure out how to do it." She glanced at the Rolex on her left wrist. "Morton Hardesty is expecting me, and if screwing him is the way to perfect this time-travel thing to the nth degree, little Morty can pop me until that poor excuse for a dick of his wears out. You'll be having more fun than I will, Lester. Guaranteed. I'm gone. But remember, before you kill Alan, tell him in graphic detail what we're planning for his wife and family and parents and all of them. Give him a moment for it to sink in, then let him have it good." Bethany shifted the purse strap on her left shoulder and started walking back to her Mercedes. There was a scuff on the toe of her left pump, and she muttered, "Damn" as she walked on.

Dawn was a palpable promise along the ragged edge of granite horizon by the time Ellen, the Bledsoe girl in tow, settled into the concealment of broad, flat rocks and focused her binoculars on the scene below her, the place from which the flashes of light had originated. She'd wanted to get closer, would have if she'd had only herself to worry about. With Helen along, she couldn't risk it.

Even without the benefit of binoculars, Ellen could easily discern the anachronistic nature of what lay in the rock depression on the other side of the mountain from the time transfer point used by Horizon Enterprises. A few four-wheel ATVs, a double-cab Ford pickup truck with a long bed, electrical generators. All of those had been readily apparent. But with the binoculars, she could see that the men guarding the facility's perimeter carried modern M-16 rifles and that submachine gun Jack had always drooled over, an H-K something or other. There wasn't a Winchester lever action in the bunch. No Colt Single Actions were slung on their hips, either; rather, she saw modern looking semiautomatic pistols.

Their clothing, as well, was from the future she had left behind. No cowboy hats, but the ever-ubiquitous baseball cap. Their jeans didn't look to be riveted denim, but the designer kind. Combat rather than cowboy boots were the norm when it came to footgear, those or track shoes.

"Shit."

"Miz Ellen!"

"Sorry," Ellen responded. "But, be quiet, Helen. We don't want those men down there to know we're up here spying on them. So, be very, very silent." If she'd been in the mood for levity, she could have added that they were "hunting wabbit," but the Bledsoe girl might have taken her seriously.

Video surveillance cameras dotted the fence line. The men with the M-16s carried walkie-talkies as well.

"Miz Ellen?" Helen whispered.

"Yes, honey?" Ellen put down the binoculars and gazed at her weary young charge. "What are we looking at? Is that what you want to ask me?"

"I ain't never seen—"

"Now, your aunt the schoolteacher and my daughter— what have they told you about double negatives?"

"Don't never use none, Miz Ellen. I know."

Ellen sighed audibly. "What we're looking at is a whole bunch of men and machinery and stuff that doesn't belong here. Its likely purpose is to cause a whole lot of trouble for a whole lot of people. Unless I miss my guess, darling, the people who paid to put that fence up and have those armed men patrolling around it aren't much different from Jess Fowler's men who kidnapped you. Just better paid, equipped and dressed. And," Ellen added, punctuating her remark by pouching the binoculars, "that is why you and I, young lady, are going to be extremely quiet and sneak out of here right now, get to our horses and ride like the devil's chasing us. For all intents and purposes, he just might be."

One hand prodding gently at Helen Bledsoe's elbow, the other on a Colt revolver, Ellen started back the way they'd come.

"I'm alright, Daddy. I'm just kind of tired."

On his knees beside his daughter's bed, Jack bent his head and touched his lips to her forehead. He looked up at Peggy. She'd almost opened fire on him as he'd approached the house, walking the done-in Barbie the last few hundred yards. When, lowering her rifle, she'd called out and run to him, he'd swept her into his arms and hugged her for a moment.

"Where's—" Jack had begun.

"Lizzie was shot. She'll be fine. She's—"

Jack started running at the first word from Peggy's lips. Vaulting the steps, he nearly smashed through the door leading from the porch.

Lizzie opened her eyes the instant he barged into her bedroom.

Jack looked once more at his daughter. She seemed pale. "How much blood—"

"I transfused her. She'll be fine, Jack."

Jack nodded. Looking at his daughter, thinking how close he had come to losing her, getting out more than a few halting words without the choked-back tears flowing as well was all but impossible.

"Fine doctor I am, Jack, but why don't you just step out onto the porch and have a cigarette, and I'll look after your horse."

"No. You relax. Come outside if it's safe for Lizzie. Tell me what happened while I tend to Barbie." Jack looked down once again at his daughter and kissed her forehead as he stood. Lizzie closed her eyes, a thin smile on her lips.

Jack washed up and changed shirts, not bothering with anything beyond that and a tetanus booster. He'd smoked several cigarettes, eating nothing, waiting while the exhausted Peggy showered and dressed. Leaving the two women alone was dangerous, especially before Ellen reached the house, but leaving Jess Fowler alive any longer than necessary seemed somehow vastly more dangerous, insanely so.

With a replenished supply of ammunition in his saddle-bags and cartridge belts, the two spare revolvers tucked into his waistband, Jack saddled a horse. There were three from which to choose, aside from the exhausted Barbie. Both of Lizzie's horses were palominos. One of them, the smaller of the two, was called Victoria, the larger male was called Garbonzo. Jack chose, instead, the little gray with black stockings, mane and tail, the one both Lizzie and David had agreed should be called Trixie.

As soon as Peggy emerged from the house, changed into a clean blue dress, her hair still wet, Jack swung up into the saddle. "Did you check on Lizzie?"

"She's fine, Jack. No fever. She'll be okay."

"Ellen should be here soon. Helen Bledsoe's going to need a tetanus shot. Make up some kind of a lie about what it is. She's got a lot of cuts that'll require attention. Ellen and I don't think she was raped, but you should check discreetly. Remember, she's got superficial wounds that'll need tending."

"So do you, Jack."

"I'll be back in a few hours. If I'm not back, well, the medical attention would have been wasted. Let's say we have an appointment for later today, Doctor." He smiled. He'd sat with his right leg crossed over the neck of his horse, his hat cocked back on his head. He shifted his leg down and lowered his hat over his eyes.

"Do you still like being a cowboy, Jack?"

Jack laughed. "With most of the important, significant things in life, there's precious little choice, isn't there? We had no choice in coming here, and I have no choice but to go after Fowler and his men, too, if I have to. They nearly wiped out our entire family. If they had, they would have gone after David and Clarence when they got back from San Francisco. Without Fowler, his range detectives will look for greener pastures—and by 'greener' I'm referring to money. But, do I like being a cowboy?

"When I was a little boy," he went on, "I wanted to be a cowboy, like most boys from my generation. I grew up on westerns. I always admired the men who were fast on the draw. When I got older, I learned that it wasn't speed so much as accuracy. But, did I ever think I'd become one of those gunmen? No. And am I happy about the fact that I did? Precious little choice. I wouldn't mind you saying a prayer for me. See ya."

Jack Naile wheeled the little gray around on her hind legs. She sprang into a trot, away from the ranch, toward Atlas and Fowler's ranch house, which lay between.

❅ ❅ ❅

Fowler and three of his range detectives were riding hard. With faded-out high grass on either side of the track, the road they traversed was analogous to a twentieth-century driveway, but a long one. From where Jack observed deep within the treeline on the slope opposite, Fowler's comparatively palatial ranch house was more than a mile distant.

One of the three range detectives spurred his mount ahead, dismounted hurriedly and barely had the gate open in time to jump aside as Fowler and the other two gunmen goaded their horses through the opening, then turned onto the road, riding toward Atlas.

The gateman vaulted into the saddle, urged his horse ahead, bent low and closed the gate, then galloped into the dust cloud that was the wake of Jess Fowler and the others. Each man wore two pistols and had a rifle in his saddle scabbard. One of the men had a Greener shotgun in a scabbard across the horn of his saddle.

If they stuck to the road, the perennial movie western option presented itself to Jack: he could head 'em off at the pass. But in this case, that would be where the road into town hairpinned around the outlet of a steep, rocky defile leading down out of the mountains.

Jack walked quickly back to his horse, slipped the Marlin into his saddle scabbard and mounted. He took out his watch, glanced at it and marked the time. "Alright, Trixie. Let's get this over with." He tugged on the reins, wheeled her around and started his cross-country run.

The distance he had to traverse was less than two miles. Fowler and his men would have to cover a little over twice that before reaching the same spot. They had an open road; Jack had to negotiate broken ground littered with rocks and deadfall trees. The little gray was sure-footed and Jack felt that he had a good chance of reaching the spot where the road turned before Fowler and his men could.

Another commonly encountered western-movie term came to mind as Jack rode, urging the horse onward but letting her pick her own way. The word was *bushwhack*. That was what he was about to do—bushwhack Fowler's men. Fowler, if the opportunity presented itself, would not be so disposed of. Jack intended to face Fowler and kill him, even if that meant risking his own life. There were some things in life that needed doing in one certain way and no other. Long-distancing Fowler would be a last-ditch option.

On one level of consciousness, Jack was counting seconds, then seconds into minutes, comparing his riding time to what he anticipated as that of Fowler and the range detectives. A fast horse could top forty-five miles per hour for a short distance on level ground. Trixie was fast, the distance was short, but the terrain to be crossed was awful.

Jack estimated that Fowler and the three men with him would cover their four to five miles in twelve minutes or so. He had to cover half that distance at two-thirds the speed in order to have time to dismount, find a spot and be ready with his rifle. He checked his watch as he reined in. Nine minutes had passed. Dropping from the saddle, he looped and knotted Trixie's rein to the trunk of a pine, grabbed his rifle and the cartridge belt of .45-70s, then ran toward the defile.

Whatever natural forces had formed the jumble of jutting gray and sand-colored rock he could not guess, but it was unmistakably some sort of violent upheaval. He found a deep niche a little under fifty yards from the road, settled into it and raised the tang sight on his rifle, set the diopter to fifty yards and slowed his breathing as he levered the first round into the Marlin's chamber. He lowered the hammer, then plucked a fifth round from the bandolier, running it through the receiver's loading gate.

Jack waited.

Jess Fowler was the first of the riders to come into view. It almost seemed odd, seeing Fowler riding another horse besides the big black that was his usual mount. Trixie whinnied, and there was the sound of a stick breaking under the pressure of a footfall.

"Shit!" Jack Naile hissed through clenched teeth, rolling onto his back, thumbing back the hammer of his rifle.

Jess and two other men crept out of the trees, revolvers drawn, except for Fowler who had a Greener double in his hands.

The shotgun was the greatest danger. Jack stabbed the muzzle of the .45-70 toward Fowler and snapped the trigger.

Fowler went down.

Bullets from the Colts Fowler's two henchmen carried whined off the jagged granite slabs around him as Jack sprang to his feet and vaulted over the rocks and half rolled, half skidded along the defile for several feet before crashing into something—he wasn't sure what—and coming to a bone jarring halt.

He shook his head, tried to think. Looking along the remaining length of the defile, he saw the fake Jess Fowler—Fowler's black frocked coat and high-crowned, broad-brimmed black hat comprising the costume—and three more of Fowler's range detectives. They were skinning out of their saddles and drawing their guns.

Jack had lost the Marlin in the fall. As he came up to one knee, he snatched the brace of short-barreled Colt revolvers from his waistband and stabbed them toward the fake Fowler and the three range detectives with him. Jack emptied the ten shots the two six-guns held toward the four men. Their ponies shied out of the hail of lead and one of Fowler's men was knocked down by his animal.

The fake Fowler went down, obviously dead or in the process of dying. One of the range detectives—a man about Jack's height and build, wearing a high-crowned gray hat—clutched his abdomen and doubled up, falling against his already bolting pinto.

Jack let the two Colts fall from his hands and drew the long-barreled Colt from the holster at his right thigh. With the revolver at maximum extension of his right arm, he fired just as the one still-standing range detective from the road below fired. The range detective's shot missed— apparently, Jack thought in the same instant, since he'd felt no bullet strike him. Jack's shot didn't miss.

Jack's bullet struck the range detective in the throat— Jack could see the wound—and the man toppled like a felled tree.

There was still the fourth man, the one caught up under his pony's legs.

There wasn't time for him.

Jack wheeled round. The two range detectives who had been with Fowler at the height of the defile were just coming into view. One of the men was executing a half-border shift, flipping a revolver from his right hand into his left in order to draw the still loaded revolver from the crossdraw holster between his navel and left hipbone.

Jack punched the muzzle of his Colt toward the other man and fired simultaneously with him. There was a flash of searing pain along the outside of Jack's left thigh, but he didn't go down. Jack's shot connected, too, striking into the chest of the man who had just shot him. The man fell back and out of sight.

Jack no longer consciously thought. It was as if all of the western gunfights he'd read about in books and watched in movies and on television had somehow synthesized in him to make him a killing instrument of consummate skill.

Jack arced his body a few degrees, the muzzle of his long-barreled Colt settling on the chest of the man who had shifted an empty revolver to his left hand and was still drawing the cross-draw-carried revolver with his right.

The man never completed his draw.

Jack shot him dead through the chest.

Jack turned around, his eyes scanning machinelike for the last remaining range detective, the one who'd had the problem with his horse.

Jack's eyes found him, and the muzzle of Jack's revolver followed. The man was standing, attempting to draw both revolvers from his belt. Jack fired once. His bullet struck the man square in the middle of the forehead, snapping his head back so violently that his flat crowned, weathered-looking hat flew from his head.

Jack turned his back on the dead and started up the defile as he opened the loading gate on his revolver, methodically ejecting the four empty shell casings, alternating ejection with introduction of a fresh round into each empty charging hole.

Jack's left leg felt on fire, but he didn't dare look at it.

Limping to the height of the jagged, rocky defile, five rounds once again filling his six-shooter, he suddenly realized that he had lost his hat, only because he saw it lying in the rocks near his feet. Jack Naile bent over to pick it up, and, as he raised his head, he noticed Jess Fowler trying to stand.

Jack holstered his revolver.

The striped trouser leg over Fowler's right knee was drenched with blood.

"Fowler. It's been a long time coming to this and I don't have the patience to let it continue. Get on your feet and we'll have this thing end right here. You don't have anyone backing you up—your range detectives are dead or dying. It's just you and me. If you can't stand up, I don't care. If you can't draw your gun, I'll shoot you dead where you lie."

Fowler's body attitude could be described with only one word Jack could bring to mind: Fowler cringed.

"I've got a whole passel of money, Naile—it's yours. You want land? Hey. All of my land is yours. Look, Naile! Listen to me! We can make a deal. Please?"

"'Come on down!' I don't think so, asshole."

Fowler managed to get to his feet, his right leg oddly bent, his face a grotesque thing, a mask of pain.

"You're used to murdering people, Fowler, or fighting it out with defenseless women. This'll be a new sensation:

a fair fight. Make sure that the hammer loop is clear of that Colt on your hip. And whenever you feel like it—but, don't make me wait too long, or you'll bleed to death first—go for your gun. With two men of close to equal skills, the man who draws first has an overwhelming advantage, almost invariably insurmountable. But I grew up on a diet of this, practiced when I was a kid until I could outdraw Richard Boone and James Arness every Saturday night on television.

"My revolver is hand-crafted. It has a fourteen-ounce trigger pull," Jack told Fowler. His voice was low, his cadence even.

"Who's them fellers? What's a—"

"It's a large box that shows pictures and sound and is partially to blame for the decline in practical literacy among the American population a hundred years hence, where I'm from. You won't live to see a television set; some might say that I'm being merciful by pointing that out. Draw your gun pretty soon, or I'll just kill you. You attack women. You don't have the balls to fight someone who can fight back."

"Anything you want, Naile! You want me to beg?"

"No. Dying will do. Draw."

Jess Fowler went for his gun.

Jack's left leg flexed instinctively, painfully, bent at the knee, his right hand flashing to the butt of his revolver. The series of motions, practiced since childhood, caused his leg to draw the holster away from the gun as his hand drew the gun away from the holster.

Jack's single shot came a split second before the shot from Fowler's gun.

Jack's bullet struck its target—Fowler's chest—and Fowler's muscle jerked and his shot went wild.

Jack Naile holstered his gun and looked down at his thigh. The blood wasn't exactly spurting out, and his conscience felt oddly sound.

Still wearing her "man" costume, packing more ammunition into her saddlebags as she sat at the kitchen table, Ellen told Peggy, "Jack should be pretty well exhausted, so he might need the help. Once he and I return, Peggy, we'll change horses and ride back to the time-transfer base Helen and I saw. Jack has to see it, and then we all have to figure out what's going on."

"What about leaving a note, even some photographs, in one of the capsules by the site of the original time base? They'd have the message and the pictures within a couple of hours at the most, and we'd have a response almost immediately."

"I've considered that, and maybe we'll do that. Maybe. But what if Alan's time-transfer operation has been compromised? I mean, this isn't supposed to happen. From what Clarence said, Alan's great-grandfather—David—passed down commentaries Jack had written, which Jack's been writing. Everything from the origins of World War I through the JFK assassination through just before the last election. Remember Jack's face when he'd heard that the Democrat had actually won?! But nothing in Jack's chronicles ever referred to a nephew coming back in time, nor to any regular communication back and forth between this time period and the future. And there was never any mention of any kind of time transfer base at all, because there wasn't one. We're in virgin territory here, on unexplored ground. We may already have screwed up the future. That time-transfer base could belong to anybody, anybody at all, any government or organization—somebody very evil." There seemed little sense in belaboring the point; Peggy already appeared ill at ease.

Ellen stood, grabbed her heavy saddlebags and picked up her cowboy hat. "How do men stand wearing these things?" Ellen queried rhetorically as she placed the hat on her head. Passing her daughter's bedroom—Lizzie was sleeping soundly—Ellen reassured herself that her daughter would recover fully.

Exhausted, but with no time to rest, Ellen stepped out onto the front porch. Resting her saddlebags across the bullet-hole-riddled porch railing, she started to say, "I'm going to grab one of Lizzie's Palominos and saddle—"

But, in the distance, she spied a cloud of dust. "Grab a rifle," Ellen ordered her nephew's wife. Ellen drew both pistols from their holsters and stepped halfway back through the still-open doorway.

Peggy was gone for less than a minute, but it seemed an eternity. Ellen's eyes were focused so intently on the figure within the dust cloud that they literally ached.

The dust cleared for a split second and Ellen smiled, lowering the muzzles of her revolvers as she sagged back against the doorframe.

Only because Ellen had insisted that he do so, Jack had taken a quick shower, washed his hair and let Peggy dress the deep crease along his left thigh and the earlier wound on his neck. The antiseptic Peggy used hurt far worse than had the strikes of the bullets. "I washed the area very thoroughly, Peggy, and it bled profusely for some time. I'm sure the wound is as clean as a whistle. Really. Are you listening to—ME! SHIT—excuse me. What is that stuff?" The wound dressed (a wise move, of course, because lead bullets picked up dirt, lubricant, more dirt and fiber), Jack dressed in a black shirt and pants and a clean pair of boots. Strapping on his gun as he stood in front of the mirror, Jack wished there was time to wait, not go to what was, indeed, almost certainly a time-transfer base that did not belong to Alan Naile, his great-great-grandson from the future.

He had cleaned his revolvers, paying the most scrupulous attention to that very special Colt holstered at his right hip. In the mirror behind him, he saw Ellen. She had showered and changed as well. Rather than the traditionally male attire with which she had disguised herself as she'd ridden out to rescue/assist him, she wore a long-sleeved pink blouse that buttoned up the front and a dark brown suede split skirt, avant-garde but socially acceptable attire for a woman to wear when she went riding—except for the Colt revolvers carried crossdraw, positioned between navel and hip bones. "You're beautiful," Jack told his wife. As was Ellen's wont, she would either acknowledge such a statement with something flippant or with total silence. She chose silence this time. "You amaze me, constantly. Knowing you, I've come to realize that the mark of the truly beautiful woman is the failure to appreciate the reality of her own beauty, which only serves to enhance that beauty, both without and within."

"Right." Ellen groaned. "It felt good to wear pants again. This skirt business gets old."

"You look pretty."

"How are you going to explain Titus Blake's death?"

Jack allowed his wife the option of changing the subject. "The truth, in a manner of speaking. He and I went after the men who'd kidnapped young Helen. Truth. Blake was killed. Truth. If he had a mother—which might be rather dubious—she'll be proud of her boy's memory."

"And Fowler and his men?"

"It seems logical that they encountered some of the same outlaw bunch and met their deaths because of it. In a manner of speaking, that's also true." His eyes dwelt on the brace of Colt revolvers his wife wore. They were Third Generation Colts, made in the 1970s. "I think staghorn grips on those six-guns you're wearing would look rather stylish, Ellen."

"You know I don't like stag on anything."

"You always liked Guy Madison as Wild Bill Hickok, and, of course, the guns Roy Rogers wore on television had stag grips, too."

"No stag grips, Jack. Wood is fine."

"Not just wood. It's American walnut."

"Keep talking about grips and I'll get Clarence and David to start pestering you again about how those black buffalo-horn grips on your gun look like black plastic."

His wife had him there. He'd never felt their remarks were in good taste, let alone funny.

"All right, we're out of here." He snatched up his hat in one hand, taking his wife's elbow in the other.

❋ ❋ ❋

Without an injured girl to look after, and riding fresh horses at a steady trot, they were able to cover the sixteen or seventeen miles to Ellen's last campsite in a little over an hour, resting the horses for fifteen minutes when they'd covered approximately half the distance.

Aside from Jack himself and his Marlin rifle, saddlebags with extra ammunition and a canteen comprised Barbie's load. Ellen rode Victoria, one of the Palomino ponies Lizzie treated more like pets than anything else. Jack's anachronistic .45 Colt Winchester was scabbarded on her saddle, and her saddlebags, too, carried extra cartridges. But slung from the right side of her saddle horn—her canteen was on the left—was a camera bag. It housed Ellen's oldest and most trusted 35mm, surrounded by plastic bubble wrap, a wide-angle and a telephoto lens, each similarly cushioned, and three thirty-six-shot rolls of her precious film. Ellen had been about ready to give in to temptation and leave a note in the capsule at the time-transfer site, asking for more film to be sent back to her. But if the original time base from which Clarence and Peggy had shipped out was somehow compromised, such conveniences might be impossible or, at least, impossibly dangerous.

Peggy was the logical person to view this suspected time base in the subjective past, the objective present. But Peggy's medical talents were too valuable to risk, especially with Lizzie having been wounded.

An errant gust of wind caught Ellen's hair, blowing some strands across her lips. She pushed them away. A hat, complete with stampede string, hung from her saddle, but she'd be damned if she'd wear a hat; hats sucked even more than skirts.

"Jack?" Ellen asked her husband, giving Victoria a little heel to bring the palomino up alongside Barbie. "If there is a time base there—and it sure looked like one—then what do we do about it?"

Thumbing his hat back from his forehead, he slowed his mount a little. "Nothing. We get the pictures. After that, we go to the original time-transfer site where Clarence and Peggy arrived. We look in the capsule and see if there's any message for us possibly explaining it. You develop your film, Peggy checks it out. We place a duplicate set of prints in the capsule and hope they don't deteriorate too badly in almost a century. Black-and-white film was a good idea for this. If we get an answer back, we make our decision accordingly. If we get no answer, we'll know that this second time transfer spot is even more menacing than we're already imagining it to be. Then we'll figure out what to do."

Jack urged Barbie ahead with his knees. Ellen let her borrowed mount fall back a stride, then gave the palomino her heels. By merest chance, the contours of the terrain took them westward for a short distance. She felt like Dale Evans, riding off into the sunset beside her cowboy hero. The sun was, in fact, setting.

The moon was bright, the sky all but cloudless.

Thunder rumbled, it seemed, from within the mountains, not without. If a storm was brewing, as indeed it seemed one might be, the tempest would be manmade. "I was trying to figure in my head," Jack Naile told his wife as they dismounted their horses.

"I still have some Tylenol for the headache."

"Very funny."

"What were you trying to figure out?"

"What time it is where we came from. I mean, the date."

"Beats me," Ellen declared. "Late 1990s, right? Like 1996."

"I got as far as calculating that it was October, there. Here we are," Jack told her, "about to reelect President McKinley, and there they are about to reelect President Clinton, at least if things haven't changed since the last time we checked the time capsule."

"It's kind of sad about President McKinley," Ellen blurted out. "You'd think we could warn him or something that there's an assassin waiting out there for him next year."

"If we did warn President McKinley that there's a bullet with his name on it," Jack mused, "then Theodore Roosevelt might never succeed him as president, might never be elected in 1904, and the history of the United States, of the whole world, could be changed in ways we could never imagine. Teddy Roosevelt was/will be one of the greatest presidents in American history," Jack added superfluously.

"This isn't fun, Jack. Knowing the future isn't fun at all."

Ellen's camera bag was heavy as Jack Naile slung it to his left shoulder. With his right hand, he slipped the Marlin from its saddle scabbard.

Ellen repeated, "Not fun at all," as she drew the Winchester from her saddle.

❉ ❉ ❉

Ellen Naile was reminded of standing once near a very large, open field, the night very dark and still. She was a little girl at the time, visiting with one set out of several pairs of aunts and uncles. This particular aunt and uncle lived in Wisconsin and had a neat house that was well away from town. Fireflies were everywhere in the field, moving in seemingly random patterns, like beautiful shimmering stars in some crazy race through the heavens. Another uncle's car started; time to go. The car's headlights switched on, the flickering lights from the fireflies instantly vanishing. This night, the moon was so bright that it was almost painful to look at, the sky perfect and clear, and the stars that would have been visible close to the moon, like the fireflies in that long ago field, were lost in the glare.

The night would have been romantic, with Jack lying beside her beneath that moon and the hidden stars, but the guns, the camera and the time transfer base about a city block or so distant from the broad, flat rocks in which they hid negated all happy thoughts.

Jack had insisted. "We can't get too close. We're lucky we haven't tripped perimeter alarms already."

"The characters in our books can always neutralize stuff like that."

"Knowing how to do it and being able to do it are two different things. I could write an article on how to swim. But can I swim?"

"You swim like a rock."

"Pumice is rock. It floats. I swim worse than a rock."

There was something visible in the spot below them that reminded Ellen of something she had researched for one of their novels. She saw it there within the time base behind the chain link fence, saw the picture from a research book in her mind's eye. The connection eluded her. "What do you call that thing?"

"What thing?"

"That thing! There!" Her mother had always told her that it was impolite to point, but if she'd heeded her mother's advice, she never would have married Jack. "That!"

That at which she pointed was a large object about three times the size of a passenger elevator, sheathed in gray metal. It hadn't been at the time-transfer base when she had observed the site fewer than twenty-four hours earlier.

"That? It looks like it's an industrial-sized generator, but it can't be, because there wouldn't be any purpose for it. You wouldn't need something that large for lights, computers, like that."

"What if this is designed to be a revolving door, Jack?"

"A revolving door? Like in a department store? What— oh, shit."

"To generate enough electrical power to really do some serious time-traveling back and forth, but in this period in history . . ."

Ellen let the words hang.

Jack finished the sentence for her. "You'd go nuclear. You're not powering a couple of states or even a city, so you wouldn't need a large reactor. You'd need plenty of shielding for the safety of the personnel."

"What did Three Mile Island look like that time you were in Harrisburg?" Ellen asked.

"A lot bigger," he advised. "What you'd probably need—we'll have to ask Peggy—but it would be something maybe the size of the reactor package that would go into a nuclear powered surface vessel."

Ellen had the old Pentax camera to her eye and was playing with the light meter and the film speed. She upped the shutter speed. The time-transfer base was well-illuminated, but surrounded by blackest night, no moonlight filtering down yet into the still-shadowy dish-shaped depression in which it was set. It was the classic case of what she could see the camera might not be able to see. She would push the film as much as possible, bracketing the shots so that—hopefully—she'd get something.

As she steadied the camera for the first shot, there was so brilliant a flash of light that it momentarily blinded her, a thunder clap so loud in the next instant that she could have sworn the ground shook with it. "Jack!"

"It's alright! I think."

Ellen blinked her eyes, blinked again, squeezing them tightly shut for an instant. When she looked again toward the time base, coronas of light appearing and disappearing everywhere within the facility, her eyes were drawn beyond the generator-looking thing to the flat surface at the precise center of the fenced-off area, in size and appearance looking like a helicopter landing pad. She brought the camera up and started clicking, hoping for at least one shot to come out.

Materializing out of the still wildly flickering light, shimmering as if, somehow, it weren't fully formed, was a capsule about the size of a 1960s Volkswagen bus but shaped and metallic in appearance like an Airstream trailer without wheels.

The shimmering stopped. Jack murmured, "Holy shit."

A side of the capsule opened, a doorway appearing in what had seemed seamless. A manshape, hooded, arms bound with heavy leather straps, tumbled from inside the capsule. As the manshape slammed hard against the flat surface of concrete, Ellen noticed that the person's hands were cuffed from behind. Someone very dangerous, or someone in very serious trouble. She guessed the latter.

A tall man stepped out of the capsule. Six feet or better in stature, he was one of those men whose build made it appear that he was suited up for a football game beneath his street clothes; his shoulders, chest and thighs were so massive, it was as if they were not muscle and bone but heavy padding. The clothes he wore were almost nondescript, expensive looking but bland. A tweed sportcoat, a black polo shirt, faded once-black jeans.

Through the telephoto lens, she saw that he had a gun stuffed in the waistband of his trousers. As he bent over the hooded figure on the concrete apron, he adjusted the position of the weapon.

Rolling the hapless person over, the big man tore the hood away. Ellen said the word as a gasp. "David!"

She looked away, at Jack. His binoculars—to be more precise, his maternal grandfather's French-made binoculars dating from 1886—were trained on the tableau below. "It's not David. He looks like David, but he isn't David."

Ellen snapped another photo, put down the camera, and picked up the rubber-armored Bushnell binoculars from beside her camera case. As she brought them into focus, seeing the figure on the ground in greater definition, she realized that Jack was right. The prisoner of this mountain-sized brute was not David, but enough like him to be . . . "He could be David's brother or son, they look so much—"

"Try David's great-grandson, our great-great-grandson. That's gotta be Alan Naile. And that brick-shithouse-sized fucker just brought him here to kill him, I bet."

"What'll we do? We've got to stop it, Jack!"

"It's perfect, perfect, a perfect crime. Take somebody ninety-six years into the past and kill him. By the time the guy turns up missing, his body will have been rotted away for almost a century. The body couldn't be identified in the past because the victim hasn't been born yet."

"This is creepy, Jack. We've got to do something."

"I'm thinking. Let's watch for a minute."

That was a sensible decision, Ellen thought, tacitly agreeing with her husband, however irritated she was by his patience.

This was her great-great-grandson. At her age, that was scary enough to consider. And it appeared he was in imminent danger of losing his life, which made matters worse.

The hulking villain of the piece hauled Alan Naile to his feet, backhanded him across the face, then shoved him into the waiting arms of three men, all of whom were dressed in cowboy clothes. A fourth man walked up behind them, leading six horses and not seeming to have such an easy time of it. The big man walked over and grabbed the reins for two of the horses, keeping the animals in check while Alan was all but thrown into the saddle of an uncharacteristically small buckskin.

Alan's hands were still manacled behind him, arms still strapped close to his sides. An ordinary rope was looped around his waist and secured to the saddle horn.

The big man—awkwardly—mounted an overweight-looking chestnut mare with black mane and tail, an animal evidently chosen because it was docile and the man riding it would be inexperienced. The other four men clambered up into their saddles, none of them looking exactly comfortable on horseback.

Jack's lips were suddenly beside her left ear. "Odds are, they're taking him some distance away to kill him and ditch the body."

"What can we do?" Ellen whispered back. "We have to do something."

"We will. Got enough pictures?"

"For now."

Jack merely nodded, touched at her elbow and started crawling backwards out of the escarpment.

This time, it would be easy to "head 'em off at the pass," the "pass" merely a place where the two trails away from the site of the time-transfer base would coincide. Not a single one of the four cowboy-looking men looked exactly at home on horseback. The big man who'd roughed up Alan seemed a downright tyro when it came to riding, however professional he might be at killing. Alan's horse was being led.

Jack swung up easily into the saddle. "We're going to try not killing all these guys, just scattering them. Too much shooting, and we could have an innocent casualty," he advised his wife, already mounted. Unnecessarily, he knew, he had held her horse for her.

"There are two of us and five bad guys."

"Exactly, and we can't disguise those numbers. We'll find a nice ambush spot as quickly as we can, position you above it. You open fire when you have a clear shot on whichever guy is farthest away from our great-great-grandson. Everybody'll look toward the point of origination for the shot. So you hunker down—"

"'Hunker'? You've been living in the West too long, Jack! Hunker?"

"Well, you know, take cover, but get over to a different spot in case you have to do more shooting. I'll take it from there. If we get separated and it's safe for you to do so, get to Alan and start for the house. I'll catch up."

"What are you planning?"

Jack wheeled his horse almost one hundred eighty degrees. "It would take too long to explain. But I'd like to get one of these guys and see if he'll talk."

"Not the big guy, Jack."

"I won't have the opportunity, but I'd love to put that schmuck in a locked room with Clarence and let Clarence beat the living shit out of him. Let's ride!"

As Jack put his heels to his horse's sides, he thought he heard Ellen calling out from behind him, "Hey, Wild Bill, wait for me!"

CHAPTER FIFTEEN

The six men rode through the steep, rock flanked defile almost painfully slowly, which was better than Jack could have hoped for. What was not good was that the big man rode alongside young Alan, and because of the snail's-pace gait at which the horses moved, all of the riders were clustered together.

Jack knew which man would be Ellen's target: the one at the far rear. Yet he was only about a half-dozen yards behind Alan. Recoil from the Marlin's .45-70 chambering would have been punishing to Ellen, Ellen never more than a casual rifle shooter when she fired a rifle at all. Ellen had the Winchester in .45 Colt, by comparison very mild against the shoulder.

Jack waited, watched, hunched in a deep crouch, more or less hidden, but little protected by sun-wasted scrub brush.

Ellen fired. The dun-colored horse under the man at

the rear of the group bucked. The rider tumbled from the saddle, and the animal took off as if fired out of a cannon. The other horses shied as it sped past. Jack rose to his feet. There was no clear shot at the big man, not with Alan and the little buckskin sandwiched between the muzzle of Jack's rifle and the preferred target.

Jack swung the rifle leftward and downward, relying on the .45-70's penetration and power as he pulled the trigger, firing through the hapless little buckskin's neck. The animal tumbled against the big man's black-maned old chestnut mare.

The chestnut stumbled, then dropped like Newton's apple.

Jack levered the spent case out, chambered a fresh round.

Alan was on the ground, his dying horse almost certainly pinning his right leg under it. The chestnut, already dead, struck by the same bullet that had penetrated the buckskin's neck, lay in a heap, legs buckled beneath it.

Jack couldn't find the big guy. Hoping the man was, like Alan, pinned under his horse, he swung the .45-70's muzzle right and shot one of the three remaining men out of the saddle of a good-sized pinto.

But the first man, the one whom Ellen had initially fired upon, who had lost his mount in the next instant, grabbed for the just-riderless pinto. He used only his left arm to reach for the horse, but wore his gun for right-handed crossdraw, which meant Ellen's bullet had probably struck him.

Jack worked the lever of his rifle.

In obvious desperation, the apparently wounded man

threw his body weight against the riderless pinto's forelegs. The horse fell as the man clambered into the empty saddle. The horse started to its feet.

Jack's eyes scanned the moonlit defile for the big man. The two henchmen so far unscathed, bouncing in their saddles as if they were trying to sustain spinal damage, were riding back toward the time transfer base, all caution concerning the steep, uneven surface of the defile abandoned. There was a shot from the higher rocks, Ellen giving them a send-off.

"Where are you, fucker?!" Jack said under his breath, still looking for the big guy. As his eyes followed his rifle muzzle, swinging back toward the wounded man and the still rising horse, Jack spotted his quarry. The big man was stabbing the muzzle of a large revolver—maybe an N-Frame Smith & Wesson, but by moonlight at the distance, it was only a guess—into the face of the wounded man clinging to the pinto's saddle. There was a single shot. The wounded man fell away as the big man grasped for the saddle and clung to it as the pinto shook its mane and snorted.

Jack fired, and the big man's body rocked with what could have been a hit or might only have been the horse shuddering under him. The pinto had its head and galloped after the two already escaping riders.

Jack levered the Marlin and fired, but the big man was so terrible a rider and the horse moving so rapidly that his shot was an obvious miss from the moment he squeezed the trigger.

Another shot from the rocks, Ellen firing, but the range was already too great for the Winchester's .45 Colt-revolver round. There were two rounds left in the Marlin, two rounds Jack would not waste on a fast-moving target he had no hope of hitting.

Instead, he drew his revolver as he walked toward the buckskin. The little horse was still breathing. Alan, under it, moaned, but that was reassuring, affirming that Jack's great-great grandson was still alive.

Jack, feeling genuine sorrow for shooting the innocent horses and wishing that he could experience sorrow— genuine or otherwise—for the vile men he had killed, put a bullet into the little buckskin's brain, then started trying to pry, push and shove the dead animal off Alan.

Almost before it seemed possible, Ellen had joined him in the effort, and worked beside him as always.

Cleavon Little, like a black Randolph Scott, rode up out of the horizon, resplendently dressed and armed, astride a magnificent golden palomino, replete with gleaming, silver-mounted saddle. Count Basie's orchestra, for some reason esconced in the middle of a southwestern desert, was belting out its legendary riff at the conclusion of "April In Paris." Alan opened his eyes. The face looking down benignly upon him was definitely not the brilliant Mel Brooks, but a woman instead. An angel's face? Was he dead and in Heaven? The last thing he remembered was a very loud gunshot and the horse that had been under him collapsing against another horse. After that blackness had engulfed him in a roaring wave of pain.

The pain was still there, and that couldn't be right, because in Heaven, as he had learned as a boy, all earthly pain would be washed away.

An angel, however. As his vision cleared, he recognized the face, yet was more amazed than if the countenance—smiling now, with a touch of worry in the gray-green eyes—had been ethereal in the literal sense. The face was that of Ellen Naile, born in 1948—or, to be born. Objectively, he knew that since the year from which he'd been kidnapped was 1996, she was forty-eight. Except for that hint of worry in her eyes, dissipating as he forced a smile to his lips, it would have been hard to imagine this auburn-haired, delicately featured woman with almost porcelein skin to have even been thirty.

"You." He realized that his voice was a dry, croaking thing.

"Don't try to talk, Alan." Her voice was a soft alto, musical to hear.

Alan shook his head: a mistake, as tremors of pain washed through him. A glass came to his lips, cool water into his mouth. He swallowed, the first sip with difficulty, the second sip more easily. The glass was taken away, and he tried again, this time successfully, more or less, to speak, the voice still not quite fully his own. "You are my great-great-grandmother."

"Yes."

"You are more beautiful than your pictures, more so than I had remembered you. I grew a beard and brought my oldest son to one of your book signings."

She didn't smile any more broadly with her face, only in her wonderful eyes, as she responded, "And you have your great-grandfather's and great-great-grandfather's ability with bullshit."

"How did—?"

"You get here? You got here by dint of perseverance, Alan. That buckskin pony that fell on you may have been little, but no fully grown horse is exactly light. Before you ask, Clarence's wife, Peggy—you remember her, that she's an M.D.?—thinks that the worst you have is a little concussion, some really nasty bruises—hence, some swelling—to your right knee and a groin muscle you may have pulled. Bet you'll know about that for sure when you try walking in a few days." Ellen grinned.

"Should I call you Great-Great-Grandmother?"

"Only if you don't value your life. Ellen will do just fine, Alan. Now, get some rest, and a little later we can get some solid food into you and talk some more. I wouldn't toss and turn a lot. Verifying the pulled groin muscle could be a real eye-opener."

Then, she leaned over, his beautiful great-great grand-mother, and kissed him lightly on the forehead.

Snippets of conversation as he slept—he'd been given painkillers, he realized—drifted to him like scents on a soft breeze. David and Clarence were back—from where? He had some sips of broth. Diamonds converted to cash successfully. Jack, his great-great-grandfather, was gone for a few days—to where? More broth, a salty tasting cracker. Titus Blake, whoever he had been, was dead. It didn't sound like anyone would be missing this Blake guy very much. Broth with soft vegetables. Diamonds and cash, again. The general merchandise store had great sales figures, up fourteen percent over the last quarter. Exciting new merchandise spotted in San Franciso. A few bites of a sandwich. House in town nearly completed.

Standing up, and the knee hurt badly; walking to the surprisingly modern bathroom affirmed the groin muscle was definitely pulled. Elizabeth, arm in a sling, pretty like her mother, only different. Peggy insisted he use a bedpan.

Theodore Roosevelt? A man's voice had spoken the name several times in low tones to Alan's great-great-grandmother. But this was 1900, wasn't it? Was it still? Had to be. Teddy Roosevelt was yet to be elected to the vice-presidency under William McKinley.

Two-way traffic in time? Variations of phrasing notwithstanding, that topic came up a lot, rising as the headaches seemed to dissipate.

Sometime later—he realized it was probably several days—Alan opened his eyes and saw a man's face looking down on him. The man's eyes were dark brown, with a hint of amusement in them. He had a wide mouth under a graying mustache that extended only to the edges of his upper lip. His hair was a dark reddish-brown, thick looking but not overly so, well salted with gray throughout, but especially on the sides. He wore a coal-black shirt, some type of pullover, but not in the modern sense, his sleeves rolled up to just below his elbows, the dorsal sides of his forearms covered in a light coating of hair, also dark red-brown.

Two realizations struck Alan simultaneously. This was his great-great grandfather, Jack Naile, and Jack was the black-clad man who had shot the horse out from under him—how many days ago?

"Welcome back to the land of the living, Great-Great-Grandson," Jack declared. "I understand you brought one of our great-great-great-grandsons to a book signing. Thank you for that. How are you doing?" The same hint of amusement that was in his eyes was present in his voice. "Peggy was a little worried with you drifting in and out of consciousness so much these last several days, lamenting the fact that she hadn't been able to do more thorough testing for the concussion she suspected you'd sustained." He held up the first finger of his right hand, a strong-looking hand, and directed, "Follow this with your eyes." Then he moved the finger slowly from edge to edge of Alan's peripheral vision.

"My head doesn't hurt anymore."

"Good! The rest was what you needed. Your knee should be stiff. Some of our reference materials contained data pertinent to physical therapy; Peggy will work with you. You'll have to go easy, though, because of that groin muscle. She doesn't think it's too bad."

"She should try wearing it," Alan told his great-great-grandfather, smiling.

"That might, I'd suppose, be instructive. Who was that really big man who was taking you out to kill you?"

Alan's eyes closed involuntarily; in the split second while they remained shut, the images of—how long had it been since he'd been abducted outside Morton Hardesty's house?—his torment coming back to him in a wash of near nausea. "My wife and family—they could be in terrible danger."

"You're a good man; that was to be expected. You should never have helped Clarence and Peggy to join us here. We all love Clarence, and have come to love Peggy. But now that the time-transfer process is duplicated, nothing and no one may be safe anymore. My mother used to quote her father, that 'the road to Hell is paved with good intentions.' Consider this a possible way station, Alan. Who was that man?"

"Lester Matthews, the security guy for Bethany Kaminsky's Lakewood Industries."

"I've heard of Lakewood—almost as big as Horizon Enterprises. Are they the ones who've built the new time transfer base?"

"Yes. She wants—Bethany Kaminsky—to sell 1990s technology to the highest bidder in 1900, become the power behind whatever government buys in, change history so Lakewood Industries will, will—"

"Be in charge of the world. Can't fault the woman for thinking small, can we?"

"We've gotta stop her."

"Indeed. 'I have no spur to prick the sides of my intent, but only vaulting ambition, which o'erleaps itself and falls on the other.'"

"*Macbeth?*"

"Uh-huh. The lady in question here, although I don't know her, strikes me as someone who uses daggers quite skillfully, perhaps gleefully. Good character analysis?"

"Yes."

"Rest. We'll talk about this soon, son."

Alan Naile saw, felt Jack Naile's right hand as it gently patted his left cheek. There was a smile on his great-great-grandfather's face, but one of love, not happiness. And, deep within Jack's eyes there was something that was at once like determination and dread.

❋ ❋ ❋

Eight days had passed since Alan's rescue from his would-be murderers. Technically speaking, Jack was, once again, Marshal of Atlas, Nevada, but the day-to-day policing of the town was something in which he had no interest; he'd appointed two deputies, both of the men cool-headed and good with a gun when need be.

Helen was recovering nicely in town, along with both her father and her mother. Sympathetic neighbors tended their stock. When all were well enough to return to their homestead, the deputies were under instruction that one of them should accompany the Bledsoes and stay on-site for a few days, just in case any of the "outlaws" had escaped and might want revenge.

With David and Clarence back from a more-than-successful trip to San Francisco, Jack, accompanied by one or the other of them, had made several nocturnal forays to the time-transfer base. David, a fine hand with a camera and armed with his mother's advice, had taken more photos.

An assemblage of over four dozen photographs of varying quality, but with fully discernable images, now existed, documenting the activity—growing nightly—at the time-transfer base.

The time-transfer base, perhaps as a result of the rescue of Alan Naile, was more heavily guarded than before. Tarp-covered emplacements at each corner of the fenced area were, almost certainly, hiding machine guns. The guards themselves bristled with H-K MP5 submachine guns and M-16 rifles; each was also armed with a hand-gun. An outer perimeter had been established to foil observation of the base as much as possible, it appeared, and to guard against the chance encounter with someone just drifting past over the mountains.

The guards at this outer perimeter had horses rather than golf carts and pickup trucks, Colt (or Italian replica) revolvers on their hips and weathered-looking cowboy hats rather than baseball caps. A few horses were corralled nearby. Curiosity was a marvelous thing, the way it could lead to terrible trouble. Jack and David and Clarence had, each of them independently, considered riding down and feigning innocence just to hear what sort of story these disguised Lakewood Industries security personnel would offer. But since there was an at-least-as-likely possibility that the guards' only response to a question might be couched in lead, discretion prevailed.

Peggy had reviewed the photos; Alan, still limping and slow to move, but clear headed, examined them as well.

Jack surveyed his assembled family as he asked, "So, guys? How can we stop the Kaminsky woman and Lakewood Industries from ruling the world?" Jack addressed the question to no one in particular, rather to all who were seated or standing in the central room of the house. This hidden room was the perfect setting for such a question. It was the only room in the entire house, likely the entire county, perhaps the state—other than the time-transfer base—that had electricity of even the most primitive sort. He was no authority on rural electrification in Nevada, but Edison had only perfected the light bulb in 1878, just twenty-two years in their objective past. There was a laptop computer, but the Internet did not exist and would not for all practical purposes for a century.

Jack's eyes drifted to the security monitor—recently

installed—that was jerry-rigged to one of the small video cameras Clarence and Peggy had brought with them from the 1990s. The possibility of attack originating from the time transfer base was very real. Jack asked again, addressing all but looking directly at Peggy and at Alan, "How do we stop Kaminsky and Lakewood?"

Peggy spoke, avoiding his eyes when he looked at her. "Clarence's loving you guys is why this happened. Maybe the last time you guys went through the time loop, Clarence didn't exist."

Alan, his voice weak, strained, said, as if thinking aloud, "My father told me that in the last cycle, before you guys—I mean the actual two of you, Jack and Ellen, this Jack and Ellen, you guys—went into the time loop, you—the earlier you—wrote that D-Day was on June fifth, not the sixth. The horrendous rains over the English Channel screwed things up so badly that Allied casualties were vastly higher. Just two changes—and there must have been hundreds, thousands, maybe millions of other changes, all for subtle reasons we can't foresee—but they affected millions of lives that affected millions of other lives. Maybe Clarence's dad didn't survive the Korean War the last time, never came home to father Clarence in 1957. Maybe, what if, who knows?"

"So, if I went back to the 1990s—"

"It wouldn't do any good, Clarence," Peggy interrupted, looking at her husband. "You've already done this, and going back to 1996 wouldn't change any of that. It isn't your fault, or anybody's fault, except this Kaminsky bitch."

"Let's say," Alan began, "that we tracked down

Clarence's grandfather. He was a coal miner in West Virginia, right, Clarence?"

"Yeah." Clarence nodded, looking at Alan rather oddly, suspicion in his brown eyes. "What are you saying?"

"Let's say we tracked down your grandfather and killed him—"

"Just one fucking minute—"

"I'm not suggesting that we do it, Clarence," Alan insisted. "But hear me out—just hear me out, huh? It's an example, alright?"

Clarence nodded, stood up and began to pace.

Alan went on. "So, if—catch the word 'if'—if we murdered Grandpa Jones before he fathered Clarence's father, then Clarence wouldn't exist, right?"

Jack was beginning to suspect the punch line to Alan's thesis, and didn't like it: They were helpless.

"Okay," Alan continued, "so we kill Grandpa Jones. Clarence never exists. If Clarence never exists, we don't know that we have to kill Grandpa Jones, right? So we don't kill Grandpa Jones. So Clarence exists. So we do kill Grandpa Jones; but, maybe he's not killed or we killed him for no purpose at all. You need more math than I've got in my head to explain this, or even think about it properly. If we knew enough to prevent Clarence from coming into the past, and somehow were able to keep him from coming into the past, we wouldn't be faced with the problem, therefore we wouldn't have taken the steps to alleviate the problem, therefore the problem would still be with us. Perhaps manifested in some other way, granted, but we'd still have the same situation. We're stuck in a conundrum from which there is no logically discernable escape."

David addressed the man who would become his great-grandson. "So, you're saying we can't do shit about this, then?"

"Well, not really. We can't give up, but we have to think way outside the box. It's just that there are certain things that might seem obvious to do which would have no effect whatsoever to alter the situation."

"Helpless?" Jack suggested. "I don't think so." He caught Ellen's eyes on him. She hated discussing time-travel theory, hadn't even liked movies about time-travel. He always had. But movies didn't help. "We know that Lakewood is going to peddle 1990s war machines to the highest 1900 bidder they can find. That'll likely be Germany. There seems to be pretty general agreement on that. If I remember my history correctly, the United States will almost go to war with Germany over Venezuela in the next two or three years, sometime in Teddy Roosevelt's first administration, I think.

"At any event, World War One is scheduled to start fourteen years from now. Germany would snap up even Korean War-vintage fighter jets in a heartbeat. Imagine just what something as simple as a couple of hundred M-16 rifles could do in no-man's-land in France a decade and a half from now? Change history on the cheap. But not this Kaminsky woman. She'll get a bidding war going between the United States, England, Germany—maybe even France'll get in on it. Germany will be the one, has to be. The United States wouldn't buy the technology to use it for aggression, not unless Lakewood gets rid of McKinley and Roosevelt and replaces them with their own man. The same with England, I think. The French are a wild-card, but Germany would just up the ante until it got the technology. Only the United States could outbid Germany, and Lakewood Industries doesn't just want a sale, it wants the products put to use. From what you say, Kaminsky isn't looking to just be richer than Sam Walton and Bill Gates combined; she wants to be the power behind whatever nation rules the world."

"And?" Ellen suggested.

"In times of trouble, who do you go to?"

"A friend?" Lizzie supplied.

"A friend, yes, because that's someone that you can trust," Jack agreed, smiling at his daughter. "Present company excepted, the only person I know in detail— so to speak—in this period in time is Theodore Roosevelt."

"What?" David gasped, sounding incredulous. "You've never met Teddy Roosevelt, Dad!"

"I've read a lot about Roosevelt, son. Teddy Roosevelt was a brilliant man. A man of letters, a man of action, someone who studied every aspect of a situation before making a decision, someone with the courage and tenacity to see a situation through to the end." Jack cleared his throat. "And he was well aware of the fact that this was a modern age, a new age. He was the first President of the United States ever to ride in a submarine, the USS *Plunger*."

"You've gotta be kidding, Daddy!" Lizzie declared.

"That's the name, kiddo. My point is, he was accepting of new things, things other people might have dismissed or ignored. We go to Teddy Roosevelt with incontrovertible evidence of what's going on. The photos, everything. We don't have enough manpower—and I'm using the word in the generic sense—to do what we have to do."

"Which is?" Clarence asked.

Before Jack could answer, Ellen interjected, "You sound like you're plotting a novel, Jack."

"Not much different, kid. We know that Lakewood has a time-transfer base here in 1900 that shares the exact space as a base in 1996."

"They may even be using the same machinery," Peggy pointed out, "existing in the same place in two different times, just like you told me that this house still existed, but in ruins, in 1992. The Japanese did some interesting experiments in quantum mechanics. They proved in experiments with electrons that, however illogical it sounds, it is possible for one particle to be in two places at the same time. Its actual position is determined by observation, observation determining reality. Two different observers would detect the same particle in two different states. Subatomic particles can exist as either particles or as waves, but in reality as both. Jane Rogers explained it all to me. She's the one who knew the math and the physics. So, the time-transfer equipment is in the same physical location, observed in 1900 and in 1996, because it was brought to 1900, built here. The wave pattern Jane discovered and we blindly duplicated, which precipitated the original time-transfer, somehow served as the medium. The time transfer mechanism, the whole base Lakewood Industries set up, exists in two separate epochs, observed differently, but the same thing."

"Headache," Ellen supplied.

Jack smiled, went on. "It would seem logical that

Lakewood Industries hasn't probably taken over the Horizon Enterprises time-transfer facility just yet, but it's also pretty obvious that Lakewood Industries has the heavily armed manpower to take over the Horizon facility or destroy it at will. I'm proposing that we take our photographic evidence and hard evidence—"

"Like my battery-operated CD player," Lizzie offered, her face lit with its customarily beautiful smile.

"Perfect," Jack agreed. "Future stuff that Teddy Roosevelt will have to realize isn't faked, is real. Some of the books we have that haven't yet been printed, like that. Everything that's necessary to prove to Theodore Roosevelt that this isn't bullshit. We get him to go to President McKinley."

"Let me guess," Ellen smiled. "Teddy Roosevelt gets together his old Rough Riders from the charge up San Juan Hill, and we take over the Lakewood time base here in 1900, then transfer ourselves back in force to their base in 1996. There's a big battle scene, and you and Teddy Roosevelt seize control of the base."

Jack laughed. "More or less."

"Then what?" David inquired.

"Yeah. What he said," Alan added.

"Kids," Ellen remarked.

Jack thought for a minute. Ellen suggested, "Then we get Alan here to stay behind in the future. We set him up with his own friendlies, of course, making sure everything is secure. Then Alan works the time-transfer machinery for one last time, zaps us—"

"Us?"

"Guys are supposed to have all the fun? I don't think so!

Anyway, Alan works the time transfer machinery one last time, we all get back after saving the world and Alan destroys the time-transfer base so no one can come along and use it again."

"There's Morton Hardesty to consider," Alan interjected. "As long as he's alive and Bethany Kaminsky is alive to finance him, they could do it again. Hardesty and Jane Rogers were the only two who knew how to do this, and Jane is dead. With Morton alive, it's just a hardware problem."

"Then, God help us, we kill the Lakewood people," Jack said.

"I never read that Teddy Roosevelt worked part time as a hit man," Clarence volunteered.

Jack shrugged his shoulders. "We worry about that when we get there, to 1996."

"Another problem," Peggy offered. "What Kaminsky is doing is sheer genius, if you think about it. We're here in her objective past. We know she's got a time-travel gizmo that will allow her to change history, but no one in her objective present will know it. If Germany rules the world and Kaminsky's company runs Germany, that'll just be the way the century worked out. World War Two will have been a bloody skirmish with Japan. Soviet Communism will probably never arise because the Germans wouldn't have any reason to help Lenin smuggle himself back into Czarist Russia, and Germany would already control Russia. She'll be able to see just how much she's changed history by simply going into the past where, if she's as smart and evil as she sounds, she'll have stored records that won't have changed over the next hundred years because they'll have preexisted the next hundred years. They'll read like fiction to her, but they'll be the truth as it was, history before it was changed. No one in her time will notice a thing. With no World War Two, no Soviet Communism, probably no Chinese Communism, the world might be a much better place. We have to think about that.

"And, we're assuming that Kaminsky will just be waiting around for us," Peggy continued. "If Germany is going to be the best potential bidder for 1990s technology, and Lakewood Industries—"

"They have a facility not far from Ulm, I think," Alan said somberly. "They could have a time-transfer base under construction somewhere in Germany right now. They could have people going out to Imperial Germany right now. This could already be so out of hand—"

"Look, son," Jack interrupted, peering intently at his great-great-grandson. "We may already be screwed. I know that. We're all aware of that possibility. Plans rarely go perfectly, even when you're just writing them in a book, let alone real life. But we have to do something. Let's say that Peggy's idea that things might be somehow better if we let this alone has some merit. I don't think it would be a better century. If the Germans control the world, even if there isn't a Great Depression, Hitler might still come to power. How many so-called 'inferior' millions would he slaughter in the name of racial purity, if he didn't have to worry about the rest of the world breathing down his neck and kicking his ass during a war? If he could devote full effort to it? If some things would be better and some things worse, it doesn't mean that we have the right to

alter the next century any more than Bethany Kaminsky
does. We have an obligation to future history, to our own
sense of right and wrong, to stop her. And preventing the
Kaminsky woman from precipitating a century of what
could be unimaginable destruction . . ." Jack stopped, not
having any words left with which to express his feelings;
he merely lowered his eyes.

Ellen spoke, and Jack raised his eyes to look at her.
He'd studied the toes of his boots for an instant, but the
exercise had neither enlightened nor soothed him.
"Unlike a book, none of us can make the ending come out
the way we want a hundred percent, because we don't
control the actions of the characters. Bethany Kaminsky
might already have people pitching Germany, promising
them nuclear weapons or something. Who knows? Jack's
right. Trying is all that we can do. So let's stop talking
about it and get started."

Ellen was never idle, Jack mused. At times, when all he
wanted to do was sit down and have a cigarette and Ellen
started doing something or other that he should help her
with, he found that trait just a little irritating. But those
wonderful aspects of her character that defied description
overwhelmed him. One thing that he had never done, in
what had become the objective future, was to get Ellen to
give a silent jukebox a slap in just the right spot, thus making the jukebox play. Secretly, he'd always believed that
his wife and best buddy might well be capable of such a
feat. She was so cool, after all, that it was like being married to a female version of the Fonz.

CHAPTER
❖ SIXTEEN ❖

The waves crashing against the seawall at the base of the Adler Planetarium were as high and wind driven as if it were a blustery evening in January, rather than the first week in November, but the breeze was only pleasantly cool, not bitterly cold.

It was, almost precisely, nine in the evening. Less than an hour earlier, Morton Hardesty—the man's timidity disgusted her, but he was cute in his own way, so proud of the bedroom triumphs she engineered for his benefit— had told her that the time-transfer facility being built in Germany would not be ready for its initial testing for another several weeks.

Lester Matthews had insisted to her, after his return from 1900, that Alan Naile had to be dead. Yet Lester could not confirm that Alan was dead. And the description of the mysterious gunman who had "ambushed" Lester and his men sounded suspiciously similar to photographs she possessed of Jack Naile, the man whose son, David, would found Horizon Enterprises.

Bethany, who had majored in business and economics, knew only enough higher math to realize that she didn't know enough. She had been standing beside her car for several minutes; bored with that, restless as she always was, she began to walk, her eyes on the crashing waves. Lake Michigan was not an ocean, of course, but it was vast and powerful, and it was here. That was enough, and driving to this place allowed her to think when knotty problems presented themselves. Since embarking upon her plan to alter the past to Lakewood Industries' advantage, she had come here progressively more often.

Time-travel theory was like a Chinese puzzle box; Morton Hardesty was the only one who could open it. She gave him that, the ability to answer her questions without reminding her that her knowledge of mathematics was insufficient for understanding. "If Jack Naile were to die, chances are still excellent that David Naile would go on, make the family store thrive, and initiate Horizon Enterprises, especially since, unlike previous time loops, this time David knows what he is supposed to do in greater detail than ever before. Even if Alan didn't survive, Clarence Jones and his wife can give—probably have given—David a pretty good picture of what Horizon Enterprises will become.

"Now, if David were killed, we'd have a problem, because Horizon Enterprises would probably never get started, and your relatives, between the two world wars, without Horizon's competition, might not have accrued the wealth and power that they did. So, Lakewood

Industries might be some third rate company, or not even exist anymore. They needed Horizon's competition in order to thrive, as something to fight against.

"So it's pretty safe if Jack and Ellen fall out of the picture. Elizabeth, too. We'd be vastly better off if Clarence and his wife were eliminated. Mrs. Jones is the only other person on earth, I believe, in this time or in the past, who might be able to reproduce the time-transfer mechanism. There are plenty of people who know pieces of it, but she and I are the only ones who know all the pieces. She wouldn't understand the theory perfectly, doesn't have the requisite skills, but she has the practical knowledge to duplicate the process by rote, if the budget and the hardware and software were available to her.

"So if you feel like it, kill them all except for David. You can't even try to control him. You need him to do his thing, as they say. Do his thing. His thing makes your thing possible."

Bethany kept walking, feeling a faint touch of spray on her cheek, smelling the water, hearing the reassuring click of her high heels beating a tattoo on the concrete sidewalk, barely audible but somehow empowering, reassuring beneath the keening of the wind.

Her research people had dug out everything that they could on Jack Naile in order to help her to computer model a second guess as to his intentions if, in fact, he was aware of the time-transfer base and had Alan—alive— with him.

Jack had been born in Chicago in 1946, which meant that this summer just past he had turned fifty. He'd married his high school sweetheart. Most women would have thought that charming, Bethany realized, but she thought it would be rather boring to bang or be banged by the same person all the time. He'd apparently developed a fascination with weapons and with typing. She'd read some of the novels penned by Jack and Ellen, things with heroes and dastardly villains and heroic feats of derring-do. Where was the angst? Where was the despair? Heroes did not now exist, nor had they ever nor would they ever; Bethany firmly believed that.

Although Naile and his wife had never published a western, Jack, at least, had always been deeply fascinated by the nineteenth-century American West. "Duh!" Bethany exclaimed into the wind as she walked, some of the lights from the Chicago Loop visible to the far west, beyond Grant Park. Anybody who believed in heroes obviously bought into the myth of the Old West.

Jack was probably grooving on this macho cowboy gun-slinger shit. Maybe his wife would just get pissed off about it, have enough of her husband's goofy crap and stab his ass to death; Bethany could only hope. "Twenty-eight years with one fucking guy," she told the wind. "She's some kinda friggin' nutball, too."

Bethany Kaminsky wondered—absently—if Jack played chess. How to run a business and how to play chess were the only two things her father had ever taught her that were at all useful. She played chess with Morty at times. He was very good, but she was always better. Sex and chess with Morty; mostly sex.

If Jack was this gunman who'd bested Lester, there might be more to him than she'd imagined. Apparently, he was capable of total ruthlessness. She liked that in a man.

Reaching her car again—she'd completely circum-navigated the planetarium—Kaminsky had made up her mind. With the facility outside Ulm, Germany, unable to become operational for what might be several more weeks, she would utilize the time-transfer base she had. Taking out her cell phone, she leaned on the hood of her car and brought up Lester's cell phone. "Here's what I want you to do. Get those guys—the salesmen—ready to travel. I want them out of here and back there and ready to get the deals rolling inside of forty-eight hours."

He mumbled something; she didn't care what because he took orders much better than he could think.

"Two teams for each prospective client, just in case this Naile cocksucker is really good. We need at least one team to get through to each government on the prospect list."

Bethany cut the transmission.

Her computer models all pointed toward Jack, if he knew what was going on, taking steps to do something about it, to contravene her efforts. He would be sensible enough not to take on the small army of men she'd installed at the time-transfer base in 1900. He'd be hope-lessly outnumbered and outgunned. The Naile family would have to find help.

In school, Bethany Kaminsky had found history boring, except as it concerned the acquisition of wealth. Lots of dead people and dates, punctuated by a few daring men who'd made fortunes or acquired so much power that they were above the concept of wealth. But Naile liked history. One of the computer models had focused on Naile's political bent. The writings of Naile and his wife showed a strong leaning toward the philosophy known as

Objectivism, as promulgated by Ayn Rand in her novels and other writings. Naile had been an outspoken supporter of Republicans for state and national offices. Nevada was granted statehood without some of the usual hoops through which to jump, it seemed, because of its strong connection to the Republican Party.

A Republican in a Republican stronghold, in an era with a Republican President—William MacIntosh? Not like the apple. McKinley. It was an election year, 1900. That same computer model—she could almost swear that sometimes the damned machines really could think—had posited that, with Jack's love for history, fascination with cowboys and penchant for Republican politics, the logical man for him to go to, if he could get to him, would be Theodore Roosevelt.

Bethany had ordered a bio punched up on Roosevelt. He'd led a cowboy life, was a military man, had organized a police department, done all sorts of macho stuff like hunting and riding and shooting and boxing and all that crap. Theodore Roosevelt was also almost universally respected for his intellectual abilities, and had a reputation for being open to new ideas.

The conclusion of the computer model's scenario was that Jack had a seventy-eight point nine percent chance of convincing Theodore Roosevelt that the time-transfer base existed, was a threat and needed to be obliterated.

The computer model was then fed the information concerning Roosevelt's life and asked to model what effect there would have been on current affairs had Roosevelt, while still Governor of New York and a vice-presidential candidate, been assassinated.

National Parks and wildlife preservation—about neither of which Bethany gave the proverbial damn—would be adversely affected. The negotiations concluding something called the Russo-Japanese War of 1905 would have turned out differently, and Japan, when it came time for World War II, might not have attacked the United States at Pearl Harbor. Antitrust legislation might have been enacted at a later date and been significantly different. There might not have been the "death tax," certainly something she would have profited from when her father died. In all, except for the tree and animal huggers, Theodore Roosevelt wouldn't be missed all that much; that was her determination and not that of the computer.

Bethany called Lester once again. "That other project we discussed?" He mumbled something. "I've decided to go ahead with that, but it's not something we should discuss right now. My office, twenty minutes." She cut the connection.

A cigarette seemed in order. It would have been far easier to light one by leaning inside her car. But easy was never fun, and she took out her lighter and cupped her hands around it against the wind, the spray stinging her face, making her feel wonderfully alive. "Checkmate, Jack Naile! I'm going to assassinate your king." She laughed.

With late 1990s technology, there was precious little difference in observing the time-transfer base during the day rather than at night; at least, Jack hoped so. With David and Clarence accompanying him, a small videotape camera pouched on David's saddle, they waved good-bye to the "womenfolk" and Alan and started toward the mountains, the sun still low on the horizon, the time barely eight.

Clarence, who cared little for firearms, holstered a Colt revolver crossdraw and had one of the Model 94 Winchester rifles sheathed on his saddle. David, wearing a hat that seemed a cross between a derby and a homburg, wore only a single Colt revolver, one of the short-barreled models with no ejector rod, but in his saddle scabbard was a Model 97 Winchester shotgun.

Jack had increasingly found himself looking almost longingly at the M-16 rifles, H-K submachine guns and assorted semiautomatic pistols worn by the men at Lakewood Industries' time-transfer base.

Just as the Suburban, however anachronistic, was stored away for emergency use, if he'd properly planned, he would have had a pair of assault rifles and semiautomatic pistols held back for a rainy day as well.

As they rode along, the sound of their horses' hooves and the dislodging of bits of dirt and rock a constant background, Jack felt himself getting into a funk. He was awaiting delivery of a telegram that would outline Governor Roosevelt's projected campaign stop itinerary. Hopefully, the man who would soon be vice-president, and, shortly after, accede to the presidency, wasn't campaigning in Pennsylvania or Vermont or even as far away as Illinois. Travel by rail would be the only option for intersecting Mr. Roosevelt's campaign trail, and rail travel, however wildly fast for the year 1900, was torturously slow by Jack's 1990s standards. If he missed Roosevelt on the campaign trail, it would mean going to Washington, D.C. or New York State in order to contact him. And Roosevelt would be swarmed over with wannabe appointees; just getting to see the new vice-president might take weeks.

There was no time for that.

Jack took a deep breath, exhaled, plastered a smile on his face and asked his two companions, "So, how was San Francisco, guys?"

"Lots of pretty girls," David volunteered cheerfully. "Never did see anybody who looked like Richard Boone passing out business cards advertising gunfighter services. But we really looked for you."

Jack laughed, realizing that they probably had looked. "Thanks, guys."

"It was as close to being back where we came from as I could imagine out here," Clarence interjected. "The streets were paved, in a manner of speaking, and there were restaurants, stores, stuff that seemed almost normal, if you ignored the funny clothing and having to turn on gas lamps in hotel rooms and things like that. Almost normal. I wanna take Peggy there sometime soon."

"That's a good idea," Jack enthused.

Neither his son nor his nephew volunteered anything else and Jack fell silent as well. Today the ride seemed interminable; indeed, observations of the time-transfer base were so regularly made, Jack felt almost as if he were commuting to and from a job.

A short stop to rest and water the horses behind them, they rode on, at last stopping where they would hide the horses. Ellen and Lizzie had made sandwiches with Ellen's freshly baked bread, and Jack and his son and nephew consumed them in relative silence. Clarence carried his own rifle and David's shotgun as the three started toward their observation point, making their way slowly.

David already had the video camera running and was whispering into a small microphone connected by a cord leading into the camcorder. "We're climbing up into a rocky overlook my father has told us is a good place to hide and check out what's happening at the Lakewood Industries time-transfer base. We're being very careful because these guys—the guards—are reportedly very well armed and probably wouldn't hesitate to kill any or all of us. If something should happen to us and this tape is found—"

"And?" Jack queried, interrupting his son's narration. "Who would know what it was, the camcorder, or how to turn it on?"

"Your father's got a point, David. If anything goes down, your Dad and I'll hold 'em off while you get that videotape outa here and find a way to get it to Teddy Roosevelt."

"If anything goes bad on us," David announced, his voice resolute-sounding, "the three of us stick together and we all get out of here or nobody gets out."

Occasionally, Jack reflected, his son really pissed him off; then there were times that his son filled him with pride. As he thought about it, Jack smiled; such an analysis could probably sum up most father-son relationships—the good ones, anyway.

Positioning themselves in the nest of flat rocks above the metal fenced compound that was the heart of the time-transfer base, David—admirably—wasted no time, but began videotaping.

There was a rumbling sound: the same "thunderclaps" that Jack and his wife had heard the night when Alan had time-transferred from 1996 on his way to an execution— his own. "Get this on tape, David. They're doing a time-transfer, I think."

There was, in the next instant, a flash of light so blindingly bright that Jack, as he looked away, had floaters in his eyes. The sound, like thunder, rang through the mountains, echoing and reechoing among the rocks, the reverberations from it making the rock beneath them pulse.

"Watch your eyes, but get this, David!" Jack hissed in a stage whisper he hoped could not be heard by anyone more than a few feet away.

Just as when Jack had watched a time-transfer with his wife, there were halos of light, rainbowlike, but flickering maddeningly, dancing across all of the structures within the time-transfer base, most concentrated around the flat expanse that looked like a helipad.

Something was happening at the center of the pad, an object materializing. Although not yet fully formed, it was clearly, obviously, the thing that looked like an old VW bus somehow frozen in the middle of mutating into a wheelless Airstream travel trailer.

"That's like the thing we came here in with the Suburban, only bigger," Clarence said through clenched teeth.

Bigger was the operative word. Much bigger than what Jack and Ellen had seen before.

Taping all the while, David remarked, "They bringing an army here, or what?"

Three white vans were being driven up from a far corner of the fenced perimeter. The vans stopped near the edge of the helipadlike surface.

The electrical activity had ceased. Jack raised his binoculars, focusing on the object that had just appeared from 1996. A portal, so seamlessly a part of the time-transfer capsule's skin that it was previously undetectable, folded open. Immediately, Jack observed not an army but a significant number of men begin exiting the pod. The men were all dressed in the same style, not that of the guards, who wore normal 1990s casual attire, nor like cowboys, but, instead, each man wore an example of decorous turn-of-the-century business attire: uncomfortable-looking three-piece suits, celluloid collars, hats of various descriptions. Each carried a small carpetbag, a folded-over leather briefcase and what appeared to be a mochilla.

"What are those things, like big saddlebags or something?" Clarence asked.

"Called a mochilla. Pony Express riders used to use things like them. The pockets and everything provide storage, and you drop it over the saddle, the saddle horn sticking up through it. Instant baggage change. These guys are planning on riding fast. It'll be saddle-sore city if they're not experienced," Jack added, recalling his own riding experiences when they had first come here.

"Why the business suits?" David asked, still taping.

Whether or not it was something that David said, Jack suddenly realized why these men were dressed as they were. "You're the salesman of the bunch, Davey. Why are they dressed that way? Think about it."

An instant later, David, his voice curiously somber,

volunteered, "They're representing Lakewood Industries to the nations this Kaminsky bitch wants to pitch her 1990s technology to."

"Give that man a cigar!" Clarence declared.

"Right you are," Jack agreed, watching as the men filed into the three white vans. "They'll be riding to the nearest railhead that will take them East."

"And we can't stop more than a few of them at a time," David warned.

"They won't all stay together." There were, by Jack's rough count, sixteen men. "They'll probably travel in groups of two, or otherwise they might attract too much attention. They'll be going to Carson City and catch their trains there."

"We try and bag some of them?" Clarence asked.

Casing his binoculars, Jack told his son and nephew, "I want to learn as much as I can about the offer this Kaminsky woman is planning to make. If we take out too many of these guys, she'll just send more teams and more after that. We want one group that we can stop, one two-man group. She's got backup groups, apparently, hence sixteen men for four countries. She's probably pretty certain we've rescued Alan and that he might be alive. So she'll figure that there's an extremely high probability that Alan has told us everything he knows about her intentions. She'll have anticipated that we'd try to stop her teams from getting through, but couldn't stop all of them."

"There's dynamite at the store," David suggested. "We could blow up the time-transfer base and go after the guys and—"

"Execute them? That'd be the only option. Couldn't

have them arrested, because there's nothing to charge them with. My telegram listing Teddy Roosevelt's campaign stops should be coming, I hope. We get a sample of the sales materials these guys are carrying—that should clinch Mr. Roosevelt believing us."

Jack Naile started crawling back from the edge of the overlook. "We make like highwaymen and rob a pair of these guys once they've switched to horses and split up. That's the best that we can do for now. Let's go," he said.

They entered through the back door of Jack Naile—General Merchandise. A sandy-haired, white-aproned young clerk came from the front of the store into the storeroom with a Schofield revolver in his hand. "Oh! I'm sorry, Mr. Naile, David. I heard noise back here and—"

"Just picking up some emergency supplies, Billy," David told him. "I'll be up front in a minute." The clerk smiled, lowered the muzzle of the revolver and closed the storeroom door. David turned to his father. "What do we need?"

He still liked the idea of the dynamite. His father was against it. "I can get the stuff, and you can help Clarence get fresh horses."

"Good idea. Okay. Each of us needs a duster, a different hat and a bandanna," his father told him. "And don't get me some goofy assed hat, okay? A regular Stetson. Remember. I have a big head."

"You're telling me." David laughed. "Go on. I'll get what we need."

As his father exited through the back door into what passed for an alley, where Clarence waited with the horses, David took off his hat, patted his clothes to shed what trail dust that he could and entered the store proper. There were three customers at the moment: two women—apparently shopping together—and a man, who looked like he was wearing Clayton Moore's old prospector disguise. The man was standing just past the pickle barrel, hunched over and ogling the glass fronted case where revolvers, derringers and the new C-96 Mauser samples were kept.

"Hey, sonny! Ya da head honcho heah?"

David looked away from the old man, searching for Billy. Billy was placing canned fruit on a shelf. "Ahh, Billy. We have a customer who needs some assistance in firearms." David turned back to the old man. "Billy will be able to assist you with any purchase you might care to make."

"Wha's this heah?" He stabbed a very dirty right index finger toward the C-96.

"It's called a Mauser, sir. It's a brand new type of hand-gun that fires ten rounds as rapidly as you can pull the trigger."

"Fotty-fie o' fotty-fo?"

It took David a beat to catch the fellow's meaning. "Forty-five or forty-four? Neither. It fires a very special cartridge called the seven point six three millimeter Mauser. Very accurate and quite effective."

"Thet don' soun' right, sonny."

Mercifully, Billy arrived. "Billy, show this gentleman the C-96 Mauser." David turned to the old man, and pasted a smile on his face as he suggested, "If you think you might be interested in purchasing the pistol, we have a demonstrator model. My assistant here can take you out back behind the store and let you fire a few rounds through it. Have a nice day."

And David was gone, grabbing three tan dusters off the rack. With them over his left arm, he scooped up three large bandannas in assorted colors, stuffing them into the pocket of one of the dusters.

David didn't know Clarence's hat size, but figured that it was close to his own. He grabbed a gray hat and a white hat. His father's head size was seven and three-quarters. There wasn't that much of a selection, but he found a broad-brimmed black Stetson with a high crown that already had what his father had always referred to as a Tom Mix crease. In 1900, it was still called a Carlsbad crease. He remembered his father watching Hopalong Cassidy movies, and this hat was identical to the one worn by William F. Boyd.

With all three hats, the dusters and the bandannas, David went into his office. He jotted down a note to list the clothing as "free samples to customers" and left his office as quickly as he'd entered.

He exited the selling floor, entered the storeroom, passed through it, opened the back door and stepped into the alley. As he was locking the back door, he heard the sound of hooves and turned. His father and Clarence had returned with fresh horses from the livery stable. David took the bandannas from the pocket of the top duster as Clarence called out, "You can bring these back and get our own horses next time you come to town, David."

David didn't bother telling his father and Clarence "Thanks a lot." Instead, he handed them their hats and dusters and bandannas, otherwise known as western desperado disguise kits. Time was wasting. He grabbed his saddle horn and swung up onto the back of the big gray mare.

Cutting cross country was the only way to keep up with the three white vans. Certain of their approximate destination, and with fresh horses under them and Jack, his son and nephew rode with abandon. David's horse slipped and fell, but didn't come up lame. David's right shoulder would bruise, but wasn't otherwise damaged. Checking the horse more thoroughly than he checked his son, Jack announced, "Let's keep going!" and climbed up into the saddle.

Using the vans this far away from the time-transfer base was asking for discovery and myriad unanswerable questions; the stagecoach road leading to Carson City was well-travelled. Yet, it was obvious why the vans were being used: in order to save time.

Distant gunshots, fired too rapidly and for too great duration to be from weapons of the period, filtered up into the high rocks through which Jack, David and Clarence forced their mounts. "The afternoon stage, I bet," Clarence shouted over the thrumming of their horses' hooves. "Probably killed the driver and any passengers. Can't leave witnesses. The bastards."

"Good point to remember," Jack called back.

An hour and a half later, their lathered horses rubbed down, grained and watered—but sparsely, lest they bloat—Jack stood in a mountain meadow, smoking a cigarette. Clarence was on watch. Equipped with binoculars, he was posted a little over a quarter mile away, keeping a vigil over the stagecoach road. Both Jack and his son watched for Clarence to flash the signal mirror, alerting them that riders were coming.

Two miles farther out on the stagecoach road, the tracks of the vans had turned off, then traveled on for over a mile before the anachronistic transports parked in a narrow canyon. A corral had been built there; horses were saddled and waiting for the occupants of the vans. Jack had crawled close enough to observe in some detail, while David and Clarence stood watch with the horses. The "salesmen" were, as predicted, breaking up into groups of two. Each man was equipped with a gun belt complete with a revolver and a sheath knife, and each pair of men was issued a lever-action rifle.

The first two pairs of riders set out at once, not seeming terribly skilled as horsemen.

Crawling back until it was safe to crouch, then moving in a crouch as rapidly as he could until it was safe to stand, Jack Naile made his way back to David and Clarence. "I just saw riders, four men heading back toward the stagecoach road," David announced. "Do we chase them?"

"No. The groups will pace each other a little. Let's find a spot up ahead where we can rest the horses and ourselves. We'll let the next four go past, too. We'll try for the third set of riders. That way, if we miss them, we've still got one more chance."

They'd urged their weary animals—animals at least as exhausted as their riders—away from the mouth of the canyon, then along the stagecoach road until they'd found a suitable spot. There were broad rocks, just high enough to shield the hat of a mounted man waiting on the other side. Up a little distance from the road, concealed from the view of any riders coming from the canyon, lay the meadow.

An hour passed before four men in period business suits, all identically equipped, rode past the rocks. David had stood the watch, Clarence replacing him.

Assuming hour intervals, by the black face of his Rolex, Jack announced to David, "It's just about time, if they keep to regular intervals."

Jack and his son and nephew had already changed into the dusters, replacing their own hats with the ones from the store. Jack noted to David, "I approve of the selection, by the way. The same style I've seen Tom Selleck use, as a matter of fact." Jack Naile thought he caught a smile flicker across his son's face, but thought nothing more of it. Their own hats were wrapped in a blanket and hidden behind an easily identified fir tree. Jack checked his saddle and set to tightening his cinch strap.

All three of them crouched in their saddles, just in case the angle of the road was steep enough that the crown of a hat might be visible to the four riders.

Jack told them, "Clarence, you've watched a lot of westerns. David, you haven't. Follow our lead." Looking at Clarence, he said, "Just like the classic thing you'd see on television back in the fifties. We're the three outlaws, hiding behind the rocks beside the stage road. That gave the effect of a robbery without having to go to the expense of filming a chase scene. Instead of springing out when the stagecoach carrying the mine payroll is passing, we're going after four men. If we can avoid it, no chase scene, because I don't want a shot fired, but don't take any chances.

"David—I want you to be the last man out from behind the rocks. I'm first, cutting them off, then Clarence on their left flank. You cross behind them and take their right flank. We want, in order of importance, the mochillas, then anything else they've got. We get them to hand over their weapons, which is what I'd prefer; it's probably safer. These guys may know nothing about older firearms and have loaded rounds under the hammers. They fling the guns down, we could have an A-D, and the noise from an accidental discharge is going to attract just as much attention as a shot being fired intentionally. The people with those vans may have automatic weapons, and we don't, so a gunfight with the Lakewood Industries guys back in the canyon is the last thing we want."

It was difficult getting used to his father as a field commander, a general, the leader of a gang. Maybe a family was, in a way, a gang, or at least a small tribe. David's only experience with his father in a leadership function beyond the scope of normal family activity was as a scout leader back when he—David—was about eight or ten years old.

So far, David had to admit, his Dad seemed to be doing okay.

Their high-crowned cowboy hats were pulled down low over their eyes, bandannas covering their faces below the eyes—his father's, of course, was black. And long tan dusters covered their clothes from the neck and shoulders to well below their knees. It would have been hard for even someone who knew them—let alone total strangers—to identify them as part of the Naile family.

David drew the three-inch-barreled Colt revolver from beneath his duster. The gun might be recognizable, but there were a decent number of these stubby Colts available. Theoretically, anyone could have had one.

His father had borrowed the '97 Winchester pump and tromboned the action, holding the weapon in his right hand, the reins to his horse in the left. Clarence drew his revolver.

There was the sound of hoofbeats from several horses.

"Let me do all of the talking," David's father cautioned. "And, Clarence, especially you, for God's sake, don't laugh."

"Why not laugh? What?"

"Later."

David closed his eyes, shook his head. What was a successful retailer and budding entrepreneur doing skulking around wearing a mask and about to pull a holdup, even considering that these four guys riding along the road were world-class bad guys? "Nuts."

"What?" Clarence asked in a low whisper.

David merely shook his head.

The hoofbeats were so loud now that the four horsemen had to be nearly upon them, ready to ride past them at any second. David's palms were sweating; his father's palms sweated even when his father wasn't nervous. Was this perspiring-palms deal a genetic trait? That was just fucking wonderful.

The hoofbeats were ringing in David's ears; the horsemen had to be about to burst into sight.

And then they were there, and the thing was getting started.

David's father rode out ahead of the two lead horsemen, the shotgun to his right shoulder. "*Sus manos arriba! Ahora!*"

The four riders reined in, holding their horses back clumsily. The Mexican accent made Clarence start to cough as he took up his position, the cough a patently obvious means—at least to David—of choking back a laugh. Then, in English, but heavily accented, David's father repeated. "Up with thee hands! Now, gringos! Thees shotgun! She has the hair trigger, *sí!*"

The four men tried raising their hands and holding the reins of their horses at the same time; they weren't doing a very good job of it as David rode around behind them and took up his position on their right. With three guns trained on them, one of the guns a twelve gauge shotgun, the four— ordinary-looking guys—appeared extremely nervous. "You dismount, *los caballos!* Off the horses! *Andale!* Quick!"

The four men, almost as one, started climbing down from their saddles.

"Do nada with thee pistolas, gringos! Or Murietta, he kill you!"

The four men stood beside their mounts. "*Miguel! Ayúdame! Toma las pistolas. Miguelito!*"

David looked at his father. It dawned on him, in the same instant, that his father was looking at him. Michael was to have been his middle name and his father, come to think of it, probably didn't know the Spanish equivalent for David or Alan.

Trying to fake an accent and simultaneously hide it

within a mumble, David used close to half his knowledge of Spanish. "*Sí.*"

Clarence coughed very loudly.

"*Cuidado, amigo!* Thee cough—it does not sound so good. *No está bien.*"

Carefully dismounting, David shoved his pistol almost into the face of the business-suited man nearest him, opening the man's gun belt at the waist and letting it ease to the ground. Gesturing with the pistol, he forced the man to step back. He repeated the process with the other three men.

"*Ahora, toma las mochillas, Miguelito.*"

The first mochilla slipped off rather conveniently. He moved on to the next animal.

"*Sus ropas, pendejos!* Your clothes and boots! Take them off! *Ahora!* Now!"

The men began to undress, right down to their proper period underwear: white one-piece union suits. David tried to dress authentically to the period, but would not be caught dead in something like a union suit; nor, to his father's credit, would he. Was Clarence wearing underwear like that? David hoped not, if for no other reason than Peggy's sake.

David's father gestured with the shotgun at the four underwear-clad Lakewood Industries men. "*Y ahora,* gringos. Now! You walk down along thee road and no look back, I think, or Murrieta, he kill you and laugh. *Andale!*"

The four men started walking, their feet obviously hurting them with nothing but woolen or cotton socks between their skin and the rocks and pebbles and ruts of the road surface.

Not one of the men looked back.

After a few moments, returned to his own voice and speech patterns once again, David's father directed, "Put all four mochillas on one of the horses. Lash them on securely. Put all the weapons on one of the other horses. Let me see one of the gun belts."

Clarence dismounted to help David. David's father carefully thumbed down the '97's hammer to full rest, then drew it back a quarter inch, just shy of contacting the firing pin, then sat with the shotgun across his saddle, taking the gun belt that was handed up to him. David's father, inspecting the gun belt, the revolver and knife in turn, declared, "All modern stuff, as I supposed. The holster and gun belt are reproductions from Rod Kibler Saddlery, the revolver is a Cimarron Arms gun made in Italy—an Uberti—and the knife is a Cold Steel Bowie. At least Lakewood Industries has good taste in equipment. This is all top quality."

David took the rifle from the saddle scabbard of the horse nearest him. "Navy Arms," David announced. It was also from the 1990s, although it was a beautiful duplicate of an 1892 Winchester.

"Same with all the rest of the weapons," Clarence volunteered.

"The boots are from Tony Lama," David added.

"All right," David's father told them. "Let's lead their horses, use them if need be, and get out of the neighborhood before anybody comes looking for us."

"One thing, Dad."

"What, son?"

"Who's 'Marietta'?"

"It's *Murrieta*, Joaquin Murrieta. Famous mid-nineteenth century bandit in California. Some people believe that Murietta was—at least in part—the inspiration for Johnston McCulley when he created Zorro—or will create him in a few years, depending on perspective. I didn't figure those Lakewood Industries guys would know what I was talking about anyway." His face seamed with a smile as he added, "*Vamanos, amigos!* Before more *gringos vienen*, hey! *Andale, muchachos!*" And he started his horse back toward the meadow, already stripping off his duster.

Clarence observed, "He just does those goofy-assed accents to annoy me."

"No," David responded honestly. "I don't think he does it to annoy you. He just thinks he does neat accents and he doesn't care if they annoy you! Doesn't that make you feel better?"

Clarence only grunted as he mounted up.

CHAPTER
❈ SEVENTEEN ❈

Sitting around the kitchen table, eating venison stew and perusing the captured documents from the mochillas by lamplight, Jack felt frustrated. He could make out some words, get the general sense of the papers—letters of introduction, maps, contracts—but could not truly read them. The men whom they had intercepted along the stagecoach road had been bound for Germany and France. Perhaps the reason that none of them had spoken a word was because they did not speak very much English. In any case, the documents were in German and French, and Jack read neither German nor French.

Clarence had summed up the situation succinctly. "Shit!"

Jack agreed completely. Rather than ruining the delicious venison stew and fresh bread Ellen had made with Lizzie and Peggy's help, Jack tried to get what he could from the documents and eat at the same time. "They're offering 'heavier than air flying machines' and '*fusils des guerre*' which are '*automatique*' and instruction in their use. That much I get from the French set. The photographs make it pretty clear. F-16 fighters and M-16 rifles." He laughed, took a swallow of Glen Livet Scots whiskey. He was grateful that this magnificent liquor had already been invented. "Whoever reads this stuff in the capitals of the world is going to think there's some special significance to the number sixteen in the future a hundred years from now. We're extremely blessed, family. If these guys had brought battery-operated video or DVD players with them and let the prospective customers actually see the planes and the rifles in action, it would have been an instant 'Where do I sign?' and things would move along much faster. This gives us a little time."

"Are they actually going to send their men to Paris and Berlin and London, Daddy?" Lizzie asked. "Traveling by ship to Europe will take forever, practically."

"I don't think they will, sweetheart. Again, as you imply, time is a factor, and especially critical for them, if they realize that we know what they're planning. No. I think they'll hit the embassies in Washington with their proposals. If they get a favorable response, the Lakewood guys will wire to somewhere near here and order up video or DVD on what they're selling, samples of some of the smaller stuff. Secret meetings can be arranged here in the United States with the ministers of war for the various powers, demonstrations set up in some desolate area— again, the smaller stuff. They'd probably pick a site here in Nevada. They might even send an F-16 through or a helicopter gunship, send them through the time-transfer point, get them out into the desert and hope nobody spots them.

"Once they get a deal in place," Jack went on, using a piece of the fresh-baked bread—it was still slightly warm—to sop the remaining gravy from the stew, "then they can risk being spotted. That would allow them to set up a small airbase somewhere near this time-transfer point in order to facilitate transportation needs until they have a new time-transfer base established in their host country."

"They'd probably destroy the base that they have here," David suggested. "Destroy it in our time and in the future, so that we couldn't reach them from here."

Jack agreed. "You're right, son. And they'd have achieved what they want: ruling the world from behind whatever seat of power becomes Lakewood Industries' partner in altering history."

It was extremely late, and Jack was exhausted from the day's events. Chasing bad guys and pretending to rob them was a younger man's game, especially when the horsebacking was factored in. "Tomorrow," he announced, "I should have an answer to my telegram concerning Governor Roosevelt's intended campaign stops. Then we can make plans." He had sent out several wires—the governor's office in New York state, the White House, the *New York Telegraph* newspaper—not knowing which, if any, of the telegrams would be answered. "Tomorrow," he said again.

There was a knock at the front door. "I thought I heard a horse coming up," Ellen noted, standing. Lizzie, her arm no longer in a sling, came to stand beside her.

Jack glanced toward her as he stood up. He'd slept late and awakened hungry, eating breakfast a rarity for him. The sun through the kitchen windows was bright.

Jack's right hand rested on the butt of his special Colt, on the table beside his plate. David went to the door, Clarence watching him. David looked out the window. "It's Bobby Lorkin," David announced. When the Naile family had first come to Atlas and its environs, Bobby Lorkin had been a teenaged delivery boy, running errands for everyone and anyone, a well-spoken young fellow who seemed pleasantly ambitious. In the intervening four years, he'd taken over management of the telegraph office and acquired part interest in the livery stable.

When David opened the door, Bobby—the once skinny kid—pretty much filled the opening, broad shouldered and tall, curly reddish blonde hair falling across his forehead as he removed his hat.

Automatically, Jack glanced toward Lizzie. In the vernacular of the day, Bobby was obviously "sweet" on Lizzie and Lizzie, who blushed as she saw him, reciprocated. It was not as if they dated, but when they saw each other, they talked, smiled, looked nervous.

Bobby said, "Mr. and Miz Naile, Miss Lizzie,—" There was a little pause that was impossible to miss as Bobby Lorkin looked at Lizzie and Lizzie looked at Bobby. "Miz Jones. David. Clarence."

It was convenient, Jack thought absently, that there weren't too many more people in the Naile family, or otherwise Bobby would have talked himself hoarse.

Ellen introduced Alan. "This is our relative from Chicago, Bobby."

Alan stood up—a little feebly still—and extended his hand as David ushered Bobby inside. "I'm Alan Naile, from the Chicago branch of the family. I had kind of an accident and came here to recuperate."

"Dry air—lots o' folks from back East take real well to dry air. Right happy to make acquaintance with ya, sir."

"Just call me Alan, please."

"Alan. Happy t' know ya." Bobby finished crossing the room. "Got ya a telegram, Mr. Naile."

"That was nice of you to bring it out personally, Bobby," Jack said, taking the telegram.

Ellen volunteered, "Lizzie. Why don't you see if Bobby would like a plate of bacon and eggs and some nice homemade bread?"

Jack Naile smiled as he opened the telegram. Lizzie and Bobby might make an interesting couple, he mused. His mind instantly left that train of thought, however, as he focused on the contents of the telegraph envelope. Governor Theodore Roosevelt would be making a campaign stop in Denver, Colorado. That was better than having to go back East to link up with him. But the campaign stop was in two days.

Ideal rail connections with an express train were the only hope to reach Denver in so short a time frame.

Jack Naile exhaled heavily and looked at Alan. "I seem to recall, Alan, that you mentioned something about having a Ferrari back in Chicago."

"Jack—" Ellen started.

Jack knew his wife was thinking he'd slipped up. Jack looked at Ellen and smiled. He went on, saying to Alan, "It was one of those Ferraris that's like a surrey, wasn't it?

Kind of sporty and fast—with a properly matched team,
of course."

Alan smiled and winked and said, "Yes, kind of like a
surrey. Why do you ask?"

"Know anything about surries and wagons and such,
besides driving them?"

"It's a hobby of mine—working on surries."

"You could use some exercise. That old Suburban
buckboard of ours in the barn? I'd admire having you and
David and Clarence take a look at it. I'm thinking of
taking it out for a little ride later today."

"Can I help, sir?" Bobby asked politely. "Since I got me
part ownership in the livery stable, I've learned quite a bit
about wagons."

"Mighty generous of you, Bobby. I'll bring it to town
some time, and you can have a proper look at it then."

The Suburban, if the treacherously bumpy and potholed
topography didn't kill it, would be the only chance to
make a connection that would get him to Denver in the
time available.

It would be up to David and Clarence to keep watch
over the time-transfer base. Alan might be able to help
Lizzie defend the house—like any Naile, he'd learned to
shoot as soon as he was old enough to hold a firearm
properly—but was not strong enough to travel. In addition
to his bruises and the groin-muscle problem, Peggy had
determined that Alan suffered from dehydration, and the
frequent beatings he had endured had brought about some
possible kidney and liver damage—bruising, again—that
would, Peggy opined, mend itself, however slowly.

Jack was going to Colorado to find Theodore Roosevelt, and Ellen was going with him.

The Suburban was fully readied. Alan's expertise with automobiles, developed from his hobby interest with sports cars, proved useful, as David and Clarence had installed one of the new batteries, administered the proper fluids to the engine block, bled the brakes and otherwise fitted the Suburban for travel. It wouldn't have to go far, only to Reno—far enough on roads that were so ill-suited to automobile use.

If memory served, Ellen had remarked, she recalled reading somewhere that, in 1900, there were approximately eight thousand automobiles in the United States. The overwhelming majority of these, of course, were in and around the major cities, predominantly in the East.

The train schedule that David and Clarence had brought back as a souvenir of their trip to San Francisco had proven helpful. If Jack and his wife could reach Reno in time to intercept and board the Overland Limited—scheduled to leave at four minutes after six that evening—they would arrive in Denver, via Ogden, Utah, and Cheyenne, Wyoming, at nine in the morning two days later, only thirty-eight hours and fifty-six minutes after departure.

"What time is Teddy Roosevelt's speech going to be, Jack?"

They were packing the last of their things. "Around four in the afternoon, which'll give us a few hours to get cleaned up and changed."

"I can hardly wait to see what a toilet looks like on a train. I remember when I was commuting from downtown

Chicago back to that apartment we had when we first got married. The toilets on trains weren't so hot in 1969, either."

"Just keep your knees together a lot and think about deserts where there's no water for miles around."

Ellen, closing her bag, said, "One more potty stop before we leave; this may be the last modern flush toilet I'll see for a very long time."

In the letter that a dying Jack Naile had written in the previous time loop to his future self, the letter found in a niche behind a loose brick in the fireplace of the otherwise burned-out ranch house, he'd warned his future self. The warning was that he—Jack—was not as good at staying alive as he thought he was and that he would need an edge, the little Seecamp .32, anachronistic as it was in 1900.

David and Clarence were off watching the time-transfer base built by Lakewood Industries. Lizzie and Peggy and Alan were in the house. Only Jack and his wife were in the barn, where the gassed and ready Suburban waited—only Jack and Ellen and a man whose face Jack recognized from a wanted poster. "You're Steve Fowler, Jess Fowler's kid brother, the holdup man and killer."

"And you's the sonofabitch fuckin' town marshal what bushwhacked my brother."

In the light from the lamp Ellen held—to Ellen's considerable credit, it wasn't shaking—Jack's eyes were able to focus with perfect clarity on two features of Steve Fowler: the burning hatred that was like a spark in his unwavering coal-black pupils and the twin muzzles of the side-by-side twelve gauge shotgun in his hands. The eyes were definitely, almost preternaturally, black, and the shotgun's barrels were nickel or chrome plated. "You know, the famous Chiracahua Apache chief, Cochise, carried a nickel-plated shotgun, kind of like that, I understand. And I didn't bushwhack your brother, although I'd intended to, since he'd tried murdering my entire family. As it turned out, he bushwhacked me. But he died in a fair fight; I even let him go for his gun first. Now put that scattergun down."

"I knows ya' pret' good from some ol boys talkin' up ya' bein' handy with that shooter. And, ya' got ya derringer sneak gun, too. But guess what this heah scattergun is a aimin' at! Yo' right arm, Naile. An' both ya's shooters is for right hand work."

At the distance, Jack realized, the minimal damage the shotgun would do if only one barrel were discharged would be to rip away the right arm, shoulder and much of the chest. Even if a gun could be gotten to with his left hand, there wouldn't be enough of him left to use it. And Ellen, standing close beside him, would be killed instantly.

To outdraw the hammer fall of a shotgun was a physical impossibility for anyone except, perhaps, the legendary Border Patrolman and gunfighter Bill Jordan, or maybe quickdraw artist and trick shooter Bob Munden. No man with ordinary reflexes, however good, stood a chance.

Jack bluffed. "I'll get you as I fall, Stevie. Sure as anything. Let my wife step aside."

The black pits that were Steve Fowler's eyes wavered almost imperceptibly.

"The bitch can move if'n ya' drops yous shooters where

ya' stand." And the twin muzzles of the shotgun slowly shifted to cover Ellen Naile.

A lot of standup comedians in the twentieth century had made/would make a good living with cracks about their wives, pursuant to the idea that they—the comedians— would have been well-rid of their spouses. Steve Fowler had guessed that Jack would be more reluctant to try anything if Ellen were certain to be killed if he did; Jess Fowler's badass little brother had guessed right.

Jack started to unbuckle his gun belt. "Left hand, no right!" Fowler ordered. Jack had been hoping for that, to get his left hand into motion. For much of his adult life, he'd carried the little Seecamp in his right front trouser pocket. But the big Colt's gun belt precluded easy access to that pocket, so he'd switched the Seecamp to his left side.

Jack unbuckled the gun belt and eased it to the barn floor. Fowler, although the shotgun was trained on Ellen, watched him. Jack caught his wife's pretty gray-green eyes. There was a slight tightening of the muscles around them, a look he knew signaled that she guessed—hoped— he had something in mind and she would back him up.

"Thet hidey-out sneak gun—drop it, too!"

The derringer was in a specially built deep riding inside-waistband holster positioned in the general vicinity of his appendix. "I've gotta fish it out from behind my pants belt, so don't get jumpy." But, of course, unless Steve Fowler was an asshole, he would get jumpy, focusing intently on the right-hand movement lest the derringer should be brought into play in some cleverly lethal fashion.

Jack fished out the derringer, held it between two

fingers and announced, "If you know guns, you know dropping a loaded derringer is an easy way to get it to go off. You could get shot, as if I cared. But my wife might get shot instead, or me. I'm setting it down nice and easy. Just watch me." Jack hoped that Steve Fowler would watch him intently.

Still holding the derringer gingerly between two fingers, not daring to risk even a glance to his wife's face, Jack flexed his knees a little and slowly bent downward, his left side facing away from Fowler's eyes. He had to do it smoothly, get the Seecamp into action, because this would be the one and only chance to kill Steve Fowler and live.

As Jack crouched, his left hand slipped into the left pocket of his trousers, his fingertips finding the worn butt of the Seecamp .32. Setting the derringer on the barn floor, Jack hesitated for a microsecond before taking his hand away from it, enough time for Fowler to start swinging the shotgun toward him.

Jack glanced toward the open barn doors and shouted, "David! Clarence! He's got a gun on Ellen!"

Ellen screamed, "It's Jess Fowler's brother!"

It was not enough to get Steve Fowler to turn around, which used to happen with considerable regularity in the old westerns, but was just enough to get Fowler to hesitate for an instant. Jack saw a blur of motion from Ellen's direction as the Seecamp cleared his pocket and he threw himself flat to the floor, under the level of Fowler's shotgun.

Something—Ellen's lamp?—went flying past Fowler's face.

One of the double's barrels discharged as Jack pulled

the Seecamp's trigger, then pulled it again, the distance between the little pistol's muzzle and Fowler's body less than ten feet.

Two shots in Fowler's midsection, one at navel level, the second below the sternum.

Not good enough to keep the second barrel from getting him or Ellen. Jack began to empty the remaining five shots, letting the muzzle rise as the pistol discharged.

Fowler's body arched back slightly.

The shotgun was vectoring downward, almost in perfect alignment with Jack's face as Jack fired the last round. Fowler's left eye and the bridge of his nose took the bullet.

A blur of motion, black skirt and white petticoats, the second shotgun barrel discharging, its shot load tearing a chunk out of the barn floor to Jack's right.

Ellen was on top of Fowler, her fingers gouging at Fowler's face, her knees planted in his chest, hammering up and down on him.

"He's dead, kid!" As Jack bent down toward her and Ellen stood up, they bumped their heads together. "Ouch!" Jack stammered.

"Ouch?! You're the one with a head like a—" Jack could barely hear, his ears ringing from the two shotgun blasts as Ellen threw her arms around him and started to cry.

Almost worse than the attempt on their lives was the precious time—an irreplaceable commodity in whatever era—that Steve Fowler's murderous intentions had cost them.

Ellen Naile cautioned her husband. "If you break an

axle or something, we'll never get to Reno in time for the train. Slow down." Seat-belted in, holding on to the overhead grab handle, she would still bounce so high that her stupid hat was almost constantly striking the Suburban's headliner. Jack had never done a great deal of off-road driving and had several times admitted that dirt roads creeped him out at any sort of speed. "How fast are you going, Jack?"

"Forty or so, unless I hit a bad stretch. Sometimes a little closer to fifty when the road looks okay."

"Your brights are on?"

"Brights are on."

"I almost wish we had airbags in this."

"I can't even remember if they were an option on the '89 models. Relax, anyway. I'm taking it nice and easy. If that rain hits, it'll slow us down a lot."

The storm clouds made it seem well past twilight, and the interior of the Suburban was in deep shadow, save for the glow from the dashboard lights. "I'm glad it's dark for once."

"Why?"

"Then I can't see the whiteness of your knuckles on the steering wheel."

Jack laughed, but his laughter sounded a little less than sincere.

While Jack had still been holding her in his arms and the smell of the shotgun's twin discharges was still heavy in the air of the barn, Lizzie—rifle in hand—had run in, Alan and Peggy just behind her.

Jack—Ellen knew that he must have been talking overly loudly because he couldn't hear properly yet—had given a quickie version of what happened, leaving off his own daring, emphasizing how she had distracted Fowler. She'd brushed herself off, Lizzie helping her, then found her dumb hat and her purse, the purse like one of those little blue sacks small bottles of Crown Royal came in. Only, it was the wrong color.

Peggy and Alan cleaned up the blood on the barn floor. Lizzie taking one leg, Ellen taking the other, Jack took Fowler's wrists and they carted the body out of the barn and toward the stream. They pitched it off the embankment and as far out into the current as they could, well past where any water for the house would be sourced. "After a while, he'll bloat up and float off—probably. If he doesn't," Jack advised Lizzie, "you send for my deputy— not the damn crook county sheriff—and tell him you discovered the body and don't know how it got there. Get him to get it out of the water and haul it into town. Hopefully, like I said, Lizzie, the corpse will just float away."

Returning to the barn, Lizzie gave them both last-minute hugs and kisses. Peggy wished them well and Alan promised, "I'll look after things as best I can, guys."

"You're a fine great-great-grandson," Jack had told him, laughing at the biological absurdity of a man of fifty having a great-great-grandson who was thirty-two years old.

Ellen envied persons who could sleep in a moving car. She could not. Instead, she peered into the deepening darkness beyond the headlights' field of illumination, the reset dashboard clock showing only five minutes after five. But the darkness was from a cloud cover more dense than she could remember ever having seen before. A storm would make their marathon drive on rutted stage roads more than doubly dangerous.

As if the storm front were some sort of malevolent spirit capable of reading her very thoughts, a barrage of raindrops larger than she ever remembered seeing cascaded through the beams of the Suburban's headlights and slammed against the windshield. In the next instant, their vehicle was engulfed.

The rain was cold, almost like ice where it pelted the bare skin of her hands and face. The goofy hat was gone, her hair covered with a heavy shawl that shielded her shoulders as well. Jack had let her out of the Suburban just past the outskirts of Reno, the equivalent, more or less, of a three city block walk from the train platform and the tiny station it fronted.

Women's clothing of the period weighed an inordinate amount under the best of circumstances, but now that Ellen was soaked nearly to the skin, the skirt of her dress and the petticoats beneath it dragged at her, weighing her down.

Ellen Naile carried only her purse and a small carpetbag, both in her right hand. In her skirt pocket was the Seecamp .32 Jack had insisted that she carry. Her left hand alternated between clutching the rechargeable Maglite flashlight—which she would have to hide as soon as she was able to rely on the meager light from the station platform—and keeping the shawl in place. She could not have cared less if she got wet under normal conditions, never being the sort of woman who cringed with fear at the thought of rain damaging her hairdo. But with the lower half of her body drenched, if her hair and upper body too were soaked, she would become uncontrollably cold.

As she neared the platform, two sconced oil lamps emitted a pale yellow light, marginally sufficient to see well enough to ascend the four steps on the near end. Ellen shut off the anachronistic flashlight and slipped it into the comparatively cavernous outer pouch of the sodden carpetbag.

As she approached the steps, she raised her skirts; the ground was softer here, the mud stickier. For once, she would have counted herself happy for the high-topped shoes of the period, had they been even remotely water-proof. Feet soaked, toes numb, Ellen Naile ascended the steps. At the height of the platform, she was instantly below the extended roofline of the station. Reno was a terminus of sorts, serviced by the V&T and the Southern Pacific. The Southern Pacific Overland Limited was scheduled to arrive for passenger boarding in under fifteen minutes.

Stepping back from the platform's edge and deeper into the shelter of the roofline, Ellen's eyes strained to pierce the darkness for some glint of light from Jack's smaller flashlight. He would turn it off sooner, of course, his night vision always vastly better than her own.

Shivering, telling herself that it would be more sensible to await his arrival in the comparative warmth of the station, she continued her numbing vigil.

At last, after what seemed an eternity, Ellen spotted her husband, his flashlight already extinguished. He was almost jogging, moving rapidly yet cautiously through the mud. As he came closer, she could see him with greater clarity, saddlebags slung over his left shoulder, a large carry-on in each hand, one a carpetbag, the other a leather suitcase, that almost looked modern.

Jack ascended the platform steps, and Ellen took the saddlebags from his shoulder as he lowered the carpetbag and leather suitcase to the platform.

"Hi, kid." Jack grinned, a torrent of rainwater guttering from the brim of his black Stetson as he leaned forward to kiss her. "Oops! Sorry about that," he amended, removing his hat, shaking it and taking her into his arms. "You freezing?"

"Aren't you?" Jack wore only a black vested suit, no rain slicker thought to be needed as they'd left the ranch house.

"I'm a little cold. You might want to change clothes, get into something warmer."

"Where?" But before her husband could answer her, she asked a more important question. "What did you do with the Suburban?"

"Well, there really is a grove of cottonwoods just outside of town, or, anyway, something like cottonwoods. I parked it as far in as I could get, got the tarp staked down over it and whacked off some boughs that I could reach. It's as camouflaged as it's going to get. Hold the good thought that nobody spots it. In this era, I don't think we have to worry about somebody coming along and breaking the ignition lock and hotwiring it."

"I hope you're right."

"Let's get inside and get tickets and see about getting you into dry clothes."

Ellen wouldn't let him take back his saddlebags as Jack regrasped the handles of their luggage.

The Overland Limited departed at precisely four minutes after six. It was so excruciatingly on time that a seventeen-year-old boy from the town of Dovia, in Italy, whose name was Benito Mussolini, would have been ecstatic—had he known about it. Mussolini and his Fascists had made/would make a big deal out of getting Italian trains to run on time.

The station master had allowed Jack and Ellen the use of a storeroom for changing into dry clothing, Jack offering the explanation—now familiar—that they had walked through the rain because of a "problem with the wagon."

Jack was reminded of the times in a subtler way when he and Ellen left the storeroom, the eyes of the other waiting passengers staring at a man and a woman openly demonstrating that they would disrobe in front of one another. In this age, many genteel people still referred to the legs of a piano as *limbs*, because the word *legs* might be misinterpreted to have a sexual connotation. Although virtually everybody had sex, it was somehow dirty to acknowledge the fact.

Using a small tarp borrowed from the stationmanager, Jack had gotten his wife and himself aboard the train without additional water damage. After returning from the bathroom, Ellen began to unbutton her wet shoes as she related, "It's kind of like an outhouse. What you do goes straight onto the track bed as you do it. You could really catch a draft on your butt in the wintertime."

"One of the principal reasons why men run the world," Jack told her, smiling. "We can piss standing up."

"Nothing to do with brains, just the ability to pee without getting your legs wet. I'm glad you admit that it has nothing to do with intellectual superiority."

"Well, of course, there's always the fact that we have superior upper-body strength."

"It's necessary to hold up the larger heads that inflated egos require. All that empty space in the brainpan area has to be filled with something."

"True enough," He laughed, taking his sodden hat and starting to manually reblock it. "Try and get some sleep. If we stay on time, we should pull into Ogden, Utah, at eleven forty-five tomorrow morning. We'll lose this Southern Pacific engine and pick up one from the Union Pacific and we're on our way to Cheyenne."

"Fine," she responded. "Let me have your arm."

Ellen wrapped her arms around his right arm and rested her head against his chest. Neither of them had eaten, but neither of them was hungry just yet. If old western movies had depicted things at all accurately, shortly someone would come along selling sandwiches.

The guy with the sandwiches came along, and Jack purchased a couple of them, saving them until Ellen woke up.

The glow from the lamplight was yellowish, stronger than candles, but hardly strong enough to read by comfortably. He looked down at his wife's face. Ellen was as beautiful in repose after twenty-eight years of marriage as she had been the first time she'd used his chest for a pillow, on a Chicago Transit Authority bus when they were still in their teens.

Jack Naile alternated between watching his pretty

wife's face and stealing the occasional glance at the other passengers, mostly male, mostly wearing business attire, mostly trying to fall asleep under the brims of their hats.

With the single exception of Indians—and not all Indians—every man wore a hat.

"The West," as it was popularly depicted, wasn't really the way that it was. There were some men who used a great deal of profanity, certainly, but as a general rule, profanity was considerably less common in the time where he presently lived than it had been/would be ninety-six years into the future. Among women, it was nearly unknown.

The formality of dress Jack Naile found even more interesting. Women, of course, were stuck with their impractical long skirts and dresses and would be considered freaks if they wore trousers. But even men, regardless of their social station, had a more rigid code. No matter what they were doing, men rarely rolled up their sleeves.

Conservatism in dress was everyone's watchword: corsets for women and union suits for men. In their store in Atlas, the only kind of men's underwear David stocked was one-piece union suits, trapdoor and all; that was all any of the store's male customers or their wives who purchased it for them wanted in male underwear. After painstaking searching, David had discovered a catalog from a New York firm that offered something close to boxers; briefs were nowhere to be found. They went nearly to the knee, and Ellen kindly shortened them.

Some one of the passengers lit a cigar; Jack could smell it, only then realizing that his eyes were closed. Men smoked everywhere; women, unless they were of the "scarlet" variety, never lit up in public. Ellen, who had smoked for a good number of years before quitting (she occasionally stole a drag from one of his cigarettes), had always been adamant in her belief that it looked slutty for a woman to have a cigarette hanging out of her mouth, equally so for a woman to have a cigarette in her hand if she was walking, especially outside.

Jack opened his eyes and looked again at his very beautiful sound asleep wife. Jack resettled his gun belt, tugged down the brim of his hat and closed his eyes.

CHAPTER
✠ EIGHTEEN ✠

After the comparatively brief train trip from Cheyenne to Denver, Jack and Ellen registered at the Hotel Grande Excelsior, taking the rather optimistically named Presidential Suite. Both bathed; then, hair still a little wet and Jack's beard stubble shaved away, they dressed.

"So, where do we find Teddy Roosevelt?"

Jack looked at his leather-cased Rolex. "In exactly three hours, his special will be pulling in at the train station, where we arrived."

"And?"

"Well—"

"Oh, we're gonna wing it."

"Well, I've got some ideas on how we'll get to meet him."

Ellen laughed. "I know. 'We're from the future.' That'll be good enough to get us hauled off to the booby hatch."

Jack smiled and reassured her, "Well, at least we'll be together, darling."

Ellen hoped the wrinkles would fall out of her dress. She didn't want to be committed to an asylum in something tacky looking.

In reality, Jack had a plan, hatched before they left the ranch, when he remembered something that he had read years earlier about Theodore Roosevelt. Roosevelt, ever the scholar, had studied in Germany during his youth. It followed that a man with such an inquisitive mind would have picked up at least a decent command of spoken German and an even better skill level when it was written.

The documents taken from the Lakewood Industries couriers hyped technology not yet dreamed of, a tantalizing taste of the future. The mere idea of something like an M-16 rifle would be irresistible to one of the few men who would carry a revolver in his hip pocket during his presidency.

McKinley had not yet been assassinated; Lincoln's death was a bitter national tragedy three and one-half decades old, Garfield's 1881 assassination was still fresh in memory. Theodore Roosevelt was, after all, only a vice-presidential candidate in an era when seeing an armed man or any number of armed men at a political rally didn't even arouse suspicion.

In such an environment, it would be possible—certainly for a pretty woman like Ellen—to rush up to Governor Roosevelt's platform at the rear of his train and shove a handful of documents toward him.

Jack freely admitted to himself that his "plan" had the

serious potential for failure, but it was the best that he had. If Ellen got the documents to Roosevelt and Colonel Roosevelt even glanced at them, he'd be hooked. Attached to the documents was a letter with little more than their names and the name of the hotel at which they would be staying until the following morning. Glued to the letter, saved from the handful of pocket change Jack Naile had inadvertently carried with him into the past, was an ordinary dime, a caption beneath it reading, "Do you recognize the profile of your eighteen-year-old cousin Franklin Delano Roosevelt? Note the date that this coin was/will be minted: 1990."

Would Roosevelt come, inquire about the strange references to future technology available to the highest bidder?

The future of history was at stake in a game of chance unlike any other ever played.

The crowd at the rail station was mixed. There were uniformed soldiers, some of whom might have served with Theodore Roosevelt during the Spanish-American War. Men in suits and working clothes. Women in their customary long skirts and dresses and omnipresent hats, some with children in their arms or held in the viselike grip of a gloved hand. There were placards waving, hand written signs of support for McKinley and Roosevelt. And there were other signs, far fewer in number, decrying "Expansionism!" and "Imperialism!" and supporting the rival Democratic candidacy of the already once-defeated William Jennings Bryan.

Ellen, standing close beside Jack, remarked, "It's

interesting, isn't it? Almost no one remembers Bryan as a political candidate, really. He's mostly remembered as the man who locked horns with Clarence Darrow at the Scopes Monkey Trial."

Before Jack could respond, a band struck up a lively air, the quality of its repertoire closely akin to that often associated with high school musicians still struggling with coordinating such things as embouchure and notation. The level of sincerity was essentially identical.

The special was coming slowly along the track, accompanied by the smell of burning coal, the hiss of steam, the squeaks and rattles and the almost human sigh as the engine slowed still more. The crowd—supporters and protesters alike—closed over the rails behind the train in a wave. Somehow, the band sounded a little better, the placards waved a little higher. Small American flags were raised at the ends of upstretched arms.

Propelling Ellen ahead of him by the elbow, Jack wriggled his way through the crowd, dodging a little girl in a pink coat and pink hat and hair bows, edging round a burly cavalry buck sergeant, slipping in front of a clerically collared minister or priest.

The door at the rear of the last car opened and the crowd went wild with noise as the forty-two-year-old military hero and governor of New York stepped out onto the small, flag-draped, balconylike structure. Arms raised, a smile on his full face, a glint of sunlight, as if on cue, catching his glasses, Teddy Roosevelt clearly reveled in the adulation.

One of the protestors shouted something unintelligible as he rushed forward, waving his placard like a sword. An army officer emerged from the doorway just behind the vice-presidential candidate and started to interpose himself between Roosevelt and the protestor.

Roosevelt shouldered the officer aside, leaned over the wrought-iron railing of his train car and glared at the protestor. In a voice not terribly remarkable except that it could be heard over the din, Roosevelt challenged, "You wish to speak with me, sir?!"

The protestor stopped his charge cold. The crowd of Roosevelt supporters pushed the fainthearted protestor back, man and sign disappearing within the mass of humanity.

Unflappable, Roosevelt was back in form, arms raised, the familiar toothy grin flashing.

The band was winding down its brassy tune. Jack had Ellen almost in reach of the train car's black railing. "I'll give it to the army officer, Jack! That'll be better."

"Okay! Now, kid!"

The band stopped.

Ellen stood outstretched, the envelope in her gloved right hand inches from the army officer.

Theodore Roosevelt looked down at her and smiled. "Thank you for coming today, madam."

Roosevelt looked up and raised his voice and declared to all present, "It is with utmost sincerity that I declare that it is a feeling unmatched by any other to return, once again, to the American West and to the city which is the jewel at the center of our continent!"

Ellen shoved the envelope against the officer's hand several times before he turned his head and looked at her. Shoving the envelope toward the man, she pointed the first finger of her other hand toward Theodore Roosevelt.

The officer—he was a captain—took the envelope from her, and Ellen sank back against Jack. Jack retreated with her into the crowd—but not too far.

Jack bent to whisper in his wife's ear, "Let's enjoy the moment for a while, Ellen."

Ellen leaned her head against his shoulder.

There came a knock at their hotel room door. Ellen answered it. As she opened the door, the face she looked into was almost at eye level with her own, and she remembered that Theodore Roosevelt, a strong and burly man, was not a particularly tall one.

"Madam. May I present myself? I am Theodore Roosevelt. The gentleman with me is Captain Rogers. I had the occasion to peruse the rather odd packet with which you supplied him for my edification. Forgive me if I assume that you and the gentleman—your husband?" Ellen nodded. "Forgive me if I assume that you and your husband wished to speak with me."

"Yes, sir, on a matter of great importance."

"Well, then I most humbly suggest, madam, that we adjourn to some more suitable location. My train awaits on a siding, and I have several more scheduled stops to make before returning to New York. Hence, time is literally of the essence."

"Time is, indeed, the essence of our discussion and the dilemma that it will present, Governor Roosevelt." Jack's voice registered from behind her. "I am Jack Naile, Governor Roosevelt." Jack extended his hand, and

Theodore Roosevelt clasped it briefly. "And, sir, may I have the honor to present my wife, Ellen."

His hat already removed, Theodore Roosevelt bowed his head slightly and took her hand as she extended it. He held it for an instant, his handshake dry, firm, exuding strength without ever exercising it: "Your servant, madam."

Ellen felt her cheeks beginning to flush.

"Please, sir, would you join us?" Jack asked, gesturing into the suite's sitting room, "and the captain as well, of course, if you feel that he can be taken into full confidence in a very delicate matter which could have unprecedented international repercussions."

"The documents written in German are to what you allude, I take it?"

"Those, sir, and the coin."

"Yes. A most fascinating coin, indeed, Mr. Naile, madam." Roosevelt glanced over his shoulder at Captain Rogers. Taller than Roosevelt, about Jack's height of a little under six foot, he was the youngest person there, no more than thirty. As he prepared to step away, he moved his head, and a perfect blond curl fell out of place and rested across his forehead. He brushed it away with the edge of a finger. "Captain, I will rely on your discretion that nothing which transpires here shall be spoken of to anyone without my permission."

"Certainly, sir."

Theodore Roosevelt stepped over the threshold, cocked his head back so that he could look Jack square in the eye and asked, "I must first inquire what fascination there exists for the number sixteen in the German documents. And then, sir, madam, what my eighteen-year-old cousin Franklin has to do with that rather interesting ten-cent piece."

"It's a very long story, Governor Roosevelt," Ellen interjected. "A very long story."

Ushering Teddy Roosevelt and Captain Rogers toward two chairs opposite a love seat, a smallish table interposed between, Jack began by saying, "I was/will be born in Chicago forty-six years from now. My father will be born in Manchester, New Hampshire, in eight years, my mother in Chicago in 1902. By then, Mr. Roosevelt, if we do not act, the world will be forever changed. In fact, at this very moment, the future may be irretrievable."

Teddy Roosevelt stood before his chair, only seating himself as Ellen fanned her skirts to sit on the love seat. Then he spoke. "I have the horrible feeling, Mr. Naile, that you are somehow not a madman, and that I may soon wish that you were."

"As do I," Jack responded, his voice like death.

Aboard Theodore Roosevelt's special car, an exchange of wires between the vice-presidential candidate and the President having taken place, Jack Naile sipped at a glass of scotch. It wasn't as good as Glen Livet, but was decent.

On a table between them were Lizzie's portable CD player—Theodore Roosevelt hadn't grooved on Depeche Mode, but had dubbed Frank Sinatra "captivating"—and a half-dozen books, the earliest of which wouldn't be published for more than fifty years. Paladin Press' *The U.S. Army Special Forces Medical Handbook* Roosevelt had found "fascinating."

Theodore Roosevelt leaned forward in his high-backed, gaudily upholstered chair. "The track will be cleared for us to Cheyenne, then Ogden, then onward to Reno. This automobile you have, Mr. Naile—it is reliable? And will seat several persons?"

"Extremely reliable, Mr. Roosevelt. It would normally seat eight, but with the rearmost seat removed it will easily accommodate yourself, Captain Rogers, my wife and myself," Jack answered.

"Wires have been sent to various individuals, their nature at once as intentionally obtuse, yet urgent in tone, as those exchanged between myself and President McKinley. By the time this train should reach Reno, Nevada, the proof of your assertions should be in hand. And forces will be assembled. Meanwhile, personnel will be discreetly stationed to view all comings and goings at the British, French and German embassies. Lamentably, similar individuals will be posted at our own War Department and in other locations throughout the capital. If these emissaries of Lakewood Industries are afoot, they will be apprehended, and the lingering—albeit wholly understandable—doubts vouchsafed by the President will be assuaged. And then, sir, madam—then we shall act against these villains with relentless vigor!"

Teddy Roosevelt's fist hammered down so resoundingly on the wine table beside his chair that the table legs collapsed.

Sleeping fitfully in the last few days, Ellen Naile at last found a comfortable spot on the bed. Still in her underwear, but minus her corset and her dress, Ellen

Naile had cuddled under a blanket in Mr. Roosevelt's generously offered bed. The future president's desire for information concerning late-twentieth century technology was insatiable, yet he had agreed that Jack should tell him nothing which might in some way alter the future, unless it was necessary to their "mission at hand."

And Jack, of course, lifelong fan of Teddy Roosevelt, was more than happy to have his hero's undivided attention.

Sleep had seemed best to Ellen; eventually Jack would join her, Mr. Roosevelt having insisted that the married couple have the train car's sole bed. When Jack felt like shit in the morning because he'd missed so much sleep, she would be her usual cheerful morning self.

The bedroom was a smallish compartment at the front of the railroad car, spartanly furnished with the bed itself, a straight-backed wooden chair and a small writing desk. There were books and sheaves of paper stacked neatly on the floor beside the desk. A mini-armoire served as a closet for Mr. Roosevelt's clothes; one of its two doors was open and her dress hung suspended from a hanger to a hook on the interior of the door.

Ellen had arrived at her decision to go to sleep when Jack and Theodore Roosevelt had begun discussing Jack's little pistol, the Seecamp .32. When conversations turned to firearms and the conversation had nothing to do with business, Ellen tuned out and shut down when possible.

A noise above her in the darkness awakened her.

She had, by this time, traveled in this train car from Denver to Cheyenne, and this was the first time she'd noticed the car's roof creaking.

Imagination? Eyes wide open, blanket tucked up to her chin, Ellen Naile stared above her, into the darkness.

Another creaking sound, seemingly a few inches off to her left, which would have placed the origin of the noise at the precise side-to-side midpoint of the train car.

She remembered Olivia de Havilland seeing the shadows of outlaws on the roof of her train car, then trying to warn Errol Flynn that Bruce Cabot and his evil minions were about to spring Victor Jory. Were there men walking on this train? At—she turned up the lamp beside the bed and looked at her anachronistic wristwatch—four in the morning? Four in the morning! Jack was still talking with Theodore Roosevelt! Jack would be worthless until well after noon.

The cute-looking Captain Rogers, a grizzled-looking sergeant of some kind and a half-dozen soldiers and Mr. Roosevelt's male secretary occupied the car immediately ahead of theirs. There was a coal car and the engine. If there were men on the roof of Mr. Roosevelt's private car, where had they come from?

Could the soldiers be up there, guarding Mr. Roosevelt? Why hadn't she heard them earlier?

Ellen kept the lamp glowing, pushed the blanket down and sat up.

"Tell Jack," she murmured to herself.

"We will actually place men on the surface of the moon! Incredible, Mr. Naile."

"Yes, sir. It was terrific to watch."

"And you saw this on what you call 'television'?"

"Yes, sir."

"If I calculated correctly, you, sir, are actually older than I. By almost a decade. Why not call me Theodore?"

"That would be presumptuous of me, sir, despite your permission. It would be like calling our first president George or our sixteenth president Abe."

"I'm only a governor, sir, and soon—if public opinion has been properly gauged—will be vice-president. When Mr. McKinley steps down, we will see what happens."

Jack would have bitten his tongue if it would have helped. Instead, he contented himself with saying, "Pursuant to our agreement concerning future history, I cannot reveal to you, Mr. Roosevelt, when you will become president, only that you will and that you'll be considered one of the greatest of America's presidents."

"I do not care for flattery, Mr. Naile."

"Only the truth, sir. I promise you that," Jack affirmed. "But, please, I'd be honored if you'd call me 'Jack.'"

"Jack. Can you tell me more about this wondrous thing of men actually walking on the moon?"

"It will be in 1969, but you must never reveal that to anyone, sir. At the time, there was/will be a great deal of international tension—"

"Germans, I'd wager. But, no, don't tell me. Go on, Jack."

"If the date were to become known, it might have serious unforeseen consequences concerning those tensions, Mr. Roosevelt."

"Does everyone in the future have one of these television devices?"

"Yes, sir, in the developed countries virtually everyone has at least one. Ellen and I were only recently married at the time and didn't have one. I got a great deal on a demonstrator model at Sears—"

"Sears & Roebuck?"

"The very same, sir."

"Bully for them! I like success. Go on."

"Well, sir, one of the astronauts—his name was/will be Neil Armstrong, a very courageous aviator—piloted the lunar module down to the surface and said—"

"There are men on the train car's roof."

Jack dropped his long since emptied glass; it landed on the carpet between his feet and didn't break. Ellen stood just inside the main portion of the train car, the bedroom compartment's door ajar behind her, a gray blanket clutched tightly around her upper body like some over-sized shawl. She jerked the thumb of her free hand toward the roof. "Up there, Jack! Men walking on the roof. I heard them!"

"Mr. Roosevelt?"

"That shouldn't be the case, my friends. Not at all."

As Ellen approached, Jack saw that the revolver from inside her suitcase was in the hand that held the blanket closed around her.

Mr. Roosevelt sprang to his feet, an odd-looking Colt revolver appearing from his right hip pocket.

Jack was to his feet as well.

"I'll contact Rogers in the next car. He'll look into this at once." With that, Theodore Roosevelt lifted a speaking tube from a wall mount, blew into it, then said, "Captain Rogers. Pick up."

Placing the tube to his ear, Roosevelt held it there for a beat, shook his head gravely, then whistled piercingly through the speaking tube. "Anyone aboard the car, respond."

There was no response.

"Shit," Ellen interjected, her voice little above a whisper.

"The appropriateness of that substance to the situation at hand remains to be determined, Mrs. Naile."

"Somebody has to check the roof of the car. Somebody has to find out why nobody's answering. That'll be me," Jack volunteered.

"Couldn't these guys have just cut the line for the speaking tube?" Ellen suggested.

"Could have, but not without one of the army guys noticing," Jack responded.

"Your husband is quite correct, madam. One soldier is posted to ride in the locomotive with the engineer and his fireman. One is posted at the forward door of this car, another at the forward door of the other car."

"Shouldn't we try the brake cord?" Ellen suggested.

"If it works and the guys on the roof didn't get alerted when we tried the speaking tube, it could alert them now." Jack's carpetbag was on the floor by the far wall of the car. He continued speaking as he crouched to open it. "Are there any weapons in this car, Mr. Roosevelt, besides those we have personally?"

"There are not, sir."

Jack took two full-size Colt Single Action Army revolvers from his bag, rolled the butts in his hands and offered them to Roosevelt. "I know that you're familiar with these, sir. Hammers are over empty chambers, of course. I'll caution you that the actions are very light, much like the revolver I'm carrying. The trigger pull's just a little heavier than fourteen ounces. They're extremely reliable."

"From your future, sir?"

"Only they cost a great deal more, Mr. Roosevelt."

Jack took the flashlight from his bag.

"What is that device?"

"A battery-operated hand torch, Mr. Roosevelt." Jack stood up and took off his suitcoat. The white shirt under his vest was not ideal for what he was about to do. But there was no time for anything else. He loosened his tie and opened his shirt collar. There was no reason to meet death while one was uncomfortable. "Ellen. You stick at Mr. Roosevelt's side like glue. Got it? I'd suggest that one of you watch each door."

"I'll take the door at the front, Mrs. Naile. You stand guard at the rear door of the car," Roosevelt ordered. As Jack started forward, Roosevelt added, "Good luck, Jack."

"Thank you, sir."

As Jack passed Ellen, she leaned up, and he put his arms around her and kissed her lips, then her forehead, and whispered to her, "You look cute wrapped up in that blanket, kiddo."

"Jack—" Ellen began as he released her.

"I know. Take lots of chances and don't be careful."

"You've got it."

Jack reached the rear door of the train car, Teddy Roosevelt a pace behind him. "There's a box with fifty rounds of ammunition in my suitcase as well, sir. You might want to get it out. Ellen's gun is also a .45."

"Luck to you once again," Roosevelt said, clapping him on the shoulder.

"Thank you. I don't have to ask—"

"No, you don't, Jack. They'll not harm your wife as long as I draw breath."

Jack nodded, drew his special Colt and put his hand to the door handle, turned it and tucked back. No one stood on the balconylike observation platform on the special car, nor on the rear of the car just ahead.

"Doesn't look good, I'm afraid," Roosevelt declared in a stage whisper.

"Amen," Jack Naile agreed, stepping out into the biting wind of the slipstream, his eyes and the muzzle of his gun turning upward.

But, before the roof, he had to know what had transpired in the support car.

Jack held on to the railing and took the broad step across to the forward car, his gaze still cast upward for any sign of men on the roof. Maybe Ellen had just heard some normal creaking sounds, and maybe there was a perfectly logical reason why no one had answered the speaking tube, why no guard was present between the two train cars. Or maybe the Easter Bunny had just hypnotized the army personnel and Roosevelt's secretary as well.

Who would do harm to Theodore Roosevelt? Why?

Roosevelt's political rivals? Jack Naile had never had a great deal of use for the vast majority of Democrats, but planning bodily harm to a Republican vice-presidential candidate wouldn't be part of the party agenda in 1900. Was it someone who had no interest in Roosevelt at all, Roosevelt only at risk as collateral damage?

Jack stopped conjecturing, noticed his hands were shaking, told himself it was the cold and stepped back from the door as far as he could. If there were men on the special car's roof, they wouldn't stay up there forever. Thrusting his revolver into his waistband, bracing his hands and his butt against the railing, he smashed the sole of his right foot against the door handle leading into the support car, dodged right to the hinge side and ripped his revolver free.

The door crashed inward, just like in the movies. There was no gunfire. There was no response whatsoever from inside the car. Whoever was on the roof of Mr. Roosevelt's car might have seen the door being kicked open, but wouldn't have heard it above the constant click-clacking of the wheels over the rails. The train moved along level ground and was an express, traveling at more or less sixty miles per hour. The wind rush of their slipstream was an incessant roar.

Jack stepped inside, darting through the doorway to his right, his gun close at his side. He'd learned years ago that the classic movie and television water-witching pose where the good guy kept his pistol at arm's length was merely an invitation to being disarmed. He took the flashlight from the other side of his waistband and raised it over his head and to his left, then flicked it on for an instant.

He saw something he didn't want to see, had only partially suspected, the horrible images lost in the darkness again.

Getting his breathing steady, changing position slightly, Jack executed the routine with the flashlight once more.

What he had glimpsed a moment earlier was reality, not the product of an overactive imagination, nor had fantasy been the impetus to Ellen's alarm concerning noises heard on the roof.

Two dead corporals, one dead private, Mr. Roosevelt's male secretary, the Army captain—Rogers—whom Ellen had called "handsome." Their bodies lay strewn in the center aisle, except for Roosevelt's secretary. He was lying only halfway out of his seat. There were various wounds, but each man, regardless of other injuries, had a bullet hole in the forehead or temple or back of the neck.

They had been methodically executed after being taken out of action. Everywhere there were spent shell casings; Jack picked one up. Modern-looking 9mm Parabellum brass.

From the number of wounds to each body and the total absence of the sound of gunfire—that would have been heard—Jack guessed suppressor-fitted submachine guns had been used. H-Ks were the best from his time, and Lakewood Industries only acquired the best.

The handguns of the dead military personnel were in various stages of readiness, some half out of their holsters, some clutched in the dead hands of the men to whom they were issued. The .38 caliber cartridge these weapons fired was next to useless against someone who didn't care to fall down and die. He grabbed two of the revolvers anyway, stuffed them awkwardly down into his copious trouser pockets, pushing his holster back. The .32 ACP cartridge his Seecamp threw was a better manstopper than these puny .38s.

Jack hurried along the length of the car, reached the forward door, stepped to its side and cautiously opened it. No one stood between the passenger car and the coal car.

Holstering his special Colt and securing the hammer thong, Jack Naile bit his lower lip, made the sign of the cross and clambered onto the railing, grabbing hold of whatever he could as he held himself there and cautiously raised his head to the level of the support car's roof.

He tucked back down in the same instant.

Three men, submachine guns slung tightly to their bodies, were jumping from the special train car's roof and onto the roof of the support car.

"They figure everybody they have to worry about is dead," Jack told himself. They were wrong.

At the support car's almost exact center, there was some sort of large object; he'd caught only a glimpse of it.

A bomb?

Jack shivered, then ducked inside the support car, dropping into a low crouch behind the nearest seat. If the men entered the support car, they would do so from the rear doorway almost certainly, unless they were masochists. Otherwise, reentering the car was not in their cards. They would have no reason to revisit the dead they had left behind.

Doubtless, there was a fourth man who had taken out the army guard in the locomotive. The fate of the fireman might have been in doubt, but since most assassins didn't have much training in how to run a locomotive, the best and most obvious course of action would have been to keep the engineer alive in order to run the train, until his services were no longer required.

The three men Jack had spied on the roof of the train car carrying his wife, Ellen, and Teddy Roosevelt, would be in radio contact with the man left to guard the engineer. They could speak *en clair*, of course, because there was no one in 1900—except, perhaps, their compatriot Lakewood Industries personnel at the time-transfer base hundreds of miles away—who had any kind of radio at all. Guglielmo Marconi's British patent #7777 dated from this very year of 1900, and in 1901 he would first broadcast radio signals across the Atlantic Ocean; nobody but these guys had walkie-talkies just yet.

One of the semiworthless .38s in his left hand, the Colt Single Action Army in his right, Jack waited.

He only realized he'd been holding his breath when he exhaled as he heard footfalls on the roof, coming his way.

They were going to come down from the roof behind him, then signal their man with the engineer to stop the locomotive. There was likely some sort of transport ready for them, a Hummer, perhaps, or maybe Lakewood Industries had dared to send a helicopter into 1900. That meant a fifth man, possibly a sixth.

If the object of which he'd caught a fleeting glimpse was a bomb, its presence answered many questions. There were only two possible reasons why a bomb or bombs would be used against this train: Lakewood Industries wished to assassinate two members of the Naile family and didn't mind killing Teddy Roosevelt in the process or Lakewood Industries intended to kill Roosevelt and Jack and his wife were merely an unsuspected bonus. Could Lakewood Industries have tried out scenarios that would have predicted Teddy Roosevelt's involvement in an effort to counter their plans?

Jack shone his flashlight along the support car's length. There were three Krag-Jorgensen rifles immediately visible. Their .30-40 cartridge was effective. There was a Model 1897 Winchester pump twelve-gauge. That was better.

Holstering his Colt, Jack moved by flashlight toward the Winchester, picked it up and gently checked the chamber: empty. The magazine tube seemed full. He couldn't remember at the moment how many shells it held. The nearest dead man had more of the paper-hulled shells on his belt. Jack took four more and put them into his vest pockets.

He racked the slide; the hammer cocked. A fifth shell he fed into the magazine tube.

His flashlight out, he approached the still-open—this was the door he had smashed—entrance to the train car.

As these men either climbed down or jumped, he would kill them, then take a submachine gun—if he could—and do the same to the man riding with the engineer. Subsequent to that, if he carried off the task successfully, would be the matter of dealing with whoever manned the assassins' transportation, and possibly the transportation itself.

As a child, Jack had pictured the West as a place where men stood opposite one another on a dusty street and someone drew, and no matter who was first to slap leather, the good guy was always faster or at least fast enough. Occasionally, Richard Boone would sustain a shoulder wound; James Arness, outdrawn every week by Arvo Ojala, got off the accurate shot that won the day.

None of the cowboy/gunmen/lawmen heroes of his boyhood ever shot a man in the back—not John Wayne, Ward Bond, John Russell or Chuck Connors, never

William Boyd or Roy Rogers, nor Gene Autry or Clayton Moore or Jay Silverheels. The newer crop of good-guy Westerners never did that, either, from Yul Brynner and his six crusader/gunfighter associates to Tom Selleck's long-range marksman avenger.

Classic Western writers like Zane Gray and E. B. Mann and, years after them, Louis L'Amour, would never have, the hero gun a man from behind.

Reality was different.

This was kill or be killed, and he already had the beautiful girl to settle down with, and they'd done more than kiss and had the kids to prove it. But Jack Naile hadn't "gone West" with the intention of living a reality that someday might haunt his dreams; yet reality imparted little choice to its participants.

There was an oft-quoted line from the western films, about a man having to do what a man had to do.

If there were explosives mounted to one or both train-car roofs, they would be remotely detonated, which meant that, as soon as the assassins left the train, the train would be destroyed. Forensic science being in its literal infancy—the eyes of one of Jack the Ripper's victims had been examined to see if, photolike, they still held the last predeath image—any sort of futuristic detonating device would, if detected, never be understood, be relegated only to the status of some inexplicable crypto-scientific anomaly.

Philosophical/moralistic concerns aside, Jack took a reassuring glance at the raised hammer of the '97. His hands did not shake anymore, nor would they tonight. What he feared was that, someday, they might. He would cross the proverbial ethical bridge when it loomed before him; should it collapse beneath him, then would be the time to worry over whether or not he would swim or flounder in a dark river of guilt. Three men. They were the immediate situation with which he must deal.

He waited, hands dry and steady.

The men were coming. The first pair of combatbooted feet appeared on the observation railing immediately in front of him. Jack raised the shotgun to his shoulder. He had never liked firing a shotgun. Handgun recoil was something he handled better than most men, and the kick from a twelve-gauge was something he found most unpleasant. He reminded himself that the Winchester was loaded only with paper-hulled two-and-three-quarter-inch shells.

The first man clambered up onto the coal car as the second man's boots appeared on the railing. As the second man sprang from the platform to the coal car, the first man looked around, upward, toward the roof of the train car full of dead men.

The first man's eyes locked with Jack's eyes.

Jack triggered a round from the '97, firing into the left ribcage of the second man in the coal car, the one nearest to him. Dead before he fell, the second man sprawled forward into the muzzle of the first man's submachine gun. A spray of blood belched from a jagged lacing of wounds in the second man's back as the first man's submachine gun fired burst after burst.

The first man was trying to shoot his dead compatriot's body away from the muzzle of his gun.

Jack already had the Winchester's slide tromboned, the paper-hulled empty flying past his line of sight as he fired for the first man's head, the only target. The lower right side of the first man's face disintegrated, and Jack's stomach churned.

Automatic weapons fire stitched across the floor inches from Jack's feet, and he jumped back.

The third man, still on the train-car roof, was firing down at him blindly, the submachine gun bullets cutting a random, zigzagging pattern. Jack swung the '97 down from his shoulder as he cycled the pump, holding the trigger back.

A peculiarity of the '97 Winchester was that, with the trigger held back, as one worked the pump, the weapon would fire. Jack emptied the twelve-gauge into the car's ceiling, averting his eyes, feeling the sting as some of the pellets of buckshot that did not penetrate through the car's ceiling ricocheted against him.

The submachine gun fire stopped for only a second, but long enough for Jack to snatch the two nearly useless .38s from his pockets and fire them out into the ceiling, toward the rear of the car.

Hoping to bait the assassin on the train-car roof into thinking that his adversary within the train car was moving toward its rear, Jack Naile leaped through the doorway at the car's front, onto the platform, jumped from the platform onto the coal car, then clambered up into the damp, rocky mass that filled it. The nearest of the two dead men was the one Jack wanted, the one whose submachine gun was—presumably—fully loaded.

Jack glanced toward the roof of the following car. He caught a glimpse of the head of a man at the roofline's horizon.

The sling from the H-K MP-5 submachine gun was cinched tightly to the dead man's torso; there was no time to loosen it, to get the weapon free.

A knife was lashed to the dead man's web gear, inverted, the Kydex sheath bound with black electrical tape. Jack snapped the blade free of the sheath and raked its primary edge across the fabric sling of the submachine gun.

Good thing the guy was already dead, Jack thought; the knife would have inflicted a painful wound.

Jack tore the weapon free of the body and hit the Heckler & Koch's bolt handle with his left hand as he found the fire-control lever.

The bolt had been closed on a chambered round that flew past him; H-Ks were among the comparatively few submachine guns to fire from a closed bolt. But a fresh round chambered. Jack had fired an MP-5 submachine gun once before in his life; the weapon, like this one, had been fitted with a suppressor. But many of the characters in his novels used MP-5s, and Jack's knowledge of the weapon was detailed.

No time for the shoulder stock, Jack let himself sprawl onto his back in the coal bin, holding the weapon with both hands as he tripped the trigger. The man on the roof was standing, submachine gun to his shoulder. Jack, on the other hand, was using a technique often described as "spray and pray," pumping the automatic weapon's trigger as fast as he could, firing three-shot bursts, turreting the weapon's muzzle in some hope of contact with his target.

Bullets pelted into the coal around Jack, coal dust spraying his face and hands.

Jack's expropriated submachine gun was very suddenly

empty. A spare magazine was jungle-clipped beside the spent one. Mechanically, he started to make the change, knowing he wouldn't have the time before his adversary fired again and killed him.

But Jack's adversary, although he stood perfectly erect, weapon tucked to his shoulder, didn't fire.

Jack blinked.

The third assassin's body shuddered, collapsing into a heap, then falling away into the slipstream, swallowed by the darkness.

Jack breathed.

He seated the fresh spare magazine and got to his knees in the coal. He looked forward, toward the locomotive. A fourth member of the team, just as Jack had predicted, was clambering up from the locomotive cab, into the coal car.

Jack started to fire, but hesitated lest he strike the engineer, a mountain of a man swinging a wrench in an arc toward the fourth killer's head. Jack went flat in the coal, a single burst of gunfire, bullets whistling past his head.

No more gunfire.

Jack's submachine gun was on-line with where the fourth man had been. But the man wasn't there anymore.

The locomotive engineer was fumbling dangerously with the fourth man's submachine gun.

"Hey, man! Don't!" Jack shouted as loudly as he could.

Then the submachine gun began to spit lead and Jack dove for what cover there was in the coal pile.

CHAPTER
✸ NINETEEN ✸

The train was beginning to slow, which might be interpreted by the assassins' pickup unit as a signal to come in closer. Jack jumped from the coal car into the cab. The fourth assassin lay sprawled half inside the locomotive and half hanging down over the coupling. The fireman was dead, executed in an identical fashion to the military personnel and male secretary in the support car.

The engineer was bleeding profusely from his left thigh and seemed close to death, already unconscious. A closer inspection of the wound revealed that his left thigh was partially severed.

"Shit," Jack hissed through his chattering teeth. He was very cold, and the adrenaline rush was leaving him.

Scanning the cab's interior, he identified the lever-like throttle and began easing it forward. The train picked up speed again.

Turning his attention to the engineer, Jack resumed his

quick triage. In the light of his flashlight, the color of the blood looked awfully dark, meaning it was very likely arterial. Considering the enormity of the wound, regardless of the blood's color, the engineer might be dead in seconds.

Jack tore the bandanna from the engineer's neck, and patched it against the most obvious bloody hole. The bandanna was instantly saturated. Jack stripped off his own vest, bundled it firmly and pressed it over the bandanna. The bleeding seemed to slow. He added the engineer's cap to the compress. Jack released the lock on the clip that held the two submachine gun magazines in place, letting it clatter to the cab floor. Using the empty magazine and the remnants of the sling from the submachine gun, Jack started a tourniquet. The fourth assassin had a knife taped to his web gear, a Randall Model 1 by the looks of it. Jack cut the sling free of the submachine gun, tightened the tourniquet again. The engineer groaned in pain.

If he let go of the tourniquet, Jack knew, the engineer would surely die. If he stayed with the engineer, they would all die when the pickup team arrived.

There was a toolbox on the floor of the cab. Jack started to reach for it, hoping to use it as a wedge against the empty submachine gun magazine that controlled the tourniquet.

Jack thought he heard his name called.

He looked up. Teddy Roosevelt, suitcoat gone, white shirtsleeves smudged with coal dust, climbed down from the coal car.

"Barbarians! To kill men like that! Barbarians!"

"Yes, sir, except that's an insult to barbarians."

"I'm glad you were able to give them their just desserts,

Jack. What can I do, sir, to assist you and this injured man?"

"Hold this tourniquet in place while I get Ellen and our stuff. We've got to lose the special car and the support car. There are explosives mounted on the roof of each of those cars. They can be radio detonated at any time. Probably soon."

"Radio—like this, this Italian fellow, Macaroni?"

"Marconi, sir."

"Indeed. Marconi it is."

"Just like television, sir, but without pictures. His invention proved quite versatile and can, indeed, be used to remotely detonate certain types of explosives. Remember to hold on to the tourniquet while I get Ellen. You may need to find additional packing for the wound."

"These dead men seem to be members of some sort of military unit. They might be carrying field kits with bandages."

"Excellent idea, Mr. Roosevelt. I'll have a look." The nearest of the dead assassins, indeed, had an individual first-aid kit. Jack opened it, took out two field dressings and applied them over the packing. There was antiseptic, but in order to have it do any good, he'd have to reexpose the wound and hasten the blood loss. "I'll see what else I can find that might help."

And Jack was moving, climbing up into the coal car as rapidly as he could, crossing to the car's rear. He jumped, nearly twisting an ankle, but reached the platform at the front of the support car. Dodging the obstacle course of dead men and their weapons, Jack reached the rear of the car, crossed to the special and shouted, hoping Ellen would hear him and not shoot. "Ellen! It's me, Jack. I'm coming in."

Jack put his hand on the door handle and twisted, opened the door and went inside. Ellen was crouched behind the overstuffed chair with a Colt revolver aimed at his chest.

"Grab whatever you think Mr. Roosevelt would want out of here, and I'll get our stuff. Hurry, kid. This car and the one in front are going to blow up any minute." Somehow, Ellen had gotten into her dress, but he would have bet a million dollars she'd skipped the corset.

The engineer was dying. She hated talk of time-travel and its anomalies, but maybe this man's death was supposed to be, or maybe time was just healing itself. With his death, the only living man from 1900 in 1900 who knew of the reality of being able to travel in time was Teddy Roosevelt.

After getting her, their bags and a hastily packed suitcase and briefcase for Teddy Roosevelt ferried across the coal car, Jack had gone back to the coal car, stripping the dead assassins of their weapons, ammunition and anything else useful. There was, of course, no identification.

With a submachine gun slung tightly at his side, he'd climbed back across the coal car one last time, to slip the pin for the coupler connecting the train cars to the coal car.

There was a sudden lurching of the engine and coal car, and Ellen Naile realized that both of the two trailing cars—the support car and the special—were no longer attached, the locomotive's full force and speed unfettered.

As Jack finally climbed down from the coal car, he looked at her in the lamplight and smiled, holding up both hands.

Despite the dying engineer, his head on her lap, Ellen almost laughed, restraining herself—but barely—only out of respect for the man's life.

The reason she almost laughed out loud was the recollection of a story concerning Jack's paternal grand-father. Michael Naile, tippling when he shouldn't have been, had lost a finger slipping coupling pins into place on railroad cars, the finger inserted where the pin should have been. Ever after that, "Mick" Naile's lost finger was kept in a jar of formaldehyde on the mantle in his home. When Mick's wife, Margaret, would move the jar in order to dust, he'd swear that he knew the exact time that she did so, that somehow he was able to feel that severed digit. Jack's showing his hands after removing a coupling pin was his way of saying "Look, Ma! All ten fingers!"

Jack crouched to the floor of the engine, where he had piled the booty taken from the dead assassins. Teddy Roosevelt was stoking the boiler and driving the train. "The people Lakewood hired for this must have brought their own individual weapons. We've got one Glock 17, one SIG 228 and one SIG 226 as sidearms. Probably work internationally, with all the handguns being 9mms. We'll give Mr. Roosevelt the SIG 226 and one of the H-Ks; I'll hold on to the SIG 228 and we'll keep the Glock for emergencies." He stuffed the smaller of the two SIG pistols—the 228—into his waistband, dropping four spare magazines for the pistol into his front pants pockets.

"Time to give Mr. Roosevelt a crash course in use of the

SIG and a suppressor-fitted submachine gun." Jack stood up and glanced behind them. "Can't see the two cars we uncoupled." As he spoke, the air around Ellen seemed to pulse, and there was a roar so loud she could barely hear Jack exclaiming "Holy shit!"

Ellen rested the locomotive engineer's head on the carpetbag as she sprang to her feet so rapidly that her heel snagged in the hem of her dress. Jack caught her, and she was in his arms when she looked back along the tracks. "It's not nuclear, is it, Jack?" Ellen heard the desperation in her own voice as the mushroom-shaped fireball lit the night almost as brightly as a premature sunrise would have.

"No, kid. No. Just conventional. Probably semtex or an even more powerful kind of plastic explosive. But they sure used enough of it. Probably trashed the whole track under the train cars. We'll need to find the first place we can where we can wire news of the wreck before the next train trashes itself with no track under it and wreckage in front of it."

Ellen turned her head and looked at Teddy Roosevelt. The explosive fireball was reflected in his glasses, his face red-tinged, as was Jack's, where the coal dust had fallen away.

Ellen wondered if Roosevelt thought that he was having a vision of Hell, and Hell was the future.

As a little girl, if Ellen had ever pictured herself as a locomotive engineer, it was not under circumstances similar to those in which she found herself now. Her husband was showing Roosevelt all about how to use a submachine gun and an automatic pistol. It was half past five in the morning. The wind around the locomotive was very cold and numbed her. The feeble light positioned between the locomotive's smokestack and cowcatcher—a headlight—provided so little illumination that the train was clearly outrunning it; by the time she might spot something on the rails ahead, there would be no time to stop the train before smashing into whatever that object was.

Nor had she envisioned herself driving a locomotive after the real engineer had died in her arms fewer than five minutes earlier.

And, to make matters just peachy, she saw a bright light to the south—a light slowly but steadily increasing in size. "Jack! We've either got a UFO coming toward us or it's a helicopter. You hear me, Jack?"

"I hear you," Jack told her, suddenly beside her. "And, I almost hope it's a UFO."

"What do the letters U-F-O stand for, Mrs. Naile?" Teddy Roosevelt inquired of her.

Ellen looked at Jack, seeing his eyes in the lamplight. She couldn't read them, but he said, "May as well tell him. The phenomenon was reported in various ways down through the centuries."

"Mysterious lights in the sky," Ellen amplified, "flying objects which move in strange ways, aerial phenomena that are unidentified. They came/will come to be known as unidentified flying objects in about fifty years from now. Some people call them flying saucers."

"Is that light emanating from one of these flying saucers, then?"

"No, sir," Jack volunteered. "You're doubtless familiar with the scientific musings of Da Vinci. Do you recall his design for an aircraft or flying machine with rotating wings above its approximate center?"

"As a matter of fact, I do, Jack. Quite fanciful, but there was no power source by means of which it could be made to fly, even if such had been possible."

"You've identified the crux of the problem, Mr. Roosevelt," Jack agreed. "Until two bicycle mechanics will achieve the first powered flight in a little over three years from now."

"Americans, these bicycle mechanics?"

"Of course, sir," Ellen informed Teddy Roosevelt.

"Bully, Mrs. Naile! So, Jack, the power problem was solved—or will be—and the origin of that light—electrical, certainly—is from a flying machine similar to that posited by the great Leonardo."

"Yes, sir. When and where we come from," Jack told him, "they are called helicopters. Sometimes they are heavily armed for warfare. This might be such a gunship, but probably isn't. More likely there will be one, possibly two armed men aboard, along with the pilot."

"If we are attacked, as it appears may soon prove out, then I would assume the object in returning fire is to disable the flying craft in such a fashion that it is forced down."

"You've got the spirit of it, sir," Jack agreed.

Ellen suggested, "If time permits when they come into range, Jack can point out the chin bubble where the avionics might be disabled, and the tail rotor, which would force a controlled landing at the very least." In the books

Jack and she wrote, the good guys had shot down many an enemy helicopter in just such a way.

As for their vehicle, one string of gunfire, if it stitched across the locomotive's boiler, could cause the engine to lose steam pressure and gradually fail. Almost certainly, had Jack Naile known a great deal more about the operation of steam-powered locomotives, there were other dangers from such gunfire that might prove more abruptly catastrophic. There were times, he reflected, when ignorance was bliss.

Theodore Roosevelt working side by side with him, Jack had taken toolboxes, coal shovels and every other suitable metal object that might slow down or stop a bullet, forming a low wall behind Ellen as she crouched before the controls of the locomotive.

Roosevelt, sleeves rolled up past his elbows, eyeglasses freshly buffed with his handkerchief, an expression of enthusiastic determination set across his broad face, had the submachine gun's stock extended, the butt to his shoulder. "Good stock length for me, Jack. Will there be much recoil impulse when I touch off a round?"

"Barely noticeable, Mr. Roosevelt. And remember— very little noise, too. It's got a sound suppressor. And, don't forget to pump the trigger, sir, as I suggested. You don't want to fire out the entire magazine."

"I await your command to fire."

Jack felt embarrassed—a seasoned man like Theodore Roosevelt following his lead. Up until four years ago, Jack's only rip-snorting adventures were the ones he and Ellen made up for their books. Aside from a few animal pests he'd had to dispatch over the years, he'd never shot a living thing. Roosevelt was a seasoned man, had been all his life, choosing the adventurous path. Jack had merely fallen into circumstances beyond his control or imagining.

He could explain all that to Teddy Roosevelt, explain about a time loop that was the cause of all of this, but instead he called back to Mr. Roosevelt across the engine cab from him, "I'll tell you when, sir," and left it at that.

The helicopter was about two hundred yards off, its outline only partially visible in the predawn darkness, the spotlight emanating from the chopper the best and most logical first target. Jack was beginning to wish that he'd brought over one or two of the .30-40 Krag-Jorgensen military rifles from the support car. Unless the chopper got in well under a hundred yards, the submachine guns and pistols would be close to useless.

"I suggest shooting out their electric light, Jack!"

"My thought exactly, sir. We have to let the machine get very close before we open fire. Even a hundred yards is well beyond any practical range for the weapons we have available to us, firing from a moving platform as we are at a moving target. We don't want to just hit the helicopter, but to disable it. If they think we're their people and injured, we might have a chance of the helicopter getting in close enough that we can destroy it."

It was a slim chance, at best, but their only one.

The helicopter was about one hundred fifty yards off, coming in so slowly that a sprinter could have outdistanced it.

One hundred yards.

Jack tucked the butt of the H-K submachine gun tight

to his shoulder. His mouth was dry. He licked his lips. He blinked his right eye as he continued to watch the chopper over his sights.

"They're getting pretty damned close, Jack!" Ellen cautioned.

"I know. Keep down and pray."

"I think I see glass on the lower front of the flying machine. Is that the chin blossom?"

"Bubble, sir. Chin bubble. You concentrate on the light, Mr. Roosevelt, and then pour as much lead as you can through that chin bubble. When I tell you to, please."

"Of course."

The air around them was freezing cold, the darkness—except where the helicopter's light illumined—impenetrable. The distance was seventy-five yards, give or take, and Jack Naile was sorely tempted to open fire.

Instead, he waited.

Fifty yards.

"Hold your fire, Mr. Roosevelt. Hold!"

"Affirmative, Jack!"

Twenty-five yards with the H-Ks would be easy, even considering that their firing platform—the racing locomotive—was moving at about sixty miles per hour and rocked slightly to one side or the other.

The helicopter was at thirty yards, Jack crouched as deeply as he could into the compartment, Theodore Roosevelt doing the same. "Like a stalk, for an animal," Roosevelt observed.

"Yes, sir, but we're the ones being hunted," Jack responded.

The helicopter increased speed slightly, swinging in

toward the locomotive to afford its occupants a closer look. The searchlight began a sweep across the locomotive.

Jack raised up slightly, bringing the submachine gun to his shoulder once again.

"Now, Mr. Roosevelt! Let 'em have it!"

Jack's trigger finger pistoned, and the submachine gun nudged gently against his shoulder as about a half-dozen rounds fired. The helicopter's searchlight went out, shattering as the helicopter radically altered course.

Orange-yellow tongues of flame licked almost imperceptibly from the aircraft as bullets pinged along the roof and right side of the locomotive's cab.

"Keep down, Ellen!"

Theodore Roosevelt was still firing, and his accuracy was just as good as Jack's had been. Sparks were flying inside the chopper, near the pilot's controls. Roosevelt had hit the chin bubble, and some of his shots had apparently penetrated the avionics.

More automatic weapons fire came from the helicopter, more bullets ricocheting off the locomotive. Glass shattered behind Jack. Ellen shouted, "I'm all right!"

In the same instant, Jack turned his attention toward the helicopter's tail rotor. He used the submachine gun bullets like a chain saw, slicing with them, emptying the first magazine. Jack found the magazine release, not as quickly as one of the characters in their books would have.

The helicopter—for the first time, Jack realized what make and model: a Bell Long Ranger—was veering away, a strange glow from within the cockpit. Fire? Jack shouted to Teddy Roosevelt. "Shoot at the tail section,

Mr. Roosevelt! We're trying to sever any hydraulic and electrical connections. Use your weapon like a saw!"

"Indeed!"

The helicopter would be out of range in another second or two, Jack surmised. He was into his third burst from the H-K, Teddy Roosevelt also shooting at the same target. As Jack made to fire out his weapon, the helicopter's motion pattern abruptly changed. The machine began to spin under its main rotor, executing rapid three-hundred-sixty-degree turns as it started downward, a roaring sound growing in volume exponentially as the main rotor strained.

In a heartbeat, the aircraft was on the ground and engulfed in flame, a body hurtling out of the cockpit as the aviation fuel blew, the sound wave drowning all other noise.

A hellish tableau unfolded beside the locomotive, red-tinged yellow flame brilliantly illuminating the night. Chunks of debris clanged against the locomotive. Jack ducked down, shielded his face with his left forearm.

There was another, smaller explosion.

The locomotive rounded a bend of some sort and the helicopter was gone from sight. "Should we try, Jack, to see if anyone survived?" Theodore Roosevelt asked.

Jack looked at the man who would, unless history were forever altered, soon become president of the United States. "If this were one of our books, Mr. Roosevelt, I would have had you shout what's reportedly one of your favorite expressions when the aircraft went down. You know—'Bully!' But no, sir, neither man could have lived through that."

Jack stood up, his knees stiff. He hugged Ellen as she

stood. Roosevelt offered his hand, and Jack took it. "You're everything I thought you would be, sir, only better," Jack said honestly.

There was a faint glow in the darkness behind them. Some parts of the helicopter would still be burning. Jack lit a cigarette and said, "We'll need to recruit some people who can keep silent, Mr. Roosevelt. The explosions involving the two rail cars back there are one thing, but the helicopter wreckage is another matter entirely. We'll have to arrange for the wreckage to be gathered up discreetly and very thoroughly. We can't have helicopter parts from 1996 discovered to have existed in 1900."

Jack inhaled, watched the glowing tip of the cigarette in his fingers. His hands weren't shaking. He was absolutely amazed.

CHAPTER
✠ TWENTY ✠

The air was crisp and cool, twilight upon them, the night promising to be clear and cold. Theodore Roosevelt had expressed considerable interest in what he persisted in calling "torchlights," so much so that when Jack had handed him one of the rechargeable Maglites, Roosevelt had flipped it on and off as often as a child might have done. As they walked the by-now customary route to the observation position overlooking the time-transfer base, Roosevelt had twice commented, "I suppose it's not time to activate the torchlights yet."

Clarence, weary of Roosevelt's seemingly boundless enthusiasm for virtually everything, however inconsequential, hadn't answered him.

Turning to Clarence's uncle, Roosevelt declared, "You'll have to let me have a go at driving that excellent motorcar of yours, Jack!"

"Any time that you wish, Mr. Roosevelt," Jack responded.

"Bully, sir!"

Clarence was amazed. Here was his uncle, Jack, palling around with Teddy Roosevelt as if they'd been buddies all their lives. Clarence shook his head, ambled on a few steps and caught up with David. "So, Mr. Bigshot of the future, think this connection with the guy who's gonna be president pretty soon will prove useful to your business interests?"

David glanced over at him and shrugged, a gleam in his brown eyes. "Never can tell, Clarence. Never can tell. William Jennings Bryan has some interesting views, though."

"If your father liked the Democrat, you'd like the Republican, David."

David made no response.

The ground Clarence walked was, indeed, familiar in the extreme. While Jack and Ellen had been off finding Teddy Roosevelt, David and he had clambered up along this nonpath on a daily basis, monitoring the progress of the time-transfer base. When the helicopter had arrived, Clarence had seriously considered taking action, despite Jack's warning not to.

It would have been easy to cripple the machine while the main rotor blades were being positioned. But David had declared, "If we tip our hand, we could really fuck things up. We need to wait and see."

Clarence, despite the seventeen-year gap between their ages, took his cousin's judgment quite seriously in certain categories, interpersonal relations not among them. But when it came to logic—so long as the issue at hand did not involve David directly, either emotionally or financially—David could have passed for that fictional alien species noted for having arched eyebrows, pointed ears and green blood.

So they'd waited.

The helicopter took off eventually and vanished toward the eastern horizon.

The following day, a number of crates had arrived, but no more anachronistic aircraft.

Reaching the height of the trail—they would have to move crouched over the rest of the way, which played havoc with Clarence's back—Clarence found himself wondering what might be arriving from the future today. He didn't wish to find out.

There would, of course, be tanks by the time World War I would begin in 1914. Brave men on horseback would hurtle themselves against the great mechanical contrivances and die for their trouble. But there would not even be tanks such as what Jack saw at the time base until well after World War II.

These were not M1 Abrams tanks from the U.S. inventory, but their Soviet counterparts, acquired on the post–Cold War black market, red stars still intact. Had his reference books been handy—they were on microfiche at home—he could have detailed the exact model, armament and capabilities.

All Theodore Roosevelt said was, "My God!"

"In World War I, which is well over a decade away, Mr. Roosevelt, Imperial German military belt buckles will be inscribed *Got mit uns*."

"God can't be with them; He'll be with us. What are those things?"

"Steel-armored motorized battle vehicles with their own built-in artillery and automatic weapons capabilities, capable of rolling over almost-unimaginably rugged terrain, impervious to any weapon of the current epoch, short of maybe a couple of cases of dynamite at the right spot."

"Then, by God, we'll get dynamite!"

"Mr. Roosevelt, it won't be as simple as that." There were three tanks, more than enough to provide an ample firepower demonstration for Lakewood Industries' gleeful potential customers. There was another rumble as of thunder and a flash of electrical energy like lightning. The capacious cratelike affair that was the focal point of the time-transfer base shimmered. Its enormous door opened and, under its own power, out rolled an aircraft Jack had never known existed, a Soviet-marked version of the vertical takeoff/landing fighter plane concept, most commonly exemplified by the Harrier jump jet. There were far more sophisticated fighter aircraft to be had in the world of 1996, but nothing like such a machine in an era before the Wright Brothers had made their first powered flight.

"That's a jet engine-powered fighter plane, Mr. Roosevelt, which is capable of a vertical takeoff, then shifting the vectoring of its engines for conventional fixed-wing subsonic flight."

"If I understood only half of what you just said, Jack, we are witnessing something at once anomalous and deadly."

"Unlike the tanks, sir, an ordinary rifle bullet hitting in the right spot could incapacitate it, bring it down, however unlikely such a scenario might prove in actuality. You're quite right about the deadly part, Mr. Roosevelt."

Jack had to congratulate Lakewood Industries for its foresight. What technology Lakewood planned to "share" with its customers was not state-of-the-art for the objective future, but equipment and ordnance that could be easily acquired if one knew the right people who knew where to look, comparative bargains on the international arms market. Jack found himself wondering how Lakewood Industries would handle getting a decommissioned Soviet nuclear submarine into the subjective past . . . .

David watched in silence, hearing the occasional murmurings of his father and his father's hero, Teddy Roosevelt.

Lakewood had irretrievably altered the course of human history. Stupid cowboy-style firearms would be no match for what David witnessed appearing at the time-transfer base. Whoever controlled such technology in the year 1900 would effortlessly master the entire world. No army, however mighty and numerous, could stand against such tanks and even one such aircraft.

The sound of thunder, the flashing of light from electrical energy, the shimmering effect, as if the great metal box that existed in two times simultaneously were shifting in and out of reality—and the door opened and another of the fighter planes emerged.

David told Clarence, crouched beside him, "This is kind of like they used to say at the end of those dumb 1950s sci-fi movies Dad likes. It's 'the beginning of the end.'"

"That Bethany Kaminsky bitch is out of her mind."

"She's brilliant. She'll rule her past and her present

simultaneously and control the direction of the future. She'll be the only person ever to rule the entire world."

His dad was suddenly beside him, had obviously heard him. "Go slow, son. She hasn't won yet."

"Are you nuts, Dad? What's going to stop shit like this in 1900, huh? Going to shoot it with that .45-70 rifle of yours? What's Roosevelt going to do? Charge up some fucking hill and get it?"

"You remember more history than you credit yourself with, Davey. San Juan Hill. Just remember. He and a bunch of wildass guys charged the Spanish guns and won. That's the same spirit that defeated Lord Cornwallis, burned inside Bowie and Travis to hold the Alamo until Sam Houston's army was ready to fight at San Jacinto, raised the flag at Iwo Jima. No, it's not 'the beginning of the end,' son—it's just another tough battle that Americans are going to win, somehow."

"It's that 'somehow' part, Dad, that kind of gets in the way, doesn't it? You believe in UFOs. What if UFOs landed in fucking Washington right now—what used to be now—in 1996? What the hell do you think all that gung-ho patriotic crap would do against a damn laser weapon or some shit like that?

"Nothing! That's what. This isn't some damn movie or one of your's and mom's adventure novels. You and Teddy Roosevelt and all of us aren't going to do squat to stop real tanks and real fighter planes. No cool guy in a tuxedo with a Walther PPK is going to pop up and stop them. No guy with a tacky looking leather jacket and bullwhip is gonna be doing it, either. No. Sure, we'll all fight, and we'll all be dead or worse. But don't lie to yourself and tell yourself we're pulling this one out of the fire, because we're fucked.

"Those red stars on the tanks and the planes mean they're Russian junk," David continued, "shit they sold after that guy with the spot on his head—"

"Gorbachev," his father supplied.

"Yeah. Him. After he said Communism was shit-canned. You know how much of that stuff is probably right there for Lakewood Industries to buy—and dirt cheap? Just by bringing it here, they've changed everything. Everything! Who are those two guys?"

"What two guys?" Jack asked, looking around.

"No! Those two guys," David insisted, "who invented flying."

"Wilbur and Orville Wright," his father whispered.

"You can't really be worrying about Teddy Roosevelt overhearing you! Shit, Dad, the future is here! By the time we hit 1996, if Lakewood Industries doesn't bring a fucking atomic bomb back here to sell, this technology will be junk. Like the stupid powered kite those Wright Brothers guys flew!"

For some reason David didn't understand, except for the fact that his father was overly emotional at times, his father hugged him and said absolutely nothing at all.

They kept their horses to a brisk trot, the gloom that had overtaken their thoughts deeper and darker by far than the nearly starless night surrounding them. Jack cupped his hands around the match he struck on the pommel of his saddle, the flickering yellow flame brilliant against the blackness through which they rode. He lit a cigarette, one of fewer than two hundred filterless Camels he had left; in some ways, they were his last personal connection to the world of the future that he had left behind.

Each of Jack's companions seemed more silent than the other, lost in the implications of what they had witnessed. To Theodore Roosevelt's credit, the man was determined that—somehow—Lakewood Industries would be stopped, that America would remain *undaunted* in the face of such dauntingly sophisticated military technology to be sold to the highest bidder.

But it was David's remarks that gave Jack pause. Sometimes the obvious conclusion could be missed. Everyone but David—including Kaminsky and her Lakewood Industries cohorts—had missed it. "It" was the inverse of the paradox that had so confounded Da Vinci with his primitive design for a helicopter, and men before him and since. The engineering to support the idea was present, but the technology with which to bring the idea to fruition was not. Once Lakewood Industries transferred future technology into the hands of engineers from 1900, that technology would be scrutinized, analyzed, duplicated, enhanced.

The past would not be static, nor would the future.

Kaminsky would wake up some morning a few years into her future, and the fighter airplanes and the tanks and the small arms would all be different, far more advanced than they had been. But she'd almost certainly never become aware of the fact. The past she altered would have changed the future without her knowing it, despite what subjective materials she left in the past to remind her of what had been. One day, all elements would come together so that everything had changed. The demands from her customers in the past would become greater, and she would supply last decade's technology to the past, and again everything would change. Within a century's time, military technology would have reached a level that, without her meddling with the past, it would not have attained for hundreds of years or more into the future.

And this arms race would never abate.

The once-innocuous time loop into which the Naile family had somehow been drawn would have become the engine for humankind's eventual destruction. And one day, Bethany Kaminsky and the billions of other people in her world would never wake up at all. The explanation was simple and would prove inconsequential in the greater scheme of things. Perhaps Russian atomic submarines, unaffected by the "divine wind" in the Straits of Tsushima, used nuclear missiles to destroy Japan and win the Russo-Japanese War of 1905. Or Imperial Germany nuked Paris in 1914.

Certainly, if the world survived into the era of Stalin and Hitler, when dictators pursued a genocidal path unmatched for ruthlessness of scale since the dawn of time itself, everything would inevitably end, because such men would not have hesitated to "push the button," and Bethany Kaminsky would have given them that button to push. And she would never be born, but the reality her lust for money and power had created would still be reality. More headache-inducing time paradoxes.

Such might be the way in which time would lick its

wounds, heal itself. Jack Naile was born in 1946, his wife in 1948. If mankind ceased to exist before he and his wife were born, then he and Ellen and the children could not travel back into time, be followed by Clarence. In that way, some might think, the technology of the future would never be transferred into the past, and the "kill your grandfather" paradox would come into play, after a fashion, and humanity might never be destroyed. Yet somewhere in the subjective middle of the paradox, billions of lives would have been extinguished or never come into being. And no one would ever conjecture that so many hopes and dreams and imaginings had vanished forever from reality.

And no one would have learned from the experience. Even if someone could, there would be no one left to learn. Hitler or Stalin or some other maniacal butcher would end all life on Earth, if for nothing else than spite and because it could be done.

Was that why true time-travel, although theoretically possible into the past, had not yet been mastered? The fluke of their transferring from one epoch to another was merely that. But was the inscrutable nature of venturing into the past some sort of divine or natural safety valve for mankind? Was true time-travel something so fraught with inescapable peril that mankind should never conquer it?

Jack reined back on his horse. After a second or so, the others reined in as well. Jack stared at the glowing tip of his cigarette for a beat longer, then crushed the cigarette against his boot heel as he crossed his left leg over the saddle. Smoke exhaling through his nostrils and mouth as he spoke, Jack said, "Gentlemen, we are at a crossroads in human history, as we are all well aware. What we are able to accomplish within the next few dozen hours will determine the fate of mankind forever. That is obvious to us all. Rather than concentrating our efforts on keeping secret what is now transpiring at the risk of its successful accomplishment, we must throw caution to the winds, galvanize whatever assets we can, damn the consequences and pray to God for the best outcome. How many troops can you muster to Nevada, Mr. Roosevelt, if you notify President McKinley of the exact nature of the crisis?"

"Within twelve hours' time, sir, I can field five thousand to six thousand men with light equipment, some heavy artillery, etcetera, and then whatever travel time should be required to reach the battle site."

"Clarence. With your background in military electronics, and everything we can possibly steal from Lakewood's time-transfer base, do you think you could rig up the means by which to track their surface vehicles—the tanks—so that we can pinpoint the location of their intended firepower demonstration?"

"Probably. If we can find or rig some balloons for high altitude aerial observation or get one of those jump jets into the air under our control. But, remember, once we hit the time-transfer base, they'll radio their people and alert them."

"I can deal with that. David. Can you liaise with Mr. Roosevelt? We'll need a half-dozen men who can be trained so well on late-twentieth-century small arms that they can duplicate that training as required, when and if additional weapons become available."

"We're going to equip a commando force. What are we sending them against, Dad?" David asked.

"If Mr. Roosevelt is willing to risk it, I'll want those six men—well-equipped and ready to die if it comes to that—to accompany me, and Alan also, into 1996. We'll attempt to destroy Lakewood's abilities to time-transfer. If we succeed, Alan will stay behind in 1996 and fuck with Lakewood's technology after we are returned to 1900. Then, win or lose at the site of the firepower demonstration, Kaminsky's people and equipment will be trapped here in their objective past. Their fighter aircraft will run out of jet fuel and their tanks will run out of diesel. They'll run out of ammo for their weapons. Eventually. However long it takes or hard it is, their supply lines will have been cut and they'll lose."

Jack lit another of his precious cigarettes. "And, Mr. Roosevelt, you should find it advisable to destroy all the equipment from the future. And you may find it advisable, after this is over and if we win, to quietly, clandestinely, get Mr. McKinley to order that all of us—and, I mean all of us, men and women—should be terminated. But, sir, should the government find such a course of action to be in the nation's best interests, be advised that anyone who comes after my family should be prepared to die as long as I have sufficient breath in my body to enable me to pull a trigger. You may want to mention that to Mr. McKinley, as well, sir.

"And now," Jack said, raising his voice, putting a smile on his face that would not be seen in the all-consuming darkness, "I suggest that we might be making a small contribution to linguistic history tonight. We may actually be coining a phrase to become closely associated with the automobile: 'Don't spare the horses.' Let's ride, gentlemen."

And Jack dug his heels into his horse's flanks, bent low over its neck and rode as if the very Devil were chasing him. But, instead, he pursued a demon of destruction, and it was far more threatening.

There were several motor homes at the time-transfer base, of varying degrees of luxury. Bethany's, of course, was the most luxurious. It had been time-transferred into the past for her use and would remain in 1900 to accommodate her needs when necessity demanded business trips between the two epochs.

Within the heavily customized motor home—well-furnished with every modern convenience, well-stocked with life's everyday luxuries, spacious with "bump-outs" on both sides—there were two particularly large walk-in closets, each filled almost to overflowing with period costumes. As a woman in 1900, if she wore her usual business attire from 1996—slacks, short skirts, etc.—she would be seen as a freak. Calling one of her political contacts in Hollywood—they'd met at a fundraiser for the seated President—she'd gotten him to do up a full wardrobe for her, his promptness not unexpected when she'd added that she didn't give a damn what it cost, so long as everything was beautiful, fit perfectly and was in her hands within a matter of days. She'd e-mailed him all the measurements he'd requested, and his greed had seen to the scheduling details.

It was no wonder to her that women had not progressed farther in business or politics by 1900; it took too damned long to get dressed to do anything. There was layer upon layer of undergarments. She'd worn corsets, but not like these and only for fun with some guy who got turned on by the sight of one.

Bethany twirled in front of one of the sets of mirrored closet doors. Yes, she looked beautiful, but the novelty of costuming herself for some goofy masquerade would wear thin very quickly. Gathering her voluminous skirts, she exited the motor home, knowing that she was not only stepping into the greatest business deal in human history, but one that would secure her standing as the most powerful person—male or female—of all time.

Using the store in Atlas because of its proximity to the telegraph line, and taking young Bobby Lorkin partially into their confidence, they established a base of operations. Bobby would race off to the telegraph office with a flurry of wires from Mr. Roosevelt, only to come running back with a flurry of responses not long afterward. The first return telegraph was from President McKinley:

> "Governor Roosevelt STOP If I did not trust your senses, sir, I would think this madness STOP Wreckage of flying machine recovered and hidden STOP Track restored STOP I have no choice but to believe situation as dire as described STOP Full support to your efforts at your disposal STOP Second Platoon Company B Seventh Cavalry under command of Lieutenant Easley arrives Atlas approximately midnight tonight STOP Reinforcements await your discretion STOP McKinley"

❅ ❅ ❅

David, upon hearing Teddy Roosevelt's reading of the wire, announced, "They were the guys with Custer, weren't they, the ones who were so successful against the Indians?"

Roosevelt had cleared his throat, ignored David's sarcasm and dictated a response to Bobby. Slapping his hat over his reddish-blond curls, Bobby took off like a shot, running back to the telegraph office.

"We'll need fresh remounts for this Lieutenant Easley's troopers," Roosevelt declared, then set about writing more wires.

Clarence enlisted the aid of Atlas's two deputy city marshals in finding the horses that would be needed for the arriving Second Platoon B Company of the Seventh, while Ellen recruited the deputy marshals' wives to get some of the other townswomen to have copious amounts of hot food and hot coffee prepared for the soldiers' anticipated midnight arrival.

By seven p.m., Theodore Roosevelt was seated on a stool at the head of the store's long main counter, Jack, Ellen, David, Lizzie and Clarence flanking him. All was, Jack hoped, in readiness for the first stage of their operation. "It seems readily apparent," Roosevelt began, picking up a mug of steaming black coffee, "that the key to this venture's hoped for success comes in three parts. First, we must seize control of what you all refer to as the time-transfer base, after that locating precisely where the weapons demonstration for the various foreign-legation members will take place. Lastly, we must utilize the time-transfer device or system or whatever the blazes it is in order to go into the future." At that, Roosevelt shook his head, removing his glasses as he did so and covering his face with his other hand. Without looking at anyone, Roosevelt inquired, "Where might they plan to hold this showing of their wares? Are there any ideas?"

"They'll want someplace really deserted," Clarence volunteered. "I've seen firepower demonstrations when I was in the Air Force."

"Air Force?" Roosevelt repeated, looking up.

"It started out as part of the Army, but after World War Two—"

"Clarence!" Jack cautioned his nephew. "Future history, remember?"

"Yeah, right. Anyway, the Air Force is like the Army, but uses airplanes more than the Army does." Clarence looked at Jack. "Okay?"

Jack shrugged, and Clarence continued. "Anyway, what was I saying?"

"About firepower demonstrations," David supplied.

"Right. Firepower demonstrations are extremely, extremely noisy. Anyone within any reasonable distance— miles in open flatlands—would be able to hear what was going on. And the airplanes will be visible from great distances away if they take any altitude, which they probably will in order to dramatize the effect of swooping in on a target. The explosions from their missiles will be another consideration."

"Missiles?" Mr. Roosevelt asked.

Clarence looked at Jack. Jack told Theodore Roosevelt, "They're rockets, maybe a few feet long, not that different from what you might see on the Fourth of July or what has been used in various wars throughout recent history.

Except they're sturdier, fly very fast, can travel great distances and strike targets with great accuracy. And the forward portion of the missile has some sort of warhead, containing sophisticated conventional explosives. There are other, worse things the warheads can contain. Hopefully, not even Lakewood Industries would contemplate loosing any of that stuff in an era before antibiotics."

"Thank you for creeping us out, Jack," Ellen declared.

Jack noticed the worried eyes below Mr. Roosevelt's tightly knit brow. Before Jack could speak, Ellen told Teddy Roosevelt, "In our time, some unscrupulous people have devised ways in which to kill or disable enemy combatants or civilians with chemicals and with diseases. Such substances can be placed in the warheads of the missiles Jack and Clarence spoke about. But if Lakewood released such chemicals or diseases in this time period, before modern medicine developed to the point of being able to counteract or defeat such substances, the death rate would be beyond comprehension."

Jack suddenly shivered, an involuntary paroxysm, the thought striking him that perhaps all of their efforts were in vain, that this had happened before and the "good guys" had lost. Had/would the influenza epidemic which followed/would follow World War One been/be the work of Lakewood Industries? Jack shook off the notion as best he could. There had been/would be millions of deaths. He lit a cigarette.

"In the future," Jack began, picking up the thread of Roosevelt's earlier question, "the United States government selected extremely remote locations for top-secret projects. Nevada—south, out in the desert—was a favorite spot. The Lakewood people will think along the same lines, be conditioned to remote areas of Nevada or New Mexico for something like this. And New Mexico is just a lot greater distance than they need to travel by ground, and offers more potential for inadvertent discovery. They'll probably take their dog and pony show south of here, into the desert. There's a possible location I'll show you on the map. It's about eighty miles north of a little Nevada town that may not even exist yet."

"One question for you, sir, before any of that, for you or for any of you. Clarence mentioned World War Two. There has yet to be any World War in the modern age, encompassing the modern world." Theodore Roosevelt looked at once saddened and resolute, doubtlessly in anticipation of the answer he would be given.

Jack let out a long breath, realizing that it sounded like a sigh; perhaps it was. "I can't tell you, sir."

"Is it, somehow, with Russia? Is that behind the references to the origin of these tanks and aeroplanes? Were these seized from some future world battlefield?"

"I can tell you that, sir," Jack offered. "As far ahead in the future as is our origin, open warfare between the United States and Russia was/will be successfully avoided. As to the other thing, suffice it to say that, in the end of both World Wars to come, the forces of democracy, the forces of good, the forces of human decency largely triumphed. But of course, what transpires in these next hours might change all of that, which is why we can't let it happen."

"You would have made a fine politician, Jack, with answers like that; but, I suppose they'll have to do."

"Yes, sir, I suppose they will," Jack agreed . . .

As in so many films, as the Seventh rode in a column of twos down the main street of Atlas, Nevada, there was the thrumming of hooves, the rattling of spurs and the creaking of tack. Clarence could almost imagine hearing the strains of "Gary Owen." As the officer in command dismounted, there was the creak of leather. And, as if somehow the youngish lieutenant—one bar, only—had seen those classic films, he saluted Governor Roosevelt, then Jack, then saluted Ellen and made a curt bow. "Second Platoon, Company B, Seventh United States Cavalry reporting as ordered, Colonel Roosevelt. Allow me to present myself, sir, and to you, ma'am, as well. I am Second Lieutenant Warren P. Easley. Is there someplace where the horses might be taken to be fed and watered and my men might take a well-deserved respite?"

Roosevelt answered. "There's a large corral down the street by the livery stable. Fresh remounts are awaiting you there. This lovely lady, in conjunction with the women of the town, has organized a fine repast for you and your men. Then, I'm afraid, in order to take advantage of the darkness, as our Indian friends might, it will be necessary to remount and be on our way in comparatively short order." Roosevelt drew his watch from the pocket of his vest. "Will forty-five minutes be adequate to your needs, Lieutenant?"

"Most adequate, Colonel Roosevelt. And, now, sir, if you will excuse me, I must see to certain matters concerning my troop." Again Lieutenant Easley saluted, bowed slightly to Ellen, then began issuing orders to his appropriately grizzled-looking platoon sergeant, the man looking for all the world like a central-casting version of a youthful Victor McLaglen as he had appeared in *Gunga Din*.

All the while, Clarence Jones had been noting the near-perfect shine on the lieutenant's boots under the thin coating of yellow trail dust, the gleaming buckle of the shavetail's pistol belt. Clarence found himself smiling. When he'd stood inspection in the Air Force in various bases stateside and overseas, never quite having mastered the aura of spit and polish, he'd more than once been accused of shining his shoes with a Hershey bar and a brick.

To a man, despite the trail dust, the troopers under Lieutenant Easley's command had the look of the proud professional. Just looking at Second Platoon, Company B of the Seventh was almost enough to make a man enlist— almost . . .

Six blue-shirted, khaki-trousered, campaign-hatted men stood awkwardly at ease beside the lamplit main counter of "Jack Naile—General Merchandise" while Theodore Roosevelt, changed into sturdy faded-brown trail clothes, outlined what, in fact, they had volunteered for. "I spoke with your Lieutenant Easley. More to the point, I spoke with Sergeant Goldberg. I wanted the best men Second Platoon, B Company of the Seventh had to offer. Supposedly, you men are it.

"So I'll get right to the point with no more shilly-shallying around." In the reddish-yellow glow of the oil lamps, there seemed almost a demonic determination in Roosevelt's hard-fixed eyes behind the omni-present spectacles. "You will see and hear and do things tonight which you must never reveal to anyone besides those of us in this room, and the President of the United States, of course. This is, perhaps, the most secret mission, as well as the most important, in the brief history of these United States. Should it fail, gentlemen, there might well be no United States. I don't have to ask if I make myself clear.

"Therefore, pay close attention to Mr. Naile, this gentleman standing beside me whom you have all met."

Jack, feeling somewhat awkward as a civilian telling six seasoned soldiers their duty, suppressed that feeling as well as he could. Clearing his throat once, he sat down on one of the stools and said nothing for a moment, looking each man eye-to-eye in turn. Then, from the counter beside him, he whisked away the saddle blanket covering one of the submachine guns. "This is called a Heckler & Koch MP-5 SD-3. It is a submachine gun, meaning that it is a pistol caliber weapon capable of multiple shots with one pull of the trigger. This particular firearm magazines thirty rounds between reloadings. It hasn't been invented yet, of course, and won't be for many decades to come. It is from the future. That's where I'm from, as well as my wife, Ellen," and Jack gestured toward her, "my son, David—the dapper-looking young guy over there—and my nephew, Clarence—that tall gentleman with the drooping mustache—and some others, as well—my daughter, Elizabeth, Clarence's wife, Peggy—both of whom helped with getting you fellows fed—and one man in particular, that fellow who just joined us." Jack pointed to Alan. Rather than trying to explain that Alan was, however unlikely, his great-great-grandson, Jack simply said, "He's also a close relative.

"We will have a mission unlike any other, gentlemen. It is simply this. After Second Platoon, B Company of the Seventh successfully overcomes a heavily armed force with superior weapons such as this submachine gun and things well beyond its capabilities, the six of you will accompany Alan and me. And, of course, albeit Colonel Roosevelt had wished to be in on any action we might encounter, I was able to prevail upon him to stay behind as the operation's overall commander.

"You six gentlemen will accompany Alan and myself into the future. It's quite safe, the process of traveling from here to there. Once we get there we'll have our work cut out for us." Jack lit a cigarette and said something he'd always wanted to say ever since he'd seen his first war movie. "Smoke 'em if you got 'em."

Exhaling smoke through his nostrils, Jack continued. "There will be an indeterminate number of hostile personnel at our arrival point in the future. They will be well-armed, but by that time so will you, trained as well as we can manage in a matter of hours rather than weeks in the use of these sophisticated weapons. The sole purpose of our mission is to get Alan access to certain pieces of equipment—machinery, if you will. In order to do this, we must kill everyone at the arrival point. Everyone. No prisoners, no woundings. Just death. Then Alan will operate the machinery that will return us to this time, to our present. We will bring with us a few items, if they are available. Alan will then destroy the machinery so that it can never be used again.

"As time goes by," Jack said, realizing the irony of his words only as he spoke them, "the six of you will learn why we are doing this. You'll be risking your lives, so you have that right. If any one of you wishes to back out, now is the time. Once you've touched one of these weapons—" Jack hefted the H&K MP-5 submachine gun again—"begun to learn why this mission is of such grave importance to the Republic and to the world, there will be no backing out. I'll add that no one will think the less of you should you choose to decline this mission. Unlike a lot of things in the Army, this genuinely is for real volunteers."

Second Platoon, Company B of the Seventh had volunteered as if one single organism when the call went out while they ate their dinner. These six—Jensen, Armitage, Goldstein, Harek, Luciano and Standing Bear— were decreed the best qualified. Jensen—short legs, thick chest and stocky build—was both the regimental boxing champion, with the semi-toothless grin to prove it, and, as his stature indicated to the experienced eye, the perfect human firing platform, he was the best rifleman in B Company. Armitage, Goldstein, Harek (his Turkish-origin name somewhat badly Anglicized) and Luciano were all standup troopers. Standing Bear was a full-blooded Cheyenne, his father and grandfather among the men who had handed the Seventh Cavalry one of the Army's worst defeats twenty-four years earlier at the Little Big Horn.

None of the six moved to leave.

CHAPTER
✸ TWENTY-ONE ✸

Teddy Roosevelt was trapped by his responsibility as the mission commander, marshalling men and materiel for the anticipated assault on the firepower demonstration Jack had guessed might be held near Groom Lake, the part of Nevada that would become known as Area 51. Superfluously, Roosevelt had said, "I wish I were going with you."

The Seventh had moved out, ridden until mid-morning, stopped to rest and feed their animals, then ridden on, minus its six volunteers, Jack and the six men staying behind. David, Clarence, Alan and Ellen rode with Lieutenant Easley's troop, guiding them toward the time-transfer base.

A picket line was set out for the mounts Jack and the six volunteers had ridden and the spare mounts that would allow them to catch up with the others; all fourteen of the animals were hobbled, lest the unfamiliar mechanical noises of the submachine guns spooked them.

The quick course in the HK MP-5 submachine gun commenced.

With the six men seated in a semicircle on their ground cloths, Jack covered operational characteristics first. "The MP-5 is a radically improved version of the basic concept of a submachine gun, meaning a weapon which fires multiple rounds with one single pull of the trigger and is chambered for a handgun round rather than a rifle cartridge. It's a delayed blowback, meaning that the gas which is generated when the cartridge is fired is used to push the bolt back. This action expels the empty brass remaining from the bullet being fired and introduces a new round into the chamber from the box magazine as the bolt comes forward." Jack held up the magazine. "The HK system incorporates a delay, brought about by a two-section bolt utilizing rollers. What all this means is that the gun works reliably, fires fast until you run out of ammunition in the magazine and is accurate in the extreme. The accuracy is in part due to the fact that, unlike most submachine guns, the MP-5 fires from a closed bolt, something you guys can parallel to the idea of the breech being closed on the old trapdoor Springfield rifles. If the breech had to close as the hammer fell, that added force would inhibit accurate shot placement.

"We will have a goodly supply of ammunition soon, we hope, when we capture the Lakewood base in this time, but for now we have scavenged all of the 9mm Parabellum ammunition from the bodies of the men to whom these weapons belonged, in order to feed these four submachine guns. I will have one of these weapons, the remaining three going to three of you. Soon all six of you will have ones like these.

"This particular variant is the SD model, meaning it has an integral sound suppressor. When you fire the weapon, most of the noise of the cartridge will be swallowed up. You don't have to worry about that. Only the mechanical noises from operation will remain, for the most part. The empty cartridge cases will be spit out. These particular models do not have what is called a burst control, meaning that they can only be fired full-automatic and semiautomatic, which means that a single shot only is fired with each pull of the trigger. This magazine holds thirty rounds. After all thirty rounds have been fired, you'll have to change magazines in order to continue making the weapon go bang!"

His previously stonily silent students laughed, the first reaction he had from them. He'd have to remember to use the word *bang* often.

Jack progressed to field-stripping, clearing stoppages and operation of the fire selector, warning the men, "Until you become proficient with these weapons, I want you to consider that there are only two positions on this lever, not three. When you're not going to be shooting for a while, put the weapon aside or must accomplish some particularly difficult physical activity, set it on safe. When you're using the weapon, keep it in the position for semiauto."

A check to his leather-cased Rolex showed him that he had about another fifteen minutes he could use before it would be imperative to get the men mounted. Jack started with Jensen, the boxer and marksman.

In all, there were twelve magazines for the submachine

guns, and, by using the pistol ammo, he'd been able to have all twelve magazines fully loaded.

It would be prudent to expend only thirty rounds on familiarization-firing, a woefully insufficient amount under the circumstances . . . .

Jack led the six volunteers into the mountains. Each man led his spare horse, keeping their animals at an easy gallop. Jensen, Luciano and Standing Bear had won the toss with the submachine guns. Each man had three magazines, plus a few loose rounds. Additional weapons and ammunition would have to be scavenged from the bodies of the men at the time-transfer base. Hopefully, they had a lot of it.

Timing would be a total crapshoot, yet its criticality inestimable. The fate of humanity, as it likely had before and would again, hung on sheer guesswork. Logic dictated that Kaminsky or her chief henchmen would not care to drag a modern motor home across a good hundred fifty miles of some of the roughest terrain to be found in North America. Nor would people comfortably used to central heat and air, running water and the like go out of the way to travel so well beyond the reach of the amenities they'd gone to such trouble to bring back to this time.

Therefore, Jack hoped, the grunts with the tanks and armored personnel carriers and Humvees and old Jeeps and anything else would set out for the site of the fire-power demonstration before the big shots did. The big shots most likely would not travel by VSTOL jet, but by helicopter.

The aircraft were the crucial element in the equation.

If they were on the ground, victory was possible; if they were airborne, or got that way, the battle and mankind's future was likely lost.

Judicious use of the remounts allowed Jack and the six volunteers to overtake Lieutenant Easley's column at almost exactly the same time that it reached the dismount point, before beginning the forced march to the time-transfer base.

Ellen, hatless as usual, one hand resting on the butt of one of her sixguns, walked forward. "You guys were pretty good in the timing department, Jack."

"Sheer skill at horsemanship," Jack responded, smiling as he dismounted and handed off the reins of his horse to one of the volunteers.

There was no fire; there were no torches. The only light was that of the nearly full moon, low on the western horizon. But it was enough, the night sky otherwise clear. Jack Naile took his wife into his arms. "I don't suppose you'd wait here with the men Easley will leave behind to watch the horses and equipment."

"You 'don't suppose' correctly. I'll be fine. I'll stick with you." Ellen patted his cheek, then leaned up and kissed his lips lightly. "Are your volunteers ready for the mission?"

"As ready as they can be to go ninety-six years into the future on a murder raid against a heavily armed force of killers with vastly superior firepower. Sure, they're ready. You are aware of the fact that you're not coming with us there? Right? Please?"

"I've thought about that a lot. Sure, somebody has to keep things organized here. But it can be somebody else.

Just don't let anything happen to that time-transfer junk so we don't make the kids orphans just yet. I don't want you trapped there and I'm trapped here. So, I'm going. Whatever or wherever happens, it's going to happen to us both."

Jack couldn't argue with that. All of their lives, since their marriage, they had done everything possible to always be together. He'd never actually counted, but a rough guess was that they'd spent perhaps as few as twelve nights apart from each other, certainly no more than twenty. For one of them to be somehow alive in the future and one alive in the past wouldn't be living at all.

"You stick beside me like glue unless I tell you otherwise. Got it?" Jack demanded.

Ellen took a half step back and feigned a salute. "Got it."

"Let me show you how one of these MP-5 subguns works, kiddo," Jack began.

Staying just outside the perimeter alarms, Jack wished he had night-vision optics. Standard binoculars had to do. What he saw as he scanned Lakewood's time-transfer base below him was unmistakable, regardless of the less than perfect lighting.

Perhaps realizing that an attack on the time-transfer base might be imminent, someone had installed something new. "Dad, those weren't here when Clarence and I were up here last."

"I figured you would have mentioned them, David."

Jack had never seen anything like the objects of his attention. They were smallish-looking guns, each mounted with a double drum magazine, the guns set on sturdy-seeming mounts at approximately chest height. Fixed atop each of the guns, scopelike, was what appeared to be a miniaturized video camera. Cables trailed across the ground from each of the guns—a half-dozen, set strategically, ringing the time-transfer base—connected to what appeared to be individual power supplies.

"If those do what I think they do," David remarked, "we're in trouble."

"They probably do and we very well might be," Jack told his son. "However, we'll have to cope." In this case, "cope" would translate into he wasn't quite sure what.

"The guns fire automatically?" Lieutenant Easley said, repeating what Jack had just told him.

"I believe that to be the case, Lieutenant, yes," Jack responded. Jack, Ellen and Lieutenant Easley crouched well back from the perimeter of rock that allowed the overlook on what could accurately be described as the enemy position: the time-transfer base. "There's something analogous to a camera, something well in advance of this time. The camera is linked to or incorporated with a small computer, which is a machine which cannot think, but can perform many functions much like a human mind, and many times faster. The computer can be programmed, I believe, to start the individual gun shooting once it has acquired a predetermined target, meaning a human or possibly animal intruder. Each gun will have been programmed to cover a specific field of fire, just like a human marksman in an infantry defensive context. The guns will be able to move right and left, up and down, will continue firing until the target has been neutralized—met a predetermined set of conditions programmed into the computer—or, until the ammunition supply is exhausted. The double drums which serve as magazines are probably .223 caliber, the current service rifle caliber from our time. If that is the case, each drum will hold fifty rounds, for a total of one hundred rounds per gun. They—the guns, I mean—are probably preset to three-round bursts for every electronic tripping of the trigger mechanism. Potentially very deadly as we try to penetrate the time-transfer base perimeter."

Lieutenant Easley spoke. "If I may interrupt, Mr. Naile, I've heard mentions of time-transferring and the future, regarding the six volunteers and now these guns. I know this is a highly secretive mission, but—"

"McKinley's people didn't tell you much of a damn thing, did they, Lieutenant?" Jack posited. "Just that you'd be briefed as appropriate, I imagine. Give the lieutenant the barebones version of this, Ellen."

Ellen started with, "We're from the future, and your six volunteers will be traveling to the year 1996 with us as soon as we knock out the resistance at the facility we're about to attack. On the plus side, the jet-fighter aircraft and the helicopter—flying machines—haven't gone airborne yet."

Outside of seeing it in a motion picture or on television, or reading about it in a book, Jack Naile had never actually seen someone's jaw drop—until he saw Lieutenant Easley's drop.

The original plan had been to ignore electronic countermeasures and simply storm the time-transfer base by force, using what would appear to its defenders to be a frontal assault while, in fact, a second element of Lieutenant Easley's force would accomplish a flanking movement that would become an envelopment.

The objectives were two, both equally important. First was to gain control of the time-transfer capsule to deny the accomplishment of a time-transfer that could alert Lakewood Industries' forces in the objective future that there was trouble and to bring high tech reinforcements.

The second objective was to sabotage the VSTOL and helicopter aircraft so that they could not get off the ground and be used to interdict either or both attack elements.

Because of the present physical layout of the base, however, both objectives could be attacked as one. Upon inspection of the time-transfer facility from their observation vantage point, it was determined that the two VSTOL aircraft had been moved to within the fenced area surrounding the time-transfer capsule. So had the helicopter. On the plus side, all of the surface fighting vehicles were absent.

Except for the computer-regulated guns, a full-scale assault was still the plan, because it was the only workable one, since no means were at hand to disable any motion or heat sensors positioned as part of an alert system. The key to the problem, Jack concluded, was to deal with the guns—somehow—and go ahead with the attack before random chance kicked in and the time arrived for the aircraft to lift off. It seemed logical—but, unprovable except in the doing—that the guns would accept the fact that an adversary was terminated and no longer classifiable as a target when the intruder dropped below a certain artificially designated horizon line—fell down dead or wounded. If that were the case, in theory it would be possible to crawl along the ground beneath this horizon line without creating the conditions that would precipitate the guns being activated. The only trouble with that idea, if indeed such functional characteristics as he imagined were, valid, was getting past what heat, motion and other types of sensors were part of the extended perimeter defense and were likely also linked to the guns and would set them to firing.

Getting past these sensors was impossible, given the constraints of time and technology.

The guns were mechanical sentries. To get past sentries, it was often necessary to disable them permanently. The only remaining option was to "kill" the guns themselves with a shot to the brain.

"Do you think, Corporal Jensen, that you and the five best marksmen in your platoon can each hit the respective target simultaneously?" Jack asked as he pointed over the rocks toward the six computer-controlled guns. "The greatest distance looks about two hundred fifty yards. You'd have to hit the little boxlike affair on top of the gun, maybe using the red diode—that's a light—as an aiming point."

"Simultane—what you said—means all at the same time, don't it, sir?"

Despite their desperate circumstances, Jack found himself smiling. "Yes, Corporal. That's what simultaneously means, true enough."

"I make the longest away of them guns at two hundred and eighty yards. Them box things with that there red light, they looks to be steel or iron."

"Probably neither, because of the weight. Most likely, a relatively thin material your rifle bullet shouldn't have any trouble penetrating. Can you and five other guys hit reliably at that range with those .30-40s of yours? That's the question."

"Yes, sir." And the stocky corporal slapped the for end of his Krag-Jorgensen rifle for emphasis.

Private First Class Wallace Standing Bear, one of the lucky winners in the first round of the submachine gun sweepstakes, would, along with Jensen and the other marksmen, be part of the "aircraft interdiction unit." Jack had drawn a crude picture of an airplane in the dirt and, by match light, pointed out things like landing gear, fuel pods, cockpit bubbles and the like. The second-element marksmen had the task of crippling whatever aircraft they encountered by the only means available—accurate rifle fire to vital components.

With all necessary watches synchronized to his Rolex, Jack watched the seconds tick by. Six shots would be fired in precisely forty-two seconds. For good or for bad, since there would be no time to verify whether or not the bullets of the marksmen had struck their targets, the assault would begin immediately.

Sergeant Goldberg, the platoon sergeant., held one squad of B Company, Second Platoon in the throat of a rocky defile twenty-five yards or so to the north of Jack's position with Easley and nine other men.

Twenty-three seconds remained.

The men of the Seventh were among the most experienced, battle-toughened men in the United States Army. In the blue-gray predawn, their faces showed the resolute hardness battle breeds. Crouched, legs like coiled springs beneath them, rifles with fixed bayonets clenched in gnarled fists, they waited. Jack's eyes drifted back to his watch.

Eight seconds.

Jensen and the five other marksmen would be letting that last breath before let-off catch in their throats, and, in another second or two, fingers would take up the slack in triggers, drawing them back to just before the break point.

For the zillionth time, it seemed, since he and his family had been swept back in time, Jack thought of a phrase attributable to the writer Ian Fleming: "It reads better than it lives." Indeed, adventure and danger on the American frontier of western books and movies and television was far less scary to experience vicariously than in personal reality. Sometimes, it seemed almost as if he had done nothing but kill since he had come to this time.

Six shots rang out almost as one.

It was time to kill again. "Let's go!"

In the next instants, it was evident only five rounds had connected with their targets. The sixth computer controlled weapon began spraying lethality throughout its field of fire the moment Jack and his men spilled down out of the rocks and charged toward the time-transfer base.

Almost louder than the gunfire were the alarms, screeching claxons resonating throughout the time-transfer base, reverberating, as did the gunfire, off the rocky terrain, the sheer cacophony maddening.

Jack raced forward, the killing ground for the electronically controlled guns made totally devoid of rocks or any other possible cover. Bullets rippled into the ground to his side. Bringing the submachine gun up to his shoulder, its folding stock already extended, he fired a long burst toward the still-functioning gun. The boxlike affair mounted above it—its eyes and brain—shattered.

Jack and Lieutenant Easley led one element of the attack force, Sergeant Goldberg the second. Fighting was everywhere, the whine of gunfire and the shrieking of the alarms all-consuming. Ellen's heart might well have been in her mouth, but she realized that she wouldn't have known, her entire being numbed by her fear for Jack and the horror of what she witnessed.

Her nephew, Clarence, and her son, David, on either side of her like protective bookends, Alan on David's right—as if two bookends weren't somehow quite enough—Ellen watched the battle for Lakewood Industries' time-transfer base in 1900, a battle of immense historical importance that would never be recorded in history books, a battle unlike any other. In addition to David, Clarence and Alan, there were three of Lieutenant Easley's men with her as well, their rifles shouldered. Clarence, Alan and David each had a rifle at the ready, the dual purpose to cover a withdrawal should one become necessary and to prevent any Lakewood personnel from escaping the time-transfer base. The goal was that none of the Lakewood personnel should be taken prisoner; that made Ellen's skin crawl, although she realized the practicality, the inevitability of such a measure.

Jack was running again, firing his liberated submachine

gun at almost point-blank range into two of the Lakewood Industries personnel. Jack dropped to his knees and Ellen knew exactly where her heart was—in her chest. It stopped dead for an instant, heavy as lead and cold as ice.

But Jack wasn't hit. Letting his own submachine gun fall to his side on its sling, he was separating the fallen Lakewood guards from their weapons.

"Oh, my God! Jack doesn't see him!" A man was coming up on Jack, blindsiding him, bringing a submachine gun to bear. As Ellen shouldered her own rifle and was going to try to shoot Jack's attacker, Jack twisted his upper body left, his special Colt revolver springing into his right hand. Jack fired, twice she thought, although individual shots were impossible to detect. The man went down. Three submachine guns slung from his broad shoulders, Jack was moving again.

Sergeant Goldberg, well off to Jack's right, shot a man point blank in the chest and reloaded. A second man tackled him. Goldberg stumbled, stayed on his feet, but his rifle fell from his hands. Goldberg took a single step back, into a boxer's T-stance. His left fist flashed out as his opponent made to open fire. Goldberg's left snaked outward again, then his powerful upper body pivoted and his right fist crashed across the Lakewood man's jaw, knocking him down.

Goldberg snatched the man's pistol, then the submachine gun. Goldberg's rifle upraised in his right hand, he shouted—Ellen couldn't hear him, but could see his mouth moving—and a half-dozen soldiers from the Seventh rallied to him. With Goldberg at its leading edge, they formed a wedge, fighting their way deeper into the time-transfer base, the fixed bayonets flashing in the brightening light. Ellen glanced to the East. The sun had winked up over the rugged horizon.

When she looked back to the unfolding battle, Ellen witnessed Sergeant Goldberg clasp his side, then hammer his rifle butt into the face of one of the enemy. Goldberg wheeled around, taking another bullet or more, hurtling himself at the man who'd fired, driving his bayonet through the man's throat, collapsing on top of him.

Jack and four of his men were fighting along what amounted to a street between more than a half-dozen motor homes lined along each side. New and improved barracks for the Lakewood personnel? That had to be it.

Beyond the "street" lay the fenced-off area within which were housed the actual time-transfer apparatus and the planes.

Jack, Lieutenant Easley and four troopers fought their way toward it, all of the men picking up weapons as they went forward. Once, Jack fired two submachine guns simultaneously, bringing down two more of the Lakewood personnel.

Four men of the Seventh appeared from between two of the motor homes, joined Jack and continued toward the enclosure.

The flat, helipadlike surface where the capsule phased in and out between 1996 and 1900 lay just ahead, the capsule itself—the width of a football field and perhaps twenty-five yards deep—at its center. There were chain-link gates, at least eight feet high, razor wire—something new, again—strung there as atop the entire fence. Two jets and a helicopter were there as well. The gates were closing.

Jack shouted to a corporal nearby, "Hold this position, if you can. I've got an idea." Without saying anything more, without waiting for a response of any kind—with the incessant gunfire and the still blaring alarms, the corporal most likely hadn't even heard him—Jack broke right, running for the nearest of the motor homes.

He spied no support jacks, no hose or sewer connections. There was an electrical line, probably leading to a common generator. Why would anybody bother to take the keys to a vehicle parked in a Nevada wasteland in 1900, an area surrounded by heavily armed guards? Why, indeed?—Jack hoped.

Jack wrenched open the driver's side door.

No keys in the ignition.

He reached up behind the visor.

"Yes!" Predictability was a wonderful thing at times, something smart people tried to avoid.

Jack stabbed the ignition key into the switch and turned it. The motor roared to life.

Jack hit the horn button, then hit it again and again. Lieutenant Easley turned around. Jack hit the horn again and waved through the open doorway. Easley prodded at the men with him, gesticulating broadly toward the motor home. Two of the men did not move, transfixed, it seemed, by the sight of such a monstrously large "horseless carriage."

Easley grabbed the more reluctant of the men by shoulders and pistol belts and propelled them forward.

Jack took a deep breath as the men of the Seventh

clambered aboard the horseless stagecoach through its center door. Counting himself, there were ten men in all. The total number of MP-5 submachine guns was six. There were a few fully loaded magazines—maybe six—and how many rounds remained in each of the in-place magazines was anybody's guess.

"Lieutenant," Jack said at the top of his voice. "Get everybody seated on the floor. Set all of those submachine guns to semi only—not full-auto. Make sure every one of them has a chambered round and a full magazine. Mine are on the passenger seat there." Jack gestured toward the other front bucket. "Impress upon these guys that this vehicle is going to be moving fast, starting now." Jack released the emergency brake and moved the selector into drive.

The motor home began rumbling forward. Jack turned the wheel left, pulling into the little street formed between the two rows of motor homes. Easley was barking orders.

"Hurry it up, Lieutenant! We're going to punch through that gate in about sixty seconds! Once we're in, pile out of the vehicle and continue the fight."

Jack stopped, threw the selector into reverse and used the side mirrors to back up. He wanted as much speed as he could get. "When I shout, everybody go flat on the floor. Hold on to something that doesn't look like it'll move."

Jack stopped the motor home, took a deep breath and put the selector into drive. Gradually, he gave the engine gas, rolling perhaps ten yards before he stomped the accelerator flat to the floor. There was a driver's side seat belt, but he'd forgotten to put it on.

No time.

For an instant, Jack found himself wondering if Jensen, Standing Bear and the other marksmen had reached the fence from the opposite side yet. Were the jump jets warming up, the noise of their engines just not discernable over the general cacophony? Was the chopper about to get airborne?

The gates, fully closed, lay fifty yards ahead. Forty. Thirty. Twenty. "Everybody hold on and be ready to move!" Ten yards. The gates looked awfully sturdy. What if they wouldn't yield to the motor home's mass and momentum? "This is stupid," Jack muttered as he grabbed his Stetson and used it to shield his face. He heard breaking glass just as his body shuddered and everything around him seemed to vibrate and his rear end started lifting out of the seat to fly forward. He should have used the seat belt.

CHAPTER
❖ TWENTY-TWO ❖

Time was dilated. In life-and-death situations, moments of great stress, life played in slow motion. He'd never believed that until it had happened to him on a suddenly icy stretch of interstate highway in Kentucky in 1979 or 1980.

"Mr. Naile! Are you still with us, sir?"

Jack opened his eyes and saw Lieutenant Easley looking back at him. Jack's forehead ached a little, and his right arm felt sore, but not broken. "Yeah—I think. Okay, yeah—everybody out!"

"You heard him! Exit that way!" Easley shouted. As Jack stood up, his knees were wobbly.

Jack looked through the shattered windshield. Parts of the fence gates had collapsed over the motor home's front end. One of the verticals for the gate had punched through the windshield about six or eight inches from where Jack's head should have been but wasn't, then continued on outward through the driver's side window.

Jack shook his black Stetson, and broken glass tinkled from it to join the glass around his feet.

Lieutenant Easley handed Jack a submachine gun as Jack finally started for the door. Jack flexed his right shoulder, rubbed it with his left hand. More broken glass fell from his shoulders and back when he moved.

A half-dozen men, perhaps more, moving from point of cover to point of cover, were running from the trailer at the center of the fenced enclosure toward the huge gray cylinder on the flat concrete apron, the site where the time-transfers actually took place. The cylinder existed in two times, simultaneously, just as did the mountains beyond and the rocks above and around Jack and the dirt and sand beneath Jack's boots. If the men could get into the cylinder and a time-transfer was already set, they would be blinked into the future and have escaped, escaped with the knowledge that the time-transfer base in 1900 had been breached, compromised and was about to be overrun. Within minutes, or no more than hours, certainly, a tank, perhaps, or several dozen men and a helicopter gunship—Jack could only guess what Lakewood Industries held in reserve—would emerge from that capsule and retake the time-transfer base.

The sole helicopter—a Bell Long Ranger, of the type used by television and radio traffic reporters and life flights and for ordinary commuting, but not a gunship—was warming up its main rotors. It was well back from the capsule, closer to the far side of the chain link fence.

Jack grabbed one of Lieutenant Easley's men. "Find Alan Naile—not my son, but the guy who looks like him. He should be up in the rocks there with my wife and the others. Get him down here to that trailer—that thing! Hurry!"

Jack buttonholed another of Easley's men. "Go with that guy! Now! Hurry." The trailer was the control center for the time-transfer mechanism. Alan was the only one of them here—Clarence's wife, who knew the procedures well, had not accompanied them—who could rightly be expected to know what he was doing with the apparatus.

Lieutenant Easley and five of Easley's men were using the cover of the motor home, advancing toward the gray capsule. Jack joined them, crouched beside the driver's side wheelwell. "We can't let those Lakewood Industries men get into the time-transfer capsule. They may have some means of operating the time-transfer device remotely, or may have the system set on some sort of timer." Unintended puns were the most embarrassing kind. "If they get into the capsule and escape into 1996, we've had it."

"Had what, sir?" Lieutenant Easley asked, his voice as grave as his countenance.

"It's a figure of speech, Lieutenant. If they get to 1996, they'll send back men and equipment we can't hope to defeat, and they'll not only retake the time-transfer base here, but also kill any chances we'd have to stop them from selling their military equipment from the future to the highest bidder in 1900."

"What if we were to destroy this capsule thing?" Easley asked.

"They could just build another one in 1996—probably already have a spare one for backup—and get here anyway. The only way to stop them is in the future, not here in the subjective present." There were seven men, actually, Jack counting as the Lakewood personnel began leapfrogging their way toward the capsule again. Three men stayed in cover, laying down suppressive fire while four men moved to the next position, a standard fire-and-maneuver tactic.

Jack touched at the skin just inside his shirt collar. Another little piece of glass. As he threw it away, he had an idea.

"Lieutenant. Take one of your men and come with me." It was a desperate idea, but one that might save the day. And, as a commodity, time was the enemy. With Lieutenant Easley and one of his troopers, Jack made his way back toward the motor home's door, hoping all the while that he could find what he needed and quickly enough.

Once inside, he started rearward. "Lieutenant, check the kitchen area. We're looking for glass bottles of alcoholic beverages. Vodka, whiskey, anything like that. If the liquor is stored in anything other than glass, we need to find some glass containers which have small openings at the top. Get your trooper to search for sheets, handkerchiefs, like that. We need fabric, material. It's no good to rip down the curtains or skin the cushions from the couch or anything because all of that stuff would be fire-retardant."

"Begging your pardon, sir, but what are we doing, Mr. Naile? What's the purpose here, sir?" Lieutenant Easley inquired earnestly.

"A man by the name of Molotov, a Russian revolutionary, will forever be associated with what we're doing, although I doubt he invented the procedure." Before Easley could ask another polite question, Jack told him, "We stuff rags down the mouths of bottles containing alcohol, then set fire to the rags and throw the bottles. When they shatter, they spray fire. In my day, we call them Molotov Cocktails and I sure hope they work as well as they do in the movies—magic-lantern shows. It would work better with gasoline."

Frantically, Jack, Easley and the trooper tore through the motor home. There was a nice little liquor cabinet in the master bedroom at the rear. Jack picked up one of the bottles. "Now, somebody find me a corkscrew! And fast!" The longer this battle dragged on, the greater the chance of Lakewood's leadership interdicting. And interdiction could translate into a helicopter gunship or a jump jet from the future, not to mention one of the VSTOLs or the Long Ranger already at the base getting airborne. If the marksmen hadn't reached the backside of the fenced enclosure yet, one of the armed VSTOLs could get airborne vertically, change to horizontal flight mode and strafe the time-transfer base, putting an end to the attack.

Submachine gun fire hammered into the motor home, blasting through what glass hadn't shattered on impact. As Jack, Lieutenant Easley and the trooper rejoined the men outside the motor home, the seven Lakewood men leapfrogged again. In another ten yards, the maneuver element would reach the time-transfer capsule. Then it would simply be a matter of laying down all the suppressive fire possible—for a matter of seconds—to bring the remaining personnel to the capsule. Once inside, it was over. The capsule was probably resistant to most conventional munitions, merely as an incidental result of the strength it would have been built with, the electrical energy it had been constructed to withstand.

Jack, Easley and the trooper handed out wine bottles stuffed at the mouth with bits of sheeting and pillowcasing. Jack took his first bottle and upended it, letting the alcohol begin to saturate the wick. In movies, lighting a Molotov cocktail had always looked a little dangerous. In real life, it was positively scary. Best cover up with bravado, he thought, striking a match on the sole of his boot. He faked a French accent. "And, on today's menu, we feature flambé of bad guy." No one caught the attempt at humor. Jack lit the alcohol-saturated wick, and there was serious flame very fast. Jack flung the bottle toward the Lakewood position. Jack was always less than gifted at throwing anything, from softballs to hand grenades. The bottle shattered some six feet shy of the Lakewood personnel, but sprayed burning alcohol all around it. The principle worked. "Who can throw better than I can? Anybody, right? The most accurate toss gets a brand new nickel-plated Colt Single Action out of my store!"

Lieutenant Easley picked up a bottle and inverted it. "Nickel-plated, you say, Mr. Naile? Who's got a match?" Flashing a grin, eyes twinkling, young Lieutenant Easley struck the match against the underside of the wheelwell beside which he crouched. "Flares up quickly, doesn't it?" Easley observed dryly, his nostrils flaring as he evidently smelled the alcohol. He stood for a split second to fling the burning Molotov. The bottle of burning beverage—vodka in this case—shattered against metal drums behind which the Lakewood fire element had taken cover. A direct hit. Easley remarked, "Now, anyone who can best me not only gets that nickel-plated Colt Mr. Naile offered, but a Winchester rifle to boot, from yours truly." He fired a glance at Jack and smiled. Over Easley's shoulder, Jack could see Alan and the two troopers, leapfrogging their way toward the control center . . .

Her helicopter would make for a spectacular—indeed, frightening—introduction to the foreign buyers. Bethany liked catching adversaries off their guard, with their "pants down" as it were. In the first few moments following such an incident, people habitually said and did things that they would never say or do if their wits were fully about them.

Vulnerability: Bethany avoided displaying it, loved discovering it.

But she was caught up in her own temporary vulnerability at the moment and cursed herself for it. The surface ordnance was already too far south of the time-transfer base to be recalled. There was no direct communication with 1996 without use of the time-transfer capsule. The two pilots for the VSTOLs—damn their chicken-shittedness—were among the seven men trying to reach the capsule rather than running for their fighter planes.

One lousy fighter plane could wipe out all of the attackers.

Because of her costuming—the long skirts and voluminous undergarments—it would have been needlessly risky for her to sit opposite the Bell Long Ranger's pilot. If an item of clothing were to snag in some control or another, disaster might result. She sat immediately behind the pilot instead, able to see nearly as well as she could have otherwise.

It was up to her to give the order to her pilot. "Steve? Can a regular rifle or a subgun take out our helicopter?"

"Sure can, Ms. Kaminsky. If this was a gunship, we'd be better set, but not immune. Bullets and helicopters—especially ordinary civilian ones—just don't mix!"

"Well, shit! That's just fucking wonderful. Then get me outa here!" The attackers—a bunch of fucking soldiers dressed like extras from a western movie and probably that son of a bitch Jack Naile and his fucking meddling do-gooder family—were going to lose her the time-transfer base. "I could be trapped here in this damn fucking time! Do you realize that?" Bethany Kaminsky's fists bunched handfuls of her skirts, and she shrieked, "Get airborne and get me out of here, Steve! Now, dammit!"

Bethany was giving a good performance, she thought. But what she knew was no one's business except her own. And, she could very well be "trapped" in 1900 without a proper shower or bathroom, without normal clothes, without any of that for—for hours.

Stifling a laugh, Bethany evaluated her position. She could obviously retake the time-transfer base once she reconnected with the tanks and armoured personnel carriers. She could radio them immediately and do just that. Or she could let the firepower demonstration go on as scheduled, get herself set with a power base at the beginning of the twentieth century just as planned.

Below her, one of the VSTOLs blew up, a fireball belching skyward. Steve banked the helicopter just in time to keep them from being swallowed in flame.

Bethany's temples pounded, and she felt vomit rising up in her throat. It was the flight, she knew; helicopter rides were never her favorite thing even under the best of circumstances.

Within little more than an hour, merely by raising binoculars to her eyes, she would be able to just make out on the horizon what would be a caravan of carriages and coaches withdrawing to a considerable distance from a dry lakebed where canvas pavilions had been erected to shield onlookers from the sun and the elements. If the range was not far enough, a great many frightened drivers would be chasing an even greater number of wildly terrified horses once the firepower demonstration got underway.

Her pilot's voice came through Bethany's earpiece. "I'm patching you through to the time-transfer base. It's a voice I don't recognize. He asked for you by name."

"Let me talk to him."

The transmission was clear, clear enough that the voice was easily recognizable as that of Alan Naile. He was gloating over how she was trapped in 1900 and would soon be out of fuel and ammunition.

While he was still talking to her, she pulled the headset off and rested it in her lap. "God, how predictable!" Steve, the pilot, just looked at her oddly. Bethany could no longer maintain the charade. And anyway, her sides hurt; the boning in her corset pinched when she laughed.

The concussion from the exploding jump jet slammed Jack back against the motor home's coachwork. Apparently, the six marksmen were on the job. Just as he mentally congratulated their skills, he looked up. The helicopter had gotten airborne and was out of range of any rifle Jack had ever heard of. "Shit!"

"What is it?" Lieutenant Easley queried.

Jack couldn't resist the impulse to try a Leslie Nielsen impression. "It's a brown sticky substance human beings excrete to eliminate waste products, but never mind that now. That's Bethany Kaminsky, the principal bad guy, getting away. That's all." Jack pulled the unlit rag from the mouth of the bottle in his right hand and took a swallow. It was whiskey.

The trooper who won the nickel-plated Colt and the Winchester rifle could pitch in the first World Series in 1903—if he made it through this alive.

Fortunately, the seven Lakewood personnel— technicians or engineers, most of them, two of them pilots—had chosen to fight to the death. Jack Naile did not relish the idea of executing someone who had surrendered, did not know if he would be capable of doing so and feared that he was.

The remaining VSTOL, its paint job smudged from smoke, seemed otherwise unscathed. Trouble was, there was no one alive in 1900 who could fly it.

Alan had reached the control trailer moments before the helicopter got airborne. After what seemed like forever, he at last exited it and announced, "We guessed right, Jack. The men who were trying to escape to the capsule had the controls set so that they could trigger a time-transfer remotely. I disarmed it. We have complete control of the capsule as far as going into the future. I can't tell whether or not there's any traffic due in to our objective present.

And I raised Bethany Kaminsky on the radio. I think she was numb." Alan laughed.

Jack nodded, saying nothing. They stood some feet away from the time-transfer capsule, David and Clarence and Lieutenant Easley and the six volunteers.

Ellen, standing beside Jack, said, "The quicker we get ourselves to 1996, then, the faster we can get back here and take care of what's left of Lakewood Industries in 1900."

Jack squeezed his wife's hand. "Understand this, Ellen, everybody. From everything Alan has told us about Bethany Kaminsky, we've got to figure that she would have covered her bet, anticipated that we might do just what we did. Alan said that she sounded numb; maybe she was just being coy. She'll have an ace up her little lace-trimmed leg-o'-mutton sleeve. Watch and see." Lighting a cigarette, Jack announced, "We'll be leaving in just a few minutes, gentlemen. Let's get all the firepower we'll need and plenty of ammo ready. We won't be able to try this again." He turned to Lieutenant Easley. "I want you to put together a detail under the command of my nephew, Clarence. He'll tell the men what to look for here."

The very fact that the seven now dead men had attempted to make a getaway into the future boded well for what Jack and those with him intended. If there were definite schedules that were followed for time-transfers and any deviation from the schedule would be met with killing force, the seven would have been better off taking their chances in 1900. Of course, they might not have known about such a schedule, but that likelihood seemed doubtful. The technician who had programmed their capsule for a remotely triggered time-transfer had to have known what he was doing, would likely have been privy to any such scheduling restrictions.

By the same token, there would certainly be well-armed security waiting in 1996; to have done otherwise would have been negligent in the extreme, madness. Since 1996 was the future, could the Lakewood people there already know the assault from 1900 had taken/would take place? Headache time again, Jack mused.

Jack was loading the last of the MP-5 magazines with scrounged 9mm ammo. Ellen came and sat beside him on the rear bumper of the motor home that had demolished the fence gate. She wore slacks and laced-up boots, and wherever her hat was, it wasn't on her person. "What do you think, Jack? Has Lakewood got another time-transfer base set?"

Jack thwacked the spine of the magazine against the palm of his hand to seat the last few cartridges—it was more habit than necessity. "I don't think a full-tilt base, because Kaminsky'd want something like that pretty secretive. And the cost is enormous, of course. No, I figure she's got a smaller facility, probably south of here, maybe closer to 1996 Las Vegas. It was probably selected here in 1900 and then built in 1996. In 1996, it could be inside a building or something. Probably is."

"So, if there's a second time-transfer base, then going to 1996, and knocking out the principal facility won't put Lakewood out of business. They can still do whatever they want."

Jack had two expropriated SIG 228 9mm pistols with thirteen-round magazines. He checked these as he spoke.

"That's going to be up to Alan, sweetheart. Once we've got him back to 1996 and we've secured the time-transfer base there, Alan should be able to quickly reestablish himself as being not only alive, but in charge. He's got political connections, as our descendants always do. His party's not in charge in 1996, but God willing, that'll change with the 2000 general election. In the meantime, he's probably still got enough clout to shut down Lakewood's time-travel ambitions. I think he can handle it on his end, and we'll pull the plug from this end. That—and tracking Bethany Kaminsky—is what Clarence is working on right now." Jack leaned over and kissed his wife on the cheek.

Jack had not wanted to risk taking 1900-vintage nitroglycerin dynamite into the time-transfer capsule. It sweated, given the slightest provocation, and was highly unstable under the appropriate circumstances. But, on the other hand, there were enough Communist bloc grenades at the time-transfer base that each man—and the solitary woman, Ellen—could have four apiece.

David, along with nine men from the Seventh, had already set out toward the anticipated scene of the firepower demonstration. All of the serious ground-based ordnance was gone, of course, but there were numerous pickup trucks, vans and a Suburban with three seats and a roof rack. David had crammed all the gear and weapons he could on to the Suburban's roof rack and into the Suburban itself, along with the nine men, the vehicle rather crowded despite its size. One of the motor homes would have accommodated more personnel and equipment but with no modern roads in existence, might have handled getting from the time-transfer base to the fire-power demonstration not at all.

Clarence, along with the men detailed to him by Lieutenant Easley, was busily scrounging electronic gear and explosives.

The interior of the time-transfer capsule—the capsule was enormous and gray inside and out and shaped like some sort of gigantic bean—beckoned with its coolness. The morning sun was strong and Jack warm.

Twenty-three minutes had passed since Kaminsky's helicopter had gotten airborne. His special Colt slung at his right hip, a brace of SIG pistols that hadn't been invented yet thrust into his waistband, one of the H-K submachine guns in his right hand, Jack took his wife's right hand in his left and took the first step into the capsule.

It was cool inside, a little dark and creepy seeming, of course, and, when he spoke, his voice echoed and reechoed, amplifying the unnatural feel of the place. "Unlike the helicopter which brought my wife and family and myself here, Lieutenant, this capsule doesn't cease to exist in one place, even for a moment, isn't that right, Alan?"

"When the time-transfer occurred the first time, the helicopter they were in—well, we later deduced," Alan said, his fingers stroking the walls of the capsule, "that the helicopter had to have ceased to exist in our time reference for possibly a nanosecond while it was traveling from the future to here.

"The people and the equipment sent from 1996, let's say, to 1900 do actually cease to exist in 1996. However, this capsule is like the mountains, like a natural feature.

The time-transfer takes place around the capsule, which is why there's the shimmering effect you and your men have probably heard us mention, Lieutenant. The problem for us has always been that we just honestly don't know what is happening or why this time-transfer thing works.

"It's a trick of nature," Alan went on, "and I don't know if we'll ever understand it. We just simply learned to imitate the trick and we can keep repeating the trick. But that doesn't mean we've gotten any smarter."

"How much longer before the door closes and the time-transfer begins?" Jack asked his many-times grandson.

Alan consulted a wristwatch taken from his pocket. "They stole my Rolex, but this is a pretty nice Omega, though. I make it about another fifty-two seconds. We ought to all sit down, I think," Alan advised.

The six men of the Seventh—Jensen, Armitage, Goldstein, Harek, Luciano and Standing Bear—all looked understandably nervous. Standing Bear, folding his legs under him and resting his submachine guns—two of them—across his thighs, was the first to sit.

Lieutenant Easley, who had volunteered to go, too, dropped to one knee, then to a seated position. As Ellen started to sit, she stopped. Jack thought he heard a noise. "I just had the goofiest idea, Jack." The noise came again, louder. "What would happen, Jack," Ellen queried, "if they decided to send someone or something into the past at the same time we were traveling into the future?"

"Good question," Jack agreed. "Alan?"

"I don't know. I don't think anybody ever considered—"

The noise came again, louder, stronger.

Easley simply remarked, "My God."

The door to the capsule began to close and the capsule itself began to shimmer almost imperceptibly.

"Jesus." Alan made the sign of the cross. "We don't start for another eighteen seconds, guys, but there's a transfer in progress."

"No shooting in here! Ricochet danger! No shooting under any circumstance unless it's point-blank and you're desperate," Jack called out.

"What's happening, Jack?" Ellen asked, her voice steady, controlled.

"What you said. They're coming this way while we're going that way."

Ellen's right hand touched to his cheek for an instant.

Jack whispered, "I love you."

About a quarter of a Soviet-era tank was suddenly just there, and the pugilist's face of Jensen was inside of it, part of it, and there was a shriek of horror and Jensen wasn't there anymore.

Ellen wasn't a screamer and she didn't scream, but she drew in her breath so sharply someone who didn't know her might have thought that she was about to scream.

Easley sprang to his feet with the speed of a wild animal.

More of the tank appeared for an instant, but Standing Bear had already gotten the other four men of the Seventh to their feet and away. As the tank flickered, Jack heard voices. Standing Bear had drawn a Bowie knife. Jack folded Ellen into his arms.

Jensen's face appeared above the growing image of the

tank. Easley reached for Jensen, said, "Here, man—take my hand!"

There was another voice, one Jack did not recognize. "I heard it again! Now I see a face! It looks like a fuckin' Indian in a damn movie!"

On impulse—insane impulse, perhaps—Jack reached out to touch the tank. He could feel it, somehow, but it wasn't there, was only empty space. "Maybe Jensen's still alive and out there!" Jack announced.

"Mr. Naile, sir! I'm over here!"

"Jensen," Ellen hissed through clenched teeth.

Harek was on his knees, reciting a prayer in a language Jack didn't know but assumed was Turkish.

"Who's out there?" The voice belonged to no one from the expedition to 1996, had to be from 1996.

"Who are you?" Jack called back.

"Are you ghosts?"

Jack shivered. By 1996 they would be—maybe.

"Get us out of here, Jack!" Ellen was breathing hard, close to hyperventilating, and her fingernails were digging into his left tricep so hard Jack knew that he was bleeding.

"If you can see us, Jensen," Easley called out, "come toward us. Hurry, man!"

Jensen's voice came again. "Who are you?"

"Who the fuck's that guy?"

"Don't shoot in here, Carpentier! Dammit, you crackhead! No!"

There was the sound of a shot, probably a pistol, but it was all around them, and the sound of the ricochet just went on and on and on. Jack drew Ellen closer against him still.

Goldstein shouted, "I'm comin' for ya', Jensen!"

Standing Bear punched Goldstein in the abdomen, doubling him over, stopping Goldstein from sacrificing himself.

The whining of the ricochet went on and on and seemed as though it would never stop. Easley called out, "Don't shoot in here! That's madness!"

The Soviet-era tank was more solid now, and Jack almost lost whatever remained from the last meal he'd eaten as Easley vaulted past him, onto the tank. Jack was a step behind the man. If ever Jack had thought of Easley as just a run-of-the-mill young officer, what transpired before Jack's eyes would have contradicted the impression. Jensen's right hand—or someone's right hand—and forearm were reaching up from within the steel on the left side of the tank turret. Easley leaped on to the turret and grasped the hand, obviously trying—somehow—to tug Jensen free of the thing.

There was a man, shadowy seeming, but real enough, suddenly grasping Easley by the throat. The man had to be from the party of Lakewood people traveling back to 1900. Easley shoved the fellow away, reached again for the hand and forearm that were disappearing more deeply into the steel of the tank as the tank's body solidified, completed itself. The shadowy man from the future was more distinct as well; he grabbed Easley by the shoulder, spun him around and thrust a suppressor-fitted pistol toward Easley's face.

The tank and Jensen occupied the same space, Jensen enveloped within the tank.

Jack had his submachine gun up, the stock folded out,

his left forearm flexing back, his right arm bending outward, snapping the weapon into a horizontal buttstroke across the jaw of Easley's assailant.

Jensen's hand and forearm were nearly vanished into the tank, and Jack feared that Easley, failing to let go, might be absorbed within the nearly completed armor-plated behemoth as well.

"Let him go, Lieutenant! Let him go!"

"I can't leave a man behind, Mr. Naile!"

"He's already ceased to exist," Jack shouted, summoning as much authority into his voice as he could, given that he was only making an educated guess. "He doesn't exist here, maybe somewhere else. Not here! Come on, Lieutenant."

There was no way Easley could have known. But calling out the last name of Naile was a tactical error. Jack knew it the moment Easley uttered it. Lakewood people from 1996 would doubtlessly know that anyone named Naile was a high-value target.

"Get that guy dressed all in black!" The voice was alien to Jack, but he knew the source. "That's Jack Naile!"

Alan's voice sounded far away, more so than it should have, as he shouted, "That's Lester Matthews talking, guys, Lakewood's chief bad guy!"

Jack and Lieutenant Easley still stood on the Soviet-era tank. Jack shuddered, but not at the realization that Lester Matthews—the big guy he'd missed killing when he'd rescued Alan from murder—was in the time-transfer capsule with them. Jack realized that Easley and he were going in the wrong direction, back to 1900. "It's the tank, Easley. We've gotta get off the tank! Jump for it!"

Jack took a step nearer the fender over the left track, With obvious reluctance, Easley let go of the hand that was still being absorbed into the tank. Where Jensen was, if he was, neither Jack nor any man could know, but that Jensen was gone forever from them was an almost perfect certainty. And if Jensen were somehow still alive, mere contemplation of what the man might be enduring would likely induce both madness and despondency.

The man that flung himself toward Jack from the rear of the tank was not shadowy in appearance, but as real looking as Easley. And the jaw Jack struck with the best left hook he could manage felt solid, fully real. Jack's hand hurt. Already, the time might have passed to rejoin Ellen and the men of the Seventh on their way to 1996. Jack might be trapped in 1900 along with Easley—and along with Lester Matthews and his Lakewood henchmen.

Jack's impromptu left—from a shallow angle and closer to a jab than a solid swing—merely deflected their assailant, didn't stop him. The man's submachine gun swung upward. Jack didn't have time to get to his own. Easley shouted, distracting the man for a split second. What Easley's intentions were—aside from fighting—Jack didn't know. Jack snatched the long barreled Colt revolver from the gunfighter style holster at his right thigh, his left hand snapping outward, palm open, straight-arming the Lakewood man in the chest. Jack's revolver cleared leather, and, punching it forward, the hammer cocked, he snapped the trigger.

The Lakewood man's eyes went wide. There was a sudden smell of burning flesh. Jack shouted, "Jump for it now, Lieutenant." Jack threw himself from the tank, hitting the floor of the capsule in an awkward roll that made his left elbow and shoulder seize with pain. Easley landed more gracefully. Jack didn't know what to do, saw no sign of Ellen and the others, just called out to Easley, "Run deeper into the capsule, Lieutenant!" Jack's elbow and shoulder hurt, but still worked. Somewhere behind them, mere feet only, were armed men who would kill them in the blink of an eye. And it might already be too late to reach 1996.

Jack heard shouts from the tank. One took his full attention. "It looks like they're disappearing, Matthews!"

Jack shouted again to Easley, "Whatever we're doing might be working! Keep running in the same direction!" The capsule hadn't really seemed that deep, but it was impossible to judge distance, the light very poor again, nothing truly distinguishable except up and down, a fog that wasn't really fog but was impenetrable surrounding them, all but ingesting them.

Jack felt something hard, and he almost lost his balance, wheeled round and started to raise his submachine gun. It was Harek, the Turk. "Allah be praised that you are alive!"

Jack only nodded. "The lieutenant?"

"Here, sir, right beside you."

Jack could see Easley clearly, standing beside him, Ellen joining them. "Alan says we are there, in 1996. The capsule will open in a second or so."

Jack Naile took Ellen into his left arm and embraced her, his elbow hurting. "Jensen didn't make it, kid. Pass the word when you can." Raising his voice so all could hear him, Jack announced, "Guns up, guys. When the chamber opens, the fight starts! Be ready!" Glancing at his wife again, Jack cautioned, "And you stay right beside me or behind me. Got it?"

This was a day for amazing things. His wonderfully independent, brave-as-they-come wife leaned up, kissed him on the cheek and said, "Yes."

CHAPTER
❊ TWENTY-THREE ❊

The capsule door began to open.

Returning to the 1990s—Jack wanted to take time, time just to breathe, to see familiar things, do things. He realized that he missed the stupid and the pleasant almost equally—everything from getting caught in an Atlanta traffic jam to junk faxes to the ubiquitous unwanted telephone solicitations to Wendy's wonderful double cheeseburgers and fries to the latest Jerry Goldsmith movie music. But he had other things to do. Save the world, or at least its history and probably its future.

Jack inhaled, treated himself to that before he would start shooting, and he kissed his wife full on the lips. "I love you, whatever time it is."

Turning to Easley, he asked, "Are you and your men ready, Lieutenant?"

"Yes, sir. With regrets for what we must do, I am ready. God willing, they're all combatants."

Jack nodded, walked toward the nearly fully lowered door, addressing it as if it were a ramp, the angle progressively gentler. Ellen was on his left side, Easley to her left, the five remaining men of the Seventh Cavalry volunteers spread out, flanking them. Somewhere along the way, perhaps while the fight at the tank had been going on, Standing Bear had etched a few streaks of black war paint to his cheeks.

A Lakewood man, dressed in urban-cammie pants, a black T-shirt and white track shoes, just stared into the capsule. "Who the fuck are you guys?" The Lakewood man drew a pistol from a black fabric shoulder holster under his left arm.

"It begins," Jack almost whispered. The H-K submachine gun was already to Jack's shoulder. It was merely necessary to fire it. Jack let off three suppressed shots, stitching a ragged line from the man's sternum into the man's throat.

Easley whispered, "God forgive us," then shouted, "Keep the lady safe. Now, follow me!"

Easley vaulted the last few feet from the capsule door into the 1996 time-transfer compound beyond, Standing Bear at his elbow. Despite the danger, Easley stared at the sky and proclaimed, "I am in the future!" In the next instant, Lakewood personnel—armed with M-16 rifles and MP-5 submachine guns—began pouring from the huts and trailers comprising the compound's structures. A single shot, followed in a split second by a long, ragged burst of assault-rifle fire, hammered against the capsule, ricocheted.

Standing Bear, a submachine gun in each hand, wheeled toward the gunfire's origin, his weapons firing from the hip. The man was a natural, Jack thought absently. Movies aside, firing a submachine gun from the hip was usually a total waste of ammunition. For Standing Bear, however, such a technique was not an exercise in futility. This man would have been a world-class fighting man in any century.

Jack, usually gifted with realizing his own shortcomings, knew that he wasn't as good at arms as Standing Bear and probably never would be. But as Jack was wont to remind himself at moments such as this one, how many novels, magazine articles and short stories had Standing Bear published? A person would excel in his or her own way; all that was necessary was to excel.

The butt of his MP-5 snugged to his shoulder, Jack Naile started to advance, Ellen beside and slightly behind him. Gunfire was general now, the number of heavily armed Lakewood Industries personnel considerably greater than Jack had anticipated.

There was no Plan B upon which they could fall back, success with this plan or failing totally the only options open to them. One of the Lakewood personnel, armed with an M-16, charged them, firing, his bullets cutting a swathe in the sandy ground a foot to the left and a yard behind Jack's feet, missing Ellen by mere inches. Anger welling up inside him—the man had been deliberately aiming for Ellen—Jack fired a series of short bursts. Jack didn't miss.

It wasn't the first time she'd almost been shot, certainly. But Ellen's knees felt a little weak as she stooped to untangle the rifle from the man her husband had just shot to death. The fellow had something that looked like a canvas purse slung crossbody to his left hip. A quick glance inside confirmed that she had just acquired four spare magazines in addition to the rifle. She had never fired an M-16, but had fired its civilian counterpart when Jack had owned one years ago.

"Put it on semi unless you need it," Jack advised, Ellen watching intently as he flicked a selector switch on the rifle. Then Jack was moving again. Sensible people would have taken cover, Ellen knew, and perhaps Jack was heading toward cover of some kind, but she realized that caution was less important for their—some would say "piteously"—small force than seizing control of the time-transfer base while some element of surprise still remained. If they lost their lives, but the mission somehow succeeded, that would be counted a victory in the larger scheme of things.

A man was coming up on her left, a semi-automatic pistol in his right hand. Ellen brought the rifle she carried to her shoulder. She noticed that the rifle's buttstock was a little on the long side for her when she lowered her cheek to bring her right eye in line with the sights. The Lakewood man was about to shoot. Ellen shot first, then fired a second shot and a third. The man went down, dead or close to it. Ellen guessed the battle had been going on for well under a minute.

Beside and a little behind Jack, Ellen ran toward what seemed the largest of the prefabricated buildings. Out of synch with the feminine stereotype, perhaps, Ellen had never eschewed violence, nor, however, had she sought it out. She remembered the day so well that the envelope had arrived at their post office box with the magazine

clipping that had started all of this—Jack Naile
General Merchandise. Perhaps, if they had never known,
somehow—but of course their destiny had already
happened and would continue to happen as long as the
time loop existed. Both she and her husband had lived
before somehow and died before and would again and
again, and she couldn't understand any part of the how, let
alone the why.

Ellen shot at two Lakewood personnel, a man and a
woman, both armed. She missed the man, hit the woman.
The man fired at Jack, and Jack fired back and killed him.

What would they do with noncombatant Lakewood
personnel? Would things work out—comparatively at
least—so morally easy that all enemy personnel would be
armed and go down fighting to the death? That was too
much like something out of a poorly written book or
movie—too convenient, she reasoned, but she could
hope.

The time-transfer technology had to be kept safe.

As she ran, feeling just a little breathless, she suggested
to Jack, "Couldn't we let the ordinary evil-henchmen
types go and just make sure the guys that are technically
in the know are the ones who have to die?"

Jack looked over his shoulder at her as, at last, they took
cover against the wall of one of the metal buildings.

As if things weren't pain-in-the-ass enough, a drop of
water touched the tip of her nose. As she looked up, she
noticed the dark slate-blue clouds closing in from the
west. It was starting to rain. "Shit."

"It's uncanny," Jack said, grinning at her. "I was just going
to say the same thing! And, yeah, maybe we can get away

with not killing everybody here—we've gotta play that by ear, though." The rain was subtly, steadily intensifying beyond just the few light drops she'd felt a moment before, and a cool wind was rising. "Stay behind me."

Jack started around the building's near corner, Ellen, her rifle at what she remembered was called high port, right behind him. More shots than she could count tore into the building's wall behind her, forcing her forward faster, and in front of Jack. Jack turned around, starting to fold her into his arms, to protect her with his own body.

Her knees were buckling.

It was possibly a different shot than that from the bullet which had struck her a split second ago. She distinctly remembered the old aphorism to the effect that you never heard the shot that killed you. She'd heard shots and plenty of them. Ellen deduced that either the aphorism was incorrect, or, in fact, she was not about to die. Aphorisms be damned; Ellen hoped that she was not about to die, but her eyelids were so heavy and just wouldn't stay open anymore . . .

Eyes locked with those of the man who'd fired the senselessly long burst from a submachine gun, Jack shrieked his rage as Ellen sank to the muddy ground, his arms cushioning her, his hands holding her face. "Fuck you, cocksucker! Fuck you! Fuck you!" The man's eyes were so dark brown they were black, he had a five o'clock shadow that looked permanent and his mouth was an ugly slash. Jack, his submachine gun hanging from its sling at his side, drew the long-barreled Colt. More personal.

Jack punched the revolver toward its target, the shooter's

face. Jack's first finger pushed against the trigger and the hammer fell and the man was already dead before Jack fired the second shot and cursed him, shouting, "Die, you motherfucker! Die! Die!"

What was left of the man's face after the first chunk of lead had struck it exploded in a spray of red and gray, blood and brain matter, and there was a deep, ragged notch roughly describing where the man's hair would have been parted had he parted it down the middle and had enough of his head still been intact to tell.

Jack, still holding Ellen, emptied the remaining three shots, spit at the dead man and promised himself to urinate on him when it would be safe to let go of Ellen. Tears filled Jack's eyes. He couldn't see much of anything except the red stain on Ellen's back. His head hurt and his chest felt tight and he couldn't stop weeping . . .

Lieutenant Easley said, "It would appear, sir, that someone was watching out not only for your wife, sir, but for you. A lot of blood, very little wound. Mrs. Naile won't be in fighting trim for a bit, I'd think, but you've not lost her."

Jack nodded. The rain fell heavily, relentlessly. The gunfire was ended for the moment, the time base won. Ellen was being treated by the time-transfer base's medic—the female medic would be spared—everyone was soaking wet, and anyone who wasn't standing around or sitting around soaking wet was dead. Only one of the Seventh had died—Luciano. Unlike his namesake of the Prohibition Era to come, there would be no reason to nickname the fellow "Lucky."

Jack walked over to the lately dead man who had shot Ellen. Jack could see himself unbuttoning his fly, unlimbering his penis and urinating on what little was left of what had once been a human face. It was a promise needing to be kept, but it would not be; being civilized really sucked sometimes, Jack reflected. Instead of pissing, he merely wished that he had and walked away.

Ellen kissed Alan as he folded her into his arms. She let herself sag against him a little, feeling a little weak, a little tired. "I'm sorry you can't wait around long enough to meet my wife and the kids, Momma Ellen. My grandfather, David's son, said that when he was little, that was what he called you."

"Since it hasn't happened yet—to me, anyway—I'll just have to take your word for it, Alan."

"I love you, Momma Ellen."

Ellen let him hold her a little while longer, even though she just wished that she could sit down. Only one bullet had struck her, grazing her back just past her right shoulder blade and creasing her right tricep. The two wounds hurt like anything, and she'd lost enough blood to make her feel woozy, but she was all right. To assume that she was going to live would, under the circumstances, have been mightily presumptuous, could be considered to border on sophistry. But between this moment and the one when the door to the time-transfer capsule was closed, barring a meteor impacting, heart attack or a major blood vessel rupturing in her brain, her survival was secure. Ellen Naile had learned a long time ago that one should be grateful for what one had; such did not imply acceptance of the status quo, however, merely that dwelling in misery ignoring what happiness was at hand while waiting for what wasn't was stupid.

Jack embraced his great-great grandson. "You sure that you'll be okay on your own, son?"

"The bad guys are all dead except for the medic and she'll stay away. I've got weapons, cars, food, money we took off their bodies. I'll get this time-transfer base shut down, and, if my own company's facility is still operational, that one, too. And I'll find Bethany Kaminsky's little ace-in-the-hole. I'll miss you guys, Grandpa Jack."

"And I'll miss you, chief."

Ellen was not a crier, but hearing Jack call his great-great-grandson by the same pet name he'd always used for their son was—Ellen told herself that it was her sinuses.

On the floor of the time-transfer capsule lay a coffin handled Bowie knife with a blade a tad under a foot long. Jack Naile breathed a sigh of relief at the sight of it. Straws had been drawn to see who would go back to 1900 as a scout. The Lakewood senior bad guy Lester Matthews and his men could have had a reception waiting for anyone coming backward in time from 1996.

Standing Bear had offered to swap with Goldstein for the short straw, but Goldstein had declined. It was then that Standing Bear offered Goldstein the loan of his fighting knife. Then, also, was an agreement struck as to how it would be known whether or not a trap had been encountered, some sort of ambush. If the knife were returned to the time capsule and left there, it would be obvious that Goldstein had been the one to leave it there.

The knife was as fine an example of the knifemaker's art as Jack had seen in the twentieth or nineteenth centuries. A bad guy victorious in a battle would be hard pressed not to keep such a knife. If a battle were ongoing, the knife would be at Goldstein's side. The only way the knife could be left in the capsule to be "found" ninety-six years away—or merely a half hour later, depending on how one looked at it—would be if Goldstein intentionally put it there.

This patched-together form of time-travel left so many unanswerable—or, at least, unanswered—questions. Why, after being left for ninety-six years in the capsule, was the knife in perfect shape, as if no time had passed at all? Obviously, no time had passed, except for the half hour or so since Goldstein had left 1996 and returned to 1900. Yet there was a ninety-six year difference between 1900 and 1996. Clearly, time was to be reckoned in more than one way, possibly more ways than anyone could count, but certainly in at least these two ways.

Ellen, leaning heavily on Jack, looked up at him and inquired, "Are you contemplating the mysteries of the universe again, Jack?"

"I had a glimmer of what somebody might someday be able to turn into a string theory concerning the nature of time, that's all."

"Nothing important, then."

Jack merely nodded and bent over to pick up the knife. He announced to Ellen, Easley, Armitage, Harek and Standing Bear, "The knife was just where it should be. There shouldn't be a trap waiting for us in 1900. Just in case, at least two subguns worn on-body by each man."

There were a good three dozen submachine guns and as many M-16s, four of these M-16/M-203s, standard M-16 rifles with independently triggerable grenade launchers mounted below the barrel/fore-end assembly of the rifle itself.

Jack had one of each principal weapon—one submachine gun, one rifle with grenade launcher—slung to his body. "I feel like a character from an Arnold Schwarzenegger movie," Jack observed.

Ellen smiled. "But you look so much better developed, so much more muscular, Jack."

"You bet," he grinned.

The capsule doorway started to close and Jack and Ellen, standing side by side, shot a wave and smiled a last good-bye to their great-great-grandson . . .

David Naile tried ignoring the man in the backseat who was saying, "I'm a gonna be pukin' heah, suh!"

"If my father were driving, I could understand that. I drive very smoothly. Your stomach shouldn't be bothering you."

"Ya jes' tell thet a mah belly, suh!"

"Aw, shit."

"Ain't the sitchashun, suh."

Under his breath, David Naile snarled, "Pitiful shit can't even speak English, and he's supposed to be a soldier." For the guy in the back seat to be able to get out, half the guys in the middle seat at least would have to climb out and guns and cans of ammunition and grenades and anything else would have to be unloaded—or, at least, a lot of it.

David stopped the car in the middle of the stagecoach road. "Okay! Fine! Hurl, then get your ass back here, Private. Corporal!"

"Yes, sir!"

David glanced at the man who'd occupied the Suburban's front bucket passenger seat. "Get everybody to do what they've gotta do. I don't want anybody asking to go potty until we're there. We're in a kind of a really big hurry. Right?"

"Yes, sir!"

David took the key out of the Suburban's ignition and climbed out. The Northwest quadrant of the inverted bowl of sky was darkening more rapidly than David Naile had ever seen storm clouds change daylight into twilight. "We're in for a good storm, Corporal."

"That's a fact, sir. A real gully washer, I bet, Mr. Naile."

David Naile glanced at his pocket watch. If his parents and the raiding party made it through safely, they'd be back.

If was a very uncomfortable word.

Clarence had been waiting just outside the doorway as the time-transfer capsule opened. After helping get Ellen inside the control shed where there was a couch on which she could rest, Clarence had immediately volunteered that the guys from 1996 who'd traveled to 1900 had come out of the time capsule shooting. Three of the men, including the apparent leader—Jack pegged him as Lester Matthews and said so—had gotten away in a Hummer, rolling cross-country almost as if the rocky terrain had been a paved road.

Two other men, who'd tried getting into the tank—an old Soviet T-62, as Clarence recounted it—died in the attempt. There were three more men in the party. After a short, furious gun battle, the enemy personnel were overwhelmed and killed. By this time, Jack had no interest in knowing more than that.

"The T-62 was kind of an evolutionary blind alley for what was then the Soviet Union. Rate of fire and fire control were inferior to NATO stuff. It went out of production. Heck, the World War II T-34 was a better tank in a lot of ways."

Jack looked at Clarence, knowing that his expression must have been something between blank and nonplussed. "How'd you get to know so much on tanks?"

"I had to learn a lot of things in the military, and that's all I can say about it. If I told you more, Uncle Jack, I'd have to kill ya."

Jack felt himself smile. "Yeah," he told Clarence. "Since you know so much, you think you and one of Lieutenant Easley's men could drive the thing and work the weapons system?"

It was Clarence's turn to smile. "I'd sure like to try."

"Just be careful—we don't have a wrecker that can put a new track on for you."

Lieutenant Easley said, "You say this isn't even a very good tank, Mr. Jones?"

"That's right, Lieutenant. Not very good at all."

"Yet I'd wager it would be essentially impervious to damage from almost anything we could field against it. Correct, sir?"

"Yes, Lieutenant, but not quite. Knock out a tread

and the tank's pretty much useless, except as a firing platform—an artillery piece."

"Maybe with this tank, despite its limitations, we'll have a chance against some of their weaponry, even against a plane if it's on the ground or just taking off. If we can find them." Jack turned his attention to his nephew. "Okay, whatchya got, Clarence? Can we do any sophisticated recon or not?"

"They had weather balloons which I can get airborne and mount with a video camera that can send back a live feed until it's out of range. I can't control direction, but I've got three of the cameras that can be rigged up and a portable receiver can go into one of the trucks. It's the best I can do with what we've got. We'll be short on drivers, only the three of us, if Ellen's okay to do it, and I'm going to be riding that tank, if I can figure it out. We get enough altitude and we might be able to spot a dust plume or maybe even a vehicle."

"Try it," Jack told him.

Despite her wound, Ellen would be able to drive one of the Suburbans, enabling the transport of more men with full equipment.

The Suburbans were even air-conditioned, but the weather at the time-transfer base obviated its necessity. Cool breezes blew down from the higher mountains and would hopefully persist, at least a short way into the desert, where the air-conditioning would prove to be a blessing.

Clarence's handling of the Soviet tank seemed to be at least acceptable. But the important thing was for Clarence to be able to get the tank to a position where it could fire on the enemy ordnance. Its use in any other tank-related role beyond that of an artillery platform was unlikely.

As Jack walked the compound for the last time, he stopped to inspect dynamite charges—as if he knew anything about explosives besides a reading knowledge. A glance at his leather-cased Rolex confirmed that a little over an hour had passed since their return to 1900, time aplenty for Alan in 1996 to destroy his end of Lakewood's time-transfer base. In another five minutes or so, fuses would be set at this end of the time-transfer base, and all structures, including the time-transfer capsule itself, would be destroyed.

Activity was everywhere, Easley shouting orders to non-coms, non-coms shouting orders to their subordinates.

Weapons were loaded, spare magazines as well, green GI ammo boxes packed tightly in the Suburbans. The supply of shells for the tank's 115mm gun was more than adequate. The odd ordnance items had been gathered up as well: one U.S. issue LAW Rocket, three claymore mines (how much "lovelier" the coming World War I's blood-soaked trench warfare might be with those) and a crate of Beretta 92F pistols, M-9s with U.S. service markings, likely stolen off a loading dock somewhere during Operation Desert Storm.

All the gasoline that could be safely carried was loaded into GI surplus-style jerricans, these packed into single axle cage trailers that would be pulled by the Suburban Ellen would drive and the one Jack would operate. Additional diesel fuel for the Soviet tank was secured as well.

The rest of the gasoline and diesel, along with the modest supply of aviation-grade fuel for the VSTOL fighter planes, was artfully arranged in the compound so that when the dynamite charges started their work, the fuel would ignite. It was important to obliterate as much of the time-transfer base as possible until Roosevelt could make arrangements for troops to be brought in and properly finish the job.

Jack clambered up onto the bed of one of the pickups and called out, "Okay, everybody listen up! Time's flying; we're not. Let's get everybody loaded in the vehicles, and those left behind get to your horses and take the extra horses with you. Remember, the three men Lieutenant Easley picked for the telegraphy unit—you'll be the only means by which we can communicate the location of the enemy firepower demonstration once we've discovered it. Hence, you'll be the only way the rest of the troops can be brought in." The number of surplus weapons in 9mm, including those brought back from 1996 after seizing control of Lakewood's base there, was substantial. Unfortunately, there were only nineteen M-16 rifles and five thousand rounds of 5.56mm ammunition—not enough for a war, but enough for one big battle, hopefully all that would be needed.

"Anybody have any questions? Now's the time," Jack advised the assembled men of the Seventh.

No questions were raised.

Jack nodded. He called to the demolitions unit, "Let's start those charges five minutes from NOW! Everybody get moving!" Jack jumped from the back of the truck and started toward the Suburbans. He spotted Clarence climbing aboard the Soviet tank and they gave each other a wave. Clarence's electronic stuff was safely packed.

Ellen was shepherding her troopers into a metallic green Suburban. "You sure you're up for this, kid?" Jack asked her. Her wound had not been deep at all, but getting shot was serious business, if only because of the body's reaction to trauma.

"I'm fine. You just be careful, Jack."

Jack angled toward her, curled his arm around her waist and planted a kiss on her mouth. "Now, remember. Try and sound like Ward Bond when I shout to see if we're ready."

"I know," Ellen said smiling, "I call out, 'I was born ready.' But let's skip the part where the Apaches chase us, okay?"

"I'll think about it." Jack kissed his wife again and started toward the black Suburban, its passengers, Lieutenant Easley among them, already in place. Jack handed his M-16 off to Lieutenant Easley and stood in the Suburban's doorway. He glanced at Clarence, visible in the tank's open hatch, then at Ellen. "Ready?"

Ellen merely called back, "Yes, we are, Jack," and gave him a wickedly pretty smile.

Ellen had ruined the whole Ward Bond thing, of course. Jack mentally shrugged, shouted, "Okay, okay. We're outa here!" And Jack waved his arm in the general direction of what passed for a road, dropped down behind the wheel and turned the key.

The engine roared loudly—it was a 454 and sounded like it might have had a bad fan clutch. Jack thought he heard one of the men of the Seventh start saying a prayer before the sound of the motor drowned it out.

Jack said a quick one himself.

CHAPTER
❖ TWENTY-FOUR ❖

Alan's first cellular phone call was to his wife. No one answered at their house, so he tried the estate in central Wisconsin after leaving a neutral sounding message on the answering machine. His wife answered the telephone on the third ring and cried the moment that she heard his voice. Promising that he was all right and that he would call back very shortly, he asked a few questions, ascertaining that he still had control of his own company and that his parents were also okay. His mother was actually at the estate, his father down in Chicago.

Alan learned that his father had literally taken himself out of retirement and was personally overseeing Horizon Enterprises' day-to-day affairs and Horizon's efforts with law enforcement and a corps of detectives to locate Horizon's missing CEO or his body. Almost oddly, Alan thought, although Lakewood Industries and Kaminsky in particular topped everyone's suspect list, it had occurred to no one that he'd been kidnapped to another time. Alan didn't mention it.

Instead, Alan told his wife to lock the doors and take the kids and his mother "downstairs," the best euphemism he could think of for the war/storm shelter built by his grandfather below the house in Wisconsin. Alan and his wife both loved gangster movies, so he added, "I want you guys goin' to the mattresses, see," and he got a little chuckle out of her.

Killing the connection, he called his father's cellular number, a number only family members had. "Dad?"

"Alan! My God, son, where have you—"

"No time to explain. I'm alive and I'm fine, but we've got work to do to help Jack and Ellen—they're still you know where, of course, but they were here with me for a little bit. Tell you when I see you, Dad. Keep my private land line clear. As soon as I find a pay phone, I'll call in. Have a scrambler on it, huh?" And Alan hung up.

Instead of a roadside pay phone—harder and harder to find in the era of wireless everything—Alan rented a motel room with a dead man's credit card. The black nylon gear bag that he carried held no socks and under-wear, but instead an MP-5 submachine gun, two 228 9mm pistols and plenty of loaded magazines for both the H-K and the SIGs.

The motel was a modest affair that probably got along based on location. It was the middle of Nevada and looked, Alan thought, more like the middle of nowhere. A remote location indeed, it was a popular one. Nevada 375 was commonly known as the Extraterrestrial Highway because it was the road to Groom Lake, the infamous Area 51.

However intriguing Area 51 might or might not be, it currently held no interest for Alan. Highway 375 also led to the far western edge of Red Raven Ranch, and this was extremely interesting because Red Raven Ranch was the location of the second and smaller Lakewood Industries time-travel base. That information was uncovered in the aftermath of the attack on Lakewood's primary time base in 1996, but only after Jack and Ellen had returned to 1900. By the time Alan had picked up on Red Raven Ranch as the site, Alan had already trashed the controls for the transfer device beyond repair and had no means by which to alert Jack and Ellen.

The base at Red Raven Ranch had to be destroyed, wiped off the face of the Earth in both times, before Kaminsky and her thugs—if Jack and Ellen were successful—could use it to escape the year 1900. If his many-times-removed grandparents were not successful, the only remaining working time-transfer base's destruction would trap the Lakewood Industries personnel in 1900, ninety-six years out of reach of resupply.

There was a bank of pay phones in the motel lobby. If he'd been spotted by some Lakewood Industries confederate, or even in the case of ordinary nosiness, the telephone in his room would be far too easy to listen in on. Alan began to dial his private number in Chicago. Unlike the room phones, the pay phones would not go through a switchboard at the motel. With a scrambler on the Chicago end of the line, chances were excellent that the conversation about to take place would be secret.

His father answered the telephone midway through the first ring.

"Alan?"

"Yeah, it's me, Dad."

"Where the hell have you been, son?"

"In 1900." Alan waited a second to let that sink in with his father, then went on. "I would have been dead if it hadn't been for great-great-grandpa Jack and Ellen and Clarence's wife—she's the doctor I told you about who was involved in the initial time-transfer experiments, helping Jane Rogers. Bethany Kaminsky and Morton Hardesty are lovers—if you can call it—"

"Hardesty? My God, son! Hardesty's got access to almost everything."

"We ought to fix that as quickly as possible."

"If we press charges against Hardesty or anybody else, we'd have to reveal the time-transfer operation, and you know what that would entail."

Alan nodded his head in agreement, even though his father was nearly two thousand miles away. If the mechanism for time-transfer—even in so limited a manner—was revealed, they would have opened the proverbial Pandora's box.

"It's a dilemma, Dad. How about some words of wisdom?"

Alan heard bitter-sounding laughter from the other end of the line. His eyes swept the lobby for signs of anything strange. He wore both SIG pistols under his shirt, but they provided little comfort at the moment.

His father spoke. "If you want me to be the one who says it, then I will. We're just going to have to—"

"No. Don't say it, but I agree. I'm going to need some help out here quite rapidly. Kaminsky's people have their secondary base out here."

"Is it even safe for you to be near there, Alan?"

An older couple wearing T-shirts and ball caps that were a perfect match were wending their way across the blue-carpeted lobby toward the polished wooden front desk. A fluorescent fixture buzzed just a little. Nothing else was even that noteworthy. "No, I'm okay for a little while, here. I'll wait, but get some people to me in a hurry."

"They're already en route, son."

Alan nodded again, his stomach churning at the thought of his only recourse concerning Lakewood Industries. "About their facility in Chicago, Dad—there's a lot of data there that really shouldn't be."

"I'm on top of that, son."

There was only one solution and it was terrible, but Bethany had brought it down on her own head.

Just as the flashes of manmade lightning that signaled the time-transfers had been visible miles away from the mountains, so too were the fires burning at the site that had once been Lakewood's base in what, to them, was the subjective past. It would be late in the afternoon where Alan was—1996. Part of the time-displacement anomaly included a difference of four hours, twenty-three minutes and some seconds. It was four and one-half hours later and early evening in 1900, dark enough that Jack Naile could easily spy the glow of the flames through his binoculars.

The small convoy—two Suburbans and an old Soviet tank—had stopped in order that Clarence could launch a weather balloon, assisted by Lieutenant Easley. Easley's father, it was discovered, had been a reconnaissance balloonist during the Civil War and had imparted an interest in aeronautics to his son. Although Clarence manned the electronics package, Lieutenant Easley was clearly in charge of readying the balloon itself.

The purpose of the binoculars Jack Naile held was not for the observation of far-distant fires, but to keep track of the first balloon. He'd lost sight of it almost five minutes earlier.

As Jack aimed his binoculars toward the subtly darkening eastern horizon, he thought he spotted it. "Over that ridgeline, about five miles to the southeast! Do you see the ridgeline, Clarence?"

"Got it! I think. Yeah, I've got it." There were a limited number of video cameras and a limited number of balloons. If they could be salvaged, it was definitely advantageous. If they could not be salvaged, at least if their location could be generally fixed, it would be possible for Mr. Roosevelt to have them recovered so they would not be randomly discovered. "The camera's picking up what must be headlights far to the southwest." The reason for waiting until near dusk before launching was the hope of spotting headlights being a better bet than spotting a dust trail. "What happens if they spot our headlights and send that helicopter back after us?"

"We might die," Jack answered as cheerfully as he could.

The air was cool, rising along the rocky promontory

near where they'd parked. The western horizon was a deep purple, the ball of sun—about the color of an egg yolk—enormous-seeming.

Clarence and Lieutenant Easley were packing up their ballooning and electronic monitoring gear, Ellen rounding up her passengers for the next leg of the journey . . .

Still in cowboy clothes and boots, Alan buttoned down the stretched black Lincoln's right-side window as the limousine skidded slightly on the hard-packed sandy dirt and ground to a halt. Three helicopters were coming in, sunset-tinged and gleaming black Bell Long Rangers, unmarked, their registration numbers meticulously taped over. Alan didn't wait for their arrival or for the bodyguard from the front seat to open the door for him. He stepped out of the Town Car and flexed his arms, his shoulders, tried loosening his neck muscles.

Red Raven Ranch was twenty miles away, a distance that a helicopter could cover in little more than a heartbeat. This land was the same as it had been ninety-six years ago, in the Old West. Only what transpired there was different. It was strange; it literally boggled the mind to contemplate that what was happening ninety-six years ago had already happened, but differently. Time, almost certainly, healed itself, as was often said in science fiction books and films; Jack and Ellen, dead by all logic, lived on in the past, and the past was happening simultaneously with the present. All pasts? All presents? Did everything just go on and on and on, repeating and rerepeating itself in alternate planes of time?

And what of the future? Alan wondered.

He'd read articles in which well-respected serious scientists had theorized that travel into the past might be theoretically—at least—possible. But that made such a vain assumption! Why was this moment in time the point farthest along in time? Had a scientist in 1900 posited that time-travel into the future was impossible because 1900 was as far as the future had yet gone, the events surrounding Jack and Ellen and himself and Teddy Roosevelt and the men from the Seventh Cavalry—not to mention Lakewood's back-and-forth journeys—would have proven the idea totally false, a conceit of the most ludicrous proportions.

The same held true in 1996, Alan felt. 1997 and 1998 and only God knew how many other futures were already out there, unreachable now, but there.

"Mr. Naile?"

Alan turned around and glanced at his bodyguard; the man looked overheated, standing there in the desert twilight wearing his nattily tailored Chicago business suit. "Yes, Frank?" The man was adjusting an earpiece, one of two, the second dangling lazily over his left lapel.

"The choppers are ready, sir, and your presence aboard the nearest of the three"—Frank gestured in the direction of the helicopters—"is requested, sir. The penetration team is in position on the ground."

Alan merely nodded his understanding and assent. Whatever the year, murder was murder, and that was what circumstances demanded of him. These murders would be for the good of all mankind, of course, but that reason was almost certainly one of the more common excuses offered for taking significant numbers of human lives.

As Alan walked toward the designated helicopter, he kept reminding himself that he was with the good guys.

David worked the squeeze bulb to evacuate the air in the transparent plastic line between the first jerrican and the Suburban's fuel tank. Among the supplies his parents had packed for their anticipated—and realized—journey almost a century into the past were numerous odd things. He remembered asking his father, "Why are we taking plastic tubing and these squeeze bulbs? Are we going to start an aquarium?" When the family had been in its tropical-fish period, identical tubing and bulbs had been used to evacuate dirty tank water into buckets; these were carried off, their contents flushed down the toilet. Jack Naile had responded that what was used to siphon water could be used just as easily to siphon gasoline.

His father had some good ideas at times.

Anyway, it amused his passengers, the men of the Seventh Cavalry, to watch the pale reddish liquid moving magically through the transparent tube. The rechargeable flashlight by the light of which he was able to see what he was doing had elicited mutterings of pure amazement, the light so terribly bright. David felt like a veritable master of illusion.

Alan retracted the M-16's bolt and let it fly forward. That he was violating countless laws was of little consequence. Dealing death from a helicopter would be the toughest rap, and he'd never beat it.

The western horizon was washed in brilliant shades of red, dissolving into orange and then into yellow-tinged pink, all edged in deeply purpling darkness. Already in the west, Alan could make out the sparkling pinpoint of Venus. The eastern horizon was so dark a blue that it was nearly black.

The desert slipping away below the helicopter was gray, neither day nor night, but in between. The leader of the raid, Del Stringfellow, was Horizon's chief of security for the southwest. His somewhat high-pitched voice was coming through Alan's earphone. "We'll be over the contact point in ninety seconds. Ground personnel—I kept to a minimum—are fully positioned. This should be quick."

"Any chance they've got us on radar, Del?"

"No, sir—we're too low. They could have us on visual by accident, but that's doubtful. About sixty seconds, now."

"You didn't have to do this, Del; so, thanks. This wasn't part of the job description."

"In a funny way it is, though, Mr. Naile. Don't sweat it."

Alan didn't answer verbally, only nodded.

Probably thirty seconds remained.

"Incoming! Surface to air!" It was the pilot's voice, shouting, not panicked, but startled.

Del's voice hit with machinegun rapidity in the next millisecond. "Evasive action. Get us outa here. Special One to Special Two and Three; we are under fire, presumably low-end Soviet-era SA-7 shoulder-mounted SAMs. Evasive action. Engage enemy at will. Prospector One and Two; commence Operation Visitor immediately. I say again, commence Operation Visitor immediately. Special One Out."

The helicopter had been climbing, then diving. It leveled

off and skimmed the ground, seeming inches over the dirt. Only twenty seconds or so had gone by. The contrail from one of the missiles flashed past the Bell's nose, missing the chin bubble by less distance than Alan wanted to think about.

A searchlight flicked on from the helicopter's nose. "They can see us by our running lights anyway, Mr. Naile."

"Affirmative that, pilot."

As the searchlight flashed across the sandy terrain, Alan spotted a half-dozen Lakewood personnel, discarded missile tubes only a yard or so behind them. Two of the men stopped in their headlong lunge and turned; one fired an M-16. Bullets spiderwebbed the chin bubble. The second had a missile tube to his shoulder, preparing to fire.

"Mr. Naile! Be careful, sir!"

It was Del Stringfellow's voice in his ear, but Alan Naile was already dismounting the door, letting it fall away in the helicopter's slipstream. Belted in, he leaned out of the chopper, the M-16 to his shoulder. Aiming at the man with the missile from the unsteady firing platform, he missed him and struck the rifleman beside him instead. The Lakewood man's M-16 fired a long, full auto burst skyward, bullets ricocheting off the fuselage.

Flying over the man with the missile, there was a flash of yellow, the missile firing. The pilot shouted, "Hold on!"

The helicopter banked sharply to starboard and Alan nearly lost his rifle as he was half flung from the machine, only his safety harness keeping him from being dashed to the ground below. The missile tracked so close to the helicopter that Alan could feel heat from its vapor trail.

Gunfire and explosive flashes were everywhere in the

gathering darkness below. Hands—Del Stringfellow's—pulled at him and Alan was fully returned to the cabin. "Thanks! Let's get that fucker!"

"Yes, sir! You heard Mr. Naile! Turn this crate around."

"Wilco that, Del."

The helicopter described a steep arc and swooped toward the ground. "He's mine," Alan declared, checking his safety belt and leaning out the starboard side of the fuselage. This time, his M-16's strap was twisted round his left arm in the classic Hasty Sling. The Lakewood man threw his empty missile tube to the dirt and ran, firing an MP-5 submachine gun blindly upward and behind him.

Alan drew his weapon's trigger back, and a long burst chewed into the ground behind the Lakewood man, then stitched up along the length of the man's body as the helicopter overflew. The Lakewood man tumbled down dead in the mini-cyclone of sand that rose in the helicopter's wake.

Alan looked ahead. Brilliant, ephemeral flashes of yellow-orange rose and fell in the darkness.

Stringfellow's voice came through the headset again. "It's estimated that resistance is over ninety percent neutralized. Enemy personnel encountered have been permanently neutralized. Estimating maybe a little over a dozen Lakewood personnel. One pocket of resistance remains near what appears to be the time-transfer control station, a capsule near it." There was a pause, and Alan looked over at Stringfellow. Short, slight, blond, with a jaw like a rock, the security man's ice-blue eyes flickered up from an aerial shot showing on the screen of a laptop.

With his right thumb, Stringfellow made a downward sign three times. "The last of the Lakewood personnel have been permanently neutralized, Mr. Naile."

"Let's get down there," Alan ordered, letting out a long breath that was almost a sigh.

The dry lake bed below them was an enormous valley, what had once been its shoreline—David had no idea how long ago, but the time would be best reckoned by a geologist—forming the rugged higher ground wherein they had concealed themselves. Through the predawn hours they'd waited. Beyond, to the east, the sun relentlessly climbed. It would be hot this day.

"The bad guys are over there," David said, addressing the nine troopers with him. He had driven the Suburban through the night on the calculated guess that this was Kaminsky's probable destination. The guess was correct. "Very bad guys," he reiterated, jerking his thumb toward the center of the lake bed, where there was pitched an enormous tent. Sand-colored and large enough to shelter a small circus, the tent had been erected with additional canopies adjoined to it. Maybe folding chairs hadn't yet been invented, or maybe a more elegant look was sought, but elaborate-seeming wooden dining-room-style chairs with cushioned seats and raised arm-rests were ranked under the canopies. Overstuffed chairs with exposed wooden trim and love-seat-sized sofas of the same construction formed a semicircle of grand proportions beneath the tent itself. At what was the exact center between the two main verticals around which the tent roof was erected were buffet tables. Several portable generators were providing power for electric chandeliers and a bank of bar-sized refrigerators and at least two refrigerated serving tables.

It was a credit to Anglo-American cooperation—strained occasionally during these times, David knew—that there seemed to be no representation for Great Britain. There was, of course, none for the United States. The French, the Germans, the Russians—they were the expected bidders and they were present. David could tell from the uniforms of the military personnel, his knowledge based on old movies his father had pretty much coerced him and his sister into watching. The Germans had the most businesslike and military-looking uniforms, and these were field gray. The French uniforms were certainly the most stylish and their headgear was the flat-topped, almost ball-cap-looking thing called a kepi. The Russians had extremely elaborate helmets, apparently not trusting to ordinary hats of any kind.

Many of the civilians—the diplomats—wore swallow-tailed coats and striped pants and tall, narrow-brimmed, shiny black silk hats. The other men—there was not a single woman visible—were evidently assistants, male secretaries and the like, attired in uncomfortable-looking suits and less formal hats, derby-or Homburg-style. Ranked socially lower still were coach drivers and footmen, exiled to nether regions beneath more spartan canopies and near where the luxurious carriages and less prestigious buck-boards were parked.

"Missah Naile, suh? What's them li'l blue houses out yonder?"

David glanced over at Corporal Gossman, the ranking

soldier, and smiled. "What do you suppose they are for, Corporal?"

"Well, suh, sho' look like the' oughta be a qua'ter moon cut in them doors, if'n y'all takes mah drift."

"I take your drift, Corporal." David nodded. "Only these are portable. When they're no longer needed somewhere, they're carted off."

"What's they do with the, the—"

"The shit? It's usually sucked up with a hose after chemicals have liquefied—" David stopped, his attention focusing solely on the motor home parked some distance back from the tent. A solitary woman exited it. As she turned her face toward the east, David could see her clearly through his binoculars. It was Bethany Kaminsky. Alan's powers of elucidation proved quite remarkable; she was as promised, even down to exuding an amazing and unmistakable deadliness.

Kaminsky's blond hair, done in ringlets, was piled at the crown of her head. Her eyes—in this, Alan's descriptive abilities failed utterly—were blue, yes, but such ineloquence could best be compared to labeling the world's most exquisite diamond as a "pretty rock." Blue, to be sure, but so much more than that. Even through the lenses of mere binoculars, the color was at once obvious and magnificent.

Women's fashions of the day were designed to accentuate a slender waist, of course, and Kaminsky's figure showed the classic and perfect hourglass. David smiled at himself as he realized that he was wondering what Kaminsky— evil bitch that she was, assuredly—looked like without all those pounds of clothes. "Oh, well," he muttered under his breath. Her coachwork looked great—what he could see of it. Her motor probably ran a little hot and fast, he guessed; but, with an experienced man controlling the throttle . . . But, lamentably, there'd be no chance for a test drive.

"Pick four men you can trust to stay here with you and not spook if they see the aircraft or any of the weapons in use before we get back. We're going to use that telegraphy kit; make sure we've got plenty of water." His father thought that he never listened. He listened—sometimes. Jack related seeing one of his half-hour western A-list boy-hood action heroes, Jock Mahoney, use canteen water and a piece of wire to short out and link up with a telegraph line. David found himself actually remembering hearing the story before when his father had recently suggested using the same technique. And his dad was actually rather impressed. "Pick your men, Corporal. I'm moving out in under two minutes." But he'd be damned if he let anyone use the barrel of a six gun to tap out a message in Morse.

David started toward the Suburban. He had topped off its tank just before parking it for the night, lest a sudden quick getaway be required.

Looking at the situation from a strictly business perspective, David could see why Lakewood Industries would not achieve quite the future prominence of Horizon Enterprises. Lakewood was making a mistake, its sales technique clearly faulty. Each of the three potential buyers for future technology would know what all the others knew. Greed manifested in the desire to up the ante to the highest possible level the first time out was sheer stupidity in the current context. Germany, according to both his father and Mr. Roosevelt, would almost certainly be the end-result purchaser. So why let the French and the Russians have intimate knowledge of what Germany would possess? Drive up the price at the expense of future sales? Madness. And what if Kaminsky set up dummy front companies, so that, after selling to the Germans, the dummy companies could sell to anyone and everyone else? More money and power, but what if these technologically naive military powers destroyed the whole world eventually, and Kaminsky and Lakewood Industries somehow wound up being obliterated along with all the rest of the future?

David didn't understand time-travel theory, so maybe what he posited could never happen. But theory was one thing, reality another.

Kaminsky was, in effect, a suicidal viper, a dangerous, deadly, egotistical asshole.

And her choice of locations proved it. She was probably one of those idiots who believed in little green men and thought that staging a firepower anachronism at this exact spot would be cutesy. David's telegraph message, which would be relayed to his father, would simply read "Area 51 STOP," because brevity was, so the expression went, the soul of wit.

Their shadows and those of their mounts stretched for yards ahead of them along the sandy stagecoach road over which they traveled, the sun low still and directly behind them. They had risen in darkness, and were mounted and moving before dawn. The stagecoach road had turned due west only a mile or so back.

Elizabeth Naile rode at the head of the column, to the

immediate left of Major Clark Davis, Army Ordnance. The air was fresh and still cool, no noticeable dust rising yet. There was a slight breeze, and they advanced against it.

Elizabeth, despite a rocky sleep in a small tent on a cot pitched on rough ground and no proper bathing facilities, was having the time of her life, an experience unlike any other. She'd convinced Mr. Roosevelt to give orders that she could accompany the forces being sent against Lakewood's firepower demonstration, promising him she'd stay well to the rear if the unit she'd accompany saw action. Mr. Roosevelt probably hadn't believed her, but gave the orders anyway. "I have a very pretty daughter named Alice, who has a rather adventurous spirit as well. You remind me of her. Be careful."

In a flat-crowned, wide-brimmed, fudge brown hat with a stampede string snuggled under her chin, white silk blouse with full sleeves, ankle-length brown-suede split skirt and lace-up-the-front brown high-heeled boots, she felt she was dressed for the part of the daring girl on her way to adventure.

Lizzie glanced at the major. He was extraordinarily tall in the saddle, so long-legged that his stirrups were adjusted well below those of any of the others of their party. Whereas she would have to take a little hop to get her left foot into her stirrup in order to mount into the saddle, Major Davis stepped onto his mount as effortlessly as an ordinary person might merely ascend a stair tread.

And she loved it when, low-whiskey-voiced, he'd order his sergeant to "Mount the men." If she hadn't found herself falling in love with Bobby Lorkin, and if Major Davis hadn't been about the same age as her father, Lizzie could have had a crush.

The pace at which the column moved was a rapid canter rather than a gallop, miles more remaining certainly before there would be a chance to rest. The pace was also determined by the rolling stock. There were three field-artillery pieces, each positioned behind a caisson of ammunition. Two men were seated on each of the box-like affairs, one of the men driving the four-horse team pulling each of the units. There were three wagons, one of these the cook's wagon, a second wagon that would serve as a field hospital and a third carrying additional supplies and ammunition for the troops.

"Ho!" Major Davis raised his right hand and reined back, signaling the column to halt.

Lizzie looked up at him as she brought her roan mare alongside. "What is it, Major?"

"There, Miss Naile. Just coming over the rise. The telegraphy party is returning." The major looked over his shoulder and ordered his sergeant, "Tucker, get a report from the man in charge of that detail and on the double."

"Yes, sir!" The sergeant called out, "corporal Redding, on the double!"

A moment later, the corporal was riding off at best speed to intercept the telegraphy party, which was still almost a half mile distant.

Unbidden, Major Davis volunteered to her, "Lieutenant Matthews and the two scouts should be getting back soon, too. If we bump into these Lakewood people and their ordnance is half as capable as you say, we'd be outgunned at the least. We're going to need all the tactical advantage we can muster to counteract their firepower."

Corporal Redding's mount, a cloud of dust around it and behind it, skidded on its haunches and stopped alongside the telegraphy party. There was a moment's discussion, and Corporal Redding's horse wheeled under him and raced back toward the column.

"Tucker, have the corporal report to me directly. You stay and listen," Major Davis ordered.

"Yes, sir!"

As Corporal Redding neared, Lizzie heard Sergeant Tucker bellow, "Report directly to the major, Corporal."

Corporal Redding made no acknowledgment except to wheel his horse a few degrees left and skid to a halt about six feet in front of Major Davis, reining in and saluting in one fluid motion. "Sir!"

"Relay your report, Corporal."

"Sir, we are to rendezvous with Miss Naile's parents and some elements of the Seventh north of a large dry lake bed in the Nellis Range about a hundred or so miles north of a little town called Las Vegas. There's also been independent confirmation from the other side of the enemy position by Miss Naile's brother. We are to make the best speed possible, sir."

"Back in the column, Corporal." Major Davis ordered, already taking a map from a leather case on his saddle. "Miss Naile, we're here," he gestured, "and we've got to get to here. We've got about two hours of hard riding, if you're up for it." Major Davis smiled, a nice smile.

"I can handle it, Major."

"I never doubted that, ma'am. Good show, Miss Naile!"

Standing up in his stirrups, he looked back along the length of his column. "Men, we've got a rendezvous with the future of the United States and maybe the world. It's two hours hard ride from here to aid the Seventh." And he said to Sergeant Tucker, "Bill, move 'em out."

"Yes, sir!"

Major Davis started his tall black gelding ahead. Lizzie drew back on her mount's right rein, falling in alongside. There was a brace of Colt Single Action Army revolvers in her saddlebags. Lizzie promised herself that, when the column stopped to rest and water the horses, she'd take them out of those saddlebags, along with the holster rig.

Of course, whatever was going to happen in 1900 at what would someday be known as Area 51 had already happened ninety-six years in the past, but Jack and Ellen had only returned to 1900 less than a day ago, and time had seemed to move the same there/then as it did in 1996. Alan felt compelled to think that—however it could be explained or might remain forever inexplicable—the same number of hours had passed for Jack and Ellen as had passed for him.

Kaminsky's firepower demonstration of modern weapons to a small crowd of early 1900s would-be despots should be getting started at almost any time, even though— by one way of thinking—it had already happened.

It was going on mid-morning in 1900, almost dawn in 1996.

If Kaminsky survived in 1900, she would attempt to escape to 1996. Alan watched carefully as the cement mixers bearing the Horizon Enterprises name and logo turned off the ranch road leading from Nevada 375 and drew up around the small time-transfer capsule.

Alan turned his back and walked away. The cement mixers began disgorging their contents into the capsule and would continue to do so until the time-transfer capsule was completely filled. Alan had decided on that as being the most certain way.

Initially, the source of the chamber music had fascinated the assembled diplomats and military personnel. Merely a CD player with perfectly placed speakers, it had seemed magical to sophisticated, worldly men of 1900.

And Bethany's assessment of the commercial possibilities for her time-transfer enterprise was suddenly and irrevocably altered. What would the rich and powerful of 1900 pay for the ordinary luxuries of 1996? What would the traffic truly bear? Finding out would be half the fun.

It was pleasantly cool and oh so civilized under the tent. Bethany's champagne glass was barely sipped from, but she placed the tulip-shaped crystal on a passing waiter's tray, then turned her attention back to the tall, very fit looking man in military uniform, the special emissary of the Kaiser.

"Whatever it is that you would wish, Fraulein Kaminsky, Imperial Germany can and will provide. The only marginally worthy opponent the Fatherland might have is Great Britain, and, of course, your United States. Upstart that it is, Fraulein—but, I mean no offense.

"No, Fraulein, the French are a deceptive lot. You have a marvelous English word: *bluster*. The French are masters of this bluster, but not of warfare. As to the

Russians, they can afford nothing, comparatively, and their country is beset with the political and social unrest which so often plagues a nation led by the maladroit, the inept.

"So, Fraulein, the only meaningful bargain which can be struck here—and we both know that—is between Imperial Germany and your firm. No other arrangement is either possible or practical.

"Who else can you sell to? The British? They would never purchase the weaponry because it would not be 'cricket' to use it. The Americans? Much the same, I am afraid. Should either of them make an initial purchase, to what end? Great Britain is more or less content with the empire it has and the Americans have never had the stomach for empire. And a one-time sale is almost as bad as no sale at all, Fraulein. Yes? You will wish to continually upgrade the weaponry which you provide for a continually rising price. That price can only be met through conquest— therefore, war. Imperial Germany is the only choice, Fraulein, for Lakewood Industries. It is your only choice, Fraulein."

"You're so forthright in your thinking and your speech, Baron von Staudenmaier! Are you as forthcoming with funds?"

"You are an incredibly lovely woman, Fraulein. That means, of course, that I should doubly distrust you." His voice was low, musical, flowed like honey.

After a moment's pause, Bethany asked, "And shouldn't I distrust you, Baron?"

"We have a commonality, then, lovely lady. Our relationship is based on mutual distrust."

"Do we have a relationship, Baron?"

Von Staudenmaier smiled, the action lighting his face, it seemed, accentuating the aquiline nose and strong jawline. He bowed slightly, the twinkle in his dark eyes ever-so-slightly masked beneath the shadow from the bill of his officer's cap. "I would hope that we might have a relationship."

"Field gray becomes you, Baron," Bethany said, glancing at him and then turning her eyes away when she realized that she was being unintentionally coy.

"Your gown—maroon, is it not?—is quite fetching, Fraulein, quite fetching indeed, but, somehow I think you would look your very best in flesh tones." Von Staudenmaier took a step back from her, looked her up and down, then said, "You will have to forgive me, Fraulein, but I was indulging my imagination for a moment. And, indeed, flesh tones—that's how I would love to see you."

"Perhaps that can be arranged, Baron. Tell me. Are you truly an expert in artillery, or are you a spy?"

"I am only expert at certain types of artillery, of the more personal kind," he responded, smiling again. "I am not a spy, but rather concerned with military intelligence. I have indulged that interest ever since my arrival in America, more than eighteen months ago. And you, Fraulein. Are you someone only interested in vast sums of money, or more in the power that such funds afford?"

"Both—of the more personal kind."

Von Staudenmaier laughed softly.

Bethany glanced at her anachronistic wristwatch.

"I noticed that before. What a fascinating way to carry a watch," Von Staudenmaier remarked.

"We do lots of fascinating things in the future. I could show you some of them if you were truly interested."

He cocked an eyebrow. "You are forward for a woman of culture and position—and, by Heaven, I like that."

"We're about to begin . . . the demonstration."

"Oh, I see."

In the next instant, a half-dozen men in surplus Soviet battle gear, most with AK-47s in their hands, rose up out of the sand and raced forward. Von Staudenmaier reached for the flap-holstered weapon at his hip, starting to draw a long-barreled, strange-looking automatic pistol from its confines. "That won't be necessary, Baron; trust me." She thought that she heard him chuckle softly as she raised her voice so that all around could hear her. "Please! This is just the beginning of the demonstration."

The six armed men, as if they weren't being watched at all, ran to a cluster of rocks some twenty yards away. As each man settled into position, suppressive fire was begun against orange painted reactive target panels that were popping up at ranges from fifty to one hundred to one hundred fifty yards distant. The leader of the squad of six men spoke into a radio handset, but a microphone amplified his voice, making it easily heard over the gunfire through the same speakers that a moment earlier had carried the strains played by a string quartet.

"Fire team Alpha to Command Post, come-in!"

The answering voice boomed back. "Sit-rep, Alpha. Over."

"Encountering heavy enemy resistance." And the "commercial," as Bethany liked to think of it, began. "Our Lakewood Industries AK-47 fully automatic thirty caliber assault rifles are working just great, but we need more firepower. We're unlimbering the Squad Automatic Weapon now, Command Post. Over."

Two of the men, one an operator and the other a helper, manned a machine gun. Bethany didn't know what kind and didn't care. She pressed the cupped palms of her hands over her ears as her eyes flickered over the crowd of onlookers. One of the uniformed Frenchmen actually drooled; all of the men, regardless of national allegiance, were enraptured—except for Baron von Staudenmaier, who seemed certainly interested, but equally amused. "Good theater!" Von Staudenmaier remarked as their eyes met for an instant.

"I thought so when I planned it."

The voice of the fire team leader could be heard again. "Requesting airpower to knock out last of enemy resistance, Command Post. Over."

"Stay on your Lakewood Industries two-way radio battlefield communication system, Alpha, so you can precisely direct the helicopter air strike. Over."

"Affirmative, Command Post. Over."

The only airpower she had left in 1900 rose from beyond the western horizon, streaking across the desert toward them. A few of the male secretaries started to break and run. Several of the onlookers all but collapsed into their chairs. Von Staudenmaier remarked, "Name what you want, Fraulein. I doubt there is enough gold in the Imperial Treasury to satisfy the price, but perhaps a little country of your very own?"

"You're serious, aren't you?"

"Deadly so, yes, Fraulein."

The helicopter completed hovering over the six-man fire team and, nosing downward, roared off in the direction of the "enemy" targets, a (hastily) nose-mounted machine gun strafing the enemy position. "Fire Team Alpha to Command Post. Over."

"Reading you loud and clear, Alpha. Over."

"We need armor in here, Command Post. And more troops. How close are the Lakewood Industries heavily armored battle tanks and armored personnel carriers? Over."

While the answer was being announced, Von Staudenmaier leaned down, his lips millimeters from her left ear as he whispered, "Never abandon your present career for that of a playwright, Fraulein. But, on the other hand, good theater does not always have to be 'good theater,' does it?"

"I like you, Baron."

"Without sounding conceited, I hope, I must confess that most women do. However, I find you equally fascinating. What shall we do about the situation, Fraulein? That is the question of the moment, hmm?"

The first two tanks—she had three in 1900—with about a dozen personnel garbed as infantrymen huddled behind them, were moving up. Earlier, Morton Hardesty had suggested, "Don't you think you should have more guys, to make the firepower demo look more authentic?"

"Who do I look like to you?" Bethany had asked rhetorically. "See? Tits, a clit, pretty hair. But you think I look like Cecil B. DeMille?"

The APCs—two of them—were immediately behind the tanks. It galled her that her two jump jets had been destroyed, but she'd bring in jump jets for the next round of sales.

Bethany glanced at the marvelous-looking man beside her. Germany really did have the inside track on the war materiel and might even position itself for a little something extra.

CHAPTER
❖ TWENTY-FIVE ❖

David swung down out of the saddle, tightly gripping the reins of his stolen mount as his father rode into sight. The noise from the automatic weapons was deafening, and the horses expropriated from the picket line were spooked by the cacophony more than David would have supposed. It was what his father would call "a miracle" that the helicopter—Lakewood's only surviving airpower—apparently had not spotted the forces of good and truth and justice observing them from opposing sides of the lake bed, let alone stealing the best horses.

His father rode a big mare, the animal's black coat lathered white with sweat.

In the second after Jack Naile dismounted and clasped David's hand in his, the cinch strap was getting opened, the saddle removed. Using the saddle blanket, David's father began rubbing down his animal. David prepared to do the same. "It's nearly high noon," David announced, "and the magnificent several dozen will have a gunfight at the OK Corral and we'll see who's still tall in the saddle when it's time to cross the Red River from Tombstone to Dodge. And I've just about used up everything I know about movie westerns, Dad."

"Not bad, son; not bad at all. Just keep reminding yourself that we're the guys in the white hats." Jack thumbed his black Stetson up off his forehead. "At least we are figuratively."

"We're not going to wait, are we, Dad?"

"We did it to ourselves, Davey. When we knocked out Lakewood's fighter planes, we killed part of the program, and we alerted our adversaries to the idea that we could do them serious harm. Your great-grandson Alan in 1996 was going to encase the backup time-transfer capsule in cement. If Kaminsky and her people escape our objective present into the subjective future, they'll be encased in cement and never leave the capsule. Not a pleasant thought, not a good guy kind of thing to do to someone, even the evil villain. But it's the only way to make certain that the Kaminsky woman and the Lakewood people never use the capsule—ever. They would suffocate almost instantly—or worse. And all of the Lakewood Industries people in 1996 who know any of the intimate details of time-transfer will be killed one way or another. Good guys in white hats don't do that; they just shoot the guns out of the bad guys' hands and get the cretins a fair trial. So, in the final analysis, son, by the time we're finished with this, all white hats will have to be permanently exchanged for black, mother-of-pearl, ivory and stag pistol grips swapped out for ordinary dark walnut wood, silver-mounted saddles discarded, guitar strings snapped, noble steeds traded in for equally serviceable but unheroic-looking horses. If we had sidekicks, they'd have to be reassigned."

"There's no other way but murder, is there?"

"We've avoided it so far, son, more or less, but I don't think that situation is going to hold. Necessity is our only option, and it's the mother of invention. But this time it's just a mother."

"So, what's the plan?"

"Clarence spearheads the thing with his tank, which will draw off the tanks Lakewood still has, and probably the helicopter. If we act while the prospective buyers are still assembled, this Kaminsky woman will try to pass off what's happening as being part of the equipment demonstration. We've got some plastique, and Clarence and Lieutenant Easley are piecing together explosive charges using the plastique and combining it with the 115mm shells from the tank. We should be able to cripple the APCs enough that the few troopers inside will exit the vehicles and our Seventh Cavalry people can pick them off."

"Still leaves Clarence pursued by two tanks and a helicopter," David reminded his father.

"I know," David's father agreed, beginning to resaddle his horse. "It's not as bad as you think. Clarence is going to get up into higher ground and abandon the tank. The two tanks pursuing him will take off after your mom in the Suburban, falling into our trap."

"You hope."

"They'll have been re-tasked once the Suburban is sighted. And the helicopter isn't a great concern. A half-dozen or fewer well-placed shots from those .30-40 Krags the Seventh is using and that helicopter won't remain airborne for long. Clarence getting out of the tank in time and escaping is the only dicey part, but if Clarence can run them out long enough, he'll be okay. Once the Lakewood people see that things aren't going their way, well . . . Who knows? They may make a run for it."

"In which case, we'll pursue. What about the eager buyers under the tent, and their secretaries and drivers and the personnel tending the food tables for the dignitaries?"

"What would you do, son?" Jack asked.

David felt his stomach churning. "Keep Mom and Lizzie out of it."

"You're a good man," his father said quietly as he swung up into the saddle. "We'll communicate by heliograph for the final coordination. Once the helicopter is down and the people inside those armored personnel carriers have been taken care of, we all close on the lake bed. Hopefully, our adversaries will put up heavy resistance and go down in battle rather than the other way. God have mercy on their souls and on ours."

David's father wheeled his mount and galloped off.

Ever since David could remember, it was always that whatever his father did required everybody else in the family to help. And, quite often, that sucked . . .

Bethany felt genuinely happy. Despite setbacks, her firepower demonstration was going quite well. The Germans would not only be the highest bidder, but the marvelously handsome Rupert von Staudenmaier was going to do his very best to screw her brains out. A breeze tugged playfully at her skirts, toyed with her hair. Clouds, nearly the same gray in color as her Imperial German officer's uniform, marched in broad columns from the west. With her left hand, Bethany controlled her clothes against the wind; her right arm rested in the crook of her dashing baron's elbow. Involuntarily, the fingers of her right hand dug into it as the third of her three Soviet-era tanks rolled down into the dry lake bed from the northeast. But it could not possibly be under the control of any of her personnel. "Shit!"

"Sheiss? My dear Fraulein, what is it?"

She let go of Von Staudenmaier's arm and started looking around for one of her security people with a radio. As she did, still another unexpected vehicle caught her eye, approaching from the northwest. It was a military Humvee, painted in desert camouflage, a machine gun mounted at its approximate center of gravity. One of the French delegation had a pair of leather-wrapped binoculars suspended from his neck on a slender strap. Bethany grabbed at the binoculars and snapped the strap in two. Raising them, focus be damned, she looked to the northwest again. Standing up behind the machine gun, ready to operate it, was Lester Matthews, her security chief. There were two other men with him, one driving, another holding a rifle.

Morton Hardesty, ridiculous looking in a tall, black silk hat, swallow-tail coat, vest, striped pants and pearl-gray spats, ran across her field of view in the same instant that Bethany lowered her expropriated binoculars. A foot or two away from her, the binoculars' owner fumed and sputtered in French. She glanced at him, using one of the only two French phrases she knew. "*Merde a vous.*"

Hardesty, barely audible with all the mechanical noise and gunfire, was shouting something at her that she couldn't understand. "Your scientist, Fraulein—he seems to be suffering upsetment."

Before Bethany could answer Von Staudenmaier, the third tank, finally in range for an artillery exchange, opened fire on her two tanks, first one, then a second artillery shell impacting only a few feet to either side of the nearest of her tanks. The helicopter spun a full one hundred eighty degrees on its main rotor axis, the jury-rigged machine gun opening fire—even she knew, uselessly—against the third tank.

The third tank fired once again, then made a quick ninety degree turn, re-orienting itself to roll off toward the northeast. Unbidden, her own two tanks and the armored personnel carriers took off after it, the helicopter flying almost directly over it, but no longer firing. Lester Matthews and his two companions in the machine-gun-fitted Humvee changed direction slightly, apparently to intercept the third tank.

"Here, asshole," Bethany snapped, shoving the binoculars toward the Frenchman. "*Merci.*" Hands on her corseted waist, shoulders thrown back, she stared after the tanks, the APCs and the helicopter. Everyone would think that this was part of her demonstration, and that couldn't hurt. There was even some applause.

"Bethany!" Sounding breathless, Morton Hardesty skidded to a cartoonlike stop and stood before her, sweat beading on his brow, his glasses held in his hands. "Look!" Morton panted. He gestured toward the north, at dust clouds by the rim of the lake bed.

Through the dust, Bethany thought that she saw a truck or a car. "Frenchie!" She snatched the binoculars from the French envoy's grasp once again, peering through them toward the dust cloud.

Morton, still sounding more than a little out of breath, volunteered, "It's one of the Suburbans from the time-transfer base, Bethany!"

Indeed, in a moment that the dust shifted direction, she could make out the Suburban—green colored— quite clearly. How many more were out there? she wondered. "The Naile family; fuck them!" She gave back the binoculars.

"I spotted the Suburban on one of the perimeter surveillance cameras. What'll we do, Bethany?"

"You've got your radio? Use the damn thing, Morty, and raise the drivers of the armored personnel carriers. Have them break off their pursuit of the third tank and go after those Suburbans. I don't want prisoners. None! Am I understood, Morty?"

"But—"

She started patting him down, searching his pockets, located the cellular-telephone-sized radio and depressed the push-to-talk button. "This is Bethany Kaminsky. Don't talk; just listen and do as you're told." She glanced once more at Baron von Staudenmaier. As appealing as he was, she wasn't going to risk anything or everything just to let him into her panties—if she'd been wearing any . . .

※ ※ ※

The armored personnel carriers made a quick change of direction and went speeding after the Suburban Jack had used as a decoy—the one that Ellen was driving. As per plan, as soon as the APCs altered course, Ellen drove over the rim of the lake bed, vanishing. The APCs rolled on relentlessly.

Using a mirror from the Seventh's heliograph kit, Jack signaled the men along the lake bed's rim to be ready to light their fuses.

Through his binoculars, Jack studied the flight of the three tanks. Clarence and Lieutenant Easley were well in the lead. The armed desert-camouflage Humvee would not intersect Clarence's tank, but would cross its line of travel a few seconds behind, leaving fewer than one hundred yards between them.

Jack swung his binoculars back to the chase scene nearest him, the two armored personnel carriers rolling hell for leather toward the rim of the lakebed.

He judged the distance as one hundred yards, and the marker they'd positioned at exactly one hundred yards was just passed by the lead vehicle. No heliograph signal was required, because the men of the Seventh would be watching through their binoculars as well.

The fuses would just be lit, timed as precisely as guesswork allowed for the improvised demolitions fabricated from Soviet-era tank shells and plastic explosives, ready to detonate when both armored personnel carriers were hopefully positioned to throw their tracks at the very least. At best, the APCs would be punctured, sustain body damage, flip over, powerless to move. When the men

inside were disgorged into the sunlight, those same
Seventh Cavalry troopers who'd lit the fuses would open
fire with their Krag-Jorgensen rifles.

As planned, Jack quit his observation post, running in a
low crouch toward where his horse was tethered. Horses
being in short supply to him—they had stolen only two in
the hopes that two missing from among so many would be
unnoticed for a short while—not only was a rein tied to a
sturdy seeming piece of scrub brush, but the animal's
forelegs were hobbled as well.

Jack dropped to one knee to undo the hobble, slipping
the knot in the rein and swinging up into the saddle in
the same instant that the explosions started. The animal
shivered, stepped sideways, lowered its head. Jack stroked
behind its ears, along its neck, spoke to his mount in barely
audible tones. "Easy, girl, easy. I wish I knew your name,
or that I could speak German." The blanket beneath the
European-style saddle bore the Eagle crest of Imperial
Germany. The animal steadied, whinnied softly. Easily,
Jack let a little slack into the reins and nudged gently with
his knees. Looking over his shoulder, Jack spied the
vaguely mushroom-shaped cloud from the combined
explosive ordnance. And as he guided his mount up onto the
lake bed rim and along its edge, he heard the sharp crack of
rifle shots. The men of the Seventh were dispatching the
Lakewood personnel from the APCs.

"Gyaagh! Let's go!"

There would be no prisoners . . .

Major Davis stood in his saddle, stirrups flared outward,
his animal's reins pulled back taut, his right arm raised, the

palm of his hand open. Lizzie watched his brown eyes as they glanced her way, his craggy features—just for an instant—re-molding into a smile. "No one will think the less of you if you stay here, Miss Naile."

"I know that, Major; but I'd just as soon be with this at the end."

"I understand, Miss. I started off in the cavalry right after the Point. That was a long time ago. I hope I remember the right commands." And he smiled again. Then Major Clark Davis shouted, "At a canter, forward, ho!" He swept his hand forward. The troop, already formed up in what she'd heard called a "skirmish line," started forward at a brisk, but easy, pace. A little triangular flag—it was called a "guide-on" or something like that, she thought—fluttered. A bugler clutched his instrument of gleaming coiled brass high against his right side, just ahead of his right ribcage, in a ready position. Lizzie felt first one, then the other of the hammer thongs on her holsters. She left them in place, lest she lose one of her Colt revolvers when the troop's pace quickened. She felt as if her hat were about to go in the wind, so she pushed it back off her head, letting it hang down her back on its stampede string. In the same instant, the gentle breeze assailed her hair.

Just ahead, Lizzie could see the lip of the valley rim, and beyond it where smoke and dust still rose following the sound of a significant explosion. The scout had reported to Major Davis that two of the funniest looking horseless carriages imaginable were damaged, small fires burning in and around them and that some oddly dressed men were being fired upon by American troopers, this all more than a half mile away to the North.

Major Davis had simply said, "I believe the battle has been joined." At his order, the skirmish line was formed, sabers drawn. The fieldpieces would be positioned to lay down artillery fire if and when the opportunity presented itself, Major Davis had told her. To Lizzie, this didn't look like the right moment.

At the top of the rise, there was no hesitation.

Major Davis aimed the point of his saber toward what Lizzie knew was the conclave of prospective purchasers. The skirmish line wheeled right and started down the sloping side of the valley that was the dry lake bed. The pace neither slackened nor quickened. Major Davis raised his voice, to be heard over the clatter of hooves and jingle of spurs and bits, the creak of boots and saddles. "Listen up! We are under orders to engage anyone and everyone in the vicinity who is not immediately identifiable as an element of the friendly force. For this operation, there is no such term as noncombatant, nor are any identified enemy personnel, however uniformed, attired or gendered to be left alive."

Lowering his voice, Major Davis spoke to the handsome young Lieutenant Adam Castle, who was riding at his side. "Castle—detail two good men to flank Miss Naile and remain at her side throughout the engagement, no matter what happens."

"Very good, sir!"

Major Davis raised his voice again. "Remember! What we do or don't do today, here, now, may well alter the course of the United States forever. We'll be bloody." Lowering his voice, he called out, "Bugler, sound the charge." Raising his voice again, Major Davis shouted, "Charge!"

The bugle call seemed to pervade the entirety of the dry lake bed, while not drowning out the thrumming of pounding hooves, the rattle of equipment, yells coming from some of the men, the snorting of animals.

Major Clark Davis' big brown gelding lunged into a low-slung run, the skirmish line—Lizzie within it—fewer than two or three strides behind him. The force of the air around him bent the brim of his hat upward and back, and his teeth were bared in what could have been mistaken for a smile—if she hadn't known better.

The enemy personnel in and around the pavilions— some few in uniform, most in civilian attire, all of them male—were moving, most running, some few walking purposefully.

Coming up over the horizon, spectral almost in appearance, heat shimmering around it from the sand and rocks, a storm of dust in its wake, was a helicopter.

Neither Major Davis nor any of his men had ever heard of such a machine, let alone seen one. The skirmish line began to break, even Clark Davis reining back slightly, his horse edging right and away from the machine.

"It's called a helicopter, Major! It's one of the flying machines from the future. It's probably outfitted with rapid-firing guns, like Gatling guns I've seen in western movies, only an awful lot faster. They use electricity to fire the cartridges, I think. It can be shot down. It must be!"

As if punctuating her plea, the helicopter opened fire, bullets stitching into the sand mere feet from the edge of the skirmish line nearest it, the sound of the gunfire like she imagined the sound would be if someone tore apart a piece of the universe, not like gunfire at all.

"Lieutenant Castle! Detail six men to assist the lady; she knows all about machines like this and will direct fire against it." Major Davis looked down at her and smiled. "I'm counting on you, Miss Naile."

"I won't let you down, sir." Already, her mind was racing, trying to recall every movie she'd ever seen in which the good guy had shot down the bad guy's helicopter. In her mind's eye, she could see Sean Connery firing a little AR-7 .22 rifle that disassembled to a size that stowed away in a trick briefcase. Somehow, she didn't think shooting down a helicopter was going to be quite that easy in real life.

Ellen's Suburban followed its carefully preselected route into the rocky escarpment on the far edge of the natural dish that was the lake bed.

Wisps of gray smoke from the explosions that had been engineered in order to disable the armored personnel carriers still hung in the desert air. Far to the North—it was probably North, Ellen figured—she could barely make out the dust trail from Clarence's tank, and a smaller trail behind it.

Hitting a rock she hadn't quite gauged properly, Ellen's vehicle bounced so hard that her head actually struck the headliner. Murmuring "Shit!" under her breath, Ellen corrected her steering wheel and rode her brakes a little more heavily.

Dangerously close, but not in any position to fire yet, as best she could tell, were the two tanks aligned with the Lakewood Industries forces. Looking ahead, Ellen reminded herself that in—thankfully—only a few more moments, she would be abandoning her vehicle and running for cover.

Ellen started braking, knowing that the preset spot where the Suburban was to be abandoned lay just ahead, around the next bend. She couldn't help glancing up into the rocks. Did she catch a glimpse of some of the personnel from the Seventh at the highest point along the bulge of ridgeline? Would the men operating the Lakewood Industries tanks see the men of the Seventh, realize what was about to transpire, what lay in store for them and their heavily armored anachronisms?

The spot where Ellen was to abandon her Suburban came upon her more quickly than she'd realized that it would, and she slammed on the brakes and skidded on the sand and gravel.

Grabbing her gear, Ellen was out of the vehicle and running. She glanced over her right shoulder and up toward the ridgeline. She heard the roar of the tanks behind her. One of the tanks plowed into the Suburban, the massive vehicle slowing the Russian tanks just enough. Ellen heard the explosion, looked back and right again. Up in the rocks, there was a puff of smoke, then another and another and another, in series. The entire face of the ridgeline began slipping away, tons of rock raining down upon what had been the road, hammering against the tanks, massive boulders striking them, bouncing off the armor—at least some of them bouncing. Ellen was running faster than she'd run in her adult life.

Ellen could barely see, the dust so thick, and she coughed, her throat dry, her mouth filled with the foul tasting pulverized rock and sand. Tears streaming from her eyes, her breathing labored, Ellen kept running . . .

Clarence stopped his tank's forward movement so precipitously that Lieutenant Easley struck his head on one of the gauges mounted to the control panel. "Watch out!" Clarence cautioned tardily, working the pedals and turning the Russian vehicle a full one hundred eighty degrees, the machine groaning in complaint, but responding. "Jack told me about that son of a bitch," Clarence declared, "the guy on the Hummer. Not the driver, but the other guy. He's the Lakewood guy who tried killing Alan. Alan told me himself how that guy—his name's Lester Matthews—had a lot of fun beating him. Look out, Easley!"

The Humvee's .50 Browning Machine gun began chattering, and the clanging of projectiles off the tank's armor was seriously unsettling because the .50 round was serious ordnance. Clarence solved the problem by aiming the nose of the tank dead on at the Humvee's hood and smashing the tank's left tread down and over it. The Humvee's rear end snapped upward several feet, the driver throwing himself from behind the wheel, Lester Matthews quitting the .50 caliber machine gun and diving for the dirt.

As soon as the tank's track cleared the Humvee, Clarence stopped the machine and started for the hatch. "I haven't been in a good fistfight in a long time—since about 1984, maybe '85."

Lieutenant Easley's face seamed with an almost ear-to-ear grin. "Enjoy yourself, Clarence."

"I intend to."

Clambering out of the hatchway, Clarence oriented

himself on the half-crushed Humvee. The driver was stirring. Matthews was already starting to stand. As Clarence jumped down off the turret, he heard Lieutenant Easley behind him. "I'll take the driver, if need be. You go ahead with the other fellow."

"Thanks," Clarence told him, nodding, and flung himself to the ground. The gravel was a little slippery and Clarence made a mental note to remember that. He began walking toward Lester Matthews. Matthews was reaching for a gun, but Clarence already had one of the MP-5s in his hands. "Touch your pistol, and I'll fucking cut you in half, cocksucker."

Mathews' fingers twitched, but his hands didn't move.

Clarence stopped, unbuckled his gun belt and put it beside the Browning .50 in the back of the Humvee. "Ditch the pistol belt, Matthews."

Lester Matthews wore a GI-style pistol belt with some sort of modern semiautomatic in a military flap holster.

"As you remove that belt, if you feel like going for the gun, hey, I'll shoot you dead."

Matthews had the belt open, held it by the buckle end, the holstered pistol, two pouches of spare magazines and a sheathed fighting knife suspended from it.

"Put the whole thing in the back of the Hummer and step away." Out of the corner of his eye, Clarence saw Easley walk up to the driver, and toss the man a revolver. The driver started to turn away, then wheeled toward Lieutenant Easley and stabbed the revolver at him. Lieutenant Easley, his service revolver in his right hand, fired, then fired again. The driver was pitched backward, on to the gravel-and-sand track, dead.

Matthews said to Clarence, "You aren't taking any prisoners, right?"

"You got it."

"I figured. Let's do it, hotshot."

"Where you made your mistake, asshole," Clarence responded evenly, "was to mess with my cousin. Nobody fucks with my cousins and gets away with it. This way, you've got a chance. Do your best, motherfucker."

Matthews lost it, which kind of surprised Clarence, Matthews being a professional. But sometimes one could hit just the right epithet that would trigger somebody into an irrational move. Head low, hands like rigid claws, Matthews charged. Clarence sidestepped, made to trip Matthews. Matthews had faked it, wheeling right in a roundhouse kick that glanced off Clarence's right ribcage. Clarence got a piece of the kick, catching a fistful of Matthews' bloused right trouser leg, jerking back on it. Matthews fell, hard. Clarence came in and went out fast, putting a kick to the side of Matthews' head. Matthews slowed for a split second, then tried a leg sweep, but Clarence was already safely out of range.

Clarence took another step back, letting Matthews up to his feet. "Bar fighter, right?" Matthews inquired.

"From Omaha, Nebraska, to Athens, Greece, with Athens, Georgia, somewhere in the middle, you'd better believe it."

"Are you good at it, kid?"

"Ask yourself—later, if you're able."

Matthews laughed, jerked a small pistol from inside his black battle dress utilities and fired.

※ ※ ※

"Testosterone," Lizzie murmured.

"Yes, ma'am. What is tess, tesstoss—what you said, ma'am?" the private soldier beside her asked.

"What it might be convenient to have sometimes, Private Hargrave. But, as a girl, I just have to make up for it with inspiration. Follow me!"

They were afoot, Lizzie, Lieutenant Castle, Hargrave and a second private soldier named Butler, their horses left with the third enlisted member of their detail at the summit of the defile. The helicopter had broken off when the series of explosions came from the ridgeline and the avalanche there had begun. Lizzie had no idea who or what was behind the occurrences, but whatever the cause, the incident had bought her several precious minutes in which to formulate a plan and get ready to see it to fruition, while Major Davis reformed his skirmish line and made a second charge toward the pavilions.

She'd viewed everybody from Connery to Mike Connors do it on big and small screens: run across a broad, open expanse, the bad guy in the helicopter in hot pursuit, trying to use the machine to knock down the hapless person he pursued. The usual thing was that the quarry got a moment's chance to bring his firearm into play and fired, either somehow or other hitting some vital portion of the helicopter's moving parts or striking the pilot himself.

Lizzie's variation on the more conventional scenario consisted of two principal points: The actual shooting at the helicopter would be performed by persons other than the party whom the helicopter pilot pursued, and the guy dodging the helicopter, like some sort of ball bearing in a pinball machine, would be a girl instead.

Lieutenant Castle veered off left, Hargrave and Butler angling right. The two enlisted men, .30-40 Krag rifles in hand, practically flung themselves beneath an overhang a scant three yards to the side of the defile. Lieutenant Castle went flat against a rocky outcropping. He would be easily visible from the air if the helicopter came that far.

It was coming along the lip of the dry lake bed, firing short bursts from its gun as if it were some sort of angry beast, snorting in contempt for its intended prey.

Lizzie poured on as much speed as she could, hoping that she'd reach the lake bed in time, before the helicopter pilot spotted Lieutenant Castle and the others. She also hoped—prayed, actually—that the pilot of the helicopter would not stop to ask himself why she was suddenly afoot rather than on horseback.

Lizzie reached the comparatively flat surface of the lake bed—she almost tripped and fell, which would have been too much the usual thing that girls in movies did, anyway—and ran as fast as she could. If she could get the helicopter safely between her back and the muzzles of the soldiers' guns, she'd have a chance. If she only had twentieth-century track shoes on instead of high-button, high heeled, hard-soled shoes. She had to maneuver the helicopter to follow her, not cut her off. Otherwise, either the helicopter's fuselage would bowl her over or its gun—it was an electric minigun—would riddle her with bullets. Either way, she'd be just as dead, and the helicopter would still be a factor in the affray.

Glancing back over her left shoulder once, she spotted the helicopter banking, vectoring toward her.

Lizzie was already running so fast that her lungs ached; she tried running faster . . .

The pistol in Lester Matthews' hand was one of the few that Clarence Jones could recognize by sight, a Beretta .25—he forgot the model designation. His aunt, Ellen, had carried one in her purse for close to twenty years, back in their own time.

As Lester Matthews pulled the trigger and there was the flash of yellow-orange light at the muzzle, Clarence remembered once bragging that it would take more than a bullet from a handgun to stop him if he was intent upon beating the crap out of somebody. The bullet struck, and Clarence's right side just under his ribcage was on fire with pain. Clarence staggered back.

This was his chance to live up to his boast.

Matthews seemed about to fire again. Clarence straight-armed Matthews in the chest with his right palm and swatted aside the little pistol with his left in the very instant the gun discharged again. Clarence felt no additional pain or numbness—there was some numbness already started by his right kidney—and his hand closed over Matthews' gun hand, twisting it clockwise, first a single quarter turn, then another. Drawing his right hand back, closing it into a fist, he punched into the center of Lester Matthews' pain-contorted face. Clarence felt his knuckles split against teeth—punching someone when there could be an interchange of blood was dangerous with someone from the twentieth century—and, in the next microsecond, blood sprayed everywhere, Matthews' torn upper lip and crushed nose spurting.

Clarence still grasped Matthews' gun hand. Abruptly, Clarence twisted it a few extra degrees and locked his own arm to maximum extension, forcing Matthews' arm upward like the hand of a clock closing in on eleven. Clarence turned a full one hundred eighty degrees, the pain in his right side entrance wound and the numbness by his kidney almost making him lose balance and stumble. But Clarence kept himself standing, his right hand flashing upward, outward, grasping Matthews' gun arm elbow. As Clarence pressured the elbow upward with his right hand, Clarence jerked the gun hand downward, hard and fast. The sharp sound of the bone snapping—actually, more like several bones—was clearly audible, and Matthews shrieked with pain.

The .25 fell from Matthews' grasp as Clarence let go of the hand and wrist but kept his arc of motion going, burying his left elbow into Matthews' solar plexus. There was a gush of breath that smelled of fear, and Clarence snarled as he told Matthews, "I learned that one in a bar fight in Greece when a guy came at me with a knife. Like it?"

Clarence didn't wait for a response, wheeling one hundred eighty degrees once again. He was inside Matthews' guard.

And Clarence did something for which he knew he would never forgive himself. He murdered Lester Matthews by smashing the heel of his right hand upward against the base of Matthews' bloody pulp of a nose, driving the ethmoid bone up into Matthews' brain, killing him instantly.

Bethany, skirts billowing wildly about her, rode low

over her black horse, rode as if all the demons of Hell were suddenly chasing her. But it was only David and his father who pursued her. She might have had better luck with the demons.

A man in a German officer's uniform, a Broomhandle Mauser pistol in his left hand, rode beside her. The horse was, quite evidently, not his own, fitted with a western stock saddle rather than a military one. Yet the German rode his mount perfectly, commandingly upright in the saddle.

There was a sharp report from the Broomhandle Mauser, like the sound of lightning striking a tree limb. Instinctively, David ducked, realizing nonetheless that the German's chance of hitting anything from the back of a galloping horse was less than negligible.

"He could get a lucky shot, son! Keep low," David's father warned, himself low over the neck of his mount, the animal's reins in his left hand, his long-barreled special Colt revolver in his right hand.

In the next instant, David watched his father bring the six-gun's barrel on line and snap off a shot. David's mount edged right, nervously. "Dad! Knock it off with the cowboy movie chase scene bit, will ya!?"

But his father wasn't listening, even if he heard.

Bethany and the German officer rode at the center of a pack of six men, at least two of the men part of the assemblage of diplomats, two others dressed less richly and likely underlings. Of the remaining two, one was clearly just a hireling, a kid with a brace of six guns and a paint horse under him. The other rider was clearly a Lakewood

Industries man, a submachine gun hanging at his side. As of yet, it was unused, the Lakewood man displaying obvious difficulties keeping his mount under control.

Jack fired one more probably useless shot, then holstered and hammer-thonged his Colt. The slipstream around him and his animal was stronger than he had imagined it might be all the times he'd watched his favorite western heroes riding hell for leather after the bad guys; Jack's Stetson was nearly blown off. He screwed it down tighter and leaned lower over his mount's neck, the animal's mane lashing at his face, foam from its lips spraying him. Jack's eyes were squinted against both.

The horse he rode with the European military saddle and Imperial German crest on the saddle blanket almost certainly belonged to the Mauser-armed German officer riding with the Kaminsky woman. "Come on, girl—we'll get you reunited with der kapitan or whatever the hell rank he is. Come on!" Jack's heels pumped against the animal's flanks, the black's pace quickening. Aside from the fact that he might get killed and be taken from his wife and family, Jack half-wished for a silver-mounted saddle and a big silvery-white stallion or a golden palomino. Live or die, this was probably the only horseback chase scene-cum-running gun battle he'd ever be in, and there was no sense not doing it right.

All the years of television westerns as a kid colored his perceptions, he thought, affected him to the point that— as surely as if he were listening to one of his daughter's CD-things through a pair of headphones—the music he'd loved so much as a child, memorized in order to retain it, to possess it, long before the days of videotape, played in his head, with a depth of orchestration he'd never before experienced. It was the music from *Stories of the Century* and a half-dozen other programs, chase-scene music, frantic, full, resonating through his soul.

The German officer fired a series of quick shots. Jack's stolen horse took a crease along the left side of its neck. Jack was angry: What kind of man fired at his own horse?

"Gyaagh!" Jack snarled, the music in his head playing louder . . .

Lizzie did it, the movie thing girls did every time a bad guy or a monster—in this case, a helicopter—chased them with evil intentions. She fell, almost flat on her face, her nose suddenly stiff feeling, but her right ankle hurting her more than any pain she could remember, even worse feeling than when she was shot. "Damn!" She tried standing up. If the ankle wasn't broken, it was doing a great imitation.

Lizzie tried again, the ankle feeling almost worse, if that was possible. She drew a revolver.

The helicopter was closing fast. There would be time for one shot, maybe two. Why weren't Lieutenant Castle and the two enlisted men firing? As she glanced right, she saw the two enlisted men, Private Butler and Private Hargrave, standing, their rifles to their shoulders. Lizzie craned her neck, spotted Lieutenant Castle. She saw his lips moving, saw a flash of gunfire from his revolver. Even above the whirring roar of the helicopter as it closed with her, Lizzie heard the dual cracks of rifle shots.

The helicopter kept on coming. More rifle shots, and maybe pistol shots, too. Hopelessly—almost—Lizzie stabbed one of her own handguns toward the helicopter. In the same instant that she fired, there was a ragged volley, coming from Hargrave, Butler and Castle.

The helicopter seemed to stop, suspended in mid-air, like a soaring bird of prey could do, its wings motionless against a powerful air current. But the helicopter, of course, had no real wings, merely its powerfully bladed main and tail rotors. These spun, but somehow not as she remembered them moving a split second before.

Her ankle screamed at her, but Lizzie got herself to her feet, started to fall. The dashing Lieutenant Castle was there beside her, catching her, propelling her away from beneath the helicopter, its gun silent, its fuselage spinning on its vertical axis, beginning to auger down toward the dry lake bed and destruction. Lizzie decided that her ankle couldn't be broken; she hadn't passed out from the pain.

Turning her head to glance behind her, just as quickly, she turned her face away. A rush of hot air engulfed her. The helicopter shattered against the sun-hardened surface of the lake bed, and a fireball flared from its fuel tank. She wasn't on fire and she kept moving, thanking God for favors large and small.

CHAPTER TWENTY-SIX

Jack was gaining on the fleeing bad guys and the bad girl who led them. David, although he told himself what they were doing was beyond insanity, would not have missed this experience with his father.

Without knowing why, David found himself wondering if there were secret orders that the Naile family should all be killed. Then, would other soldiers kill the soldiers who had killed them, like some sort of Ancient Egyptian security precaution taken when the great tombs of the Valley of The Kings were sealed against a presumed eternity? He'd seen that old Boris Karloff movie about a mummy on the loose.

And, riding like a madman, bullets periodically whizzing around him, the uneven ground enough to make his horse snap an ankle and pitch him to the rock-hard lake bed, dead, crippled or concussed, was it that one's mind turned to unadulterated crap in the moment before death?

The mysteries of life and death perhaps unfolded before him. "Fuck it," he murmured, kicking his heels into his mount's sides still harder and getting with the spirit of the thing, firing his Colt revolver uselessly and shouting, "Giddyup!"

If his old friends could have seen him—David shuddered at the thought . . .

Lieutenant Castle's hands were at Lizzie's waist, Private Hargrove's left hand under her good foot, Castle saying, "On three, Hargrove! One. Two. Three!" Then Lizzie was up into the saddle, and the pain in her ankle—it wasn't broken, she told herself—only felt unbearable for a split second, then began to subside.

The battle raged on a mile or so ahead of them in the dry lake bed, and Lizzie wasn't going to miss it. "Let's go, Lieutenant!"

"Yes, ma'am!"

He was cute, she thought.

Clarence leaned heavily against the side of his tank; he'd miss the tank, actually. Easley asked him for the third time in the last few minutes, "Are you sure you're all right?"

"I've never been shot before. Have you?"

"No, Clarence, I haven't."

"So I don't know if I'm okay or not. But there isn't a lot of blood. My wife's a doctor from my time. Once we get me outa here, she'll fix me up quick as anything." Easley was either moving, swaying back and forth, or Clarence's vision was starting to go. He felt a spasm of pain, clutched his side, fell forward into darkness.

❅ ❅ ❅

The Lakewood man reined in his horse, half fell from the saddle and tried holding on to the terrified animal's reins as he swung his submachine gun forward on its sling.

The guy had watched too many movies, Jack observed to himself, realizing the mere thought was the pot calling the kettle black. The MP-5's butt stock wasn't extended, and the weapon wasn't even steadied at his hip. He just held it up, jerking the muzzle side to side and firing like somebody in a Middle Eastern terrorist group or something, his bullets stitching into the ground, making a lot of noise and frightening the horses—especially his own—but doing nothing to stop the men who pursued him. David's horse reared; David held on, then spurred the animal into a lunge that took rider and mount perilously close to the Lakewood man.

Jack reined in tight, his stolen black skidding on its haunches.

Jack swung down out of the saddle, hauling the animal downward, tugging hard on the right rein to turn the horse's head away from him as his left hand went to the horse's near-side elbow and pushed. The animal laid itself down, belly toward the man with the submachine gun. Jack dropped behind the saddle, knowing he had a matter of seconds before the horse might bolt to its feet. Jack drew his revolver and fired one shot, hitting the Lakewood man in the throat. Jack fired again, the second shot striking the man in the forehead.

Jack stood, stepping back as he tugged at the reins and let the horse rise to its feet. Jack stood on the reins in the next instant, quickly replacing the spent cartridges in his revolver, holstering and hammer-thonging, then catching up the black's reins in his left hand. "Easy, girl. Nearly through here."

Jack led the less skittish animal quickly toward the dead man. He dropped into a crouch, holding the reins under his boot once again as he rapidly opened and removed the dead man's pistol belt, then the strapped bag of spare magazines. There were three thirty-round sticks remaining. Jack examined the magazine in the weapon. Three or four rounds appeared to remain. There would be a round in the chamber.

Jack inserted a full magazine up the well, slinging the submachine gun to his right side well behind his revolver, the magazine carrier already slung to his left. The pistol on the man's belt was apparently the man's own and a brand that Jack didn't fully trust. He cleared the weapon, dismounted the slide, pulled the recoil system and dropped the springs into the magazine case. He flung the weapon's slide and frame in opposite directions, dropping the dead man's belt.

Jack eased the cinch on the dead man's mount, tethered the animal to some scrub just off what passed for the road. Swinging up into the saddle again, his own animal starting to shiver from its sweat—no time to rub the black down—Jack turned in toward the pursuit, but not taking the trail. What Jack intended to do in order to make up the lost time was dangerous in the extreme, something that could result in a broken leg for the black and a broken neck for himself. The shootout with the Lakewood man had been at a hairpin along the ridge road, the road turning back on itself into the next valley. A steep incline separated the two sections of road, cutting off, Jack calculated roughly, close to a mile and a half.

Jack made the Sign of The Cross and murmured "God help us," then started the German's horse down on to the loose gravel and sand that formed the slope. Errol Flynn or his stuntman did it in the classic film *Virginia City* and Jock Mahoney, one of the greatest stuntmen who ever lived, did it in 1958's *The Last of The Fast Guns*.

Jack tried to concentrate on the ride. He no longer actually controlled his horse's movements, nor did the black control its movements, either. What he and the animal beneath him were engaged in could best be described as a headlong downhill lunge. To stop would be suicidal for them both.

A sudden dip—like a pothole from his own time—loomed ahead of them. In vain, Jack attempted to exert control via the reins. The animal didn't respond. Jack realized that his lips were moving and he was saying the Lord's Prayer. The German officer's horse wouldn't swerve right or left; Jack was certain that the black was going to fall and pitch him over its head. At the last microsecond, the black leapt up, jumping the depression, its hind legs half folding under it, Jack's left hand going out to grasp the saddle's smallish cantle. The black righted itself and dove onward and downward along the face of the slope.

Jack dared to glance away from the terrain and look at the road below. The woman, the hired gun from this time and the German officer and two other men were almost directly below him. Following behind them, low over the neck of his sweat-gleaming mount, rode David.

More than halfway down the rock-and scrub-strewn

slope, Jack thought of the first of William Boyd's classic western adventures when "Hoppy" was riding down a slope much like this and fired his revolver from the hip off the back of his still moving horse, shooting the revolver out of the hand of a bad guy maybe a hundred yards away. "Poetic license," Jack Naile murmured to himself and the horse.

Bethany Kaminsky judged that the second and smaller time base had to be over the next ridge. The animal she rode was beginning to falter and couldn't go on much longer. Young David Naile was about two city blocks behind them, and his madman father, Jack, would be reaching the road in another moment or so.

Bethany licked her dry lips. "Baron," she shouted over the labored breathing of the animals and the thudding of horses' hooves. "We might need the extra horse. Shoot the kid on the paint horse!" She still wondered where the young punk had gotten the twentieth-century woman's wristwatch he wore on his left wrist.

The oddly shaped automatic pistol Von Staudenmaier held in his right hand flashed fire twice, and the local punk with the two pistols all of a sudden had a third eye just under his hatband at the bridge of his nose and an instant tracheotomy from the second shot.

"Get that horse!" Bethany shouted to her men as the dead kid slumped out of the saddle. "Baron! Do you want to come with us to my time? I could use a man like you in my organization."

"I should travel through time!" he shouted back. "You are mad!"

"What've you got to lose, Baron? And you've got me to gain!"

As Bethany glanced toward him again, she caught his lips curling into a smile. "As you say, Fraulein, what is there to lose?! Yes? Ha-ha! Yes!"

"I like you, Baron!" Turning her head toward the two remaining Lakewood men, Bethany ordered, "Stop the Nailes. Kill them! We'll wait for you at the alternate time base. But be quick!"

The two Lakewood men reined back on their mounts, Bethany, with Baron von Staudenmaier riding beside her, Maier leading the dead cowboy's paint horse, headed toward the ridge.

Of course, she had no intention of waiting for anyone.

"I'll be fine," Lizzie gasped as Major Davis and Lieutenant Castle helped her down from the saddle.

"This man needs medical attention, and fast, really fast!" Lizzie heard her mother shout. Lizzie began looking around to find her. Davis and Castle helped her to stabilize, to stand on one foot. Hopping a little bit to turn around, to see better, she at last spied her mother standing in the midst of a sea of dusty, uniformed shoulders. Ellen dropped to her knees in the dry lake bed near a blanket stretcher. Clarence lay on it, looking like he was dead. "Get a medic here! Now!" Lizzie watched in horror as her mother began to beat on Clarence's broad chest.

Jack marveled at his own folly; never again would he think it at all even remotely odd that someone might be so moved at journey's end as to kneel and kiss the ground. As the German's big black mare bounded on to the roadway, nearly abreast of David, Jack would have done so, time permitting. Time was accepting of less and less. The easy thing would have been to rein in, fall back and let the two Lakewood men—perhaps a quarter mile ahead—just wait there. Jack had ridden to catch David, to keep David from going at the bad guys alone. Kaminsky would not wait for her two hapless minions. Any enemy personnel not dying in combat would have to be executed. Jack, in this short period of years, had accumulated a lifetime's worth of things he did not want to remember, knew he would never forget. Albeit that he and his family were, literally, saving the world from veering into an alternate historical path, one more bloody than the original destiny which lay within the years ahead, murder was still murder, however noble the reason.

Kaminsky would literally—and figuratively, as well—seal her own fate.

Jack reined back a little, letting his horse slow. David did the same.

"When this is all behind us, son," Jack began, looking at the fine and strong man who had once been a little baby in his arms, "let's plan a family trip to New England. A few years down the road, here. I'd kind of like for you to meet your grandfather. He won't be born until 1908, but still . . ."

"I'd like to meet your dad—Dad." David laughed.

Jack glanced up the road. The two Lakewood men had their submachine guns at the ready. Jack looked again at his son. He extended his right hand. David did the same. They held the handshake for a moment, exchanged a nod,

Jack offed the safety of the submachine gun he'd liberated from the Lakewood man he'd killed. David had one, too, shifting it into a firing position.

"Let's be done with this, son."

"Agreed, Dad."

Jack and David—a calm having settled over them—urged their sweating mounts slowly ahead . . .

Bethany dismounted from the paint horse she'd expropriated and glanced behind her. Looking silly running in his high riding boots and funny uniform pants, Von Staudenmaier was about a city block's distance away. His horse had collapsed under him. In the distance, on the other side of the ridge, she could hear gunfire, and lots of it. She turned away from the road and toward the large shack about a quarter of a block off the road. "Better hurry, Baron," she called over her shoulder. Raising her skirts, Bethany started toward the shack.

The old-looking cabin had been built only weeks before, torn down from a location several miles distant, brought to this spot and reassembled, with an addition put on at the rear. This addition contained a compartmentalized cylinder about the size of a large bathroom, shaped like a loaf of bread. She had been rehearsed in the cylinder's use dozens of times. Everything was automated, computerized. Push this button, that button, this other button. Enter the code—known only to her now that Morty was probably dead or about to be executed. The power would come on-line, and the machine would be activated.

Bethany could hear the Baron's heavy breathing. Still, he was in remarkably good shape.

"There'll be a lot of rebuilding to do, Baron, my organization and all."

They opened the cabin door. Inside was darkness. She'd forgotten a flashlight. "Baron? Got a match? We need some light." He struck a match as they stepped through the doorway and out of the wind, the smell of sulfur unmistakable. "On the far wall. There's a deer's foot shaped like a clothes hook."

"I see it," Von Staudenmaier volunteered, striking a second match as he dropped the first to the dirt floor.

"Good, Baron. Give it three twists to the right—full twists—and jerk it downward."

"Is this some sort of—"

"It opens a panel in the wall."

Her baron turned the repulsive looking clothes hook three times exactly, then pulled it downward. The right side of the rear wall slid a few inches inward, then left, disappearing beside the other half of the shack's back wall. A light mounted above the chamber, powered by emergency batteries, came on. The baron dropped his match to the floor and stepped on it. "I am impressed, Fraulein, once again."

"You think you're impressed now, wait until we get between the sheets, Baron."

There was a smooth metal surface beyond, forming the back wall of the building, seamless in appearance. A smallish panel—like a keypad for a miniaturized cellular telephone—was at eye level on the far left side of the metal wall. She heard gunfire from outside, perhaps the two men she'd left behind shooting it out with the Nailes.

Bethany tapped out a series of digits on the panel. There was a hum, and a piece of the metal surface slid away. This exposed the combination lock to the outer chamber door. She twirled it, swung back the rest of the metal panel and turned the handle, then opened the vaultlike outer door of the bread-loaf-shaped metallic gray pod through which she would escape. At the touch of a button, the rest of the lights came on. "Close that door behind us, will you, Baron? Turn the handle." She stepped over the threshold, the baron behind her. He began to turn the small, four-spoked wheel, the outer vault door locking bolts—twelve of them—sliding back into the frame. "We're impregnable now, Baron."

"We are locked within an enormous bank vault. I do not understand how this benefits us tactically."

Bethany was already booting the computer for typing the entry code giving access through the inner vault doorway, readying the power for the surge that would carry her and everything within the time-transfer capsule to her own time.

"What is this humming sound?"

"Electricity, Baron. A special kind. It will carry us away from here. I'll have a tech explain it to you when we get there."

"What is a tech, my dear?"

"Tell you later, Baron." And she leaned up on tip toes and kissed him hard on the mouth. He was salty-tasting from sweat. She liked his flavor.

The inner door opened. "Come with me," she beckoned, passing over the threshold. He followed. She closed the door from an activation panel on the inside wall to her right. "Hold my hand and walk slowly, and we'll be in my time when we reach the other side of the chamber."

He took her hand. Bethany began to walk as the chamber began to shimmer, looking at once of substance, yet shapeless. She felt the pressure of the baron's hand closing around hers in the instant before she realized that her body was merging with something unrelenting and hard and the air was pushed out of her lungs and—blackness.

CHAPTER
❊ TWENTY-SEVEN ❊

Father and son, Jack and David, prepared to mount up, their horses tired, sweat soaked, close to used up. The two Lakewood men who had been left behind had made a good, quick fight of it. Jack had gotten a terrible scare when David was hit. But it was only a flesh wound across his left tricep. Cleaned properly, it would amount to little more than an inconvenience.

"The war's still going on out on the lake bed, Dad."

"I suppose we should, shouldn't we?"

David swung up into the saddle. "Shit, that hurt!"

"Pain makes a great reminder, doesn't it, son?" Jack observed. He was securing the captured twentieth-century weapons to the mounts the two dead Lakewood men had ridden. Jack climbed up into the saddle, feeling his fifty years a lot more than he usually did. He lit a cigarette. Pretty soon, he'd be back to rolling his own again.

"You ought to quit those things, Dad, before they kill you."

"When I smoke the last of these, I promise I'll try. One last battle?"

"Sure. Maybe they'll be through by the time we get there, huh, Dad?"

Exhaling smoke through his nostrils and mouth as he spoke, Jack smiled at his fine son. "I wouldn't bet on that."

Jack Naile thwacked his heels against the black's flanks, but not too hard. The mare would go down dead if she went too fast. And they didn't have to hurry.

Jack and David turned their horses toward the heavily occluded horizon and rode together to the sounds of the guns.

Enemy combatants were considerate enough to fight to the death. If there were any survivors, they eluded the troopers sent against them. The only disturbing thing was that no corpse had been found to match the description of the renegade scientist Morton Hardesty. But there was no reason to suppose the traitorous Hardesty had survived. Beyond what information concerning future technology had been cabled to the French, Germans, Russians and the British, nothing of the Lakewood "sales kits" survived, the men who had carried them already intercepted. Their fate had not been discussed. It took months of meticulous checking and rechecking to accumulate all the weapons, cartridge cases and miscellaneous equipment, including the tanks, the remains of the armored personnel carriers and the bodies. Everything was gathered together at what Teddy Roosevelt had described as "an undisclosed location, buried under tons of rock."

Jack had voted for William McKinley and his brash

running mate, Teddy Roosevelt. Ellen couldn't vote. Women would not have the vote in Nevada until November of 1914. Although election results wouldn't be "known" for quite a while, compared to the speed with which election winners were announced in the 1990s, Jack and Ellen already knew the results as they sat together on the front porch. Ellen wore no corset under her dress and no apron over it—and no stupid hat. Jack was rolling a cigarette. A rifle rested against the door frame. Jack was smoking far fewer cigarettes than he had; Ellen held out hope that he would really, finally quit.

The citizenry of Atlas was so confident that the McKinley/Roosevelt ticket would be triumphant, they were holding a party hosted by Republican leaders in the town. Ellen had made her venison stew—Jack raved about it—and sent a huge pot of it along as her contribution to what amounted to a town-wide block party. Bobby Lorkin had picked up Lizzie, showing off his new spring wagon and the matched pair of dapple gray geldings pulling it. Clarence, recovered from his near fatal wound, and Peggy were in the secret room, watching a movie and just keeping company. Eventually, the tapes would wear out. Clarence was a political conservative, but Peggy, a lifelong Democrat, as had been/would be her parents, could not make herself go to a Republican rally. As Ellen reflected upon that, she realized that the Naile family could accept this one terrible flaw in Peggy's otherwise fine character.

As to David, his politics were a mystery, but he'd liked Teddy Roosevelt. And he liked parties. There was a girl he'd been seeing, as pretty as she was smart. Good daughter-in-law material. The store was a runaway success. David had just returned from a business trip two towns over, where he'd opened up a second Jack Naile—General Merchandise store. The family's fortunes, in David's hands, were on the increase. Horizon Enterprises was on its way to its destiny.

Jack fired his cigarette, and Ellen moved to stand beside him. The stars shone so brightly over Nevada in 1900 that, on a clear November evening, Ellen no longer considered herself night-blind—almost, at least.

"Gimme a drag," she told Jack, taking the cigarette from between his fingers. She inhaled deeply; then, as she exhaled, told him, "This roll your-own-stuff is nowhere near as good as a Camel."

"Yeah, I know. Boy, would I walk a mile for one."

"Do you miss it? Besides the cigarettes, I mean?"

"Yeah, I guess. But I'm way ahead of anybody else in this time or any other. Come here." Jack snapped the cigarette away over the porch rail, folded Ellen into his arms and kissed her hard on the mouth.

After a long moment, Ellen leaned her head against his chest and said, "I thought a good cowboy hero was just supposed to kiss his horse."

"No see, those are the kinky cowboys. Real cowboys kiss girls and that's how you get little cowboys and cowgirls."

"Whoa, pardner!"

"Don't fret none, ma'am. I recollect how I got the sawbones to fix me up a few years back." Jack tilted her chin up, smiled and whispered, "We can fool around all we want."

❖ AFTERWORD ❖

The beginning of this novel is true. We went to the post office, and a reader—we've lost track of the man's name, and we apologize for that to him—actually sent us a page out of the April 1993 Nevada—*The Magazine Of The Real West*. On page 19, there's a photograph of a very busy boomtown street scene in the early 1900s Tonopah, Nevada. Men, women, children, dogs, all manner of wagons, horse-and mule-drawn, fill the photograph. On the farside of the street, at the center, is a light-colored building. Fanned out in a crescent at the top of the building front in big block caps is JERRY AHERN and underneath that, GENERAL MERCHANDISE. This street seemed like a good location with lots of business.

The photo got us thinking, just like the Naile family, about what would happen if, somehow, our family got swept back in time. Our son, Jason, really was heavily involved with work that summer and was even then and is now one of the most intelligent businessmen we've ever met. Our daughter, Samantha, sweet and loving with plenty of pluck, helped us plot out the story. We actually called the historical society and discovered further proof of Jerry Ahern having lived there. We have a nephew—George—who has always been like an older son to us. At the time, after a stint in the Air Force, he was managing a theater, just like Clarence. As anyone who ever got into a fight with George could attest, he's always been very good at taking care of himself.

Many readers will know that, aside from writing novels, the Ahern family has always been involved with firearms, just like the Naile family.

We carefully research in order to make the story as accurate as possible. A good example of that is the train schedule, when Jack and Ellen go off to intercept Teddy Roosevelt. Assuming the train didn't break down or a trestle wash out, the times for those train trips are exactly as they would have been, and so is the route.

Lastly, however time travel may someday be accomplished, it will likely start out as a trick, occuring by mere chance. Let's hope it will be looked at serendipitously.

JERRY and SHARON AHERN
May 11, 2010

THE FANTASY OF
ERIC FLINT

THE PHILOSOPHICAL STRANGLER

When the world's best assassin gets too philosophical, the only thing to do is take up an even deadlier trade—heroing!

hc • 0-671-31986-8 • $24.00

pb • 0-7434-3541-9 • $7.99

FORWARD THE MAGE with Richard Roach

It's a dangerous, even foolhardy, thing to be in love with the sister of the world's greatest assassin.

hc • 0-7434-3524-9 • $24.00

pb • 0-7434-7146-6 • $7.99

PYRAMID SCHEME with Dave Freer

hc • 0-671-31839-X • $21.00

pb • 0-7434-3592-3 • $6.99

PYRAMID POWER with Dave Freer

hc • 1-4165-2130-5 • $24.00

pb • 1-4165-5596-X • $7.99

A huge alien pyramid has plopped itself in the middle of Chicago and is throwing people back into worlds of myth, impervious to all the U.S. Army has to throw at it. Unfortunately, the pyramid has captured mild-mannered professor Jerry Lukacs—the one man who just might have the will and know-how to be able to stop its schemes.

And don't miss **THE SHADOW OF THE LION** series of alternate fantasies, written with Mercedes Lackey & Dave Freer.

AMAZONS 'R US
The Chicks in Chainmail series,
edited by Esther Friesner

Chicks in Chainmail

"Kudos should go to Friesner for having the guts to put together this anthology and to Baen for publishing it... a fabulous bunch of stories... they're all gems."—*Realms of Fantasy* "For a good time, check on *Chicks in Chainmail*.... In its humorous exploration of the female fantasy warrior, this anthology does its best to turn every stereotype on its ear. There's something to offend everyone here, so bring your sense of humor and prepare to be entertained."—*Locus*   0-671-87682-1 • $6.99

Did You Say Chicks?!

Smile when you say that.... Stories by Elizabeth Moon, Harry Turtledove, Esther Friesner & more.   0-671-87867-0 • $6.99

Chicks 'n Chained Males

"This anthology is a hoot!"—*Affaire de Coeur.* Stories by Rosemary Edghill, K.D. Wentworth, Lawrence Watt-Evans, more.

0-671-57814-6 • $6.99

The Chick is in the Mail

Neither rain nor snow nor hail shall stand in the way of these chicks! Stories by Charles Sheffield, William Sanders, Robin Wayne Bailey, Nancy Kress, Eric Flint, more.   0-671-31950-7 • $6.99

Turn the Other Chick

These babes were born to battle. Stories by John G. Hemry, Jan Stirling, Wen Spencer, Selina Rosen, Jody Lynn Nye, more.

hc 0-7434-8857-1 • $20.00
pb 1-4165-2053-8 • $7.99

And don't miss:

E.Godz by Esther Friesner & Robert Asprin

Dow Jones meets dark sorcery—no holds are barred in this family war for control of the Wal-Mart of the magic world.

hc 0-7434-3605-9 • $17.00
pb 0-7434-9888-7 • $6.99

Available in bookstores everywhere.
Or order online at our secure, easy to use website:
www.baen.com